THAT DAY IN JUNE

Martina Reilly, formerly known as the author Tina Reilly, lives in County Kildare with her husband and two children.

Catch up with Martina on her website www.tinareilly. info, on Facebook or on Twitter @MartinaReilly

Also by Martina Reilly

Martina Reilly

That Day in June

HACHETTE
BOOKS
IRELAND

First published in 2015 by Hachette Books Ireland
First published in paperback in 2015

A CIP catalogue record for this title is available from the British Library

ISBN 978 1444 794 458

Typeset in Sabon by Bookends Publishing Services
Printed and bound by Clays Ltd, St Ives plc

Hachette Books Ireland policy is to use papers that are natural,
renewable and recyclable products and made from wood grown in
sustainable forests. The logging and manufacturing processes are
expected to conform to the environmental regulations of the country of
origin.

Hachette Books Ireland
8 Castlecourt Centre
Castleknock
Dublin 15, Ireland

A division of Hachette UK Ltd
Carmelite House, 50 Victoria Embankment, London EC4Y 0DZ

www.hachette.ie

To Mam and Dad, Tom, Mary, Pat, Marie,
Leanne, Laura and Rachel
Thank you

And to Deirdre Hyland – because she loves my stories

Part One

SANDY

1

He didn't come today. I knew by half eleven that he wasn't going to show, but I held onto the fragile hope that I was wrong, that some part of his important job had held him up or that he'd been waylaid by the girl he'd been telling me about, the one who kept turning up outside his house and sending him texts. He laughed uneasily when he talked about her and I liked his white teeth in his wide mouth. The straightness of them, the evenness. I don't know what my teeth look like; not as good as his, that's one certain thing.

His name is Max, short for Maximus, which is a pretty awful name if you ask me. He's thirty-four and he's not married. When I look up at him, his legs seem long and lean. He's got hair as shiny and sleek as the coat of a seal and big hazel eyes. His eyes remind me of my mother.

Max comes every day at eleven. I know this because I sit opposite the church and the church has a clock and it chimes on the hour. When eleven comes, Max strides up the street towards me, shiny haired and white toothed, carrying two cartons of coffee and some sandwiches. Or maybe some days he'll have cakes. He crouches down beside me and gives them to me. Sometimes, if he's in a hurry, he just says, 'Here you go, Sandy' and rushes on. Other times he sits in beside me and we drink our coffees together, blowing the steam away and sipping it down bit by bit. I don't really talk to people but I like to listen to him. Sometimes he talks a lot, other times hardly at all. He always smells nice, like the sea.

But today is day four and he still hasn't come and the sun is slipping away from the sky and the dusk is creeping in like a cat after a mouse. I wonder where he is. If he doesn't come tomorrow, I'm going to find him.

The thought scares me.

2

Sandy Lynch is my street name. How I ended up on the street and homeless, I don't quite know. The whole thing started with a lie told long ago. Now I don't know where the truth ended and the lie began. For me, there was once a house with a mother of sorts, then there was Dublin with a job of sorts and now there's this. Three months and counting of Shitsville.

I left home at seventeen with a burning desire to run. Just run. Anger propelled me out the door, anger has kept me from going back. Maybe there was a point where I could have returned, where I could have demanded the truth, but each time I backed off because I wasn't sure I could have coped with her refusal to tell me, or even worse, with her telling me more half-truths. If I had gone back and it had come to nothing, what could I have done then? I might have crumbled. I might have torn myself up with not knowing. Or torn myself up with knowing. No, I told myself, better to stay away and keep strong. Better to stay away and not get sucked back in to her ways of thinking. And I have stayed strong. Just keep moving, never look back, that's the best thing to do.

I left home on June 5th, eight years ago. I took a rucksack

and filled it with money I'd stolen from my mother. I figured
she owed me that much. I pulled on my jacket, even though,
at four in the morning, the heat from the previous day still
lingered.

I vanished off the face of the earth that day in June.

3

The town I sleep rough in is called High Hills and it lies, as you might guess, at the base of a very high hill. It's not large, having a main street and a few smaller streets feeding off it. The main street is filled with restaurants and pubs and a few newsagents and a lovely coffee shop cum bakery. I would never know how lovely it was only for Max. The smell on the main street at three on any given day is bread and garlic and coffee, the most wonderful combination imaginable.

It's a pretty town, the sort of place tourists like to visit for a short while. In the summer, they arrive with haversacks and hiking shoes having climbed the hill from the other side. Before they make the trek back, they'll have a meal or a snack in one of the restaurants. I like looking at them, peering at them from across the street, warming myself in their sun. I like to watch parents and children especially – it makes me sad and happy all at the same time, which is kinda weird.

It's not a young town, as a lot of people in their twenties and thirties seem to have left it to work elsewhere. I suppose there are not a lot of job opportunities in small-town Ireland, even one that's not too far from Dublin. I worked in Dublin for years in a crappy cleaning job that kept me below the radar. If I paid fifteen euros a day, I could bunk down in a flat with about twenty other girls. Now I don't even have that. I hate being homeless but I like being alone. It's safer for me that way.

Homelessness in High Hills is just me as far as I can make out, which suits me fine. At first, no one living here seemed to realise I slept in the park and now that they do, they don't look so friendly. I get the feeling they think I might encourage all my homeless buddies into their pretty town. And if I *had* homeless buddies, I sure would – serve them right. If people glare at me, I glare at them right back and they turn away. I don't like meeting people's eyes but glaring is the quickest way to scare someone off.

Around nine, I climb the really low fence that surrounds the local park. I sleep under a hedge and while it sounds totally shit, it's actually sheltered and safe. No one can see me when I'm inside and the rain very rarely gets in. I don't know what winter will be like, though maybe I'll have another crappy job by then.

Tonight, though, it's warm; the sky is a little cloudy, but through the break, bright stars glitter. I take out the magazine I nicked and use my torch to see the words. I'd always liked reading. My mother was – is – a poet and I guess she'd given me a love of words. I used to read lots of books but not anymore. It's not like they're real life. Magazines are better.

Tonight, just as I'm about to reach the part where the woman got plastic surgery that went wrong, Margo and her son Keith arrive. They've started bringing me soup; I think someone told the local Simon Community about me. I don't treat them too good – it doesn't do to get too close – but they still keep coming. And the soup is good.

They hand me soup and a sandwich and ask how I am.

Margo is a big woman with a loud voice and a huge laugh. She never seems to mind that I don't talk. She fills in the gaps for me. Keith, her son, is quieter.

'How's Sandy tonight?' Keith asks.

I shrug. I told them my name last week, now they keep using it.

Margo sits beside me, making herself comfortable on the grass, while Keith hops onto the lower branches of a nearby tree. He sits there every night, peeling the leaves off and tearing them into pieces. 'Busy night tonight,' Margo tells me, 'we're a bit late getting to you, sorry about that.'

I take a sip of the soup. I have a vision of a horde of homeless people moving into the town. Like Zombies.

'The van broke down and Keith had to fix it. The pressure.' I watch as she fans herself with her hand.

'It was a puncture, Ma.' Keith rolls his eyes. 'If the van broke down I'd be next to useless.'

'The van *was* broke down,' Margo insists. 'It would not go, that's what I meant!'

'Yeah, well, technically a puncture is not a breakdown.'

'Technical, my arse!'

They always go on like this.

'So, have you any news for us?' Margo breaks off the impending debate on what a breakdown is to nudge me with her elbow. These days, she is the only person who touches me.

I don't react. Playing it hard ass is best.

There is a pause then and I'm good at pauses. Pauses generally mean danger or that someone is about to suggest something you wish they wouldn't. There was a big pause when my job went. Clara, the girl I'd worked with, had shouted up a storm, but I'd just walked out. I think Clara went home to her family, though she swore once that she never would.

'Love,' Margo says, and I think she is talking to Keith, but nope, it's me, 'would you not think it's time for you to try and get yourself into a hostel? Sheltered accommodation. There are some lovely ones and after a bit you'll get back on your feet and into the world again.'

I stare at my sleeping bag, wrapped around me. It's a new one. They gave it to me a month ago. I like it.

'You could get a few bob for yourself and set yourself up nicely.'

I had a few bob. I rented with twenty other girls. It wasn't nice. 'Give it a rest, yeah?'

'But a young girl like you, sleeping here, it's dangerous.'

'This way of living isn't right.' That's Keith.

How do I explain that I don't know any other way of living, not really. I'm happy enough. I just say, 'Fuck off.'

'OK,' Margo says, not sounding too bothered by my hostility, 'I said I'd ask and I have.'

I feel mean about it. To make up, I stumble out a 'Thanks.'

They can't hide their astonishment and I almost laugh only for it's kinda sad. I'm not like my outside self inside. Not always anyway. I watch them walk away and I think suddenly of how lucky they are to have each other. I wonder if Margo has a husband. I wonder if they love each other. I wonder if it is just the two of them, Keith and Margo.

I wonder do they wonder about me.

4

Vanishing is easier than you'd think, even when you just have the vaguest plans. When you vanish at four o'clock in the morning from an isolated cottage in Wexford, disappearing can be effortless. I watched the sun rise and headed west. I stuck inland to fields and ditches, of which there were plenty, avoiding roads and people when I could. By the time morning came, I had travelled about fifteen miles. I wasn't sure when I'd be reported missing so I hurried through that night.

By nine, I was sleeping in the middle of a hedge in a field. It was thorny and tore my clothes, I got scratches on my hands and down the sides of my cheek but I was tired and the adrenalin which had prompted my flight had long gone and I slept the best I have ever slept since I was ten years old.

For what seemed like weeks, I walked by night and slept by day. At that stage I had a bit of a plan, I knew where I was going. Sometimes, I stole blankets and clothes from people's lines. I stuffed them into my haversack. I took shampoo if I spied a downstairs bathroom window. I nicked soaps. One day, I stole a designer top from a line. I never wore it, I just took it, buried it deep in my haversack. I used to take it out and admire it from time to time. It's not always wrong to steal, I don't think.

Disappearing, I soon realised, was all about bravado. If I let myself get too dirty, people noticed me. The trick was to stay reasonably clean. And so I washed in the public toilets of shopping centres; I assumed confidence and walked into hotel lobbies and used their facilities. I became a fan of McDonald's and it was there, maybe ten days later, that I found the newspaper. The sight of it gave me a jolt, my eyes transfixed by the photo and the headline: *No Sign of Runaway Ruby. Mother Appeals for Her to Come Home.* A picture of my mother, looking shellshocked, stared out and guilt swept through me. I damped it down before studying the photo of me. It was one taken by my mother a while ago. The picture didn't look like me now. The girl in the picture had long dark hair, caught up in a ponytail, the ends of which could be seen snaking down her shoulder. I gazed around the diner; no one was looking, and so I picked up the paper and took it.

I read that I'd been discovered missing fairly early. Mam had gone into my room to check that I was OK as we'd had a tiff the night before. When she'd found me gone she'd rung the police, who hadn't taken her too seriously. Seventeen-year-old girls, they'd said, tend not to tell their parents when they go out. They hadn't realised that this particular seventeen year old was very different. Or at least, her mother thought she was. Eventually, probably because of my mother's hysteria, they'd issued an appeal.

Apparently, the whole place was involved in the search for me. People came from neighbouring villages to help out. More guilt. Two weeks later, I saw another headline: *Ruby Fairbrother's Double Life Revealed. Boyfriend Questioned.*

It brought my disappearance to a whole other level. Numerous pictures of my bewildered mother adorned the newsstands. Pictures of Louis soon joined her, only not the Louis I knew. This one looked mean.

I almost went home. I mean, she was my mother and I loved her. I really did love her. She'd sung me to sleep when I was small, read me stories all the time, bought me books, given me piggy backs. She could kick a football over the roof of our house, she surprised me with a giant teddy bear when I was four. She didn't deserve this. But on the other hand, what had she expected? She had lied to me. About every single thing that mattered.

But still the guilt lingered. Compared to other girls I've met, my life didn't seem so bad. But, like them, I too had been betrayed by someone I trusted. I thought maybe I'd send a note to say I was OK, only it meant buying a stamp in a shop and at that stage, with my face all over the place, I couldn't risk it. After a bit, I disappeared from the front pages and other news took over, and though I started off letters to her, I never sent them. I couldn't say what I wanted to say. Not in writing. So I never sent anything. Like when you have a pain and you mean to go to the doctor and then the pain goes and you forget about it. I made myself forget. And I never did get recognised because no one ever really looked that hard at me. I've since figured that people never really look at others. Certainly not at the ones like me, floating about on the margins. But we're on the fringes precisely because we don't want to be looked at, which makes us worth looking at, I think.

I left myself behind in Wexford and became someone else on the journey here. And you know what? Me and my mother should have been looked at a lot earlier.

5

Despite the fact that I have nothing now, my life is more ordered than it ever was. I get up early because breakfast is at eight in the shelter and I have to walk a couple of miles to get there. Keith and Margo told me about it and first off I thought it was a trap, but then a month ago I was so hungry, I thought, *Why not?* So I go there every morning now. On good days, when the world hasn't quite woken up and everywhere is hushed, like something great is about to happen, I even like the walk. Early mornings are sacred, safe times. All the shitheads and ratbags are still asleep. Mornings are for the newly homeless. The ones who haven't yet been lured by the skank on the streets.

The shelter is not a place for sleeping or for staying during the day: it just does a big breakfast to keep you going. The first time I had breakfast here, I was blown away by the size of it. A fry-up, cereal if we wanted, and some fruit to take with us for the day. I wear a jacket with big pockets now. There are shower facilities too and I normally take one after breakfast. The rules are that you have to leave it clean and dry and that the towel you use must be left in the basket.

And then it's just the whole day and me. The wet days are the worst – finding shelter, trying not to get soaked, feeling the rain eat away at the protection of your clothes bit by little bit. Trudging through the streets, dripping, hoping someone will let you into their shop so you can get warm. I only go back to the hedge on the really wet days. Most times I like to be out and about. It makes me feel normal.

On warm days, the world is my oyster. I can go anywhere. Sit in the park and be just like all the other people there. Though I never quite am. It's like they sense I'm different and they haul their kids away if they get too close. They even did that when I was working, so I guess I've never managed to fit in right. I don't mind. I like having a no-go zone around me. Most times. Other days, I weaken; I get so lonely, I'll ask directions from someone just to have contact with them for a few fleeting seconds.

Today, after breakfast, even though it's raining I head for the square. I'm bundled up in my rain jacket and warm boots and colourful scarf. I take up position on the bench, opposite the church clock, and wait. The rain gets heavier as the slow minutes tick on by. It drum-drums on the hood of my jacket and I put my gloved hands up into my sleeves in an attempt to stave the weather off.

When you spend many days sitting on the same patch, you get to know people's legs and feet. You know this shoe or that trainer or this way of walking or that way. Certain legs walk by at certain times. Ten o'clock comes and goes and as eleven nears, my heart starts bodhrán-beating in my chest. I raise my eyes and scan the street. It's emptier than yesterday because of the rain. I see the old woman with the nun's shoes pitter-pattering towards me. She always walks straight at me and then at the last minute makes a big deal of moving away. She's carrying a shopping bag. She goes shopping once a week in the Lidl up the town. She has a dog because she buys lots of cheap dog food. I like dogs.

The joggers go by, and the guy who cycles with one hand while he balances boxes with the other. The butcher beside the church comes out for a smoke. The lady with the brand-new baby power walks with her three-wheeled pram. Cars and buses pass. Max does not go into Maguire's coffee shop and come out with sandwiches. I wait an hour but I know he's not coming, just like he hasn't the past four days.

I think back to the last time I saw him. He'd been in a hurry; he looked like he was worried about something, maybe that woman who was after him. He gave me my coffee and kept checking up and down the street. He didn't even sit down, like normal. He just hopped from foot to foot, looking at his phone. Then he said a weird thing: he asked me what colour was guilt. That was so weird. I said I thought it would probably be purple, dark purple like a stain, and he said that was right. There was purple everywhere. Then he left.

Does anyone miss him except me? No one in the street has marked his absence. Other people are not looking at the door of the coffee shop waiting for him to emerge with his grin and his piping hot drinks. How can someone who has made such a mark on me go unmissed by everyone?

At least now, though, I can do something about it. I am grown up. I'm twenty-five, I think. I'm going to find him.

The thought hammers me to the seat. My head swims a tiny bit. I gasp.

'Are you OK, love?'

There's a woman peering at me.

I nod, avoiding her eyes.

'You sounded as if you were in pain.' She is concerned.

'No.'

She hesitates. I can see it in her, wondering if I'll savage her. Finally, to my surprise, she sits beside me. 'Here.' She fumbles in her pocket and pulls out a fiver. 'Get yourself warmed up.'

Kindness always catches me around the throat. Inside, I feel angry but I know that, in a few minutes, the anger will turn into something else. Something softer and more pliable. I can't name it. So I allow her to press the money into my palm. I say nothing.

She seems unsure what else she should do. 'You can get a coffee over there.' She points to Max's coffee shop. 'Bye now.' She hops up. 'Take care.'

I watch her leave.

I say nothing because I might cry.

I have to find Max.

I followed him home once. I hadn't meant to but when I saw him in the distance, I just thought, *Why not?* It wasn't as if I had anything else on or a pressing engagement I had to make and so I just fell into step behind him. I'm good at being invisible so he never noticed me, or if he did he never mentioned it again. He lives in another town, over the mountain, maybe about four miles away. The walk is branded in my memory.

I turn out of High Hills at the corner of the Lidl and start up a steep hill. I wonder if maybe he is sick. Or if he has

moved away. I hope not. Aside from Margo and Keith, Max
is the only other person who has talked to me in months. I
would not like if he has moved on and left me. I would not
like that at all. I can't even go there in my head. The road
is very steep and I find it hard, especially in the rain as it
lashes my face and makes it hard to see. At the top of the
hill, I have to turn right and I'm walking along the edge of
the town, seeing it from the top, like as if I'm walking on the
invisible roof of it. It's a narrow road, only enough for one
car with lay-bys carved into the hillside here and there. I'm
still climbing, only it's not so steep. The higher up I go, the
quieter it gets until all I can hear is the faint murmur of cars
and the patter of rain on my hood. The sky is grey and the air
smells heavy. I trudge on. The heat builds, the sun peeps out
from behind clouds, the road levels out and, finally, I start
to descend again. I arrive at the place where I'd seen Max
that time. He'd been jogging really slowly with headphones
on. At first I'd lost sight of him, but there was only one road
and I eventually saw him in the distance, bent over, gasping
for air. I'd watched as he'd hobbled home on shaky legs. The
road gets busier as I descend, as it's on the way in to Dublin.
The town Max lives in is on the edge of the city, but Max
told me he comes to High Hills especially to buy coffee. It's
the nicest coffee anywhere, he says. I stand for a second in
the middle of Max's town, trying to get my bearings. I've
always been better in quiet places, towns confuse me. Finally
I spot the library that I turned up by last time. Max's house is
in a little laneway somewhere behind it. Number six.

6

The first time Max had bought me coffee, it had been snowing. Early April snow. I was huddled up in my parka jacket, flakes piling up on the ground beside me. I was about to move, to try to get some warmth into my body, when a coffee was placed beside me, followed by a pre-packed sandwich. I thought I was hallucinating. I looked upwards and saw the figure of a man, all bundled up into a furry jacket, staring down at me.

'OK?' he said, before walking on.

The coffee was cold by the time I gave in and drank it. I tucked the sandwich into my pocket for later. When I left my pitch, I almost had to unpeel myself from the seat, I was so cold.

The next day the man gave me a different type of coffee. This one was frothy and sweet. The sandwich was cheese. Again, all he said was, 'OK?'

He didn't expect anything of me and that was good.

This continued for a while. I don't know how long for. A few weeks anyway. Different coffees, different sandwiches. Sometimes, he'd leave a bun.

One morning, the coffee was placed under my nose as usual but instead of an 'OK?', a voice asked, 'So which one is your favourite?'

The question was so unexpected that I jerked up my head and found that I was looking into the most beautiful face I had ever seen. Angular, sallow, with a dimple in one cheek. I took in the casual clothes and the Doc Martens. Weak sunlight broke just above his head and he looked like he had a halo. I averted my eyes.

He was undeterred. 'That one there,' he pointed to the coffee, 'is hazelnut mocha. My personal favourite.' He waited.

I lifted the cup up and took a sip. There was silence. 'It's good,' I said. Whispered, really. You get out of practice. Like learning a language. Use it or lose it.

'Your favourite?'

I was overwhelmed. Who cared what my favourite was? They were all warm. I shrugged.

'And which sambo did you like the best?' He had crouched down to my level now, his hands clasped loosely in front of him. I didn't know if I liked him being so close. I glanced sideways at him. I shrugged again.

'All of them?' he prompted.

I gathered courage about myself like a robe. 'All except for the one with the black chopped-up bits.'

Max gave me a funny look. 'OK, well I won't get you one with olives again,' he promised. Then he held out his hand. 'Max,' he said.

'Hello.'

I didn't tell him my name that day. I didn't shake his hand. I didn't tell him to fuck off either though.

7

Nobody enters or leaves number six all day. I know because I've hung about, going up and down the little road, hoping no one will notice. Only that's not really possible in such a small street. Max's house is in the middle of a row of houses and they're in the middle of a short laneway. Opposite, across the narrow, uneven road, there are more of the same. The houses are made of red bricks, they have doors with stained glass, with one window downstairs and two windows upstairs. They look old. The houses could be broken into quite easily, just push the windows in ever so gently. Lots of elderly people live on the street. At one point during the day, a woman goes up the driveway and into the house beside Max's. She carries a shopping bag. She knocks on the door and a man answers and invites her in. He says, 'Hello, Patricia, you look ravishing.' She doesn't, so that's funny. Then he brings her inside, saying his mother was wondering where she'd got to.

There are a few cars parked along the road too but no one gets in and drives away. A flock of pigeons make me jump as they take to the air. Down the street, the sound of someone singing floats out a window. After more time, the street quietens and I walk straight up to Max's and ring the doorbell.

The minute I do so, I want to run off. Say he's in there and just doesn't want to buy me coffee anymore? Then I think, so what? But just say he is … The choices I have flash through my brain. I hear the bell echo inside the house but no footsteps approach the door. Gaining courage, I ring it again. Nothing. Maybe he is on holiday. Maybe he's moved. But I know he hasn't. He doesn't know me well, but he tells me things. A while ago he told me he was going to meet an old friend of his. He would do the same now. Wouldn't he? He couldn't just drop me as if I never existed. But sometimes people do that and it's a puzzling thing. How can they like you one minute and not the next? Do they suddenly see something in you? Had Louis seen something in me that had made him pull away? My neediness, I suppose. I shove Louis out of my head. That was so long ago. I don't need anyone now. Not really.

I take the risk of calling out Max's name. Only it doesn't sound that loud. So I do it again. 'Max!' I call. It's funny hearing my voice so loud.

Nothing.

In the house beside Max's the curtains twitch upstairs and the woman I saw earlier peeps out. Then the man's face appears. They look at me and I look at them. I'm tempted to give them the finger but think that these are Max's neighbours and he might get mad, so I don't.

I ring Max's bell again and just ignore them. I take a chance and peer in through the window set into the door. I see a small hallway with a door at the end and a door off it. I peer in through the front-room window, a little curious and braver now that no one has come out to challenge me. It looks like an office, as I can make out a computer and a chair and some files which are scattered across a little desk. A bookcase crammed with books. A TV. A cup stands on the computer desk beside the remains of some cake. It's as if he stepped out for a second and forgot to come back.

'Excuse me,' a voice says from behind, and I jump.

I whirl around, glowering, hoping to intimidate whoever it is.

It's the man I saw from next door. He's tall, lanky, with floppy hair. His face is narrow and pale with a long nose and his clothes hang on him as if he bought them a couple of sizes too big. He carries an umbrella in one hand and rain splatters off it and onto the ground.

I become aware of just how wet I am. Water is dripping from the sleeves of my jacket.

'Are you looking for Max?' the man asks. He sounds posh.

I make an 'isn't it bloody obvious?' face.

He studies me, long narrow head held a little to the side. 'D'you want to come in?' He indicates his house. 'It's very wet out here.'

I'm not going in there. I stand my ground. 'I just want to know about Max.'

'Are you a friend of his?'

Would we be friends? I don't know. 'Yes.'

Another long pause. I want to shake him, tell him to hurry up. What is the problem here?

'No one told you? His father wasn't in touch?'

I don't answer. *Isn't it obvious?*, I want to say. Would I be here if I knew where Max was? A thought hits me and then I say, 'Is he dead?' My voice shakes, without me knowing it was going to.

'No.' The man rushes to reassure me. 'Oh, I'm sorry if I gave you that impression. I—'

'Where is Max?'

His mouth opens and closes like a fish. 'In hospital,' he blurts out quickly, like as if my snappy question squeezed it out of him.

'Why?'

He waits a second. 'Max had an ... accident.'

I don't like to think of him having an accident. 'Is he OK?'

'He's in hospital, which is the best place for him,' he says firmly.

'What hospital?'

'St Lucy's.'

I never heard of it. I wonder is it far away. 'Where is it?'

'He doesn't want visitors,' he says. 'He won't even let his father visit. Do you know his father?'

'St Lucy's,' I repeat. 'Is it far?'

'He won't let people visit him.'

I say nothing. I probably won't visit him anyway.

'It's about a mile from here. Just follow the road out of town, keep walking and you'll see it on the bend before you hit the road for Dublin.'

'OK. Thanks.' If I decide to visit, I'll go tomorrow. I'll retrieve my sleeping bag, hitch up somewhere nearby for the night and go then.

'If you do get to see him,' the man calls after me, 'tell him Charles and his mother say hello. If he wants post collected or anything, to give me his key.'

I wonder if I'll have the nerve to visit. I should try, I think. He did bring me coffee when no one else saw me.

'Max is a ...' the man hesitates, 'a grand fella.'

I say nothing, just leave.

8

In the beginning, and for a long time afterwards, I loved my mother with all the love my heart could hold. She filled my world. Her smile, the pale skin of her face, the smudge of blue in her hazel eyes that I inherited. Hers was the face I saw first thing in the morning and last thing at night. We shared a house, we shared our lives, she told me stories of old Ireland. She showed me Ireland on a globe and pointed out the south east. We lived in Wexford, she said. Wexford was on the coast of Ireland, which meant it had beaches. She described for me the sound of the sea and the swell of the waves and the tang of seaweed in the air. She told me that the smell of chips drowned in vinegar on a hot summer evening would lift your heart. She showed me pictures of the sea on the computer that she bought for me to use for my lessons; she described to me how the sea was thousands of times bigger than a bathtub. Water, she said, as far as the eye could see. And way beyond that too. The sea knew its boundaries and rarely encroached on the land. Everything had boundaries, she said.

I wanted so much to go there and see it.

My father, she said, loved the sea. He was a fisherman. He caught trout and would bring them home for us to eat. Did I remember, she asked, the way he'd bring us off to the seaside? Did I remember how we'd splash and kick water at each other? I'd already seen the sea, she said. Did I remember my dad's cuddles, the way he'd hold both of us tight and tell us how much he loved us? I did remember, I told her. I remembered the smell of him, the salty sea smell of him. I could hear his voice in the way she spoke of him. Gravelly and deep, full of love for us. My father was a wonderful man who tragically ended up making my mother famous. They'd met when she was eighteen, fallen in love and married a year later. He'd wanted her to live far from the sea; the sea was dangerous, he said. He wanted her to live somewhere that was quiet, that was just going to be the two of them, and so they'd found the cottage and bought up some fields and there they'd lived and I was born and my father had thought I was the most beautiful girl in the world. At night, my mother said, he'd wrap me in a blanket and curl up with me on the sofa and she would make tea and they'd have it together in front of the fire, or if it was summer and there was no fire, they'd eat with the window open and let the breeze through the house.

Just the two of them and baby me.

When I was four, my father died at sea. His body was never found. That's when my mother said she began to write. Laments for him. Love poems for him. I didn't remember my father's death or his funeral. I didn't remember the mass or anything like that. But I remembered the trips to the seaside and the smells. I even remembered being a tiny baby and being wrapped in a rough blanket and cuddled.

9

Rain is pouring down the next day. I wake up to the sound of it gurgling in the nearby stream and hammering off the tight branches of the hedge. The space where I am hidden is gloomy and feels cold. I hop out of bed and poke my head out. Immediately I'm battered by water. I think that maybe I won't bother with breakfast this morning. Then I think that if I don't go, I'll have no food for the rest of the day. I wait a few minutes, just to see if it will ease off. All is silence outside except for the rain. I lie down, finishing off another magazine, one I'd found in a bin. I read about recipes I will never cook and music I will never hear. At what I imagine must be around ten, I crawl out. The rain has eased a little and I head for the shelter, half running, trying to get there before it closes up for the day.

Only thing is, I must have got the time wrong because it is all shut up. The smell of fry still drifts on the air and my stomach rumbles. I can't go and see Max in the hospital with my stomach rumbling. He'll think I've just come to get food from him.

In my head I have two options. Starve until the next day or do something about it. Clara, my friend from the cleaning business, was good at doing something about it. She taught me some neat tricks to help me survive on the crap wages we made. OK, they got us fired in the end but they worked for a good long time. One of the things she taught me was how to steal. I know it's not a great thing to do but sometimes, as Clara said, it was necessary. I figure that right now, I have to steal something to eat and if possible get my hands on some fruit to bring into Max. People bring apples and oranges and sometimes grapes to others who are in hospital because when I was a kid, my mother was in hospital and my granny brought her fruit. I can't walk into a shop and lift a load of apples, so I figure, I'll take a wallet instead.

The first thing I have to do is find a crowd. If the hospital is near the city centre, I should start walking towards there because the city centre is full of crowds. I begin retracing my steps, leaving the shelter, heading back towards High Hills, back over the mountain and into Max's town. Out through Max's town and on towards the hospital. And hey presto, a set of traffic lights. A pile of people waiting to cross the road. I pull up my hood so people won't notice my scraggy hair. I want to look like a regular person waiting at a set of traffic lights. I join the queue in the back and scan the people in front. I'm looking for back pockets. It is amazing how many people keep their wallets in the back pocket of their jeans. This time, I don't see anyone. Everyone is wearing long coats because of the rain. But then, in front of me, I see a girl wearing a haversack slung low on her back. And right there in the front of the haversack is a little pocket for a purse. In fact it says in fancy writing 'money pocket'. Have you ever seen anything so stupid? But maybe she's not a stupid girl, maybe her money isn't in there, but she looks the kind to do what she's told, all neat and precise. So I sidle up behind her and get in real close and pretend to be pulling up the zip on my coat and quick as anything I pop the popper on the haversack and dip my fingers in and just as she moves off, the purse slides out, right into my hands. I keep walking right behind her but take a left as she takes a right on the other side of the road.

I make fifty euro. I drop the girl's wallet in a place where it will be found and hopefully returned. It's a nice wallet, pink and glittery. I'm tempted to keep it, just because it's so pretty, but that would be really bad. Instead, I take the fifty euros and, finding a café, I buy myself some breakfast. After that, I head into a supermarket and buy some apples and grapes and oranges and bananas to give to Max. Then I have to buy two bags because there is such a lot of fruit. After all that, I have ten euro left, which I pocket; that'll keep me going for another few days.

Taking a deep breath, I head for the hospital.

10

We didn't get many callers, my mother and I. There were three regular ones. The two women who always came together, the postman and the man from Casey's, the local supermarket, doing deliveries. We called him Casey's man. The two women scared me most because, despite what she said, I knew they scared my mother.

They came irregularly, sometimes not for months, sometimes twice in a day. Through a tiny gap, where the curtain didn't quite meet the wall, I knew that one of the women had short yellow hair and the other had grey hair. The blonde one drove a blue car. It was always the same: they'd drive up, and on a signal from my mother, I'd jump over the newspapers and run on shaky legs to my position. As the two women banged on our door, calling out my mother's name and imploring her to answer, my legs would tremble in terror wondering what awful thing they would visit on us. When we didn't answer, they'd walk around the house and I suppose they peered in the windows. Each time they called my mother's name, my heart would jackknife in my chest. I didn't let my mother see how scared I was because she was scared too. In time, I buried my fear and assumed a cockiness about their visits that I didn't feel. It was easier to cope that way.

One time, after they'd banged on our door for over fifteen minutes before driving away, I asked my mother who they were.

'Nobody,' she said.

'They must be somebody.'

'Nobody important,' she said.

I fancy that I knew she was lying, but maybe I didn't.

The postman was next scariest. He put things through our door that made my mother gasp. Each time letters plopped onto our mat, my mother would tear through them frantically as if she were looking for traps. She hated the pink envelope the most. Unopened, she'd throw it into the bin. Once, unable to help myself, I fished it out. I was very young at the time. I remember staring at the large writing, the stamp in the corner, marvelling at the colour of the paper.

'Never ever take things out of the bin, do you hear me?' My mother snatched it from my hand. 'Never.'

From then on, she took the pink letters and burned them.

The third regular caller, Casey's man, wasn't scary. He came once a week, always at eleven, and he left our shopping outside the door. He was strong, able to lift three boxes at a time, and he was always whistling. We still hid when he came but my mother didn't seem to mind if I waved out at him.

One time there was a note with the shopping. I think I was around eight. I spotted it first and picked it up. It said, *I threw in a few lollipops for the little girl. My treat.*

And there, right at the end of the bag, were seven lollipops in rainbow colours.

From then on, I got rainbow lollipops every week.

There were some nice people, my mammy said, just not that many.

The world was a big, scary place and the only thing we could be sure of was that we were safe in our home.

11

St Lucy's is a psychiatric hospital. That's a surprise. As I enter the large hallway or whatever it's called in a hospital, an announcement blares out telling people to wash their hands on the way in. I jump and a man behind me laughs. 'Gets me every time,' he says.

I try to smile back but I'm annoyed at myself. Showing fear can get you into trouble.

I watch as he scrubs his hands with some weird gel. I do the same. Then I look around. The place is enormous. There's an information desk over to the right and I join the queue. Eventually it's my turn. The woman behind the glass looks bored. Her eyes flick to me. 'Yeah?'

I understand I have to be normal. 'I'm looking for Max.' Even though I try my best, it comes out like a growl. So I add, 'Please.'

'Surname?'

'Mine?' There is no way …

'His.' She flicks a glance at me.

'I don't know.'

'Well, you'll need to know. We search under the surname first, then the Christian name.'

She looks at me as if I'm stupid.

'That's a thick way of doing it,' I say, and realise that I've just burnt my hope of finding Max.

'That's not my fault.' She's already looking beyond me to the next person.

'You can check on a Christian name surely,' the man behind me says. It's the same man I met on the way in. I thought I'd seen him get into a lift. 'Max isn't exactly a common name. I'd bet there is only one Max in the whole hospital.' He smiles at her.

The receptionist waits a beat or two as the man keeps smiling. It works. She sighs a bit, glares a little at me and presses some buttons.

The man winks, and before I can help it, I grin back at him.

'There's one Maximus,' the receptionist pronounces as if she's reading something incredibly distasteful, 'he's up in St Jude's. Top floor, turn left.'

'Now,' the man says cheerily, 'that wasn't so hard, was it?' He winks at me again. 'You've moved my daughter,' I hear him say to the receptionist as I walk away towards the stairs.

I'm panting and puffing by the time I push the stair door open on the airy corridor of the fifth floor. I take a second to get my breath before looking for a sign for St Jude's Ward. There is one, pointing left, and I follow it. My trainers make squelching noises on the floor, like the sound of a cartoon character, echoing up and down the mainly deserted halls. I wince with each squeak. More signs for St Jude's, and I walk past walls lined with artwork, some of it good, some of it terrible. When I finally reach the ward, I'm startled to have to ring a bell set into a doorframe to gain admittance. I wonder why Max is here. He didn't appear to have any mental health issues. I wonder now if it's the right Max. Maybe it's another Max. I steel myself and press the bell and then I'm so flustered that when the door buzzes to let me in, I make a bit of an eejit of myself by pushing it instead of pulling it while a disembodied voice keeps telling me to 'Pull'.

Eventually a nurse comes out from somewhere and pushes the door forward. 'Pull,' she says.

'I was,' I lie.

She waits a beat before saying, 'What can I do for you?'

For a second, I don't answer. I'm so used to not answering. Then it dawns on me that, like downstairs, I have to say something. I swallow hard. 'I'm here to see Max.'

'Max Coyle?'

'Yes.' Hopefully it's him.

'He asked to see you?' Surprise.

I shrug in response.

'Really?'

'I want to see Max,' I repeat.

'I'll just check with him.' She sounds suddenly suspicious. 'You better not be a journalist. Your name?'

'Sandy.'

'Stay here. Don't move.'

The place is bright and airy, like the rest of the hospital. It's hard to tell the patients from their visitors as everyone is dressed and walking about. Some people have bandages over their wrists, which is weird. I wonder if I should have come. I feel I should run but something keeps me waiting.

The nurse arrives back. She's smiling a little. 'He'll see you,' she says.

A small beat of panic hits me. *Shit. What am I doing?*

'Third door on the right.'

I feel her eyes on me as I slowly make my way down the corridor. I could be sick right now. The third door is blue, number three, and is slightly open. I knock.

'Come in.'

Pushing open the door, the first thing I see is Max, the right Max, sitting on a chair, dressed in jeans and a black T-shirt. His face is badly bruised and his arm is in a sling. He regards me with his massive brown eyes as I stand like a spare in his doorway. We eye each other.

'Sandy,' he says after a bit.

'Hi.' I try for nonchalance.

I've never said 'hi' to him before.

'Come in. Sit down.' His voice is quieter than I remember.

There is nowhere to sit, so I perch on the bed. We look at each other. It's weird to see the whole of him, rather than just a glimpse of foot or a profile of face. His room is small, closed in. I can't decide how I should look. My usual defensive glower seems wrong. And yet, I don't do smiles and I don't want to smile anyway. I try to pull myself out of the situation. Make my expression neutral. 'Here.' I lay the fruit on the floor.

He seems surprised. 'For me?'

'Yes.'

He peers into the bags and I think he smiles. 'Did you rob a fruit shop?'

'No.' That's not very nice.

'There's quite a lot of fruit here.'

'I know.'

He looks back up at me. 'You should take some for yourself. I'll never eat it all.'

'No, thank you. It's yours.' My mother never gave her fruit back.

He seems overwhelmed. 'Well, thank you, Sandy.'

I just nod.

'You look good,' he says then.

I don't, though. I'm all wet. And my hair is scraggy.

'How did you know I was …?' He stumbles to a halt. 'Why?'

I shrug and fiddle with the ends of my scarf. I think of 'why?' I barely understand myself. I can't talk for that long even if I did understand. I settle for, 'You never came.' I bring my eyes to meet his.

Silence.

Finally he mutters, 'That's nice.'

'So was the coffee.'

He laughs a little. I wasn't trying to be funny. Then more silence. I look away, I don't know if I should have come. I wish I could go but I've only just got here.

'I'm not mental.'

I don't know what to say to that.

'I fell down the stairs,' he says. He is cross. 'I was drunk and I fell down the stairs and they think it was, you know, like a suicide attempt.'

I wonder why they think that. One time, a guy I cleaned for fell down the stairs. He tripped on a toy one of his kids had. He broke his leg.

'But it wasn't suicide.' Max is still talking. 'That's private health insurance though.' His finger jabs the air. 'If I was just a public patient they'd have me out of here by now.'

He sounds cross. I blab, 'Your neighbour says if you want anything done, let him have your key.'

I suppose he wasn't expecting me to say that. His mouth opens and closes. 'You talked to my neighbours?' He makes a face. 'The people next door?'

'Yep.'

He gives me a look that I can't fathom.

'The key is under the stone at the front door. The spare one. The code for the alarm is ...' He frowns. Then he pulls out his mobile phone and reads out, '1234. Can you remember that?'

I wonder if it is a joke. 'Yep.'

Silence falls like feathers on the room. I realise that Max has a stack of books piled beside his bed. Thrillers mainly. I used to like books. Romances and short stories. I wonder who gave Max those books or did he take them from his house. He has a CD player and some music. His leg jiggles up and down to some invisible rhythm.

'It's hard to work in here,' he mutters, catching me looking at the books. 'I have no computer. They won't let me have it. Being in here is not exactly good for business. And they,' he nods in the direction of the doctors outside, and his voice rises, making me wince, 'hate me doing it. Say it stresses me out. But it keeps me sane.' He drags a hand through his hair. 'I could lose business. Clients don't want their agent to be in a psychiatric hospital, do they?'

It's not a question though because he goes on, 'I look after a few well-known people, try to keep them in the public eye in a good way, mop up their relationship mistakes, sell their books, stuff like that.' His words are rapid. 'Master of Spin, that's me.' Then he gives a laugh, only it doesn't sound much like a laugh.

'I'm glad you're OK,' I say then because I don't know what he's talking about. 'I'll tell your neighbour that you're OK.'

His mouth clamps shut. Then he says, 'Thanks.' He chews on a nail. 'Thanks, Sandy.'

I don't know what else to say so I stand up to go.

'Will you come see me again?'

I'm taken a little by surprise. And trepidation. And a little bit of joy. I must be a good visitor. 'Sure.'

'It's just ...' He stares at his feet, scuffs the toe of his bright red trainers on the floor and makes a squeaking noise, then says, 'Nothing, doesn't matter.'

'I'll come back soon.' It means I'll have to find a hedge somewhere near here for a bit. Or see if there are any crappy jobs going, though there doesn't seem to be.

'Grand.' He smiles the smile I'm used to and he seems like Max. 'Bye, then.'

'Bye.'

12

When I was ten, my life tipped sideways. At first I thought it was another of my mother's tests. She did that to see how I'd cope in an emergency situation. She'd fake a burn or a pain and I'd have to do first aid. She'd fake a fire and I'd have to know how to escape. She'd fake unexpected visitors and I'd have to find a suitable place to hide. She always made it very exciting. Most of my childhood was spent on the edge of panic.

When I was ten, she got sick. Not just ordinary sick, but stay in the bed and get worse sick. I decided after the third day of feeding her food she couldn't eat that this was not a test. For the next couple of days I sat by her bed and tried to spoon drinks into her. I wiped her face with a damp cloth, sang little songs to her, but it was no good. A week on and she wasn't even able to walk. She had pains, she said, in her bones.

Eight days later, she fell asleep and I was glad because it gave me a break. Only she slept for a long time and when I tried to wake her, I couldn't. She was still alive because I could see her chest going up and down really fast. I remember standing at the foot of her bed as panic rushed headlong through my body. 'Mammy!' I called. Nothing. I grabbed her foot and shook it. Nothing. I climbed up beside her on the bed and shouted out her name. How could she not hear me? I shouted louder, making my voice hit the rooftop. I was shaking her harder than I'd ever shaken anything.

'Stop it!' I yelled then, just in case it was a test. 'Stop!'

From outside, someone called, 'Is everything OK there?'

I froze.

'Hello?'

Soft as a cat, I dropped my mother's hand and snuck to the window. I popped up real quick and saw the Casey's van outside.

'Is everything OK?' Casey's man was at our door. He gave it a bang. 'Is everything OK?'

Bravely, I opened my mother's bedroom window and shouted down, 'Go away.'

'Is everything all right?' He pushed his cap back on his head and shaded his eyes as he peered up at me.

'Yes.'

'I thought I heard you scream.'

I looked back at my mother, hoping she'd tell me what to do. I was not supposed to talk to people. The sight of her so still sent tears spurting from my eyes.

'That's it,' Casey's man said, 'I'm coming in unless you tell me what's wrong.'

I couldn't have him come in, my mother would kill me. 'My mammy isn't moving.'

'Is she asleep?'

'I don't know, I thought she was.'

'Is she sick? Do you think she needs a doctor?'

'She was sick, now she won't wake up.'

'OK, pet, don't panic.' He pulled a phone from his pocket. 'I'm calling an ambulance. You'll have to let them in, OK? I'm going to stay here until they arrive.'

'No one is allowed in our house. There's boundaries. It's private.'

'Do you want your mammy to get better?' On my nod, he said, 'Then let them in.'

Next thing I knew, Mammy was on a stretcher, things attached to her, and the ambulance men were bringing her out of the house. I thought they were stealing her. I got hysterical and the rest of the night is a blank until I met the puppet woman.

'I'm Lucy,' she said. 'What's your name, honey?'

I stared at her. I stared around the room I was in. It was yellow and bright. I couldn't remember how I'd got there.

'Can you talk? Bill, the man that came with you in the taxi, he said you could. Would you talk to this?' And from behind her back came a puppet. I stared at it. I had the exact same thing on my wall at home. The woman put on a voice, only she made it sound like it was coming from the puppet, and asked me my name again.

It didn't seem so bad to talk to a puppet. 'Ruby,' I said.

'Can you tell me what happened, Ruby?' the puppet woman asked.

So I did. And I told her that I wanted to see my mammy right now. I pretended that I wasn't scared, the way I did when the two 'nobody importants' called.

She said that my mammy was very sick, but that she would

get better and that I might have to go live with someone else for a while and how would I feel about that?

'You don't go live with strangers,' I said.

'You do if you have no mammy or daddy to mind you,' the puppet said.

I never knew that. My mammy had never told me that.

They brought me to see her. They let me look at her through a glass door. She was lying real still on the bed, her hands outside the covers with machines all strapped up to her. They said that she was too sick to mind me but that I could go live with someone in my mother's family if they were prepared to have me.

'But you have to stay in your own house,' I said. 'There are boundaries, like the sea.'

They put me in a room with a TV and some food and some other children who I didn't want to talk to. The children were singing along with a song on the TV. I never saw TV before: it was good. There was a woman minding us but I didn't talk to her either. I fell asleep and next thing, the puppet woman came back and told me that my Auntie Susan was here to collect me.

I knew that an auntie was a sister of your parent. That meant my mammy had a sister. I screamed when I saw Auntie Susan. It was the blonde-haired woman who visited our house and knocked on the door. It was the 'nobody important'.

MAX

1

I'm sitting across from the counsellor and I know I'm not being very co-operative, but I'm not in need of counselling. I blame the private health insurance. If I didn't have it I'd have been shipped out of here by now, but instead they want to analyse me, they want to figure out why I drank a load of booze, took a load of pills and then tried to kill myself. I didn't try to kill myself, I keep saying, I just drank too much and fell down the stairs.

This counsellor – 'Call me Ian' – looks at me and says nothing. I know what his game is: he hopes I'll say something instead, then he'll pounce on it like a cat with a mouse and try to 'read' stuff into it. I've seen the movies. So I lean back in my chair and cross my legs and smile at him. It's hard to smile when you've a massive bruise on your face. Like, I mean, massive. It covers one eye and runs down by my nose. But I smile as best I can and I cross my legs, just like Ian. At least my arm is out of the sling. Not that I even needed it in the first place.

Ian waits. He's good at waiting. I'd imagine if he was on a blind date and the girl didn't show, he'd hang around forever, just waiting. He looks like a counsellor, like a shrink you'd see in a movie, a lot of beige and a calm voice that grates.

I wonder what I look like.

Time ticks on.

I see my leg is jittering so I stop it. I've never been able to sit still. That's just me.

'You seem agitated,' Ian says, his voice pouring out of him like smooth caramel. 'Why is that?'

I shrug. The rain pelts off the window, smashing onto the pavement below. This is officially, as far as I'm concerned, the crappiest Spring ever. My gaze darts around the room. It's pretty bare. Just a desk and two chairs and some pictures of landscapes. A smell like incense. Tissues and a notepad.

More silence.

I think Ian has the best job ever. Sitting on a chair, saying nothing. Better than my job anyway, thinking up spin for clients that frankly deserve to be roasted in the press.

'When can I go home?'

He seems prepared for the question, though in fairness I have been asking it since they've put me here.

'Is there anyone there for you when you go home?'

'I don't need a babysitter. I fell down the stairs.'

'After you took dangerously high amounts of drink and pills.'

'I was celebrating. I didn't realise it was dangerous.' That's good, Max, I tell myself.

'Celebrating? What?'

'My birthday. I was thirty-five.'

'And your friends?'

'What about them?'

'Where were they?'

'They'd left.'

He sits back. 'Do you and your friends normally take pills like that?'

I shrug. 'When can I go home?'

'You were unconscious for a day. It wasn't just the fall down the stairs that made that happen. You're a lucky man, Max.'

I nod. I am lucky, I agree. A terrible thing. So stupid. When can I go home?

Ian writes something down in his folder. Then he looks at me. 'Do you remember what happened in the weeks before you fell down the stairs, Max?'

'I guess you'll tell me.' I pause. 'Again.'

'Do you remember?'

I remember Sandy, that's what I remember. I remember her whiteness and her stillness. I remember the smell of coffee and the heat from the bakery. 'Bits.'

'You were in the papers a lot, do you remember that?'

'I'm always in the papers.'

'You verbally attacked some of your clients in public places. You got thrown out of nightclubs. Adam Brown, the actor, he took a restraining order out against you. Remember?'

Ian eyeballs me hard. I try to hold his gaze. Truth is, I don't remember, not exactly. He's been churning this stuff out each session and I think it's a trick. I think he just wants me to spill my guts because it all sounds so bad. And yet, there is something at the back of my head, tapping away, telling me that it could be true because I've lost all my clients except one.

'Julie Winterson said you ruined her last book promo. She said it in the newspaper two weeks ago.'

'I never liked Julie anyway.'

Ian says nothing to that. Then, suddenly, he changes tack. 'I believe you had a visitor yesterday.'

'Yep.' The change of subject is a relief.

'Was she a member of your family?'

I laugh, and he doesn't ask why.

'So, who was she? Girlfriend?'

'Nope. Just a …' I don't know what to call Sandy. 'Friend,' I finish.

Ian nods. 'And why did you agree to see her?'

What would he make of me buying a homeless girl coffee every day? Would he think it creepy? I know for sure he'd ask me why I did it and the reason why sounds bonkers now. It wasn't pity. I have no way to explain it that sounds sane. I just say, 'Because I was surprised she came to visit. She wasn't on my radar to visit.'

'So you don't know her that well.'

'I don't know her at all, she barely knows me.'

'So you're happy to have someone you hardly know visiting you?'

Yes, I think. *Yes, I am.* 'I liked that she came,' I say.

Ian nods. 'Will she be back?'

'Yes.' I know that much about her at least.

And apparently that makes Ian happy and I can go.

2

I first saw Sandy a week or so before I started getting her the coffee. I remember it had been one of those shit-hot, sunless, muggy days. The sort of day that gives me a headache. The sort of day when the sky presses down like a quilt, suffocating you. The sort of day where people walk with their heads bent and no one looks at anyone and before you've even walked ten feet, sweat is dripping down your face and your feet are fat and heavy in your shoes. That kind of a day.

I hadn't planned on leaving the house, but I couldn't stand it inside anymore. It was just me and the computer and all those people connected to me by my computer. That day, I was having heated exchanges with this person who wouldn't leave me alone. I don't know how she got my email but she was sending me messages telling me she was watching me. It was freaky, but even that wouldn't have made me leave the house. What made me leave was that I'd just been fired by Neil Foster. You know the singer, more famous for his revelations on his battle with depression than for his songs? He was real angry with me because, apparently, I had messed up his career big time. He said he hadn't wanted to talk about his depression only for I pushed him into it. It's true. That is totally true. Only I didn't push him into it, he made his own mind up. I just told him it would be a good move. I told him his single wasn't strong enough without some sort of a personal tale to back it up. The song, if I remember, was called 'Blue', so the whole depression story fitted right in. His label were delighted when it went to number one in four countries. Neil said that he never should have done it.

What did he expect me to do? I was only doing my job. I was good at my job.

So he decided to fire me. He was one of my biggest clients.

Then a guy from home contacted me. After I got his email, I left the house and started to walk. I normally drive to High Hills. Sometimes I go out running. I'm a good runner. I could run forever if I wanted. That day I just walked. High Hills is nicer than where I live. More colourful, vibrant. Not so many old people. There's a great coffee shop too and I like to grab a coffee and a cake and sit on the bench opposite and just enjoy it.

Watch the world go by, as it were. Brainstorm with myself if I want to.

That day, there was a girl on the seat that I sometimes sat on. First I wasn't sure if she was real because no one ever sat on that seat. Or at least no one I'd ever seen. It's a seat that faces into the wind, so it's not the warmest. Anyway, this girl, in a white coat, was sitting there, still as an ice statue, and I thought – and I know this is mental – that she looked like an angel. It was probably the white coat and the white hat and her stillness. I watched her from the door of the coffee shop, my takeaway cup in hand, and she just didn't move.

I liked that. Her stillness.

I went back the next day and the day after that and all the time she was there. It took me a while to realise that she was spending all day there. Just watching the world go by. And when I realised that, I bought her the coffee.

I thought she'd drink it right up. But she didn't and I was disappointed. But after a bit, she started to look up at me and her face didn't look as calm as her body. Her face had lived, if that makes sense. Her eyes were flat. Like she was looking out of them from far away. I feel like that a lot. *A lot.* Finally, we talked. And she told me her name was Sandy. I took that as a sign. I like the beach.

I kept buying her coffees and stuff after that.

3

Not much happens in the hospital. Days are all the same. We do art and drama and shit, but none of it interests me. And the fact that I'm in a mad fucking hospital is a bit freaky. I'm not mad, in fact most of the people on this floor, ward, whatever, are not mad. I mean the ones I've talked to at least. No one is too out of it or too inside themselves to not make sense. But I really don't know why I'm here. I am normal compared to some of them. One guy doesn't eat. Like seriously refuses to eat. I thought only girls got that. He says that he just can't, that if he does he'll lose control of himself. He's only about twenty. Another guy says he got depressed, one day he woke up and he was depressed. I seriously doubt that but you wouldn't argue with him. His name is Sam and he's a monster of a man, big thick biceps and tree trunks of legs. He says he used to play rugby and I believe it. In fact, it looks like all he did was play rugby and when he wasn't doing that he was probably devouring protein. Another guy, Vic, twitches all the time – if it's not his mouth or eyes, it's his feet and hands – and he has the weirdest laugh, like something out of a horror movie. There's Evie, who I liked until she befriended Norm. I don't like Norm. He's a bit of a dork. Post-traumatic stress, that's what he says is wrong with him. Only his is real bad so he has to come in here. Boo hoo.

When they ask what's wrong with me, I just say that's what I'm paying the doctors to find out and they all laugh.

It's true, though. I have no clue. I guess swallowing a load of tablets and drinking a load of booze is pretty reckless but I must have had a good reason to, only what with my booze and tablet-addled brain, I don't know what that was.

The hardest thing about being in here is: number one, no booze, and number two, trying not to let my one remaining client know that I'm in here. I don't know how it came to that. I had at least forty people on my books, big names too. I was the guy people wanted, if you can believe it. According to Ian, who I don't believe, they all left me because I was flaking big time or else I attacked them in public. I would never do that. No one stays with anyone anymore. My last client is a singer, apparently. I say 'apparently' because I actually don't remember taking her on. She says I met her in a nightclub and told her she rocked and gave her my number. Not a clue. No memory. I never take on people that way so I think she's a bit of a con artist.

My phone rings, and one look at caller ID and my heart hops about like I took speed. It's the singer, Laura is her name. Think of the devil – my one client. Imagine, I thought about her and she rings, that's got to mean something. I wonder why she's calling. I close the door to my room and decide that I'd better answer. 'Laura,' I say, and my voice sounds normal, 'great to hear from you.'

'How's the mental hospital working out?' Laura asks. Her voice is husky, pleasing, though the question less so.

'You know I'm in here?'

'Everyone does. It's been in the papers. So, can I come in or what? We can chat about my career. I'm so excited.'

If I admit that I don't know who she is, she won't be impressed. And the thoughts of launching someone right now, well, to be honest, I don't have the energy. So I say, 'I'll give you a bell when I'm sorted, Laura, OK? Won't be too long.'

If she's disappointed, she doesn't say. 'OK. Take care.'

We hang up.

4

I left home when I was nineteen. I came from this little seaside place in Wexford and basically I spent all my childhood messing about on the beach with my friends or family. In summer, if the weather was even a quarter way good we'd meet on the strand, togs on under our jeans, sandwiches wrapped tight with clingfilm to stop the sand getting in. As the years wore on and we became teenagers, we took to the beach armed with booze and crisps and loud music. Our winters were spent hiding out in the sand dunes, sheltering from the wind, daring each other to take the plunge into freezing water. We spent the days of our childhood pier-jumping, sailing, surfing and fishing. The smell of seaweed and the call of gulls were the backdrops to my life. By the time I was ten, people said that I could swim better than I could walk.

I had four close mates. Our core group, the ones who were always on for a beach ramble: Paddy, Tom, John and Shane. We grew up thinking it would never change. We swapped girlfriends and stories, we got drunk together, we lay down, full of booze, in the sand dunes staring up at the sky in which the stars had suddenly begun to spin. We filled each other full of bullshit stories of our daring with girls. We had that easiness between us that I've never ever found since.

It kind of fell apart when Shane drowned. Shane was the quiet one and though sometimes he was overlooked when he was there, when he wasn't, there was a gaping hole in the centre of our group and it was either be swallowed up by his absence or leave the hole behind and move on. And so, without actually saying it to each other, the days behind the sand dunes diminished, the loud music was turned down, and even though we all drank a bit more, we did it with no joy or sense of rebellion. It was just a means to take the edge off the grief and guilt, for at eighteen, we were unable to handle the feelings of loss and though we'd talked about so much, we couldn't ever talk about that. That would open a whole other set of wounds that we might never have handled.

There is a 'before Shane drowned' phase in my life and an 'after Shane drowned' phase.

So I left at nineteen; the lads gave me a send-off in the local pub. They were on their way to colleges around the country. Paddy, the clever one, was doing some sort of social justice thing, John was doing sport in Limerick, Tom was doing Arts and I was taking up a job in PR. I had no clue what PR was, only that there seemed to be a lot of partying and meeting famous people involved.

I liked the sound of that.

5

Sandy seems even shyer and odder than she did the first time she visited. I don't think she'd been expecting me to ask her to come again and I suppose it was a strange request; after all, we really have nothing in common other than the flavours of coffee we like.

I wonder what we'll talk about this time. I think I did most of the talking the last time, telling her about my job and stuff.

I watch her as she stands in my doorway with all the awkwardness of a new-born colt. She's a funny-looking girl, long-limbed yet childlike. I get the feeling that she knows squat about the world and a lot about life, if that makes sense. Her eyes are large and wary and she wraps her arms about her body as if she's trying to stop herself from flying into pieces. She only talks when she absolutely has to say something and if she wasn't so weird, she'd be, like, my ideal client. The only joyful thing about her is a massive multi-coloured scarf she has wrapped around her neck. But it's June and warm so she doesn't need it, which makes it a bizarre choice. She's dressed in jeans and a blue top and her brown hair is pulled right back in a ponytail, which makes it seem like she's had a facelift. She looks clean. Well, cleaner than normal. 'Hi,' I say.

'Hiya,' she says, as she edges her way into the room. 'You didn't finish the fruit.'

Damn. I'd meant to hide it so she wouldn't be offended. I don't do fruit. Eating an apple is way too much of a commitment for me. 'Not yet,' I say.

'It smells.'

'Only a bit.'

We look at each other. She holds out a bag. 'I got you some more.'

She got me a lot more. 'Great.' I take the bag from her. 'That's very kind of you.' I want to ask where she got the money but I'm afraid she'll be offended. I put the fruit with the other fruit. 'You don't need to get me fruit every time.'

'OK.'

She seems relieved. She looks at my bed. She looks at me looking at my bed and she sits on it. Then she looks like she shouldn't have. And it does look odd, her on my bed. I think that the best thing I can do is what I always do for her. 'Come on,' I jingle some change in my hands, 'we'll go to the canteen and I'll get you a coffee.'

There is a canteen on our floor; it's a bit shit but the cappuccinos and muffins are decent enough.

She smiles, or at least I think it's a smile, and it lightens up her face and I think that maybe if she hadn't been on the streets she'd have been pretty.

She follows me down to the canteen, again in a sort of awkward shuffle as if she isn't used to being accompanied by anyone, which maybe she isn't. We walk a good distance apart along the corridor, like as if we're not even together. When we reach the canteen, I tell her to find a seat while I grab us some coffee. The seat she finds is miles away from everyone else and I have to negotiate my way past table after table to get to her. It's like we're marooned on an island in the middle of the room. I pass the coffee across the table to her and I note the way she cradles the mug in her hands as if she's warming herself up, though she must be roasting in that scarf.

I wonder at the wisdom of asking her to come visit. I wonder what had possessed me. We look briefly at each other before she lowers her eyes.

'Thanks for coming,' I say.

''S OK.' She pauses, then adds, her voice jumping and spurting out of her like it's stuck in her throat, 'I have some post for you.'

Her voice has a familiar twang to it that I can't quite place. I watch as she digs into a pocket and passes me some envelopes. One of them is a cheque I'd been waiting for.

'I appreciate that.'

'Good.'

Silence. We both take a sip of coffee. I like her being there, I realise. Just someone to have coffee with, not one of the nutters, which is how I think of my fellow inmates. I know, uncharitable, but they think the same of me, I bet. And Sandy doesn't really know me either, so that takes some pressure off. And she's nice and still and calm. I like calm.

I have a sudden idea, like a spark in my head. 'Can I ask another favour?' I venture.

She shoots me a glance. One of her eyes has a blue patch. She has a scar on her lip.

'Well, I was thinking, you need a place to stay, I need a house minded, would you like to house-sit for a while?'

She jerks, coffee slops out onto her hand. 'Stay in your house?' she says.

'Yep.' I thought she'd be thrilled – she just looks confused. 'I need someone in it, to mind it.'

'And you want me?'

'It'll suit you, won't it?'

'I guess.'

'Well, then.'

'I won't rob off you,' she says.

I laugh and some people look over. 'Good. I appreciate that.'

'Some people are quare bad,' she clarifies.

The use of the word 'quare' catches me unexpectedly. And that twang … 'Are you from Wexford?'

It's like I've just made a sudden move on a frightened animal. More coffee slops from her cup and she stares at me as if I've somehow betrayed her.

'Sorry,' I apologise hastily, though I don't know what I said. I hand her a napkin to mop up the spillage but she just lets it lie there. 'It's just that I am too.' I pick up the napkin and start to mop the spilt coffee. 'That's all. That's if you *are* from Wexford. Maybe you're not.'

She doesn't reply and I continue to clean the table. 'Sorry,' I say again. I realise that I don't want to lose my only visitor. 'None of my business. It's just the word "quare" reminds me of home.' I sit back down, table done.

'I—'

'Are you harassing this woman?' Sam has appeared from nowhere and for such an enormous man that is some achievement. He slaps me on the back and, I swear, I can hear my spine crack. 'He's a terrible man,' he says loudly to Sandy as he holds out a shovel of a hand. 'You're the only one brave enough to visit him, from what I can see.'

'You need your eyes testing so,' I say back. I'm glad of the interruption, not quite sure how to make things right with Sandy. 'She's the only one I let visit.' I try out a smile.

Sam's hand dangles in mid-air. Sandy stares at it, looks to me. I think she wants to know what to do so I nod and she shakes Sam's hand. I have never touched her. She wouldn't take my hand the one time I offered it.

'Sam,' he introduces himself.

'Sandy,' she says back.

'Nice to meet you,' Sam says, like he means it, and lumbers off.

'Depression,' I whisper to Sandy, though why I feel the need to tell her, I don't know. 'That's what Sam has. He doesn't look depressed, does he?' I sound like a dork.

'I don't know what depressed people look like,' she says.

'Sorry about your coffee,' I say, having run out of steam on Sam and reluctant to go on about people being depressed.

'It's OK.' She doesn't look at me and I think I've cocked up, only I don't know how.

'I won't ask you about yourself again,' I say.

'Good,' she says. Then, a bit crossly, 'I left Wexford long ago.'

'Me too.' Then I add, maybe to give her something to make up for my blunder, 'My family are still there. There was me and my dad, my aunt and my sister. My mother's dead. I lived in Rossclare.'

A pause. A flick of her eyes. 'I was from near there.'

'Yeah?'

'I have to go.' She startles me by standing up abruptly.

'And you'll come again?' This is one strange stranger.

A hesitation. 'Yes.'

'You remember the alarm code?'

'Yes.' She almost runs out of the canteen.

6

At the beginning of my new PR job, I spent my days running around with files and meeting people who were famous, and leading them into offices. I'd sit in on some meetings and take notes and type them up. I knew which celebs were having affairs and who with, whose marriage was in trouble, who was planning to bring out a new album, who was suing who. I learned how the truth of things can be twisted to expose another angle, how the truth wasn't necessarily the truth, how to apologise without actually apologising. When I wasn't working, I joined the rest of the staff for a few jars in the local pub. Then one evening, when I'd been there about a year, the boss called an after-hours meeting. I had to be there to distribute files and take notes while at the same time staying below the radar and being easy to ignore. It transpired that one of our clients, a high-profile singer, had been caught having an affair. The boss wanted to brainstorm on how a positive spin could be put on it. Various suggestions were put forward. It couldn't be called a 'moment of madness' because it had been going on for four years. This man had three children all aged under six.

Eventually, I said, 'Can he not just deny it?'

Everyone looked at me. The boss was not happy. 'It's an affair that's been going on for four years, Max,' he said, and I swear, he sounded as if he wanted to throttle me. People like me did not speak up in meetings. 'Now—'

'Who says?' I spoke again.

Through gritted teeth, he said, 'Pictures have been leaked to the papers. You saw them. You photocopied them for us.'

There was a titter through the room.

'Yeah, pictures of him going in and out of this woman's apartment. Big deal. If he denies it, who can argue, especially if,' I leaned over and thumbed through the file and found the name of his mistress, 'Lena backs him up and I think she will. She says she loves him and she has a lot to lose too. She's a counsellor, for Christ's sake.'

There was a pause. Surprisingly, to me at least, none of them had considered the woman.

'Get them both to lie?'

'Is it a lie?' I made a face, I spread my arms. 'There is no real proof here. It's not pretty but denial is your best bet. Get him to issue a non-apology apology. Something like, "If my behaviour caused hurt to my wife or suspicion among my colleagues, then I deeply regret it."'

'And what will we say he was doing, going in and out of there for four years?' someone else asked.

'She is a counsellor. Maybe the poor sod needed counselling for a trauma, or a sadness in his life that he felt unable to tell his wife about. It's easier to spin a sob story for him.'

There was a silence. I walked out.

The following week, I was given my own office and the week after that, I was given two mid-list clients. It was my job to make them famous.

And I did.

Part Two

SANDY

1

Max's offer to let me live in his house makes me feel bad. Because, you see, I already had moved in. I didn't plan it. That's important to say. Other times, before, when I had the cleaning job, I did it on purpose. Like if people were away on holidays, Clara and me would move in for a couple of days, just to get a proper shower and watch some TV, but I would never ever take advantage of Max, especially as he's sick.

Only I did. I did take advantage and though I know it's wrong, it's right too, because I'm on the other side and I'm looking at me. And I know that I'm not going to do anything bad, like run up a big bill or steal stuff. I'm not going to break things or mess up the gaff.

I was just going to live here for a bit. That's all.

The lure of a roof and safety is like the siren call of a pied piper to someone who has lived on the street, to someone who has shared a crappy apartment and one bathroom for fifteen euro a day with twenty other people, some of whom would kill you for a tenner. And when it's a roof that you have some control of, well, it's pretty much irresistible.

It happened like this. I went to call on Max's neighbour to tell him where the key to Max's house was and when he wasn't in, I hung about for a bit. Then it started to rain and

I had no shelter and so I thought that maybe I could get the key and collect the post myself. What was the big deal?

So I did. And the minute I set foot inside the door, it was as if the house wrapped itself around me and that was it. I just sort of moved in. It's not like I was doing any harm.

I hadn't even realised that my shoulders spent most of their time hunched round my ears until I stood in Max's hallway and breathed in warm, dry air. Now they ache with how tense they were.

That was five days ago.

Max's house has two bedrooms, one that is Max's because it's filled with loads of stuff: CDs piled in the corner that look as if they're about to topple over, books thrown under the bed, socks and discarded clothes. Trainers of all colours line the skirting boards; some of them look as if they haven't even been worn yet. There's a flat-screen TV on the wall, the remote control on the bed. The room smells musty, as if no air has ever got into it. The floor is wooden and a little dusty, the walls cream.

His other bedroom just has a bed and an empty chest of drawers. That's where I sleep. It's hard to get used to a soft bed, so I mostly sleep on the floor. At night I lie there in my sleeping bag, with the curtains open, and peer up into the sky. On clear nights the moon shines right in and I just want to stay here forever.

In return for staying here, I've decided that I'll clean Max's house top to bottom. It could do with it. It just seems as if Max never loved it enough. At least the house is not carpeted, it just has wooden floors throughout. Right at the very bottom of the stairs, just after the last step, there is a patch of red. I figure that's from when Max fell down the stairs. I'll scrub that. Max has a super shiny kitchen with a massive fridge. Only there is no food in the fridge. If I get a job, which might be easier now, I can buy food for the fridge. On the upside, there are loads of cans in the presses. Maybe about fifty cans of beans and thirty cans of spaghetti. Packets and packets of soup and stock cubes. And about ninety packets of marrowfat peas.

He also has a washing machine and a dryer. Two days after I moved in, I put my sleeping bag in the washing machine. I found some powder and dumped it in too and then sat and watched as my sleeping bag was spun around and around. When it came out, the smell of freshness from it nearly made me cry. I pulled it right to my chin that night and fell asleep to the scent of roses.

Max's bathroom, which is a bit skanky, has washing gels. Loads of them in a little drawer underneath the bath. They smell good too and I use them. Once I get a job, I'll replace them. I try not to use too much electricity so that he won't have a big bill.

From Max's bedroom, I can see into his neighbour's garden. It's really pretty with colourful flowers tumbling out of flowerbeds, bushes in full bloom and grass smooth enough to play sport on. Max's garden looks like he fought a war in it. I think at one time it must have been looked after because there is a flower bed and some hedging. Now though, the grass is as high as my hips. Right down the back, there is a wooden shed and I wonder what is inside. Probably a lawnmower. Halfway down, there is what looks like the remains of a bonfire. I think that maybe I'll tackle the garden too, just mow the grass if I can.

Of all the rooms, I like Max's office the best. It's full of books and magazines and bits of paper. His books are mainly biographies, which I think I might read. I prefer that to fiction. Max's computer is still on and I haven't dared to turn it off in case I break it. If I touch it at all, a picture of a beach pops up. The first time it happened, I couldn't look away. I've never seen a beach in daylight. The computer sits on an old desk with loads of drawers. I haven't looked inside the drawers because that's private. On the walls, there are photographs of Max with various different people. I guess they must be his family or friends.

The day Max asks me to mind his house, I pick up his key from under the stone and let myself in through the front door, in daylight. It doesn't matter who sees me now: I can come and go as I please. I open the door, walk into the hallway, close the door and lean against it.

I am free for a tiny while.

I'm scared to feel the enormous relief I know I should, because this situation won't last and sooner or later I'll have to leave here and get back to my real life.

2

The street. That's what everyone calls it. And it means everywhere and just one place. In the city, the street is alive, bright and dangerous. It's tempting and frightening. It's loud and deathly quiet all at the same time. It sings with tension and keeps secrets like a grave. I spent a month in the city, in doorways, after I lost the cleaning job, trying to be normal, trying to hang onto myself, though I had no idea what either one was. I'd tried to find other work, though I couldn't. Being off-radar means no PPS number so people won't employ you or if they do, the wages are shit. That month almost broke my hope. I remember one night, sitting in a doorway, knees scooped up into my chest, head bowed, rain sleeting down and no one asked how I was. People walked on, the thrum of the city pulled them to their clubs and jobs. And the night passed and by morning, I was a new me. Fashioned again from the mess of the gutter.

I left that day, just as dawn broke over the Liffey and the wheeling gulls. I set my face west and I just walked. I don't know how long for but after a bit I found High Hills. It's pretty, but in the quieter towns the streets are slow and easy, a lullaby compared to the raucous chorus of the city. And time stretches out like a blue ocean, on and on, forever. Just like it had when I lived at home. Each day is quiet but endless, each hour becomes a city day, each minute, each second is felt keenly. Street living in High Hills is for the terminally ill who want to feel they've made their lives that bit longer. But it's as safe as you can get in this life.

Once upon a time I thought I knew the world. Then at ten, my world tipped. It never righted itself again. So at seventeen, I ran. And in running, I went from a frying pan straight into a furnace and the old me was burnt up and someone else was re-fashioned from the ashes. A stronger me, a more resilient me. A me that will fight hard if I have to. A me that takes no messing. A me that sometimes can't feel anything beyond the loss of knowing how to feel.

Max with his coffee and sandwiches was the first person to rap on the wall of glass that seems to separate me from everyone else. It's like I opened a window and let him in. And with him came fresh air and more hope.

And now, I'm very much afraid of letting him go.

And very much afraid of him staying.

3

Max's town is a nothing kind of place. The only thing it has that High Hills hasn't is a library. On impulse, I decide to go in. It'll be warm and dry and it'll kill a couple of hours. I think that maybe I could find some magazines and come here every day and just read them for free. I miss my magazines.

Inside, the library is dim. There's a noticeboard at the door which I busy myself looking at in order to get my bearings. I have no idea if anyone will question my presence here. Maybe I might need to show ID. There are a few older people sitting at tables reading the newspapers. A mother with a toddler is busy trying to interest him in a couple of books. She's on her hunkers showing him the pages while he keeps slapping the book away and going, 'No'. The mother has great patience, her voice is calm. I watch as she pulls him into her embrace and, despite his protests, cuddles him hard, then tickles him, making him laugh. I find myself smiling, then she catches me looking and I hastily turn back to the noticeboard.

An ad, in big bold red letters, catches my eye.

Wanted: Reader for an invalid. No experience necessary. Call Charles for an interview. Ten euros an hour for two hours a day.

My eye slides over it before coming back for a second look. I could do that job, I think. And it'd probably be cash in hand, so I wouldn't need any sort of tax stuff, which has been a big problem for me before. I stare at the ad. It's dated yesterday. My heart whumps. It'd mean going into someone's house, talking to them, hoping they wouldn't recognise me. But it's been eight years, it's hardly likely now. Dare I?

I glance around. No one is looking. Reaching up, I take the ad and pocket it.

I've a list of things I owe Max for taped to the fridge and I add phone call to the end of it. After that I use Max's landline to dial this guy Charles. I get as far as 'I saw your ad in the library' before being interrupted.

'You'll be reading to my mother mainly in the late afternoon,' Charles says. 'Where are you living? We're in Hill Walk.'

'Me too.'

'So you're local. That's brilliant.' Charles sounds as if I've done him a huge favour. 'Tell you what, call around tomorrow at two and we'll see how things pan out. Number eight, Church Terrace.'

That's next door. The house beside this one. That man with the lanky body and the floppy hair must be Charles. I wonder what his mother is like; I haven't seen her. I wonder if I should say that I'm beside them. It'd look weird if I don't. 'I'm in number six.'

There is a pause. His voice when it comes is muted, 'Max Coyle's house?'

'Yes.'

'Oh.'

I think then that maybe I shouldn't have said it. 'Is that OK?' I venture.

'Are you the girl in the white jacket that goes in and out?'

'Yes.'

'Oh.'

I don't know how to respond so I just say, 'I'll call in tomorrow, then.'

'Yes,' he seems to recover, 'we'll see how it goes. There might be more people calling so don't get your hopes up.'

It sounds like he just made the last bit up so I say nothing, just hang up.

4

Clara was a couple of years younger than me but seemed way older. She was thin with spiky limbs that seemed to stick out in every direction. Her hair was choppy and dyed blacker than night. Her nose and ears had rings and she had a tattoo of a spider on the back of her hand. She wore jeans that made her legs look like sticks and t-shirts that hung off her like washing on a line. On my first day, she took me aside and said that I'd better toughen up or I'd be eaten up and spat out. She said I should say 'fuck off' often and with menace. She said that chewing gum was a good tactic to make people think you didn't care. She said that the wages were crap and that in this job you had to take the bonuses when you found them. Then she tapped her nose, said she'd see how I measured up and if she felt I deserved a little more help, she'd give it to me.

I don't know what I did to measure up – maybe it was when I managed to glue a vase together that she'd broken by accident without leaving so much as the trace of a crack. Maybe it was the day I ended up in a fight with one of the girls in the flat over the shower and won. Whatever it was, Clara decided that I was a worthy pupil.

The first thing she did was teach me how to supplement our income. Her words. I remember it was the day after

Christmas and she'd been away somewhere. She'd found me in the flat and dragged me outside where it was freezing. 'I trust you,' she said, looking me up and down, arms folded. 'Am I right to do that?'

'Yep.'

'Come,' she said.

I had nothing else to do so I went with her. She talked all the way down Grafton Street and into D'Olier Street. Then she patted a bench for me to sit beside her, so I did. For a while, she did nothing and the two of us people-watched. The shops were open again and it was busy. I was cold, but she was the first person to seek out my company since I left home and I liked that so I stayed where I was and waited to see what she would do. After a bit, she stood up and sauntered down the street towards the traffic lights. They went green for the pedestrians and everyone except Clara crossed the road. Instead, she turned back and came towards me, trying not to grin.

When she reached me, however, she smiled. She sat down beside me and pulled a black wallet from her jacket.

I stared at her, amazed.

'Let's see.' She flipped it open and found sixty euros. 'Yes! Christmas breakfast for us two, I think. And a sleeping bag for me.'

'How did you do that?'

'Come on, let's move before he realises it's gone.'

'Who realises?' I ran to catch up with her.

'The guy I took it from.' She talked rapidly, high on success, I guess. 'Did you see him? Jeans, short puffa jacket?'

I nodded.

'Well, the stupid idiot had it in the candy pocket.' She laughed. At my look, she explained. 'Back pocket of jeans, the candy pocket,' she said. 'You leave your money there, you deserve to be robbed.' We crossed over a busy road, cars honking us, me half-running to catch up.

I didn't think anyone deserved to be robbed, but I didn't say it.

We arrived in George's Street and Clara pushed open the door of a café and ordered us both a full Irish breakfast.

'Who taught you to do that?' I asked.

'What? Order a breakfast?'

'No.'

She grinned. 'I mostly learned myself.'

Two plates of steaming sausages, rashers, pudding and eggs were laid in front of us. My stomach rumbled; it was a long time since I'd eaten anything this big. We dived on the food.

'Happy Christmas,' she said.

'Thank you.'

'Payback for the vase.'

'Cool.'

We ate in silence before she asked, 'So, what's your story? You leave home or what?'

Her directness wrong-footed me. 'Yeah.'

'Me too,' she said. 'Why?'

'Wanted to.'

'Same here,' she said. 'Respect.' She clinked her fork off mine and it struck me as a cool thing to do.

We ate some more, both of us enjoying the heat and the

warmth of the diner and the food, wincing a little too as feeling returned to our frozen fingers and toes.

'I have ideas for more money if you want to stick around,' Clara said.

I shrugged. As her face fell, I explained, 'When I came to Dublin, someone stole all my money. It sucked.'

'Yeah, well, maybe they were hungry too. Maybe they needed a sleeping bag.'

'I suppose.' I'd never thought of that before. It was wrong for me but right for them, maybe.

More silence.

She fanned out some money on the table. 'It's all very well working for the cleaning company but a bit of a rob now and again is necessary. Everyone needs clothes.'

She was the first friend I ever had. We'd been mates until I got us fired.

5

I sit across from Max, two coffees in front of us. He's bought us an enormous bun each, which he says are called muffins. The chocolate muffins are his favourite and he reckons they might be mine as well, but I think the chocolate is too sweet. I don't want to say it though, because that would be rude, so I'm picking on it using my fingers and making loads of crumbs.

'How you getting on?' Max asks. He leans towards me, elbows on the table, his face cupped in his palms. His eyes are bright, alive.

'Good.'

'The house is OK?'

'I haven't broken anything.'

'No.' He waves me away. 'I mean, is the house OK for you?'

What a ridiculous question. I almost laugh. 'I was homeless,' I say.

'You can make it your own,' he says. 'Like, listen to my music, whatever. What music do you like?'

That's a weird question. How would I know that? I haven't listened to music in years. I know all about different types of music because I used to nick music magazines from the newsagent's but I discovered that reading about music is not the same as listening to it. Max looks so expectant that I don't want to let him down so I think hard and a memory surfaces. A teenage boy, a guitar. 'There was a band from Wexford once, The Unconventionals. I liked them.'

'They're huge.' Max nods. 'They got a good agent. What's your favourite song of theirs?'

'Dunno.' I can't remember any of their songs. My mother and I listened mostly to classical music and, now, whenever I hear a Vivaldi or a Mozart my stomach lurches in recognition and the longing to go home is excruciating.

'I'm sure I have a couple of The Unconventionals' CDs in my room. Have a listen. You can listen to anything you want, OK? There are loads of books too. Do you read?'

'Not anymore.'

'Not anymore?' He sounds amused.

'I don't like fiction.'

He seems surprised at that. 'There are lots of different types of fiction.'

I shrug. 'Yeah, but it's all fiction.'

He grins. I don't know why. 'OK. Well, I've biographies too. Have a look at them.'

I don't tell him that I spend my time mostly watching his TV. There's a show on about people who let cameras follow them around and they live their lives on TV. They're weird sort of people and they're from America and they eat hotdogs all day. I'd love to try out a hotdog. My mother used to tell me that America was ruining culture, but that is a great programme. I also like the talent shows, especially when someone has had a really hard time, like their granny who brought them up dies and her one wish was for this person to appear on TV singing and they do and nobody thinks they'll be any good and suddenly they open their mouth and, hey presto, they can really sing. I love that. It's like fiction, only better, because it is real life. I must miss what Max says next because then he waves his hand in front of my face and asks me if I'm listening.

'What?'

'I forgot to say the other day that if someone rings the house, don't answer, OK?'

I wouldn't have anyway. 'OK.'

'Good. So, anymore news?'

I think hard. 'I'm going for a job interview.'

'Hey, great.'

'And it's next door to you.'

'Next door to here? The hospital?'

'No, next door to your house. It's reading for an invalid.'

Max goes suddenly quiet. It's a little unnerving.

'I've never seen this person,' I say. 'Is she nice?'

'Did you by any chance say you were a friend of mine?' Max asks. His gaze drops from my face.

'I said I was in your house.'

'Tell them I employ you. Tell them you don't know me.'

I gawk at him.

'Be better for you.' He gives a half-smile. 'Trust me.'

'Why?'

He shrugs. 'I'm not sure, but I think they don't like me.'

'You're not sure?'

He raps his head. 'Fuzzy.'

I feel sorry for him. It must be awful not to be able to remember things. I change the subject. 'Is there a key to your garden shed?'

'Why?'

'I thought I might clean up your garden.'

'You don't have to.'

'I would like to. I like cleaning things up. I used to be a cleaner.'

'You did?'

'I got fired.' I don't tell him why, he might think badly of me. 'But I was good at the job and I would like to clean your garden.'

'Why did you get fired?'

'I'd rather not say.' I stare him down. Then I add, 'It was for nothing, really.'

He lets it go. 'The key to my garden shed could be anywhere. I think it's probably in the garden somewhere.'

'In the garden?'

Max nods. 'Don't ask.'

So I don't, because he didn't ask about me. I tell him I'll look for the key and he tells me not to bother and I say I will and he says he'll pay for the hire of a lawnmower. Then we have another cup of coffee and then I have to go because he has a therapy session with all the nutters. That's what he calls them. Which isn't very nice, I don't think. But Max is nice so I'm sure he doesn't really mean it.

'Good luck with the interview,' he says at the end. 'And remember, you don't know who I am.'

I don't tell him that I already met Charles that first day

when I came looking for Max. I think Max has forgotten that bit. But I'd never say I don't know someone when I do. That was the sort of thing my mother did.

At two, I ring the bell at number eight. Like all the houses on the small street, bar Max's, it's beautifully cared for. The knocker on the door sparkles and my reflection looks all wobbly in it. That's the way I feel actually.

The door is opened by Charles, who looks even taller and skinner than the last time I met him. His jeans are way too big and pulled tight at the waist by a big brown belt.

'Hello.' His voice is sunny and bright, like a rabbit hopping about. He pulls the door wider to let me in. 'It's Sandy, isn't it?'

'Yes.'

He scrutinises me. 'You look even younger than you did the last time we met. Are you sure you're free every afternoon?' He's walking ahead of me into the house. He bounces along. He's just wearing socks. The left one has a hole in it.

I know that I have to follow him, so I do after closing the front door. It amazes me the ease with which people invite others into their home. 'Yes, I'm free,' I say. 'I do nothing all day.'

'Sit down,' he says, 'I've coffee in the pot.'

I sit and watch as he pours me an enormous mug of coffee and pulls packets of biscuits from a press.

Everything about him is rapid and jerky and done with lots of energy. 'Sorry,' he snorts, as he comes to sit opposite, 'I never even asked if you like coffee. Tea? Would you like that instead? I have some somewhere.' He hops back up again.

'Coffee is fine.' I'm unsure how to respond to all this liveliness.

'Sure?'

I nod and take a sip. It's awful coffee, not that I'm an expert. I've only drunk it since Max started buying it for me.

'Good.' He sits back down. 'So, you're Sandy?'

'Yes. And you're Charles.'

'That's right. Top marks already.' He takes a sip of coffee and spits it out. 'Bollix, that's vile. Do you really like it?'

'Yes.'

'Seriously? You like that?' He hops up again to make a fresh cup for himself.

I thought it was a test. I'll have to drink what I have now.

When he's satisfied that he's made a better cup, he sits back down, takes a sip and sighs in satisfaction. He sprawls his legs in front of him and crosses them at the ankles. 'Right,' he says, 'so, tell me about yourself. You live next door now?'

'Just while Max is in hospital. He asked me to mind his house for him.'

Charles nods. 'And how is he?'

'Good.' I wonder if he wants me to say more. He looks as if he does. 'He's good,' I say again.

'He's still not letting his father visit, you know,' Charles says. 'My mother rings his dad now and again to ask how things are.'

I have nothing to say to this. I think my silence flusters Charles a little.

'It's just that my mother is really fond of Pierce,' he explains, then adds, 'Max's dad.'

'I see.' I don't actually.

Charles holds his hands up. 'Anyway, all that has nothing to do with the job. Basically, it's my mother you'll be reading to, she loves her books and her poetry. Patricia, a neighbour, does it at the moment for free, but her eyesight isn't great and my mother is a bit exacting.' He takes another gulp of coffee. 'Molly is my mother, she's bed-bound. I'm her son and carer. The only pleasure she has now really is her books and poems so I'm looking for someone good. Do you like poetry?'

'I do.' I used to, so it's not a lie.

'Good,' he beams. 'I'm banking you read well?'

'I'm banking on it too.' He laughs. It wasn't a joke. 'I really am,' I say, and his smile dips a bit.

Then there is silence, before he stands up. 'Come in and meet my mother. See if you'll both get on.'

Get on? I'll only be reading to her.

He leads me upstairs and raps on a bedroom door. It's the bedroom I use in Max's house. 'Come in,' someone calls, and Charles pushes open the door.

'Mam, this is Sandy, she's hoping to read for you.' He beckons me forward.

I walk into a dim room which is totally taken over by a large double bed. Beside the bed, various medicine bottles stand on a dresser. A vase of flowers adds some colour along with rows and rows of CDs. Music is playing. Beethoven. I say, 'Hi,' because you have to.

The woman in the bed looks me up and down with bright blue eyes. She isn't a real old person, she looks young enough. Probably the age my mother is.

'Sandy,' she says, 'come over here.'

I walk towards her. I try to look like I'm not nervous, but I am. I'd really like this job.

'That's good, I can see better now,' she says. Her voice slurs but is strong and I can understand her.

I'd say she was quite a good-looking woman at one stage, but now her face is twisted. I wonder what is wrong with her. 'So, Sandy,' she says, 'why would you want to read for me?'

'Because I have no job and I live at the moment next door.'

'In Max Coyle's house,' Charles says, and I feel that his words are loaded with meaning.

'How is the volatile Max?' Molly asks. 'Is he any happier now?'

That's a weird question.

'Such a sad boy,' she says, before I can answer. 'I always said that about him, didn't I, Charles?'

'Among other things.' He grins, then backs out of the room. 'I'll leave you two to get to know each other, see if it suits you both.' He closes the door and it's just me and Molly.

We eye each other up.

'Sit down.'

I do.

'You like books?'

I jump at the way she fires this at me. 'Yes.' I used to.

'What sort of books?'

'All sorts,' I lie.

'Name the last book you read.'

I gawk at her.

'Well?'

I can feel this slipping away. Desperately, I try to think of

one book I've read. It's been so long. I stopped reading fiction
when I left home, sick of happy endings, sick of people doing
the right thing. I needed reality back then, tools to live by.
'It's been a while,' I eventually admit. 'I had no time.'

Molly appraises me. 'You should always have time to
read,' she says. 'Name one book you read and liked.'

'*Wuthering Heights*.' I liked it at the time.

Molly nods her approval. 'And you're used to reading out
loud?'

'I read to my friend,' I say, which is true. I'd read magazine
pieces to Clara.

'Hmm.' She looks me up and down again. 'You're bound
to be better than Patricia anyway. She can't see and she refuses
to wear her glasses. I say to her, I can't walk so that's why I
have a wheelchair, you stupid woman.'

'That makes sense.'

She laughs for some reason, then says, 'Don't you want to
know what's wrong with me?'

'No.'

'Really? If I saw a woman in bed, I'd wonder.'

'That's you.'

I think she's laughing at me. She says, 'I have motor neuron
disease. Basically it means that my muscles are fucked.'

I don't know what to say to that. She doesn't look like the
sort of woman who would say 'fucked' but you never can tell.
I go for, 'Thanks for letting me know.'

'So, to books,' she says after a beat. She reaches over and
shakily pulls a piece of paper from her locker. The medicine
bottles rock and I make a dive to stop them from falling.

'Plastic,' she says to me as she unfolds the paper. 'Now, see here.' She passes me the page. 'These are the books I want you to get from the library. Julian is the librarian there, he'll help you. Tell him the books are for Molly.'

I scan the list. Oscar Wilde's short stories, A few Brontë novels, a couple of more modern ones. And some poetry.

'Get the books. We can start the day after tomorrow.'

'I have the job?'

'Yes, you have the job.' A pause. 'For now.' Then she says, 'Aw, a smile at last.'

I realise that I'm smiling. Then I glower because she has embarrassed me.

'Tell me about yourself,' she says, not bothered by my scowl. 'Having Mad Max as a friend is not much of a recommendation.'

'Max isn't mad,' I defend.

'Sorry.' She doesn't sound sorry. 'I wasn't thinking. I always called him Mad Max, mainly because I had a bit of a brawl with him. Where are you from?'

This wasn't part of the plan. 'Wexford.' The word causes a hitch in my throat.

'And what brings you here?'

'I walked, mostly.'

She laughs.

'Why did you come here?' She stresses the 'why'.

I think I go red. 'I came looking for work. I got some for a while.'

'Like?'

I have to answer. It's as if I'm stepping out into a cold wind. 'Leaflet delivery, sandwich board, paper seller and then a cleaner.'

'And you gave them up?'

She's nosey. I eyeball her. 'Yep.'

She changes tack, sort of. 'And did you go to college or anything?'

'No.' She wants more. I want the job. 'I was home-schooled. Never did the state exams.' Then in case that'll turn her off me, I add, 'But I can read well.'

A pause, then she nods. 'Get those books and we'll see how it goes.'

'OK.'

'You can go now.'

As I stand, I say awkwardly, 'Thank you.'

She smiles. 'See you in two days with an armful of books.'

That evening, I stand in Max's back garden and take it in. I have a roof over my head and a job of sorts. My body feels different and I realise that most of the tension in my belly and shoulders seems to have lifted.

I stand among the knee-high grass, the overgrown flowerbed, the numerous dandelion clocks and daisies and I realise that for the next couple of weeks, maybe more, I won't have to worry about a thing.

It's then I realise that I'm smiling.

6

I went on the rob a few times with Clara. I did it because she was my friend and also because I liked it. I didn't want to but it was a buzz, a way to break the monotony of my day. Plus, I made money out of it and it kept me alive.

'It's easy,' Clara said, when she broached it with me. 'And you won't be doing it, I will.'

'So why do you need me?'

'Because no one knows you. And you look like you can just wander into a shop and everyone will believe who you are.'

I liked that she said that. 'What would I have to do?'

She grinned and explained the job.

It sounded quite easy.

The next day the two of us walked into Gordon Black's, a really expensive shop in Dublin. We looked like two friends on a shopping trip. Clara looked good, she'd managed to grab the shower before anyone else that morning. As we wandered about, marvelling at the designer bags and shoes, Clara pointed out the security cameras to me. On no account must I ever look in their direction.

The next day, we did the same. On the third day, I had to point them out to her.

I realised that Clara was a bit of a pro at this, which probably should have reassured me, but it didn't. It just made me think that whatever she was going to steal would have to be worth all the planning.

On the day she'd decided to carry out the robbery, she managed to acquire some respectable clothes from the hostel. Five minutes before I entered the store, Clara swaggered in. I watched her from the window of a neighbouring shop and I had to smile at the arrogant way she walked. It was a little over the top.

At ten to eleven I entered the store. The plan was that I'd be over at the jewellery section by eleven. I had to take a few deep breaths before beginning a fake browse through the make-up. An assistant asked me was I OK. Five minutes to go and she was advising me on lip colours. Three minutes to eleven, I stopped her sales patter and told her I'd be back when I'd checked a few things out.

I walked on shaky legs towards the jewellery, my heart walloping like mad against my ribs. More deep breaths before I spotted Clara a little way up the shop. I began to follow her at a distance, looking at her but not looking, making sure I was close but not too close. I watched her mosey into the bag section. I fingered a few scarves. I saw her pick up a bag and try it on for size. I draped a scarf around my neck. I saw Clara look at herself in the mirror and begin innocently to move away, the bag still on her shoulder. When she reached the shop entrance, I let out a shriek and collapsed onto the floor.

They let me leave the shop ten minutes later when I assured them that it was just vertigo and that I'd only screamed to make sure people got out of the way before I toppled over.

There had been so much commotion by my fall that when the alarm went off for Clara's bag snatch, the reaction had been too slow for Clara to be caught. Clara was whooping with delight when she caught up with me an hour later. In her hand she had one hundred euros.

'Our commission,' she grinned.

After that I did it a few more times and we only came close to being caught once and that scared me so much, I told Clara that I couldn't do it anymore. She was pretty OK about it, I think she knew our time would have run out eventually.

Our modus operandi never varied. The day we almost got caught was my fault. Clara had decided to rob an electronics store. Someone she knew wanted printer cartridges. It was the usual routine: she entered and then after five minutes it was my turn. Clara had told me to go to the back of the store, that it was so small that I'd see her from there. There were only two security cameras in the place, one at the front of the shop and one in the middle; there were none at the back. Because the shop was so small it meant that I wouldn't have to follow her, all I'd have to do was see her from where I was standing and my faint would not be captured on any camera.

I walked in and did my usual meandering around, looking at iPads and fancy cameras and laptops. I tried pressing buttons on a few of them. Finally, I made it to the banks of TVs at the back of the store. And I came face to face with images of my mother appealing for information about me. I'd been missing five years at that stage, and seeing my mother magnified on the screens of those enormous televisions shocked me so much I was totally unable to move.

And it wasn't just seeing her that stunned me, it was the fact that she'd gone out into the world to make the appeal. And she didn't look like she used to. Her face was thinner than before, her hair was greyer than I remember and her eyes had no spark. *You have done that to her*, I remember thinking.

She was hunched up in a studio chair telling the interviewer that she knew, just knew, I was out there. 'Please, Ruby,' she said, 'please, please come home. I just want to hug you. Or even just phone me. Just a call to say that you're OK. Please.' Then she looked as if she was trying not to cry. 'We all miss you,' she said. 'Me and your granny and Susan and all your friends.'

I had no friends. She didn't talk to Susan.

'Have you got a picture of her?' the interviewer asked.

She pulled a picture of me and her from her pocket and the camera zoned in on it.

I don't know how long I stood, mesmerised, in front of the TV. It was probably seconds but it felt like years as emotions ripped through me. The next thing I remember was the sound of an alarm going off and when I whirled about, the look of panic on Clara's face as she realised that I hadn't done my job. And then she was gone, flying down the street with someone chasing after her.

She didn't get caught but she was furious with me and I didn't blame her. 'What the fuck were you doing watching that TV?' she snapped. 'I thought you were being really clever about it, I didn't realise it was going to hold your fucking interest so hard. He was this close,' she made a tiny gap with her thumb and forefinger, 'this close to catching me.'

'I'm sorry, I really am. I don't know what happened.' I was so relieved she hadn't been caught.

'You were looking at that woman talking about her daughter.'

'Yes. Sorry.'

Clara took a deep breath and said nothing for a bit. Finally she said, 'I outran him, big fat eejit.'

I was forgiven.

7

The next morning, bright and early, I head for the library. It's pretty deserted except for one old man reading the newspapers and a dapper-looking librarian complete with dicky bow energetically filing books onto shelves. He smiles at me as I pass. He looks like a Julian. 'Are you Julian?'

'Yes, yes I am.' He almost stands to attention. 'What can I help you with?' His face is as eager as a puppy's.

'I have a list here from Molly—'

'Molly Stephens?'

I realise that I don't know Molly's surname. 'Molly from Church Terrace?'

'Molly Stephens,' he repeats with pleasure.

I hand him the list and he scans it. 'She loves the classics,' he tells me, as he walks through the library with a little swagger. 'She's read them all. I don't suppose she told you that she founded our book club?'

'No.'

'Well, she did. And now, here we are.' He plucks out an Oscar Wilde and hands it to me and walks on. 'She is a wonderful woman. How is she?'

'She's in bed.' I don't know how she is.

'Full time?' Julian shakes his head and tuts. 'Such a pity. Such a pity. A dynamic woman. She was always in here, life and soul, that's what she was.' He plucks another book from a shelf and hands it to me, without so much as a glance. I don't know how he knows where everything is. 'So you're going to be reading to her?'

'Yes.'

'Charles told me he was on the lookout for someone. You're younger than I thought you'd be.'

'Unemployed.'

'So sad. And what did you do before you were made unemployed?' He puts the final novel into my hands and looks at me.

'Nothing.'

He laughs, only half-listening as he swivels to the left. 'Poetry,' he says, and I follow him until he stops in front of a bank of shelves. 'Seamus Heaney,' he mutters, looking up and down.

And then I see my mother's poetry books, face out. One of the covers is a black and white photo of her and the image startles me. I drop the books I'm holding and they scatter over the floor. I barely notice. Only half-aware of what I'm doing, I reach out and pluck the book from the shelf. It's called *We Wait in Vain*, which I don't even remember. It must have been published after I left. I flip to the title page. The dedication reads, *To Those Who Wait*.

Heart sore, I turn the book over and am faced with a colour picture of her. She looks fabulous with her large eyes and her hair up in her customary bun. She's smiling without showing her teeth – she never showed her teeth – her head is thrown back at an angle and suddenly I'm ambushed by the memory of her laugh. I see her flinging me into the air as I shriek in delight. The day is yellow and bright and I'm small. Swallowing hard, I flip to the first poem. I scan it and turn to the next one and then the next one. All in all, there are about thirty poems.

'Are you OK?' Julian asks.

'Yes.' I bend down to pick up the books, but he has got there before me. 'Sorry about that.'

'No bother.' He lays the fallen books beside me on a shelf, then straightening up, he peers over my shoulder. 'Melanie Fairbrother.' He draws out the name, piercing me again. 'What a poet!'

'Yes.'

He moves closer, invading my space, and peers at the book I'm holding. 'Not her best book.' He deftly removes it from my hands. 'No, no, no, the poetry in it is not as good as the earlier volumes. Now this,' he reverently hands me *Ruby Slippers*, which was the book she'd dedicated to me, 'this is the best, in my opinion.'

I rub my hand over the front cover, unable to say anything. I know she loved me in her own weird way.

'You can feel the love in your bones when you read these,' Julian says. 'This,' he waves the other book in the air, 'well, it got panned by the critics when it came out. And really it's not surprising.'

That *is* a surprise.

'It's a pity she published at all,' he says, shaking his head. 'What were her publishers thinking?' He looks at me as if expecting an answer, then says loudly, 'Ker-ching.'

'Sorry?'

'Money. If you ask me, happens a lot. A lot.' A sigh. 'The

poetry in this,' he shrugs, 'well, it's not at all good. No,' he taps *Ruby Slippers*, 'you stick with that now.'

He nods at me and I feel obliged to open the book. *To Ruby, with all my love – Mammy.* A lump the size of America lodges in my throat. I push it down. The first poem chronicles me as a baby. I pretend to read it.

'Here.' Julian leans over and flips through the book until he gets to a poem entitled 'Fear'. 'This is her masterpiece,' he says.

He stands, hands on skinny hips, looking expectantly at me. I have no choice. I scan the poem. Nothing goes in. I get the gist that she's writing about how scared she is for me in my life. That she's giving me advice. That she equates childrearing to driving on a motorway with no lights in a fast car at night. How one small false turn of the wheel could result in a catastrophic injury.

'Always the violent imagery in her poems,' the librarian says. 'Very visual, she's a master of onomatopaeia.'

'Yes, I know,' I say. I go to put the book back. 'I'm actually not a member of the library, so …'

'That's no problem, I can check it out on Molly's lists. You're hardly going to run away now, are you?' And he laughs.

I almost laugh at his choice of words.

There is no way I will read those poems though.

8

Of all the jobs I had, I miss my cleaning one the most. It wasn't just that I liked imposing order on mess, it was because being in different houses gave me glimpses into other people's lives. It allowed me to examine how they lived and find out what normal people did with their time. I wasn't totally shocked to discover that no one else had ten locks on their front doors or shelves upon shelves of daily newspapers. No one else had an 'Emergency Visitor Alert Protocol' pinned to every wall in the house.

My favourite houses to clean were the ones that belonged to families. There was something warm about stepping into a hallway littered with drawings the children had done in school. Some parents framed everything – that's what I would do if I had a child – while others just left them hanging on the wall or the fridge for a week before dumping them. The pictures were usually of big stick-like mammies and daddies with happy smiles.

And the photographs …

I used to examine them in detail, staring at the faces of these people and their children, marvelling at the apparent normalcy of their lives. There was generally a First Communion photo in most houses along with pictures of kids with messy ice-cream mouths and holiday snaps of swimming pools and beaches. Different people but the same stories all over the city. Then dumped in corners or in a utility room were the sports shoes and the tennis rackets and the dancing costumes. Children who went out into the world and enjoyed doing stuff. I used to imagine how I would be if I lived in this house or that one. What would I be doing? The nicest house I was ever in was the Molloys'. They had a picture on their wall of a smiling child performing on the stage. There was a big close-up of the child as a tree, with her face painted all green, posing with her dad. I used to spend so much time looking at that picture that Clara would get mad at me.

In the end, it was that picture that got me fired.

Clara and I weren't bad people, I don't think. We just had a chunk missing that we couldn't fill. For the time we worked together, we became each other's best ally. I robbed with her and after a time she trusted me enough to share her other secret with me: when people were away, Clara moved into their houses. She'd copied their keys. It was beautiful really. We were like caretakers. We didn't mess the places up, we didn't run up big bills and we stayed out of sight. All we did was watch a bit of telly and stay warm and safe, pretending that where we were was home.

It was wrong but it was right too.

Last Christmas, the Molloys went away. Under cover of darkness, Clara and I moved in. I luxuriated in just being there. For three days things were good. The only thing I moved was the tree picture. I took it from the wall and put it on the countertop where I would see it each morning as I walked into the kitchen.

Then, on the fourth night, I woke to water dripping on my face. Opening my eyes, I saw that water was running across the ceiling and pouring down through the light. Already there was a sizeable puddle on the floor. I shook Clara awake and she insisted that we pack up and leave. I did as she said but I was in a daze. The house would be destroyed. The pictures might be ruined. The happy family wouldn't smile so much. Clara dragged me out the back door and locked up.

An hour later, unable to bear it, I rang my employer, told her what I'd done and begged her to get someone out to the house. I knew I'd lose my job but what I forgot was that Clara had all the keys on her so when they investigated, she lost her job too. I ran, not wanting to be on anyone's radar. I left my last bit of cash for Clara along with a note of apology.

I lost the only friend I ever had.

9

Later that night, just as the reality TV show woman is about to face her deepest fear and have a spider crawl in her hair, a man calls. As I open the front door, he's leaning over to ring the bell again and we both jump back a little.

'Sorry!'

'Sorry!'

He looks respectable and neat, dressed in a grey suit with an open-necked white shirt. He's tall and tanned, as if he's been away. The only quirk is his hair, which is a mess of dark curls. He takes a step back, checks the number and turns to look at me. 'Is this Max's place?' His voice has a twang of Wexford with a touch of other places mixed in.

'Yes.'

'So, who are you?' the man says. 'Where's Max?'

'I'm … I'm Max's friend,' I answer, and it feels good to say it. He quirks an eyebrow, wanting more. 'I'm minding Max's house for him while he's … away.'

In the TV room, the woman screams. The man at the door jumps, then says, 'Max is away? Where?'

He must be the only person in Ireland who doesn't know that Max had been in an accident. I'm unsure whether to tell him. Then I decide that if Max had wanted him to know he would have told him himself.

'Just away.'

'Away?' A crease appears between the man's eyebrows as he scrutinises me. 'I've been waiting to hear from him for a while, so when he wasn't in touch, I took the opportunity, seeing as I was in the country, to come here.'

I'm not sure what he wants me to say.

He chews his lower lip. Slowly, he says, 'He's not answering his phone either.'

I have the weird feeling that he thinks I've disposed of Max. 'Maybe it's powered off.'

'Surely you can tell me where he is.' He gives a small laugh.

His laugh isn't real. 'If he wanted you to know, he would have told you himself.'

He doesn't like that. His jaw tightens. 'Forget it, it's fine. I'll find out anyway. In the meantime, tell him Paddy McIntyre called.'

'OK'

'I'm a friend of his too.' He doesn't look friendly. 'I'll be back.' It sounds vaguely like a threat. He raises his hand in a goodbye gesture and moves off down the path.

I say nothing, just watch him leave.

Max had given me his mobile number in case of any emergencies. I dial it from the house phone.

'Hello?' He sounds chirpy. 'This is a late call.'

'It's Sandy.'

'Hiya, Sandy, what's up? Is the house OK? Are you OK?'

'A man came to your house just now. Paddy McIntyre.'

Silence.

'Do you know him?'

'What did he say?' Max's voice has changed and it gives me goose bumps.

'That he was waiting to hear from you and hadn't.'

'He was?' Max sounds surprised.

'So you do know him?'

'Yeah. He's a ...' Max hesitates, 'an old friend.'

'I didn't tell him where you were. Should I have?'

'No. No, I don't want to see him.' He sounds pretty definite about that.

'He said he'd find out and be back. He was quare suspicious of me.'

'Paddy's grand.'

'I think he thought I'd done away with you.'

Max laughs, then stops abruptly. 'Shit.'

'What?' I've got goose bumps again.

'He might think you're ... that girl who was stalking me.'

I vaguely remember him telling me about some girl who was hassling him, ages ago.

'See, I told him who the girl was but he said no. But now, now you see, he thinks ... and oh, he offered me work!'

It's like he just remembered that bit.

'I'll give him a shout,' Max says. 'I'd forgotten that he offered me work. I had to turn it down.' Without even saying goodbye, he hangs up.

I can't get Paddy McIntyre out of my head. I know I should get a good night's sleep, be on form for reading to Molly when I go to her, but finally, at about three in the morning,

I get up and I flick on Max's computer. I don't like doing it but after thinking about it for so long, I reckon it's probably the safest thing to do. Max can't seem to remember much from before he went into hospital and I don't feel too good knowing that some woman was stalking him. I mean, how do I know she won't start coming after me? And how do I know who else will turn up on the doorstep? That Paddy guy sounded pretty mad. Years of living with my mother has had its effect. Paranoia for me is always just around the corner.

The computer has been on all the time so I don't even need a password. It's different from the one I used to have at home so I'm not that sure how to work it. After thirty minutes, I find a 'Documents' folder. It seems reasonable that this is where Max would store things. I don't know what I'm looking for, only that Max told this Paddy person about the girl who was stalking him. I find a search box and key in 'Paddy McIntyre'.

Diary entries pop up, as do emails. Feeling a bit shit, I go into Max's diary. It takes me a while to figure out the programme, but after a bit, I have the hang of how it works. I flick through it and see that, yes, Max has met with a Paddy McIntyre a few times in the past year, the most recent being six weeks ago. I click on a 'results of meeting' that Max has associated with every appointment but it is blank. Maybe he never bothers to fill it in. I flick on another result of meetings for a 'Dadra Conway' whom Max seems to have met a couple of weeks before that and see that he has written extensive notes about that meeting.

Another meeting and another set of notes.

Since Max met with Paddy that last time, there have been

no meetings with anyone. I suppose the main reason for that is since then Max has been in hospital. To my vaguely suspicious eyes, it looks like Max was doing fine until he met Paddy that day. It was as if, after that, Max's career started to unravel.

I sit in Max's computer chair for what seems ages, not knowing what I'm looking at really, not even sure why I'm looking, yet something is driving me on.

I hesitate only briefly before going into Max's emails. The first mail, dated eight months previously, reads:

> *Hey, Max, it's Paddy. From home? How are you these days? I'm hearing great stuff about you. D'you fancy meeting up to discuss some work I could throw your way? I'm in Dublin next week.*

Harmless.

Max had replied that he was very busy and probably wouldn't be able to. Thanks anyway. Paddy had responded a few days later with another email asking when he'd be free. Max had said that his diary was chock-a-block and that maybe one day he'd be down in Wexford and could meet up then.

Max's diary was not that full.

Paddy's next email came a few days later:

> *From: pmce@gmail.com*
> *To: max@maxcommunications.ie*
> *Hey, Max,*
>   *We both know you're never home in Wexford these days*
> ☺ *I'm not home much either.*

I really do need a guy for my company and, ideally, one
I can trust.
Come on, for an old pal.
Paddy

Max had replied that he'd have to wait and see how stuff
panned out. But Paddy had been persistent and eventually
Max had agreed to a meeting. They'd swapped a few more
emails, and then I find this one from Paddy:

From: pmce@gmail.com
To: max@maxcommunications.ie
Hey mate, are you OK? Just checking in after yesterday.
Also, I didn't know you didn't know. Thought you might
have heard through the jungle drums that are Wexford.
You OK? At least you know it's not her stalking you and
anyway, why would she? We'd all drifted apart and I
didn't think you'd be so upset. Sorry about that. The job
is still open.

Max had replied:

From: max@maxcommunications.ie
To: pmce@gmail.com
Take my ideas, use them. I can't do it.
Best of luck.

Paddy had responded:

From pmce@gmail.com
To: max@maxcommunications.ie
Come on, Max. Let's meet up. I'm in Dublin again
Friday?

Max hadn't replied.

Two days ago, Paddy had sent another email asking if Max was OK and saying he was going to call on him.

I wonder what it was that Max hadn't known that upset him. I also notice that the day after Max had told Paddy to keep his ideas was only a couple of days before he ended up in hospital. Is there a connection? And if so, what?

Then next thing I do is I scan Max's emails for threats from a stalker. Nothing. I go to his 'Deleted items' folder, his junk mail, his recycle bin. Nothing. He obviously got rid of them.

Then I go into his photographs. If Paddy is a close friend, there might be a picture of him there. Or I might find pictures of some woman who might be a threat. And if I'm being truly honest, I want to know more about Max. From that very first coffee, I've wanted to know more about him.

But his pictures are only of Wexford. The beaches. The sunsets. The boats. He has pictures of the water, of glistening fish being hauled onto decks, of market days and strawberries. There are pictures of dark sea and low clouds, pictures of the roads, the harbours. Pictures of the towns and the narrow streets and the festivals. My heart squeezes up tight with each new image. It's a collage of love for a county. It's the cry of someone who is away and can never go back.

I know, because I feel it too.

Both of us, it seems, want to go home some day.

Max

1

Sometimes the edginess takes me over. It blocks out my thinking and looms like a cloud in my head. I either sit real still in order to think it out, or I jitter. My foot moves up and down, my hands clasp and unclasp, my words come out jumbled 'cause I'm thinking of the thing that's bugging me and trying not to talk about it.

Ian is having none of it. He's sitting with his legs crossed in this pair of wanky beige trousers, showing off his white hairy ankles. The notebook is open and his pen is poised.

'Why don't you tell me what's wrong, Max?' he says. 'We both know something is.'

'I'm in here, that's what's wrong.'

'You've been in here a while now so that's not it.'

'You calling me a liar?'

Ian shrugs. 'I merely said that it must be more than just being in here.'

It's Paddy fucking McIntyre, that's what's wrong, I want to shout, but I can't. I can't because then I'll have to explain why it's wrong. Deep down inside, there's a part of me that knows why but dragging it up into the light will only make everything worse. 'I'm fine,' I say.

'All right.' Ian nods. 'Can you talk about what happened at the group session last week?'

Shit. 'I can but I don't want to.'

'Apparently you got into a bit of an argument with one of the other patients.'

'I wouldn't call it an argument.'

'I heard you upset Norm.'

'Why do you want me to talk about it if you know?'

'I know the facts, I don't know it from your perspective.' He leans towards me. 'Come on, Max, give me a break.'

Maybe it's the plea that gets to me. The vulnerability. The fact that he's not all-knowing.

'Am I being difficult?' I chance a grin.

'Very.' He grins back. 'Sorry about that. It was unprofessional.'

'It was honest,' I say.

'You value honesty, then?'

Fucking tears in my eyes. I blink and hope he doesn't see them. 'Yeah, I do, yeah. Or at least in my head I do.'

Ian nods. 'That's good. It's a good thing to value.'

'I said I value it, doesn't mean I *am* honest.'

'You don't think you're honest?'

I'm aware that I'm talking to this guy but I'm not talking about what he originally asked me about, which is fine. 'I'm in PR, spin, how can I be honest?'

'Meaning?'

'People do stuff, get drunk, get into fights, have affairs. My job is to cover it up or make it go away or justify it.' Something inside me flares briefly. I lean towards him. 'Basically, in my heart, I want to hang these guys. I want to tell the fucking world what they're doing, but I can't, because it's my job and I'm good at it.'

'So you hate your job?'

That's the thing. I don't, actually. I love my job. I love the rush of it. The way, when I've to jump to someone's rescue, the adrenaline fills my head and chases its way through my veins. I love the way it's all systems go, plugging the dam and building another one in its place. I love helping someone be great, like the way I helped Julie Winterson, my only novelist, be great. That was careful micro managing, telling her where to go, how to dress, what tasty words to drop to the press. Julie is the one I'm most proud of and yet I fucked that up too.

'Do you hate your job?' Ian asks.

'No.' I shrug. 'No, I don't hate it. That's what I hate. I hate that I don't hate it.'

Ian studies me. 'You can't help the way you feel,' he says. 'No one can.'

The words touch my skin like a balm. The truth of them, the simplicity of them. I can't help my feelings.

It's the first bloody helpful thing he's said. Accepting it is harder.

2

Shane liked Imelda, that's the way it was. Well, liked was an understatement: he fancied the arse off her. I think most of us fancied Imelda but Shane had said it out loud so until she told him to feck off, none of the rest of us would try anything on.

I was confident that she would. Tell him to feck off, that is. Shane was nerdy. Clever. So bloody clever. He was tall and skinny too and when he stripped off to go swimming you could have taken a spoon to his ribs and played them like a xylophone. I spent days in my room doing core exercises and weights and working on my six-pack. Each day, I'd stare at my torso and tell myself that it wouldn't be long before I'd have the girls of Wexford chasing me down the main street, mad for me. In my head, though, I only saw Imelda and I wasn't running that fast.

She wasn't a beauty the way you'd think of, but she had that 'thing', that indefinable sexiness, laughter, humour, ease with which she lived life and it drew us to her like lemmings to the side of a cliff. She knew it too; I think she played with us, dangled us, worms on a hook, casting her eye one way and then another.

She had a friend called June whom none of us noticed and, looking back, June was the better-looking girl. She was probably nicer too, but the four of us were not into nice girls. Not then. We liked them loud with a hint of madness.

The summer before Shane drowned, there was a beach party. All I can remember from summers before Shane drowned are beach parties bathed in heat. Even now, the smell of a barbeque brings such a rush of nostalgia and regret that I can't breathe.

Paddy had built this massive fire on the beach. He was the doer, the guy who spent ages searching the beach for stones to ring the fire, the guy who cooked, the guy who looked after us when we got drunk. Paddy was the guy who studied and had his life mapped out before he'd even started to really live it. Anyway, that night, it was coming to the end of the summer, the days were not as long as the week before and I don't know what time of the morning it was. The dawn was edging in past the stars, though, I do remember that. The sky was pink and the air smelled washed. I could tell by the sound of the tide that it was coming in. There were a few of us left still, the rest had gone home. At the height of the party, there had been about fifty, now only a handful remained.

I watched from my position on the flat of my back as Paddy dampened down the fire. Of all my mates, Paddy puzzled me the most. He was probably the best-looking of us but never bothered much with girls. He was easily offended, liable to take the most harmless comment the wrong way. Of course, feckers that we were, it made us pick on him all the more. But, I like to think, our good-natured jibes did loosen him up a bit.

As he cleared up, I pretended to be asleep. There was no

way I was helping; I was way too lazy for that. Shane was opposite me – I could see him across the smoke that was still drifting upwards. He was just sitting, cross-legged, swilling from a bottle and telling Paddy to relax and chill and sit the fuck down. Paddy ignored him as he tossed away the hot stones. John, by this stage, had disappeared.

I saw Imelda, through my half-closed lids, creep up behind Shane. Maybe my memory is faulty but I remember she put her hands on his shoulders. There was a second before he looked up and then she knelt down in the sand beside him and kissed him. Paddy kept tossing away the stones and I tried not to look. I tried to push down on the searing hot wave of jealousy that shot right through me. I told myself that they were both drunk, that she'd regret it. Then when I could bear it no longer, I hopped up and strode away across the sand.

3

First thing in the morning, my dad rings. I'm at breakfast with Sam and Vic. Sam has been told he's getting out in two days and I'm so pissed angry at him. Vic is too. Don't get me wrong, I'm glad he's getting out, but I'm pissed too, because he's leaving me. He's finally out because he realises that he is who he is and he can't change it. And now at fifty-eight, he doesn't want to.

That's what he's told me anyhow.

When he goes I'll be stuck with the really serious nutters and there are so many of them here. Vic for one, though at least he laughs at my jokes. Norm, who looks like a rat and can't talk above a whisper. The guy who won't eat. Evie, who came in all meek and mild, carrying books about breastfeeding, and who now shouts me down every time I go to say something in group session. She's the worst. Totally nuts.

Sorry if I'm insensitive. Anyway, my dad rings.

'You getting that?' Sam says, looking at my phone. 'It's your auld fella.'

'I can read too, thanks,' I say.

'Ouch. Someone's in a shit mood.' Sam stands up and leaves the table, bringing his tray with him. I reckon he's been told to leave those who will bring him down. I regret my words as soon as he leaves. I like Sam.

My mobile stops ringing and I start spooning flakes into my mouth again. Ten minutes later it starts up again.

'You getting that?' Vic asks.

I still don't pick up. And then again.

'Will you knock that fucking thing off!' someone says from another table.

'I'll knock your head off,' I mutter back, but not too loudly. I'm still in disgrace from wrecking the group meeting last week. I had to apologise but then I went and copied Norm's lisp and got thrown out again. In my defence, Norm called me an asthole and I told him I wasn't an asthole.

The phone stops and starts once more.

I wonder suddenly if something is wrong at home. Then I think that my dad would have rung the hospital to tell them this first, but it's too late by the time I think this. I have the phone to my ear and a 'hello' out.

'Max?' my dad says and he sounds cautious.

'Yep.'

'Just calling to see, you know, how you are.'

'How I am?'

'Yes.'

'As well as can be expected for someone whose family dumped him in here.'

My father takes a deep breath at the other end of the phone. I think he'd like to kill me.

'We had to, Max,' he says, and he sounds weary. 'And behind it all, you know that.'

'I do not.'

'You were raving. You were—' He stops. 'I was talking to Paddy. He called over at the weekend. He says there's a girl living in your house.'

'Yes.' I knew it. I knew Paddy would do that.

'He says she said you were away.'

'Yes.'

'I told Paddy where you were.'

I wince and snap out, 'Thanks for that, Dad.'

'It's nothing to be ashamed of.'

'It's also none of your business to go around telling everyone.' I want to hang up, but I can't. Me and my dad were close once.

'I only told Paddy.'

'Did Paddy tell you that he offered me a job? What was that all about? Did you put him up to it?'

'That's ridiculous.'

There's a silence.

'Can we visit?' he asks eventually.

'No.'

I put the phone down.

Sandy calls in. When I spot her, weaving her way between tables, I find I'm smiling. But then something about her closed-in body language makes my grin fade quicker than a cheap tattoo. 'What's up?' I ask as soon as she sits down. She opens her mouth to answer but before she can reply I ask if she'd like my uneaten chocolate muffin.

She darts a look at me. 'No thanks,' she says.

'You'll have a coffee?' I hop up and head to the counter.

Whatever she has to tell me can wait. I don't want bad news. I'm served way too quickly and, in less than a minute, I'm back, sitting opposite her, pushing the coffee towards her, my heart drumming with anxiety. I watch as she curls her hands around the mug and I reckon if she squeezed any harder, she'd smash the mug clean in two. 'I have a confession to make,' she says.

'Bless me father for I have sinned.' I crack a smile.

'I looked at your computer.'

'Yeah?' I don't know what she's getting at.

'At your files and stuff?'

I feel a little bit outraged. A lot relieved. And, weirdly, kind of flattered. 'Why?'

She squirms. 'That Paddy McIntyre guy was pretty mad at me. He said he'd come back. I wanted to know who he is.'

I almost laugh in relief. 'He's no one. He's not going to attack you any time soon with a machete.' At my words, I have a sudden flashback. Me. Top of the stairs. A woman. Then it's gone. Like a sudden illumination in the dark.

'Are you OK?' Sandy asks. 'You've gone pale.'

I shake my head, dislodge the image. 'Paddy is cool,' I say, getting back on track.

'But who is he? And if he comes back what do I tell him?'

'He knows I'm in here, my bloody father told him. He won't be back to the house.'

'How do you know?'

'Can you leave it?' I do not want to talk about Paddy, and Sandy going on about it is like someone jerking me on a choke chain. I bring my voice down. 'Just leave it, OK?'

She looks like she's about to agree but then says, 'I'd just feel better if I knew something about him. I know nothing about this man.'

'I know nothing about you and you're living in my house.'

I've hurt her, I think too late. She pulls back and seems suddenly unsure, like as if I've slapped her.

'Sorry,' I stumble out. Then add, 'It's OK that I don't know you. I like you.'

'What do you want to know?' She stares at me defiantly.

'Nothing. I trust you. Now trust me. OK?'

She stares at me for ages. 'I'm from Wexford, like you.'

'Honestly—' I try to interrupt.

'I am twenty-five, I think. I used to be a cleaner.'

'Well that'll come in handy for the state of my house. Honest, Sandy, there's—'

'And I miss home like a limb but I can't go back.'

I close my mouth and stare at her, her words hitting me. I miss the bloody place too. 'Why'd you leave, so?'

It takes an age. Finally she says, 'A lie.'

I swallow hard. 'A lie,' I echo. The walls waver a little. I see her nod.

Then she asks, 'Do you think a lie is a good reason to leave home?'

It's like she wants validation. I can't talk, my throat is dry. She keeps on looking at me.

'Sorry,' she says abruptly, 'forget that. Forget I asked. Do you miss home?'

'Yeah.' I nod. 'Yeah, I do.'

That seems to satisfy her. 'Do you ever visit?'

'Nah.'

We're whispering.

'Why?'

'Too busy, mostly.'

Then she smiles, which is odd, I think, and she says, 'The night I ran away, the first thing I did was find a beach, just to say goodbye to it.'

It's like she's echoing my loss. 'That's nice.'

'Yeah.'

We stare at each other across the table. I think I could look at her for a long time and not get bored.

'If you did go back,' she asks, chin propped in the palm of her hand, eyes studying me, 'what would you do?'

'I dunno.' I've never planned on it. This is the longest conversation we've had and way more bizarre than I'd have liked.

'I'd swim. I've never swum, can you believe it?'

My stomach lurches. I try to keep the expression nailed to my face as I nod. I haven't swum since Shane drowned. I miss the sea like a friend who betrayed me.

Sandy talks about some stuff after that but I can't concentrate, the tablets make me fuzzy after a while. I like that she's talking, though. She's come out of her shell a bit. There's an innocence about her, as if the world hasn't touched her or something. I'd hate for the world to hurt her, I realise suddenly. And then I think about the woman. 'Has there been a woman hanging about outside?' I ask. 'She wears a red scarf?'

Sandy is startled; whatever she has been talking about has nothing to do with women in red scarves. She shakes her head. 'Is that the woman you told me about before?'

I remember then that I did confide in Sandy. Ages ago. When I met her first. 'Yes. She hasn't been around?'

'No. I'll keep an eye out for her.' She seems about to say something but stops.

'Stay away from her,' I say.

She nods.

'And trust me on Paddy.'

A moment before she nods again. 'OK.'

I wonder what she'd make of the fact that half the reason I'm in here is down to Paddy.

4

My dad was a fisherman and I was a fisherman's son. It could be a song or a book title. I had one sister, Maya. She was three years younger than me and, until she was about ten, she followed me about the place. I always found her a nuisance but when she stopped following me and worshipping me, I missed it. We got on OK for a brother and sister and as we grew older she'd sometimes hang about with my mates, though I didn't encourage her to.

My mother died when we were young; I barely remember her. Dad says she got really sick but was brave right to the end. Everyone says she was. She raised funds for counselling others, for medicines, for research into cancer. In short, she did all the stuff that you see in films that brave people do when they are dying.

Dad says that he was so proud of her that his heart almost broke each time he looked at her. I'm glad I'm too young to remember.

When she died, her sister came to mind us. Auntie Marnie. She minded us when Dad was at sea. When I turned twelve, in summertime, I'd head out to sea with him. I sometimes think that they were the best days of my life. There were three crew and me on board and the work was hard. I often came home with a split head or bleeding hands, but it never put me off. I was at home bouncing up and down on the waves with the wind hammering my face. Dry land always seemed so pedestrian afterwards. All I'd ever wanted to do was fish from the boat.

Dad and I grew apart after I came to Dublin. I suppose so anyway. I mean, there is no definite moment in time that I can pinpoint and say this was the start of the rot or that was when we split. We were like two buoys drifting on the tide, suddenly we looked up and we were divided by an ocean.

At first, when I came to Dublin, he visited me a few times, stayed in my spare room, but I was always busy, rushing about, solving the catastrophes in other people's lives, so that maybe the drifting was my fault. I just remember being too harried in those days to talk to him.

He kept coming up, though, which was how he found me at the bottom of the stairs that night. Apparently. I can't remember.

I was way too busy to visit Wexford. PR work is intense, and especially after I set up on my own; there was just no time for holidays. I read ten papers a day, listened to every news bulletin, having to be on top of all the breaking news in the world of celebrity. In this kip, they only allow me one newspaper a day, but I have my mobile phone and all my apps and I read my Twitter feed. It's not the same though as having a beer or a coffee beside you and scanning pages and pages of newsprint. I'm old-fashioned like that.

My sister never bothers visiting. That is entirely my fault. The last time we met was about two years ago. She called up just as I was going out. I'd forgotten she was coming, if I'm to be honest. She walked in my door as I walked out. I told her to make herself at home, that I'd see her later.

It was two days before I got back to the house and she was gone with a 'Fuck you, Max' note on the table.

I debated ringing her but I thought that she'd get over it. She didn't.

I guess I can be a bit of a shit. I don't know why I do it.

I keep up with Maya through her Facebook. All her stuff is public, which is a mad mistake, and every time I log into her page, I'm so tempted to tell her so, but I don't, because she'll probably unfriend me or bar me or whatever it is they do. I've learned that she's got a boyfriend. There are pictures of the two of them posted all over her pages. They're drinking wine or sitting on chairs or laughing. He's tall, she's tiny and she looks a little like me. His name is Oliver, which is a totally pratish name. He's from Wexford and she lives with him in a small house just outside the town. She's a teacher and I don't know what he does. He doesn't have a Facebook page. They look happy. I'm glad about that.

I wonder how I became so isolated. No family, and the only friend I seem to have at the moment is a homeless girl I know very little about.

Oh, and Paddy, of course. The guy who told the first lie.

5

My one remaining client arrives at eleven o'clock on Wednesday. I'd asked her to come in in an attempt to keep my career going. I told her to tell the nurses at reception that she's my friend. If anyone here thinks I'm working, I'll be in trouble.

It's a testament to my addled brain that when Laura walks into the canteen, I have no recollection of her at all. In fact, it's the first indication to me that I must have been off my head for a while, because if I'd been sane, I would never have signed her. I must have been mad. The thought sends chills racing up and down my body. Laura, to put it bluntly, is an eighties throwback. High boots, tight black leather trousers, huge boobs, lips, earrings and with enough fake hair to eradicate baldness. Am I that desperate? I watch, struck dumb, as Laura slides into the seat opposite.

'Hiya,' she says, putting an enormous fake leopardskin bag in front of her on the table. 'This is great. I'm like, honoured. Hiya.' And she shoves out her hand. A hand sporting enormous rings and long fake nails. Am I that desperate?

I shake her hand and my own is enfolded in a grasp of such magnitude that I gasp. Laura is oblivious.

'I'm in awe, like. You can ask me whatever you like. Anything you want. I'm all yours.' She flicks her copious hair

back over her shoulder and immediately the air near me is
filled with the jangle of earrings, bracelets and necklaces. The
smell of perfume wafts from her.

I try to return Laura's bright, hopeful smile. I think of
all the things I used to say to potential clients. In the face of
Laura's awfulness, they vanish. 'So, Laura,' I say, 'you, eh …
what is it you want to do?'

She looks confused. 'Sing? I told you that night at Black's?
Remember? You were shouting out that you wanted a singer
and I said—'

I hold up my hand. Way too much painful information.
'Of course, you'll have to forgive me, this place messes with
my brain, literally.'

I'm rewarded with a laugh that's way too hearty.

'So you want to sing. What do you think I'll be able to
do for you?'

'Get me to number one, get me on all the TV programmes,
make me famous.'

'No pressure, then.'

Another hearty laugh.

I'm not sure what to do with this girl. I don't want her and
yet … something niggles at the back of my mind. What is it?

'I'm not sure I can work with you, Laura,' I say. It feels
right to tell her that.

She stops smiling. She blinks and I notice that she has
nice eyes. 'Why? I can sing. I'm a nice person.'

I hold up my hand and her voice drains away. I can't look
at her, miserable fecker that I am. 'I know you are. Well, no,
that's a lie, I don't know that. Maybe try another agent.'

'I only wanted you. You're the best.'

'Laura, I'm in a psychiatric hospital.' I try for a joke.

'I don't care, the most brilliant people are mental,' she says with a charming lack of PC. 'And also, you represent Julie Winterson.'

That she knows that impresses me. 'Not anymore. She fired me.'

'Bitch. Was it because you're in here?'

'No. Julie is a total lady. I'm sure she had a good reason, I just can't quite remember it.' I try out a laugh that doesn't quite come off. 'Anyway,' I wave my hand about, 'that's not the issue. The issue is, I can't work with you.'

'Why?'

It's so hard to explain, so I opt for, 'I just can't.'

'You can at least tell me why.' The smiling, babbling girl is gone. In its place is a bit of hard steel. She folds her arms. 'I'm not budging from here till you tell me why you can't work with me.'

Evie, one of the women from the group session I got thrown out of, chooses that moment to pass by and, totally invading Laura's space, leans across the table towards me, her slim hand flat down on the table's surface. 'You are a bastard,' she hisses, surprising me and Laura with her venomous tone. 'Poor Norm is so upset at you copying his lisp. Do you not care about anyone?'

I'm so taken aback, I'm struck dumb. Attacking me in group session is one thing: this is another step up in her 'I hate Max' campaign.

'Everyone here is trying to get better,' she says. 'Everyone here has awful stuff going on. You don't need to make it worse for them.'

I glance at Laura, try to smile like this is normal. Say to Evie, 'And you think my life is a bed of roses, do you?'

'I wish it was,' she says. 'I'd love to see you get ripped apart by those thorns.'

I laugh at her wit. 'That's very good.'

I think she doesn't know whether to be outraged or pleased. 'Yes, well,' she straightens up, 'the sooner you cop on, the better you'll get.'

Then she walks off.

'One of my charming fellow inmates,' I explain to Laura, whose mouth is hanging open like the tail end of a ship. 'Anyway,' I say opportunistically, seeing as she's still a bit shocked, 'I really do think you'd be better with another agent.'

'You haven't heard me sing.'

I don't want to hear her sing. If she's good, I'll be too tempted. 'You want to know why I won't represent you?' I eyeball her hard. 'You look awful.' I feel like a heel but sometimes honesty is the best policy. Or so I've heard.

'That's not very nice,' she says.

I shrug. I know that. I'm not very nice.

'Julie Winterson was a big frump until you took her over,' Laura says. Her voice suddenly sounds far away. 'She wears skirts with big slits in them now. And you told that country singer fella to talk about his depression to promote his single and it went to number one.'

'I know.' I don't like to be reminded.

'I can do that too.'

I stare at her. The walls start to waver. Those bloody tablets.

Then she starts to sing. It's like her voice is coming from really far away and the walls are swaying. Her song is something I've never heard before and, to be honest, the lyrics are a bit crap – all about someone leaving a small town – but her voice is pure. There's a cracked, broken sound from it and it's raw.

Then she stops. Someone in the canteen claps.

I close my eyes to stop the spinning. Maybe it is OK to mess around with the truth of someone a little, to make it more attractive? A ray of hope lights inside me. If I can work from here, I might distract myself from the reality of the place. 'You'll do what I ask?'

A hesitant smile. 'I will. Well, once it's legal.'

'OK, then.'

Laura lets out a shriek.

'Just for a trial,' I clarify.

She shrieks again and I wince.

When she goes, I have to lie down for a long time. If only I had a drink.

6

The girl started following me a few months ago. Maybe she'd been following me longer only I never noticed her before. I was in a shop one day and caught a glimpse of her out of the corner of my eye, just a flash of a red scarf. I turned, liking the colour of the scarf, and she ducked quickly away, which made me think she had to be following me – why else would she try to hide? I couldn't think of any reason why anyone would follow me, but there it was.

She didn't appear for a few more days, or again, maybe I just didn't see her. The second time I saw the red scarf was when I was walking over to High Hills to grab a coffee. It was raining, I was wrapped up, my hood covering my face. Again, from the corner of my eye, a flash of red, and when I looked up, she was gone. It was as if she'd been watching me approach and when I neared, she'd ducked into the undergrowth. I did nothing again. The road was deserted and maybe it was someone who was scared of running into a lone man on an isolated road. I didn't want to make things worse for myself by calling out.

As the winter drew in, I began to notice her more and more. She would stand opposite my house and disappear between the time it took me to get from my front room out into the street. She'd be in High Hills watching me buy coffee. She'd be on the road as I passed in my car. Always I just saw the red scarf and the bleached blonde of her hair. But I recognised the frame and the height and the fact that when she walked, she walked quickly.

At first I wasn't too bothered. I mean, it was a woman, after all, and a small enough woman. But as the days wore into weeks and the weeks into months and she began to get more brazen, I was a little freaked. I did my best to ignore her, to pretend that she wasn't there. I ignored her if she passed me in the street, she always averting her head so I could never catch a good look at her face. One time, while stuck in traffic in Dublin, I saw her, standing at the kerb, looking over at me, and I jumped from my car and let out a roar. People looked, but I didn't care. I ran and ran and ran after her. I had her within touching distance, but then she disappeared into a shop and was gone.

Afterwards, I made my way back to the car and it had been smashed up. I'd left the door open and someone had taken my phone and my radio. Things happen fast in the city.

A week or so later, I got the first text from her. It read, *And you still don't know who I am.* It wasn't signed but I knew it was from her. After a few more texts, I changed my phone number. But somehow she got it again. *And still you don't know who I am.*

I tried to think of any women who would do this to me. As far as I knew, I hadn't offended anyone so much as to have them stalk me but you can never tell what goes on in people's minds. I thought of my slush pile of girlfriends, most of whose names I don't remember. I doubt they'd remember mine either. Girlfriends from home, girlfriends from Dublin. I counted the ones I could recall on my fingers. At least ten. One serious. But we'd broken up about a year ago and I'm still struggling to understand why. I think it had something to do with me being unavailable, but that's work. So if our breaking-up had been her decision, it didn't seem reasonable that she would stalk me.

That left Imelda. Imelda Green. From Wexford. Shane's girlfriend. She had worn a red scarf once. Maybe she had found out what had happened and decided to come after me. And the more I thought about it, the more convinced I became.

Imelda was after me.

Sandy comes in to visit again. Time plays tricks on me in this place. Sometimes it feels like I only saw Sandy an hour ago and at other times it seems as if kingdoms have been toppled since I last saw her. I'm just out of Art Therapy, where I painted night time. I was trying to be smart, pasting the page with black, but everyone now thinks I'm depressed.

Sandy seems to float on air as she moves towards me. She's wearing her white coat, the one she had on when I thought she was an angel. Her hair is loose and it flows over her shoulders. It shines. She shines. 'Hi.' She smiles. 'Here.'

She passes me over some newspapers, for which I could kiss her.

'They said you'd be OK reading these.'

'I could kiss you.' A beat as she looks a little awkward, so I add, 'But I won't.' Sandy's sense of humour seems a bit underdeveloped or something. It's like she takes things literally. 'So, how's the job?' I remember she has a job at least.

'Good. Molly hasn't got rid of me yet.'

Good? Reading to Mad Molly? Sandy's life must have really been shit. All I say though is, 'She'd be mad to get rid of you.' I wonder how she'll take that.

She flicks me a look and changes the subject. 'I found the

key of your shed. It was in the middle of the dead bonfire in your garden.'

I'd forgotten about the bonfire. Now I remember, in a weird kaleidoscope of images sort of way. I see myself throwing armfuls of Neil Foster's CDs onto it and screaming abuse as the flames lick their way across them, while playing his biggest rival's songs at full volume. Charles and Molly had not been happy. Probably because it was about two in the morning. And the guy on the other side of me, the one who keeps pigeons, had rung the police. I told him roast pigeon was next on my menu. Oh, shit.

'Max?' Sandy is shaking me. 'Max, are you OK?'

I have to take a few deep breaths. In and out. In and out. Grind my feet into the ground. Slowly, the present comes back. I raise my eyes to Sandy. 'Can I ask a favour? A big one?'

She nods without hesitation and I like that.

'Just tell Molly and Tar I'm sorry about the bonfire.'

'Tar?'

'Tar is the guy who lives on the other side of my house. And basically the bonfire was a lapse of saneness.'

She doesn't ask any more, just pats me on the arm and my whole body fizzes with the contact. Maybe because no one touches me in here. In fact, I can't remember the last time someone touched me.

'So you found the key.' I get us back on track.

'My mother burned my clothes on a bonfire once,' she tells me. Her voice dips. 'And she never apologised.'

I don't know what to say. I go for 'Yeah?'

'Yeah,' she says, and the silence stretches and just when I

think she's going to say nothing else she says, 'So it's good to give an apology. I think Tar and Molly will like that.'

I don't share her optimism so instead I say, 'Sorry about your clothes.'

'I never told anyone before.' She seems surprised. Like she might cry or something.

'It's OK, I'll probably forget it anyway what with the drugs they give me here.'

I'm rewarded with a smile.

'So, key?' I say.

She grasps the subject change. 'I unlocked your shed and you have a lawnmower and shears and all sorts of gardening tools.'

I do? 'Right.'

'I'm going to try and fix up your garden if you don't mind?'

'You don't have to.'

'I'd like to.'

'Go for it.'

She smiles at me. 'Why did you buy all that stuff and never use it?'

'The truth?'

She nods.

'I can't even remember buying it.' Even though I sound flippant, it hurts to say it out loud.

Sandy flashes me a smile and, bending down, she pulls a notebook out of her carrier bag. 'I thought that might be the case.' She sounds delighted with her deduction. 'I mean, who buys ten pairs of shears? So I made a list of everything you have so you'll know all about it when you get home.'

I have to swallow a huge lump in my throat.

8

Imelda cast a spell on me all through that year. I don't know if it was imagination or not, but even when she was with Shane, I thought she was looking at me. I tried to ignore it, I tried to pretend it wasn't happening, but every time I looked at her, it was as if she was looking at me. Imelda with her blue, blue eyes and her long hair and that expression on her face that said she just didn't care.

Shane was oblivious. He was mad about her, the way any fella would have been. The two of them walked hanging out of each other, she with her hand in his arse pocket, him with his hand loped about her shoulder. They looked good together, I had to admit, and she brought Shane out of himself.

He'd always been quiet, the kind of guy that spoke rarely, but when he did, we always listened because he could make us laugh. Or he could clarify things with that sharp brain of his. Now, though, he cracked jokes and slagged Paddy off, the way the rest of us did. Shane did piss John off though by dropping out of the soccer team they were both on. John refused to talk to him for a week and from what I can remember, it was a pretty awkward time. Their friendship was never as easy afterwards.

The only one not caught up in Imelda's spell was Tom,

and later on my dad told me he was living with another guy, so that's obviously why.

Imelda and her mate became honorary members of our group. I'd spend nights just listening to her, my heart a bit wrecked every time she turned to Shane for a quick kiss, every time she smiled at Shane. But it was an exquisite torture because at least I could look at her. And in the back of my mind, I kept thinking that my time with Imelda would come.

The months went by and still she gave me those sidelong glances that I thought were invisible to everyone but me. *Wait*, they seemed to say, *wait until I let Shane down gently. Wait.* And I did wait. Not wanting to spoil any chance I might have with her, I didn't get involved with anyone. Not that they were queuing up or anything.

The weeks turned into months and it was Paddy who said it to me. I remember it was around Christmas and we were all in a pub. Shane and Imelda together, though to my eyes, she didn't look as happy as before. Shane though was more entranced than ever, staring at her even when she was talking to someone else, smiling at everything she did, even when she sipped her wine. It was as if he was in a bubble and he didn't care that the rest of us slagged him off as a big saddo.

I had to leave when she put her hand to the back of his neck and began to curl his hair around her finger, when she put her lips to his ear and whispered something that made him smile. I told them I was going for a smoke and outside I went and lit up. I leaned against the pub door, my head resting against the jamb, and I closed my eyes. How the fuck, I wondered, would I get through that night? How could I stand it? I loved that girl, I was sure of it. I'd never been in love before but the way she made me feel, it just had to be love.

I sensed someone else beside me.

'She's teasing you,' Paddy said. 'Don't fall for it.'

My eyes snapped open and I was glad the night was dark because I flushed. 'Who?'

Paddy took a drag on his cigarette and blew the smoke upwards before he answered, 'You know who. She's a bloody cock tease. She's going to destroy Shane if she doesn't watch it.'

'That's a bit over the top,' I scoffed.

Paddy shrugged. 'Maybe, but it'll never last. She loves herself way too much.'

His words gave me hope. I said nothing more. But to my shame, I hoped he was right.

SANDY

1

Molly is odd. That's what I think. She seems to spend every day in bed watching TV or listening to me read. Her room is always dim, the blinds pulled down even on the sunniest days. I itch to ask why she has shut herself away from the world. I know she's ill but she has a wheelchair and a ramp. There is nothing keeping her inside except herself, as far as I can see.

I don't say any of this though as I have a job and it pays me twenty, sometimes thirty euros a day. I enjoy it too, reading on and on into the silence of a room. I'm on the final chapter of the first book I've read her, Jane Austen's *Emma*. As I finish, Molly heaves a sigh. 'Wonderful,' she says, and she's smiling. 'What did you think, Sandy?'

I'm not prepared for the question. 'It was OK.'

'OK?' I think my answer has disappointed her. 'Only OK?'

'It's just a story. It's not real.' Two hours are up. I reach for my coat.

'I know it's not real.' Molly half-laughs. 'But it was well written, yes?'

'Sure.'

'And Emma was very well drawn?'

I make some sort of an answer. I don't want to offend her in case she fires me.

'What does that mumble mean?'

Her sharp tone makes me flinch. 'It means,' I hesitate, reluctant to agree, 'that, eh, she was OK.'

Molly's eyes widen. 'But?' she prompts.

'But what?' I am lost in this exchange. I've read the book, now I want to leave.

'What did you think?' She taps her head with a sort of urgency. 'I want to know what you think. You must think something.'

'No.'

'You have no opinion at all on the book?'

I feel like a deer in the sights of a gun. This is unexpected. 'I was just reading it to you.'

'But you must have an opinion?' Her eyes search my face. 'You read it so well. You got it.'

No one bar Max has asked me my opinion in a long time. The time before that, I'd given my opinion to my mother and it had ended badly. Opinions, I learned, can be dangerous. 'I have no opinion on it,' I say very firmly. I zip up my coat and wrap my scarf around my neck.

'Sit back down and I'll tell you mine,' Molly says. She glances at the clock on the wall. 'It should only take an hour or so.'

I don't know if she's joking, but I sit, happy to earn another ten euros just to listen to her. Molly folds her hands together and eyeballs me serenely. Then she begins to talk. And talk. And how annoying it is. Her analysis of the book is so completely at odds with mine that I have to clench my hands and take deep breaths in order to stop myself contradicting her.

'Emma as a character is so entertaining,' Molly goes on. 'And so concerned with others that—'

'She's a busybody,' I blurt out, then clamp my mouth shut.

'Pardon? Was that an opinion?' Molly sounds amused.

'She has so little going on in her own life that she spends her time matchmaking her friends. Huh, I'd have loved her to see a bit of the real world.' My crossness surprises me. I brace myself for Molly's annoyance.

'What do you mean "the real world"?' she asks, sounding curious.

Her interest wrong-foots me a little. 'This,' I say, indicating Molly, me, the world outside the window. 'If she had real problems, matchmaking would be so low on her agenda.'

'You're looking at it from a twenty-first-century perspective,' Molly challenges. 'Girls in those days had sheltered lives.'

'D'you think the ones working in the mills were concerned with matchmaking? Or the ones living in tenements?'

'I suppose they weren't but this book is set in a particular world, so within that world Emma is entertaining.'

'She's a pain in the arse.'

Molly claps her hands. 'So you *do* have a reaction to the book,' she says gleefully. 'Right, next one up is *The Picture of Dorian Gray*. If ever there was a pain in the arse in fiction, it's him.' She beams at me. 'I think I shall enjoy our chats.'

I wasn't aware she'd require me to chat. I just want to read. I don't respond, instead I change the subject. 'Max asked me to apologise for the night he lit the bonfire.' I'd been saving it until I was leaving because I thought it would avoid any personal interaction.

Molly makes a face. 'That's nice of him.'

'He's a nice man.'

'I think they must have done a personality transplant on him in there.'

'No. He's just nice.'

'Or else, you bring out the best in him.'

'I have to go now.'

I make it to the door before she says, 'Are you his girlfriend?'

'No.' I turn to see she that has hauled herself up in the bed.

'His father was wondering who you were.'

'I'm just his friend.'

'How did you meet him? He's a bit of a high flyer, isn't he?'

I shrug.

'Were you a client?'

'I just met him one day on the street,' I murmur. I indicate the door. 'I really have to go.'

'On the street? Here?'

'High Hills.'

'Tell him I accept his apology about the bonfire.'

'OK.'

'Tell him that when he lets his father visit, then I'll really forgive him.'

'OK.'

'And tell him that you should be his girlfriend.'

I shoot her a look and she cackles.

Instead of going straight back to Max's after the reading, I turn into Tar's house and knock on the door. I've seen him from the top window of Max's pottering about in his garden, cleaning out his lofts, talking away to his birds. He answers the door, a small, bald man in old brown cords and a tatty shirt. He wipes his hands on a rag and looks at me questioningly. 'I've no need of an upgrade to my internet,' he says.

I'm flattered that he thought I was selling something. 'I'm from next door,' I say. 'Max's house.'

'I've no need to be insulted either,' he replies. His face darkens and he frowns at me.

'Max told me to tell you he's sorry about the bonfire.'

Tar doesn't respond, just continues to hold the door aloft. After a bit, I nod a goodbye and move off.

'How is he?' Tar splutters out as I'm halfway down the drive.

I turn. 'Getting there, I think.'

A pause. 'Right, well, tell him thanks for the apology.' He closes the door.

In Max's I flick on the kettle and flop into a kitchen chair. With my wages from the reading, I've bought some nice biscuits and I have two every day with a cup of tea after I get in from Molly's. The range of biscuits in the local shop bowled me over and I'm aiming on buying a different packet each week. Today it's the turn of the shortbread ones.

The phone rings. I ignore it. It stops and then starts up again. Wearily, I cross towards it and look at caller ID: 'Dad'. It must be Max's father. It stops and starts again. For the third time I ignore it. This time he leaves a message. I play it back because I know it's for me. He sounds like a nice dad, his voice soft. 'This is Pierce, Max's father. Hello, Sandy, Molly has told me about you. I'd appreciate some information on how Max is getting on.' I hear him swallow hard. 'Please.' He leaves a phone number before hanging up.

I'm an inch away from ringing him but I don't. If Max wanted him to know, he would have told him. Families are funny.

2

It was a moment of raw terror when I discovered that my grandmother was the other 'nobody important'. After my reaction to Aunt Susan, the puppet lady decided that my grandmother's house might be a better place for me to stay while my mother got better.

The fact that I reacted the same way to my granny led them to believe, I think, that I was unused to adults in general. Which was true. I spent the car journey back to Galway pressed into the seat of the puppet lady's car, trying to make myself as small as possible. I can still see the blue puppet with the dungarees saying, 'Your nana's will be nice and quiet, just like your mammy's house at home.'

'It's nothing like her mother's house,' my grandmother said. 'That place is a death trap.'

I don't think I was meant to hear that, but I did. I said nothing, though, I was too scared. In the space of a day, my mother had been taken away from me and in her place were two people she was scared of. What would happen if I got cross with them?

So I allowed the puppet woman and my grandmother to bring me to Granny's home. It was in Galway, which was a long way from Wexford. When she opened her front door and I saw what seemed to me to be acres of shining tiles, I backed away.

'What's the matter?' my grandmother asked. There was nothing in the space, just a floor. They waited for me to answer, but I couldn't.

'Come.' She walked ahead of me. Her shoes click-clacked on the tiles. You did not just go and march into people's houses. My grandmother turned around and came back to where I stood in the doorway. She crouched down to my level. 'I know this is scary,' she said. 'And I know you'll miss your mammy.' She took a hankie out of her pocket as I started to sniff. 'But I promise you will go home to her. And I promise I won't do you any harm. Well, I might feed you too many sweets by accident.'

'I won't eat them,' I said defiantly. 'I'm big. I can do things. I know first aid.'

'Well, good.' I think she was laughing at me. She held out the hankie but I didn't take it.

'Would you like to see your bedroom? You can bring teddy?' I was carrying Harold, he was as big as me.

'Let's have a look, shall we?' the puppet lady said. I followed her up the stairs. My grandmother was behind us. The stairs were enormous.

'In here.' My grandmother pushed open a bedroom door and all I could see was floor and more floor with a huge bed in the middle of it and some toys. The walls were white. The curtains at the window were white. The ceiling looked like it was up in space it was so high.

'I don't want this room.' I just wanted to go home. It was as if I was unanchored. Bobbing about. Like my dead daddy in the waves. I started to cry.

They whispered for a bit before my grandmother pushed

open a door at the end of the hall. 'This room, maybe?' she said. The room was cosy and had a hoover and an ironing board and lots of boxes in it. There was a tiny bed all tucked up nice against the window. I had to climb over boxes to get to it.

'OK.'

I stayed in my room day after day, looking out at my grandmother's back garden. It was pretty, big but not too big. It was surrounded on each side by walls so you knew just how far it went. I could see lots of different-coloured flowers and shrubs all in neat little rows. There was a tree with a swing and little steps going up into another part of the garden that I couldn't see from the window. In the early weeks, I spent a lot of time watching my grandmother, her back bent over a flowerbed and sometimes, when I was too slow disappearing out of sight behind the curtain, she'd see me looking and wave. I never waved back.

Even in the rain, the garden looked good, the grass seemed greener and I liked the way the swing creaked back and forward as if someone was playing on it.

At mealtimes, I only ate what my grandmother ate, that way I knew I wasn't going to be poisoned. At home I ate loads of bread and cheese, but in my grandmother's, she had a big fridge full of everything and each day we had a different dinner and lunch. I knew what most of the vegetables were from flashcards my mammy had used to teach me, but it was hard to know what some of the meals were meant to be. They looked like plates of poison, that was for sure. After I ate, I'd go back upstairs again.

During the day, people called in to my grandmother. I

would hear her inviting the people in before offering them coffee and biscuits. 'I'm making coffee, Ruby,' she'd call up to me. 'Would you like something?'

Sometimes I answered, 'No', sometimes I didn't answer at all.

One day, ages later, when my mammy was still too sick for visitors, my grandmother knocked on my bedroom door. I held my breath. Kept real still.

'Would you like to help me in the garden?' she said. 'I can show you a tree your daddy planted for me if you like.'

My daddy? Planted her a tree?

'And you can help me prune it.'

We worked in silence for the first hour, me chopping bits of a tree she said my daddy had given her. She told me that my daddy had done her garden for her. Then she let me plant some flowers, telling me how far down to dig and praising me when I got it just right. I pretended not to hear her, just like I did when she started to tell me funny little stories about my mammy when she was little. She had a good way with words and even though it was a bit shocking that she was sharing private information, I couldn't help laughing at the one where my mammy had baked a cake and put in salt instead of sugar and everyone had to eat it and pretend it was nice. She asked me if I had any funny stories like that. I wasn't sure about telling her stuff but she didn't mind, she just kept talking on and on. So I told her one about me eating a bit of an onion my mother peeled because I thought it was an apple and she laughed. I liked making her laugh. I told her about Mammy's newspapers falling out her window and how we had to run around the field at the back of our house, catching them all before they blew away. Then she asked about my mother. I told her about our lessons in the mornings. It was called 'home schooling' and was better than going to a real school where you had to compete with a lot of uninterested students who might pull you down. I told her the way Mammy made brown bread because you couldn't trust shop-bought bread. I told her about my mammy's poems and how it was Daddy that she started writing them for. I told her about my daddy and how he died and that no one ever found his body. Of our trips to the beach. She listened to it all.

One Sunday, my Aunt Susan came for a visit. She brought three girls with her who I learned were called my cousins and she brought a man who was their daddy, my uncle and her husband; his name was Dan. Such a lot of things.

The three girls, Nan, Nelly and Nora, stood staring at me. They wore bright summer dresses and all of them had their hair up in pigtails of such shininess that I couldn't believe they were real. They had shoes, which I learned were called sandals, and their toenails were painted. If someone had told me that these girls had flown in from outer space, I would have believed it.

'Hello,' Susan said, 'I brought my girls to meet you, Ruby.' She turned to the tallest girl. 'This is Nan.'

Nan, in a short red dress, smiled at me. 'Hiya. I think it's great to have a cousin my own age. All my other cousins are dicks.'

'Nan!' That was her father.

The other two girls giggled.

Nan smirked and I smirked back, liking her a lot. I had no idea what a dick was.

'I'm Nelly,' the next one said, pushing herself forward. 'I'm nine, nearly your age. Have you any games we can play?'

'I have a teddy.'

They laughed like I'd made a joke.

'And this is Nora, she's five,' Susan said.

'And she's my little angel.' My grandmother, who was obviously their grandmother too, scooped Nora up and brought her over to the fridge. 'Now, Missy, pick whichever ice-pop you'd like.'

The other three started clamouring for an ice-pop too. I stood apart and observed them. Was this how it was, then? I couldn't wait to tell my mammy that there was no need to be scared of Susan and Nana.

Nana had photo albums in a drawer underneath her bookshelves. She took them out one day, asking if I'd like to see some snaps of my mother when she was young. Side by side we sat on the sofa and she showed me pictures of my mother as a baby. Then pictures of Aunt Susan as a baby and then pictures of a little boy. 'Who's that?'

'He's my son,' Nana said. 'He would have been your uncle. Your mother was eight when he was born and she spoiled him rotten. His name was Robert.'

My uncle Robert had a big smile and blond hair. In one picture he was wearing shorts and a stripy T-shirt and had a huge ice-cream cone in his hand. 'Where is he now?'

'He died,' Nana said, and her voice hitched up at the end. 'He fell off a roof when he climbed up to get his football back.'

'Climbing on a roof is dangerous.'

'I know, pet.'

I put my hand in hers because I thought she might cry, and she squeezed it. 'I'll tell my daddy in heaven to mind him,' I whispered. She smiled and leaned over and kissed me and said that that was a big comfort to her. The day Robert died was the saddest day of her life, she said. Robert was the sort of boy who never walked if he could run. A boy that had a loud voice and always laughed. It was like there was a big hole in the family when he was gone. I found it funny to think that my mother had a brother like that.

There were pictures of my granddad in the album too. He looked like my mammy, Nana said, but I didn't think so. He drowned at sea, which was weird, as so did my daddy. I wondered if they were on the same boat and Nana said that no, her husband's boat was called *Melsuerob*, which was clever because it was all the names of his children jammed together. I didn't know what my father's boat was called.

At the back of the album, there was a picture of a little girl with my mammy, Aunt Susan and my nana. The little girl is in my mammy's arms but her hands are stretching towards Aunt Susan. She looks like she's crying. 'Who's that?'

'That is Ivy. She was two then.'

'Is she dead too?'

My nana made a sound, I wasn't sure if it was a laugh or a sob. 'No. She's in England. She's as alive as you are.'

'Did she come on a visit to you?'

'She did, and that's when we took this picture. This is one we took of her last year.' She pulled out another photograph and in this picture Ivy was bigger than me. Her hair was brown and sleek and she was wearing a short skirt and high shoes. They looked like something an adult would wear.

'I like her shoes.'

Nana laughed.

There was a woman in the picture with Ivy, standing behind her with her hands on Ivy's shoulders. To the left of Ivy was my nana and to the right was Aunt Susan. 'Why isn't my mammy in this picture?'

'Because your mammy wasn't there,' Nana said. 'You and your mammy haven't visited me in a long time. You've never been here before.'

The words hung there between us, and I wondered why we'd never come for a visit. And also, it occurred to me that there was not one picture of me in this album.

'Will you take some pictures of me so you can put them in here?' I asked.

Nana smiled. 'Of course we will. Starting tomorrow, I'll take a picture of you every day until you go home.'

And she did.

Mammy was a pale ghost in the bed. She had lost weight and her hair had been chopped. When she saw me, she smiled and reached out her hand. 'How's my baby?' she said, and her voice was so small, I had to lean in real close to hear.

It felt like years since I'd seen her. 'When will you be

home?' I kept my voice steady as my grandmother said it was important for me not to get upset as it would only upset my mammy.

'Soon. I hope you're being a good girl.' She shot a look at my grandmother, who was standing behind me.

'She is,' my nana said. 'A great help in the garden.'

'Daddy planted a tree in Nana's garden, did you know that?' I asked.

There was a silence. At the time I thought it was because my mother hadn't known.

'And I saw a picture of your dead brother. And I met my cousins,' I said. 'Nan, Nelly and Nora. Nora's so cute. I'd love a sister like her.'

My mother started to cough and immediately my grandmother poured her some water. My mother's cough sounded like a rumble of thunder. My mother said something to my grandmother, who said something back. I don't know what it was. Then my grandmother straightened up and said, 'I've got a room, you can have it, no strings.'

'I've got a house,' my mother said. Then added, 'I'd like to talk to my little girl on her own.' Mammy sounded cross but she gave me a wink.

That was our wink! I looked at my grandmother but she was looking at Mammy. After a bit, she left, ruffling my hair on the way out. I climbed up onto the bed beside Mammy and as she smoothed my hair back down, she said, 'I'll be home soon, OK?'

I felt as if I could burst into song, I was so happy.

'My mother is very nice, but she lives her way and we live ours, isn't that right?'

'That's right.' I wondered if we could change some of our ways, though.

'I don't like you staying away from me but I have no choice.'

'It's OK. Everyone is very nice to me.'

'Good.'

'And Nana lets me bake and, oh,' I giggled, 'she told me a story of when you baked.'

'What did she say?'

'That you made buns and that you put salt in them instead of sugar.'

Mammy smiled. 'Yes, I knew there was salt in them actually, but it was just too hard to get it out, it looked so like the flour, so I just left it.'

I laughed, though I didn't find it that funny.

3

I have spent the last couple of hours shovelling up the remains of Max's bonfire into a wheelbarrow and dumping it out on the far corner of the garden. Being a cleaner has in no way prepared me for gardening, my limbs ache with the effort. Still, at least the big slag heap is gone from the middle of the lawn now and instead all that remains is a black circle. I'm sure I'll be able to dig it out and coax some grass into growing there.

The front door bell rings and I jerk a little, spilling dirt from the shovel onto the ground. Even though Max has assured me that Paddy won't be back, I'm still a little wary. Putting the shovel down, I move cautiously inside. A tall person is silhouetted against the glass in the front door. Paddy hadn't been as tall as that, I'm sure. And besides, I tell myself, I've a right to be in this house. Max gave me his permission. The bell rings again and I answer. The instant I see the caller, I know who it is. His hair is grey, but his features are all Max. He's taller than Max though, standing about six three in the doorway. There's a moment of silence as we take each other in. Then the man says, 'Hello, I'm Pierce, Max's dad.'

'Hi.' My hand on the door, I shuffle about a bit awkwardly. I don't know what to do.

'And you are Sandy?'

His tone is pleasant but firm. I remember Molly saying she told him about me and I feel a little more confident. 'Yes.' My voice comes out in a croak.

'Max never told me about you,' Pierce says. He leans against the door jamb. 'May I come in?'

I desperately don't want him to. How can I refuse to tell him about his son if he's standing in front of me? 'I have no proof that you're his dad.'

'I'll get Charles next door to vouch for me,' he says pleasantly. 'He met me the night I called the ambulance to take my son's almost lifeless body out of here. I'll go get him.' He makes to leave.

'OK,' I wince, pulling the door wider, 'come in.'

He steps inside and pauses just as he is about to pass me to go into the kitchen. Standing in front of me, he eyes me up and down. 'Look,' he leans towards me and his voice drops, his eyes narrow, 'my son is an ill boy. I don't know what he told you or what impression he gave you but he's not well. He's liable to give all his money away to a dog the way he is now. So whoever you are, you better not get used to being here. This is his house.'

I suppose he's trying to sound intimidating, but there is such sorrow in the way he says it that I can only pity him. I can't even feel offended. Maybe I look like a house-grabber to him. 'I am Max's friend,' I say, stressing the 'friend'. 'I am not taking advantage of him.'

He pulls a little away and nods, though he looks sceptical. 'OK, let's say you're telling the truth—'

'I am!'

He ignores my outburst. 'If I come in perhaps you'll tell me how my son is.' He doesn't wait for me to reply, just goes on into the kitchen, where he stops and stares out the window.

'So you're cleaning up his garden for him,' he says.

'Trying to.'

'It's hard work.' He looks at my skinny arms.

'I know.'

'That's a nice thing to do.'

We eye each other up, not as warily now.

'Tea?' I ask, not actually sure this is the done thing. This is the first visitor I've ever had in my whole life. So I copy what Charles does for me.

'Thanks,' he says.

I turn from him and put on the kettle. I feel incredibly self-conscious doing this for a man who has probably been in this room hundreds of times before.

'Look,' he says, 'sorry if I was a bit heavy-handed at the door, but I worry about Max.'

'I understand.' I put some milk and sugar in front of him and the kettle clicks off. He doesn't say any more until I sit opposite, having handed him a large mug of tea.

'Since he came to Dublin, he's been unravelling. Did you notice it?'

'No.' I take a sip of tea, biding my time, before admitting, 'I haven't known him that long.'

He winces.

'He appeared totally normal to me, though,' I blabber then. Which is a bit ridiculous when I think about it as I've never known normal.

'He used to be such a …' he pauses, and his smile is sad when he says, 'such a great kid. Funny and kind and …' He stops again and spoons four sugars into his mug. 'How is he?' he asks. His tone is neutral and he doesn't look at me.

I hesitate. 'I'm not sure he'd be happy with me if I told you.'

He stops stirring his sugar and meets my gaze. 'Please?'

And just like that, I get a flashback to that shop all those years ago, when I saw my mother on TV. The desperate look on her face, the guilt that ate away at me for a few nights afterwards. The guilt that is ever-present when I think of how upset I've made anyone who did know me. The guilt at everything I've done since to stay alive. And the desperate love of a father for his son. Oh God, I envy Max that. I am unable to do anything about my own situation, but maybe I could help Pierce now.

'Max seems OK,' I say, and watch the look of relief spread over his face. 'Like he's talking and he makes sense. Sometimes his head is a bit all over the place but then the next time, he's grand.'

'And he knows who you are and how he knows you and everything?'

'Totally.'

Pierce closes his eyes briefly. When he opens them, he looks me straight in the face. 'Thank you.'

'Why won't Max talk to you himself?'

To my horror, the man's eyes fill with tears and he looks upwards to stop them falling, I think.

Oh God, I shouldn't have asked. I'm about to say it doesn't matter when he says, 'Because I'm the one who put him in there. I signed him in.'

I don't know what he means.

'I had to, don't you see?' He seems to be pleading with

me. 'He was a danger to himself, I couldn't stand by and see him hurt himself. He's been running on empty for years. I should have seen it coming.'

'What do you mean "running on empty"?'

Pierce looks at me. 'It's as if he's trying always to run from what happened. That's what I think anyway.'

'What did happen?'

There is a pause. 'Didn't he tell you? Does he not talk about it?'

And I think how little I really know Max. 'No, he never talks about before.'

'Then maybe you should wait for him to tell you. It's not my place.'

'Fair enough.'

We finish off our tea in silence and as he stands up to leave, he looks out into the garden again. 'Do you want a hand with that wheelbarrow? It looks very heavy.'

'Are you not in a hurry home?'

'It won't take long.'

To my dismay, he strides out the back door and starts unloading the wheelbarrow. Then he begins hefting up the large rocks and stones from the lawn and throwing them into it.

I come out to watch him and he tells me that if I like I can start chopping down the overgrown grass before mowing it. I feel I have no choice.

'Max hates the garden,' Pierce eventually says, panting. 'When he bought this place, his sister and I were relieved because it had only a small garden. Maya, that's Max's sister, she calls him the germinator terminator.'

It makes me smile.

'Maya came up and planted a lot of stuff for him but it's all dead now. D'you like the garden yourself?'

It's funny, I barely know what I like. Cappuccinos, The Unconventionals, sandwiches without olives, reading aloud. 'I'm not sure. I haven't done it too often.' I cut down a swathe of long grass and seeds scatter everywhere.

'Well, you stick with Max and you'll soon find out.' He laughs. Then says, a little awkwardly, 'You must be special if he lets you visit.'

I meet his gaze. 'I think it's the special people he's not letting visit.'

Pierce considers this. 'Really?'

I nod.

He stands, observing me, his hands on his hips, saying nothing. Then quite suddenly, he resumes clearing the garden. A couple of seconds pass before I begin cutting down the grass once more.

'I'll order a skip once this is cleared,' he eventually says. 'Then I'll be back to load it up.' A pause. 'OK?'

'Sure.' Max might be out of hospital by then and I'll be gone.

We work in silence for another while until the light starts to fade from the day. Pierce heaves a sigh and wipes his hands along his trousers. 'I'll pop back some day next week and finish up,' he says. 'Don't kill yourself, it's heavy work.'

I really wish he wouldn't but it's like my mother used to say, you let people in and you can't shut the door ever again. 'OK.'

Pierce flashes me a brief smile and says he'll see himself out.

4

The lure of three girl cousins was impossible to resist. Even though I told myself that they would only want to know my business, that the way they stomped around my grandmother's house was rude, I found that it ceased to matter, I still wanted to know them. After standing on the fringes for a while observing the way they went on, I dove in, like a thirsty person in the desert soaking up the water of friendship. These girls did things that I'd never known existed. My favourite was family night when they all sat together and watched a film and passed around a bowl of popcorn from which everybody ate. Some nights I barely watched the movie, preferring instead to look at everyone's faces. These were my family, I thought.

Nan adopted me. She would suddenly pull me aside and whisper her secrets to me, driving Nelly into a temper. She told me that she had a boyfriend who kissed her. I didn't know if that was good or bad but she seemed to think it was good. She asked my opinion on her nail varnish and I, who barely knew what nail varnish was, gave it. She asked me if I had a Friends Reunited page.

I couldn't bluff that. 'Friends Reunited?'

'Yeah. You said you had a computer.' She made it sound like I told her a lie.

'I do.'

'Well, then.' She heaved a sigh and pulled me upstairs to her room and closed the door. Her voice dipped to a whisper. 'I'm on it but Mammy doesn't know, so you can't tell her.' She went into Friends Reunited and showed me all her pictures and all the groups she belonged to. She explained to me how you could get loads of friends on it and how you could chat to people. I didn't believe her but she said she'd set an account up for me and then I'd see. So she set up an email address for me and then an account. She lied about my age. Then she put up a picture of us lying in the grass that her mother had snapped on her phone. 'Now,' she instructed, 'seeing as you don't go to school, you can join our school group, we use the secondary school one, and you can be friends with me and all my friends. I'm going to be your first friend, OK?' I watched as she accepted her own friend request. Then she smiled at me. 'And when you go home, we can stay friends.'

That simple statement filled me up. 'I will go on it when I go home,' I told her with fervour.

Then she showed me other things that the computer could do. I wondered fleetingly why my mother hadn't shown me any of this. Maybe she hadn't known.

Maybe.

Two weeks before I went home, my grandmother treated me to a shopping spree. She said that she did it for all her grandchildren. Once a year she brought them into town and they could buy whatever they liked. The budget was a hundred euros. I almost collapsed with excitement. One hundred euros! I told my nana that I wanted clothes, just like Nora's. I wanted sandals just like Nora's and I wanted my hair done just like Nora's.

That day is a fairy tale etched on my memory. Even now, I recall it with huge nostalgia: the bright sun, the crowded city streets, the way she held my hand in hers and I danced alongside her. The shops we visited, the clothes I tried on, the lunch we shared. Never had I a day like it. I enjoyed the rush and hum of traffic, I loved knocking against people as we made our way up the street, I wondered if you had to be eleven before such a day was given to you. By the time the shops closed, I was the proud owner of pink glittery sandals, long white socks and an assortment of dresses and jeans. I had a new winter coat. My hair was curled up in ringlets. Walking past a window, I glanced at myself and realised how good I could look.

'Mammy won't know who I am when I go back,' I told my nana, and a part of me hoped she wouldn't. A part of me hoped she'd reject me and say that I could live in Galway forever. And I didn't understand why I thought that and I felt bad for thinking it.

'You and Susan are so nice,' I said to my nana as she treated me to a fizzy orange.

'Thank you.' She smiled. 'It's only because you're so nice yourself.'

'I'm going to tell my mammy to answer the door to you and Susan from now on.' Even back then, I knew by her silence that I'd said something that touched a nerve. 'Why doesn't she answer the door?' I asked.

My nana didn't say anything for a long time and I began to wonder if she'd heard me. 'I think you should ask her that,' she said.

'I did. She just says that you're nobody important.'

And again, that stab of silence, the way she closed her eyes at my words.

'But I think you *are* important,' I said hastily, not wanting her to be sad.

'Thanks, pet.'

'Is she afraid of you?'

My nana smiled and touched my cheek. 'You're a very perceptive little girl.'

I didn't know what that word meant. 'Is she?'

'I think so.'

'Why?'

It took ages before she answered. 'Sometimes,' she said slowly, 'life makes people scared so they think that by staying in the same place and doing the same things nothing can harm them.'

'Like in the cottage?'

'Yes.'

'So if she doesn't go out, she can't trip over or hurt herself?'

'Yes, sort of.'

'But she could trip over inside. She got sick when she was inside.'

'Yes, she did.'

I smiled and said, 'I'll tell her that that is just silly.'

My nana smiled back. Then she got serious. 'Just remember, no matter what happens, she's doing it because she thinks it's the right thing.'

I nodded. Somewhere along the way, though, it became too hard to believe.

The puppet lady drove me home some months later. I went back with new clothes and shoes and, unfortunately for me, a new way of living.

As we drove up the driveway to the house, something in me stirred. An uneasy feeling that I couldn't place. It was as if there was a scrabbling in my tummy, an itch under my skin. I saw the high grass on each side of the rutted lane brush the edges of the car. As we turned the corner, the cottage came into sight. I saw it as if for the first time. A tiny building huddled in on itself. The front door a little crooked. The whitewashed walls not so white. No gleaming tiles or full fridges, just glimpses of a flagstone floor and a block of cheese and some milk.

'Are you OK?' Puppet Lady asked.

I stared ahead, hugging Harold, missing my grandmother already and feeling guilty about it.

The door of the cottage opened and my mother stood there, framed in the doorway.

The unease lifted when I saw her and only joy was left. Forgetting that the car hadn't quite stopped, I flung myself from the vehicle, tripping slightly, but righting myself, I hurtled up the drive towards my mother.

She let out a gasp and, bending down, scooped me hard against her.

I was crushed in her embrace.

Over and over she said, 'Thank God they let you back. They let you back.'

Puppet Woman stood looking at us. 'May I come in, Melanie?' she asked.

My mother hesitated. I felt her arms loosen about me.

'Much better to talk out here,' she said, standing up, 'and let Ruby get settled back in.'

I should have seen it as a mark of what was to come, but I was only going on eleven.

5

'I met your dad,' I say to Max the next time I see him.

He flinches but doesn't seem all that surprised. 'He called to the house, then?'

'Yes. He was asking about you.'

'I hope you told him nothing.'

'I said you were doing OK.'

His face darkens. 'You shouldn't have. You shouldn't talk to him.'

I say nothing to that. Max's dad is going to call again, I'm going to have to tell him how Max is.

'You'd talk to him again, wouldn't you?'

'He helped me clean your garden. He says you're a hopeless gardener.'

'He put me in here, do you know that?' His voice rises and he has to pull it back. 'Did he tell you that?'

'He said it was for your own good.'

He winces. Then he turns and stares at the table.

'He says you've been unravelling since you came to Dublin.'

His eyes meet mine. They're angry. 'You had a good old chat about me then, eh?'

'No, he's just worried.'

'I am fine,' Max hisses at me. 'OK, so I got a bit stressed but I'm grand now.'

'Did something happen in Wexford?'

It's like the air stills with the question. Max seems to freeze, he eyes me warily. 'Why?'

'I don't know. It's just your dad—'

'Forget about him,' Max snaps. 'Just forget about him. I don't want to hear about him. He put me in here. I don't want to be here.'

'Sorry.'

'It's not like I go asking you all sorts of questions about yourself, is it?'

He has a point.

'Like, I don't go asking you about the lie that made you leave Wexford, do I?'

'You've made your point.' I feel a flash of irritation.

'I don't even know your second name.'

'I said you've made your point.'

'What *is* your second name?'

He's goading me now and I don't like it. He's in a shit mood because I talked to his dad. I glare at him.

'Well?' He regards me cockily.

'Fairbrother,' I grind out. And the shock of saying my name blasts me from the feet up so that I rock a little. 'Happy?'

'And the lie that made you leave Wexford?'

I can't believe he's just asked that. I stare at him, willing him to take it back.

He crosses his arms and cocks an eyebrow. 'Spill.'

I stand up and leave. I ignore him calling after me. I have to blink hard to rid myself of the tears.

I spend the day battling fury and upset mingled with curiosity. I hadn't liked the look on Max's face as he'd challenged me to reveal my second name. There had been something predatory about it. And I hadn't liked the way he didn't acknowledge the fact that I'd told him my surname. It was the first time I'd uttered it in eight years and just saying it had sent shivers through me. This was who I was; no matter how far I ran or how long for, I would always be 'Fairbrother'. There is something powerful in saying your name like that. And he'd just discarded my honesty for another smartass question.

After I get back from reading to Molly, I check Max's landline for messages from his Dad. The voice at the other end tells me that there are ten unheard messages. That's surprising. None of them are from Pierce though. I listen as Max, at first nonchalant and then wary, issues excuse after excuse for his behaviour. He doesn't apologise once. I gave him something true about myself, the first real true thing I'd said to anyone in years, and all I get in return are a lot of crappy excuses. Bastard. Without thinking, I turn to his computer and for the first time in years, I log onto the internet. I think about what to type into Google and I start off by typing in Max's name.

'Max Coyle.'

Loads of information pops up. Images of Max with well-known people. Images of Max at important events.

Articles Max is mentioned in. Articles about Max. In all the photographs he looks the picture of a hugely successful businessman: happy, well groomed and suave. There is nothing to say how it all fell apart. At least his clients haven't talked about him to the press.

But this is not what I'm after. I'm looking for what his dad referred to. The thing Max is running from. It was something that happened when he was at home, so I add 'Wexford' into the search engine and once again a glut of information pops up, a lot of it the same as before.

I drum my fingers on the table, thinking hard. Finally I key in 'tragedy' because I reckon a tragedy is the only thing a person would try to escape from.

And bingo! Right down at the end of the first page of search results I come across a headline from the *Wexford Bugle*: *Tragedy as Teenager Feared Drowned After Fall From Pier*. The headline is repeated again by a national paper.

Unease grips me. I wonder if it is right to pry like this. Maybe I should let Max tell me himself. And then I think back to the look on his face as I said my name, and with a mixture of upset and determination, I click on the link.

Five young lads, arms about each other's shoulders, grin out at me. They are listed as Paddy McIntyre, John Judge, Max Coyle, Shane McEvoy and Tom Byrne. Max is instantly recognisable, while Paddy has filled out and is no longer so skinny. They all look ridiculously carefree. It's a really lovely picture of five friends and I can't stop looking at it. I never had friends. These look as if they've known one another forever, as if they share each other's lives. I envy Max right then.

After a bit, I turn to the article.

Teenager Shane McEvoy (18), pictured above, is feared drowned after falling from Rossclare Pier, Wexford, yesterday afternoon. There was a strong current at the time and despite a valiant attempt by his friend Max Coyle (18) to save him, the current was too strong and Shane was dragged away. The search for his body continues. His friends were brought to Wexford general hospital and were treated for shock.

Poor Max. How horrible to see your friend being pulled away and not to be able to do anything. It's no wonder he doesn't want to talk about it. There is another article, shorter, dated the following week.

The body of Shane McEvoy was recovered from the sea yesterday evening, approximately twenty miles from where he fell in and drowned in a tragedy that has shocked the local community. Shane was well known in Rossclare and was a talented football and soccer player. His soccer manager called him 'a superb addition to the team who will be sorely missed'. Shane was due to get his Leaving Certificate results in August and he had hoped to study medicine in Trinity. He is mourned by his parents and his two sisters Lisa (16) and Amy (15). His parents have thanked all who were involved in the recovery of his body and paid tribute to his friend Max, who did his best to save him.

This piece is accompanied by a picture of Shane and his girlfriend, a plump, serious-looking girl named as Imelda Greene.

The minute I finish reading, guilt sideswipes me. I'm as bad as Max. I've spied into a private part of his life, one which he chooses not to visit. And I didn't do it out of concern, I did it out of anger, a desire to lash back. On impulse, I shut down the search. As the computer returns to its screen picture of a beach, it strikes me that I can spy into *my* old life. The thought sends the blood rushing to my head and I feel a little sick. Should I? No one will ever know. And I can stop whenever I want. I don't even have to look if I don't want to.

Fingers shaking, I log back onto the internet and key in 'Ruby Fairbrother'.

Like Max's name, my own brings up reams of results.

Ruby Fairbrother Still Missing.

Is Ruby Dead?

Reward for Ruby.

Mother Appeals for Information on Ruby.

It goes on and on. Gaining courage, I call up some of the pieces, but there is nothing new in them.

Then I think of my old Facebook page and I wonder if I can get into it. I'd joined Facebook because Nan had announced on Friends Reunited that she was joining it. She'd never accepted my friend request, I remember with a stab of hurt. None of her friends had. Louis and his band had been my only friends on it. I key in 'Facebook' and go to 'Login'. The computer wants my email and password. They are branded onto my mind and my fingers fly over the keys as I type.

My profile picture is exactly as I remember. Me and Nan lying on the grass in her back garden. My eyes flick to the posts and I don't know what I'd expected but I'm shocked to see that my page is alive with messages. I'd just wondered what my last ever post was. But just looking at this it appears that people post every year on the day in June that I ran off. Most of the posts are from people I don't know. I scroll down through them, numb with shock. Someone writes, *Ruby, if you ever log onto Facebook, know that you are missed.* And someone else says, *Come home, Ruby.* Of course there are the horrible ones, like *You fucking scumbag, worrying your poor mother like that.* But in the main, it consists of complete strangers trying to reach out to me. And then, like cold water on a hot day, I see Susan's name and picture. And she has written: *Dear Ruby, you didn't just leave Wexford, or your mother, you left us. Me and your cousins and your mother can never go back to where we were until you come home. Please. Please. Come home. Xxxxxxxx*

It was written a few weeks ago.

I can't take my eyes off that post for ages. I want to cry but I can't. It's as if the tears are too far down inside me to come out. I think I might be sick. Susan, I'm so sorry. I'm so, so sorry.

This is another time I won't answer her. I think about sending a note or making a call, but reject it. I've thought of nothing else through the years and each time, it was too risky. I cannot get pulled back into my mother's world. I have tried to write letters but each time, I got bogged down by the words. A letter could not bridge the enormity of the betrayal that lay between us.

I wonder if Ivy has a page. I'm about to do a search when I realise that I don't know her surname. I spy on Nan. She hasn't posted on her page in years. Neither has Louis, though he's probably got some kind of band page now. Everything has moved on.

I sit and stare at Susan's post. And it moves down the screen as someone posts something new. I take a deep breath and scroll back up.

Ruby, I log on every year, I hope you know that wherever you are you are not forgotten. Bill Jackson

I have to think who that is. Then I remember that it was the name of the man from Casey's who used to leave the lollipops for me when he delivered the groceries to our house. I reach out and touch his post, running my fingers along the words. I sit there for ages.

About an hour later, the phone rings. It's Max again. I pick it up, not thinking of our row, just feeling sorry for the boy who saw his friend drown.

'I'm bloody sorry, OK?' Max snaps into the phone. 'I was being a shit. Is that what you want to hear?'

Here is the apology I wanted and I couldn't wait for it – I had to snoop into his life. But if I hadn't, I probably wouldn't have answered the phone just now. 'Thanks,' I mutter.

He is silent for a few seconds. Then he says, in a gentler tone, 'I *am* sorry.'

'And I'm sorry if me talking to your dad upset you but he called to the house and he really wanted to know.'

He ignores this. 'And thanks for telling me your second name. I couldn't find any Sandy Fairbrothers in Wexford, though.'

'You googled me?' I'm appalled, then realise I'm way worse. At least I know his name.

Max laughs gently. 'Sandy, I'm a PR man, of course I googled you. Anyway, you're like an anomaly. You must be the only person in Ireland who isn't on the internet.'

If only he knew. Part of me wishes I could tell him.

'So,' he interrupts my thoughts, 'can we move on from here? I don't want to lose my best visitor.'

'You won't,' I say, and I wish he was in front of me so I could … I don't know … touch his arm or his sleeve, something to show him that I would never not visit.

'Good.'

'Thanks for the apology.'

'I should have done it with the first phone call.'

'It was worth waiting for.'

He chuckles softly. 'You've got very cheeky.'

'What can I say? You bring out the worst in me?'

He laughs, then lapses into silence, which stretches. Both of us, I think, are reluctant to hang up.

'Well,' he finally says, 'goodnight.'

'Goodnight to you too.'

And we hang up.

6

For the first couple of weeks I fussed over my mother, thrilled to have her back. I watched her every move. I told her when the postman was coming so that she could be in position by the door when the post plopped through. I spent my days staring out the window in case we'd have unexpected visitors. I was determined not to have her stressed. The only person we didn't bother to hide from anymore was the man from Casey's. The first day he delivered our shopping after my mother came home, he knocked on the door. Then he stood back and pointed. 'For your mother,' he shouted out to me.

It was a small bunch of daffodils.

The next week, my mother wrote him a little 'thank you' note and I slipped it under the door as he drove up in his van.

The honeymoon period ended about six weeks later in the first row we'd ever had. She was obsessing over her newspapers, convinced that while she'd been in hospital some of them had been stolen. She was marking them off in a jotter to see which ones were missing. Everything about her was a bit frantic.

'You can trust no one,' she said. 'What date is that paper?'

I gave her the date. She jotted it down.

'You had to trust doctors when you were in hospital,' I said, 'to make you better.'

'Trust the doctors?' She made a comical face. 'Sometimes I didn't even take the medicines they gave me.' She started flicking through more papers.

I stared at the top of her head, feeling really cross with her. 'No wonder you were sick for so long then.'

She paused in her search. A silence settled on the room. 'What did you say?' She sat up straight and eyeballed me.

I stared down at the bundle of newspapers, at my hands, black from thumbing them with her. 'I said,' I took a deep breath, anger and hurt ricocheting through me, 'that if you didn't take your medicines, no wonder you were in hospital for so long.'

'I was not staying away deliberately,' she said, eerily calm.

I didn't answer. Not taking medicine seemed a good way to stay away.

'I was sick.'

I shrugged.

'I did not go off and leave you.'

'I didn't say that.'

'You might as well have.' In one swift movement, she grabbed my arms and poked her face into mine. 'Did they tell you that I left you?' she hissed urgently. 'Did bloody perfect Susan with her hippy happy kids say I left you?'

'No.' I tried to pull away. 'I only said—'

'"Susan says, Susan says," that's all I've been bloody hearing from you since you came back. From now on,' she let me go and slammed her hand down on the newspapers, 'no more talk about Susan.'

'You won't let me talk about her anyway.'

'Because they're trouble, that's why.'

'They were nice!'

'You'd rather live with them, wouldn't you? You'd rather go and live with perfect Susan.'

'No!'

'You would.' She started to sob. She pointed to the door. 'Well, go on then, if you want. Go on. I'm obviously not a fit enough mother.' She picked up a book and flung it in my direction. It flopped open at a poem called 'Vanished'. I wanted to vanish. 'Go,' she screeched again.

'I don't want to.' I wanted to cry, but I wouldn't let myself. 'I don't want to go, Mammy.'

She sat, her shoulders heaving with sobs. I kept telling her I didn't want to go. Her sobs grew louder and she buried her face in her hands and rubbed her eyes with her palms. Finally, in desperation, I reached out and rubbed her shoulder. She grabbed me, reaching for me like a blind person. 'I'm sorry, Ruby. I'm so sorry.'

'It's OK.' But it wasn't. Not really.

'I think I'm afraid I'll lose you.'

How could she lose me, I thought. We never go anywhere.

7

Dorian Gray is a pain in the arse. At least Molly and I agree on that one. Then Molly asks, 'Did you think he was going to die when he stabbed his own portrait?'

I hadn't thought about it at all, but now I do. 'I guess it was the only thing that could happen,' I say. She looks interested so I go on. 'You can't wipe away your past, can you, no matter how hard you try. His portrait reminded him of who he really was and he couldn't bear it.'

Molly nods. 'I think you're right. And without our pasts, we are nothing.'

'Tea?' Charles pokes his head around the door. 'I've bought some nice lemon cake too if you'd like?' He looks at me hopefully.

'Lovely.' I smile.

'Mum?'

'Yes, and do join us.' Molly pats the bed. 'We're discussing Dorian Gray.'

'That pain in the arse? I'll pass.'

I laugh.

Charles leaves and when I turn back to Molly I see her staring at me, her lips curved upwards.

'What?' I ask uncomfortably.

'You have a great laugh,' she says. 'You don't smile too often, you know?'

I flick my gaze to the pages of the book I've just read.

'Have I upset you?' Molly asks. 'I'm sorry if I have.'

My answer is a shrug. I wonder do people look at me and see sadness roll off me like rainy mist.

'It's just …' Molly says, 'for a young girl you're very different.'

I thought I'd kept the different part of me hidden away but obviously not too well.

'Most young people are loud and brash, with opinions on everything,' Molly goes on. 'It's what being young is about, I always thought. You're not like that.'

I was never young, that's why. I've spent nearly all my life, bar the past few weeks, on the edge of hysteria, doing my best to keep afloat in a world whose rules were alien to me. As tears prick my eyes, my stomach clenches up in horror. I cannot cry.

'Sandy,' Molly sounds alarmed, 'please don't cry. I didn't mean to upset you.'

'I'm not crying,' I hiccup.

Charles chooses that moment to come back. He shoulders in the door, balancing a tray of tea and cake which he puts on the side table. I turn my face away but he must notice because the next thing he says is, 'What's happening here?' He crosses over and surprises me by putting his arm around my shoulder. I realise that I am crying. 'Mum, what have you said to her?' He sounds angry. 'You told me you liked her. You can't keep doing this to people.'

'I didn't do anything.' Molly sounds bewildered. 'I really didn't.'

'You never do,' Charles barks. 'Honestly, you don't make it easy for us, do you? If you got out of that bloody bed and went outside you wouldn't take your frustrations out on a lovely girl like Sandy.'

'I didn't,' Molly snaps. 'And thank you very much.'

'She didn't,' I say hastily, not wanting the two of them to have a row on my account. 'It's just me, I was silly.'

'She must have said something.'

'She didn't, honestly.' I scrub my eyes.

'Now,' Molly pronounces triumphantly. Then to me, 'Please don't cry, Sandy. I like that you're not loud and brash. Really.'

'Was she commenting on your personality?' Charles sounds appalled. 'Mum, will you stop mouthing off.'

'She wasn't.' I feel a bit sorry for Molly. Charles is pretty angry at her. 'It's just me. This isn't very professional of me.'

'Fuck professional,' Charles says, and hearing him say 'fuck' is a shock and makes me smile. 'Once you're OK?'

'I'm fine.'

'I like Sandy,' Molly says with spirit. 'She's the nicest person you ever employed.' She turns to me. 'Charles is not a good judge of character.'

'You are just not the easiest to get on with,' Charles says back, moving away from me and beginning to pour the tea. He milks mine just the way I like it before handing it to me with a large slice of lemon cake.

'I can do without your comments,' Molly says. Then she goes on, looking at me, seeking to make amends, I think, 'I have been difficult. I found it hard to accept this.' She nods at her legs and arms. 'Very hard. I was always on the go and then to be told that I'd lose the use of my limbs and body in a short time, well, it wasn't easy to hear.'

Charles caresses his mother's shoulder and she reaches up and catches his hand.

'I couldn't bear to be seen, I didn't want pity.'

'No one pities you,' Charles says. 'They pity me having to put up with you.'

Molly laughs gently.

Charles goes on, 'Poor Patricia never comes now, you scared her away.' To me, he says, 'She's from number eighteen, she used to visit every day.'

'She told me I should get some fresh air. It was not her business.'

'Patricia was right. What do you think, Sandy?'

I really don't want to cause a row. 'Whatever suits the person,' I say, and then think what a bloody hypocrite I am. That it's not the best thing if it's the wrong thing. 'Actually,' I blurt out, just as Molly is beginning thank me for agreeing with her, 'I think you can't shut out the world no matter how much you want. And if you try, then it only hurts you.'

They gawp at me. 'Fair play,' Charles says.

Molly looks a bit taken aback. 'Yes, well, I'm quite happy,' she says.

'My arse,' Charles says, and silence descends.

'The last time I went out,' Molly says, breaking the silence, 'was the night your friend had his bonfire. Two months after I'd been diagnosed.'

Charles grins. 'You should have seen her,' he says to me. 'There was almost fire coming out the back of the wheelchair.'

'Yes, poor Tar was getting a right earful from Max and I

was so angry I forgot about myself and made Charles wheel me outside to confront him. I took all my anger out on him that night.'

'Wow!'

Molly grins. 'Yep, it made me realise that I was still the same pain in the ass I always was.'

'So Max being an asshole helped you.'

'He was invaluable.'

'I'll let him know.'

She smiles.

'You should go out then,' I say.

There is the longest pause. 'Not like this,' she says. 'I'm a lot worse off now.'

'It's still you,' Charles urges.

'No,' she says, 'it was anger that time and it was good. And I could stand up then. But now ...' Her voice trails off. 'Not like this.'

Charles and I look at each other.

Maybe, I think, maybe she just needs a reason to go out, like my mother.

8

A few weeks later, Susan and my grandmother called. I saw them pull up in Susan's blue car. Hot excitement ran through me and I scanned the car to see if they'd brought Nan, but there was no one with them. 'It's Susan and Nana,' I said, making a dash for the door.

'What are you doing?' My mother pulled me away and pushed me to my position behind the curtain. 'You can't let them in.'

'But Nana says she loves you. She loves you very much.'

'Didn't I say no more talk about Galway?'

'Yes, but—'

'Hello?' Susan knocked on the door. 'Mel? Ruby? Anyone home?'

I looked at my mother. She turned away.

I made a move to the door and she whispered fiercely, 'Don't answer that.'

'Why?'

'We don't need them.'

'But it's nice to see them.'

'I said no.'

I felt like I imagined her dead brother had, balanced on

a garage roof, about to fall. No matter which way I fell, I'd hurt myself.

I saw Susan and my grandmother through the small gap in the curtain. They looked at the house, looked at each other and shook their heads. I saw my grandmother hug Susan. Then Susan lifted her head and shouted, 'Damn you, Mel, open the bloody door.'

'See?' my mother said, as if she'd just proved a point.

I heard them tromping around the house, rattling windows and calling out, and with each step they took, I felt they were walking over my heart. Feeling like that was worse than being frightened of them. Feeling like that was worse than being wary of my mother. I waited until my mother was occupied staring at them through her own gap in the curtain, until she was relaxed and not able to react as quickly as normal. When I saw her shoulders slump a little, I jumped over the pile of newspapers that were blocking my way, raced across the front room and into the kitchen at the back. I ignored my mother's shout as I pulled at the locks on the back door. One. My mother was running. Two. She had entered the kitchen. Three. She was right behind me but I had the back door open and was flinging myself out. I was thinking, if she just gets to meet them, she won't be so scared of them. If she just gets to meet them, we can have them in our lives. Hope was a rainbow I was chasing.

My mother caught me just as I turned the corner of the house. As the door slammed on Susan's car, she pulled me back, making me trip. I shouted, but they wouldn't have heard over the noise of the car's engine. My mother dragged me back into the house. She slammed the back door and flung me into a chair.

'What were you doing?' she screamed, and I had never heard her sound so shrill, so furious.

'I was going to say hello to Susan and Nana,' I shouted back.

'I told you not to.'

'You said they were nobody important. And they are. They are important.' My throat hurt.

'They are not important to us. We have our own lives.'

'I want to see them. They were nice to me.'

'Well, tough. Don't you ever do that again.' She poked her face into mine. I saw how thin her nose was, I noticed the crease between her eyebrows. She didn't look so pretty close up.

'I will.'

'You won't.' She marched across the kitchen and up the stairs.

'You're just afraid to go out,' I yelled after her but she didn't answer.

I ran to the bottom of the stairs. 'You can still have bad things happen inside,' I yelled again.

I heard her stomping about upstairs and next thing she came back down with armfuls of my new clothes that my nana had bought me on our shopping trip. Fear hit me like a steamroller. 'What are you doing with those?'

'You don't need them.'

'I do.'

I ran alongside her as she flung open the back door and made her way up the garden. 'Where are you going?'

She strode quickly, ignoring me. At the part where our garden met the hill to the forest, she dumped all my clothes onto the ground. I dived on them.

She ignored me and strode back into the house.

She re-emerged with the petrol can for our lawnmower and a box of matches.

'No.' I couldn't believe it. 'Don't, Mammy, please, I won't ever answer the door again.'

'This is for the best,' she said. 'Those clothes will only make you sad, they'll only make you miss Galway, but Ruby, you're back here with me now. That's all that matters, isn't it?'

Big fat tears started to roll down my face. 'I like being back,' I said, not moving, 'but I want these things. Nana bought them for me. It was our girls' day out. We went for ice-cream and I got my hair cut and she bought me new shoes. Please, Mammy.'

'Up.'

I didn't move.

She reached down and grabbed my hand, and though I shrieked and yelled she held me firm as she poured petrol all over my new clothes. Then she let go of me and struck a match.

'No!' I cried out.

But she didn't listen.

The clothes went up in a flash of bright light and I wailed.

And then, I don't know what, something happened in her and it was like she realised what she'd just done and she started trying to get the clothes off the bonfire and so I did too but it was too late and the ones we did save smelt all wrong.

I left her crying in the garden by herself.

From then on, my teeth clenched every time my mother tried to influence how I saw the world. Each time she proffered an opinion on how mean or petty people could be, I would get a flashback to her burning my clothes.

And so, in defiance or desperation or something, I began to spend a lot of time on Friends Reunited messaging Nan, who seemed to be so busy she never answered. But it didn't matter. It was an escape.

I did wonder what would happen if I just walked out the door. If I just turned the handle and walked outside and on down the path.

But I didn't. Not for years. I wasn't angry enough.

MAX

1

I'd told Laura to ditch the eighties clothes but I don't think she really got what I meant. She's in the paper today, holding hands with some guy who looks like he should be on one of those children's TV shows wearing orange trousers and dancing. Both of them are waving at the photographer. The idea was to pretend he wasn't there. I text her. *Crap clothes, crap picture, ditch the floppy-haired dweeb.* I press 'Send'. Then I text, *BTW, GET A STYLIST!*

A cheer goes up in the canteen and I glance up. Norm has just walked in with his 'say the wrong thing and I'll deck you' wife. If you ask me, most of Norm's problems come from her. Norm is happy and smiling and holding her hand. He's going home. I watch as he says goodbye to everyone in the place. Doctors and nurses and patients. Well, he says goodbye to everyone except me. I don't care. If I was Norm, I wouldn't say goodbye to me either. I've been a bit of a shit to him and I don't know why. I think it was because he doesn't look like the kind of guy who'd save a girl from a fire and yet he had. Then he'd spent group session moaning about his post-traumatic shock. I wanted to yell in his face, *Get over it, for God's sake,* but I didn't. Instead, I'd been horrible to him.

I watch as Norm embraces people with an ease I envy. He's a popular guy.

I stick my head down and pretend to be absorbed in the awful picture of Laura. She's described as an 'up-and-coming star', which isn't too bad. I've got her a spot on morning TV next; the presenter owed me a favour and, in fairness, didn't even refer to my breakdown when I asked if Laura could appear on her show. Laura bloody well better dress a bit better though.

Norm is sharing chocolates about. Everyone crowds around to take one. The guy who starves himself, he takes one and I see him push it into the back pocket of his jeans. I wonder how he'll get rid of the sweet, will he forget it's in his pocket and will it melt or will …

I look down as Norm and Evie cross towards me.

'Seems unfair to leave you out,' Norm says as he shoves his sweets under my nose.

'No, it doesn't.' Evie is at his side. 'Not unfair at all. You're just being gracious, Norm.'

'Chocolate, Max?' Norm ignores her.

It would be very ungracious of me to refuse. 'Thanks …' I stumble on the words, 'and good luck.'

He nods. 'To you too.'

He walks off, Evie trailing him.

When he's not looking she turns and gives me the finger.

I just grin.

2

Paddy had been pestering me for ages to meet up. When I'd seen his email pop into my inbox, I'd experienced a lurch of my stomach and my hands had shaken uncontrollably for the day. Lighting a cigarette had been impossible, pouring a drink had resulted in it slopping out over the glass.

I get like that about things from time to time. I think it's when I'm unexpectedly confronted with them. Initially, I'd ignored his emails, then he'd started to ring me. His number had been private and so I'd answered his call. Hearing his voice after so long had resulted in another bout of the shakes, but he seemed to be the same old Paddy. There had been no weirdness in his voice that I could tell, and so, hoping for I don't know what really – redemption? – I'd agreed to meet him. I felt as if I was pulling a plaster off a wound. How hard could it be? It was just Paddy. And Paddy knew …

So we'd met for lunch. Both of us trying not to look like we'd made the effort. I was awkward, stammering, stuttering. It was as if I was watching myself from a distance, seeing myself pour the drink, eating, chatting. It was forced; sometimes I could barely get the words out of my mouth. Paddy appeared to be the way he always was: solid, dependable. He had an impressive job. No one could have achieved what he had without some serious hard graft. He had decided, he confided in me over some sauce-covered chicken that I could barely eat, to go out on his own. He wanted my advice. No, actually, he wanted to employ me. I told him 'own' was just an anagram of 'won', which I thought was terribly clever. He agreed that yes it was and would I work on his publicity campaign. Or whatever it was he called it. Marketing, maybe? I let on I had to think about it and told him I'd let him know. In reality, it was my dream job. I'd finally be repping something I could be proud of. A human rights organisation. It'd be a challenge too, to get it into the public spotlight. If it had been anyone but Paddy. But then anyone but Paddy would never have asked the master of sleazy spin to represent them. Paddy saw beyond who I had become ... to what? To the snake I'd once been.

Why had he asked me? I wondered if he was setting me up.

Then the woman started to follow me. I thought it was Imelda. It freaked me out a bit. Then I got a text from her telling me not to work for Paddy and it creeped me out. But it was Imelda, and I owed her that much at least. I was glad she'd asked something of me. Glad I could do something for her. Maybe she'd leave me alone if I turned Paddy down.

So as calm as I could, the last lunch I had with Paddy, I told him no, I couldn't work for him.

I think he was shocked. He'd leaned over the table and I'd tried to hide, not physically, but mentally. I felt my mind shrinking away from his careful scrutiny. 'Why?' he'd asked, and my heart bled at the Wexford accent. I didn't have any accent left, I'd eradicated it. Better to sound as if you could be from anywhere.

I opted for the truth. He might understand the truth, not think I was such a shit. I don't like people thinking that about me. 'Imelda doesn't like it,' I found myself blurting out. Then I glanced around the restaurant, scared in case she was there. But she wasn't. There were only two other people in the place. A couple, holding hands.

'Imelda?' Paddy asked. 'Imelda who?'

'Imelda Greene,' I said. I had to whisper. 'She's not happy about it. She doesn't like that I'm meeting you, that we're working together.'

I'd seen the way he jumped at the name. 'Imelda Green?' he said, and his face wrinkled up. 'From home?'

'Uh-huh.'

He stared at me for a bit. Wary. I wondered if he knew. Maybe this was a set-up.

'She's after me,' I remember telling him. 'I knew she'd come after me one day.'

'Max,' Paddy said, 'Imelda's in Australia.'

'No, she's …' My voice trailed off.

'She went last year, she emigrated with her husband and two kids. I keep in touch with her. She couldn't be following you.'

I don't know what happened after that.

3

Ian asks me about Sandy. About my dad. I wonder did my dad talk to Ian or something. I tell Ian that I don't want to talk about my dad. Ian writes that down. Then he looks up and taps the pen on his teeth. 'When you were admitted here, Max,' he says, 'you were convinced a woman was following you. Have you seen her since?'

'No. How could she follow me here?'

'So you still think she exists?'

My head is clearer these days. I think they've managed to balance the drugs, that's what they do, apparently. When my head is working right, I think about the woman with the red scarf, I wonder about her. Mostly I wonder if she was real. I have half-forgotten memories, like something from a sluggish nightmare, of seeing her in strange places. 'She felt real,' I say. 'I thought she was a woman from down home.'

'And she isn't?'

'No.'

'How are you so sure?' He pins me with his gaze.

I used to think he was an idiot, but I see he's not. Now that my head is clear, I see him as a man trying to help me despite my best efforts to thwart him. I swallow hard. 'Because the woman I thought it was is living in Australia.'

He nods. 'Did someone tell you that?'

'Yes.' I remember something suddenly. 'Yes. Then I looked it up, in case he was lying to me. Her Facebook says she lives there.'

'And why, Max, would this woman have followed you?'

'She didn't, that's what I've just said.'

He pauses, shifts himself on the chair. 'I know she didn't,' he says, 'but why were you convinced – and you *were* convinced, make no mistake about that – why were you convinced that she would?'

I'm suddenly unreal again. The walls waver and sway. The light above my head flickers. I'm finding it hard to breathe.

'It's OK, Max,' Ian says, and his voice comes at me. 'Take your time. All you have to do is keep breathing, feel your breathing, in and out.'

I cling onto his voice, like a raft in an ocean. I hold onto it, I focus on what he is saying. I breathe in and out, in and out. My mind is melting, I think.

'In and out,' Ian says.

Slowly, very slowly, the room comes back into focus. My heart is still hammering and I'm ashamed to look at my hands, which tremble like a Parkinson's patient.

'All right?' Ian asks.

I can only nod.

'Think about what I asked you.' Ian is calm, balanced. 'We can leave it there if you like. I think you need to voice it, though. It's holding you back.'

How can I leave this room knowing I'll have to come back and talk about that day? Maybe today it would be best to say it. To say part of it. My mind is suddenly clear, clear as a bright crystal, refracting my thoughts into prisms, into pieces. My mind is glowing with light, brightening with the possibility of revealing the truth and I wonder if I should. Will I change? Will the world suddenly be more enjoyable? Will I be free finally from the burden of guilt I've carried all the years? I step towards the light and it blinds me.

'And it's safe to tell me here,' Ian says.

Hurts my eyes. 'I failed to save her boyfriend,' I blurt out. It's a quarter true. I hate my cowardice but it's all I'm capable of right this minute.

'Failed?'

I tell him how Shane drowned. 'I was on the pier with him and another friend. Shane,' I choke on his name, 'fell,' I choke on that too, I take a deep breath, 'into the water. I jumped in after him. He was a shit swimmer, I was the best.' I take a breath, continue. 'So I plunge in and I swim as hard as I can, and I can feel it, the undertow, pulling me out, pulling me along, and I still keep going. And then, I'm … I dunno … five feet from Shane and, like, I can see his face and …' My voice trails off.

'And?' Ian prompts.

I wince. 'That current was strong.'

'You felt guilty about letting him go?'

'Of course I did.' I snap. I think I might be sick. 'He was my friend. I wanted to save him.'

'You were the best swimmer. If you couldn't save him, no one could have.'

'He wouldn't have given up, though. He wouldn't have …' I stop. Too much.

'You don't know that.'

'I know he was a better friend to me than I ever was to him. That's what I know.'

'What do you mean by that?'

Then I do get sick, all over my jeans and Ian's office.

4

Shane was a clever guy. The cleverest of us all. His dream was to do medicine; I don't know if he really wanted it or if he was doing it for his parents, who seemed to be big into education and results. We used to discuss it among ourselves when he wasn't there and the general consensus was that his parents were too pushy. He didn't even let his relationship with Imelda get in the way of his study. From around November of sixth year, Shane hit the books big time. And for the next six months, he was rarely seen with us. He came out sometimes on a Saturday night, Imelda breaking my heart by holding tight to his arm, but during the week, when we'd hang about the beach or go drinking on the seafront, Shane was not there and Imelda was.

Then one Saturday morning, when the sun had risen and it looked like being one glorious day, cold, fresh and windy, I headed out, surf board under my arm, and found Imelda sitting on a wall a little down from my house. She was casually swinging her gorgeous legs to and fro, wearing tight jeans and a jacket. As I approached, she popped a sweet into her mouth, hopped off the wall, her breasts jiggling underneath her coat, and offered me a sweet too. I took one, though my mouth was dry.

'I'm bored,' she said. 'Can I come see you surf?'

'Yeah, sure.' Then because I was trying hard to be a decent guy, I asked, 'Is Shane not around?'

She made a face. 'He's studying. He's turned into a right swot.'

'I thought you wanted to go out with a doctor?'

'Not right this minute.' She linked her arm through mine. 'I'd rather, right this second, go out with a guy who's a bit of fun.'

'That's me so.' I tried to say it like it was all cool, like I was doing her a favour, but my voice hitched up at the end and I flushed.

She didn't seem to notice. She laughed and rubbed my arm and my whole body literally spasmed with desire. 'Let's have fun so.'

And we did, just fun, though. That day.

The weekends wore on and I found myself, every Saturday, hanging out with Imelda. Paddy, John and Tom would come by later and sometimes Paddy and Imelda would head off and buy chips for us and we'd sit in the dunes and eat them. Sometimes, Imelda and me hung about the arcade, hoping to win some money for a burger and chips; other days we were on the pier from early morning to late at night. My dad was going a bit mental, chewing my ear off about doing some work, my aunt telling me I'd never get anywhere just hanging around the beach. But all I wanted to get was into Imelda, if that doesn't sound gross. My brain was full of her. Each time she was with Shane, I died a bit; each time she smiled at me, I felt elevated.

Then, the Saturday night of my eighteenth birthday, I was on the beach with a few mates. It was late and, though

I should have been in good form, I was pissed off because Shane had managed to leave the books to come to wish me happy birthday. Then two hours later, he'd left, Imelda wrapped around him. I watched through a drunken haze as they'd made their way unsteadily home.

I walked home on my own, a bit drunk, a bit morose, a lot determined not to let Imelda get to me.

She was waiting outside my house. Sitting on the wall, in her tiny shorts. 'Thought you'd never get back.' She came towards me.

I couldn't move. I thought I was dreaming. It was the first time I experienced that unreality that haunts me. 'Here I am.'

'So I see. I never got to give you your birthday present.'

As a line it was a bit shit, I remember thinking from somewhere.

'Here.' She held out a small box.

Oh. Right. Disappointed, I took it from her. 'Cool. Thanks.'

'Are you going to open it?' She was right up beside me now. I could smell her perfume and the sea spray from her hair.

'Sure.' I fumbled with the small box, my fingers suddenly clumsy. She took it from me and opened it. There was nothing inside. 'I always wanted an invisible present,' I said, glad I could make a joke.

'Aren't you going to thank me for it?' she asked.

This was too much. I couldn't take much more. 'Imelda, I can't—'

'Thank you, that's all you have to say,' she said.

'Eh, thanks.'

'You're welcome.' And she stood on her tip toes and kissed me lightly.

And that was it. I cupped my hands about her face and turned the kiss into something way more. And my heart sang. And I didn't give a fuck about Shane.

Imelda said nothing, she just pulled away when I was finished.

'I like you a lot,' I stumbled out.

She smiled, turned away and was gone.

I think I knew then that I was doomed.

5

I haven't been able to get up in days. Getting sick in Ian's office had been a low point. And besides, since that meeting, my insides have been churning non-stop. Maybe it's because I have some kind of a bug. I can't even eat my breakfasts, which they bring to me in the room when they discover that I haven't got up. I want to stay in the bed, with the curtains pulled and the world safely outside my door. I turn off my phone and when anyone knocks, I tell them to go away.

There will be more questions, more probing, more explaining to do for Ian. More introspection. I can't manage it. All I know is that before that kiss with Imelda, I had been an average Joe, happy with my life, happy in my fantasies about my mate's girlfriend, not ever believing they'd come true. Then when they did, I was happier still, but there was an undertow of disgust running through it. And after Shane drowned, well, the whole deck had collapsed, hadn't it?

Knock. Knock. Knock.

'Go away!'

'It's me.'

It's Evie. What is she doing here? 'What do you want? Come to laugh at me?'

'Well, yes, I'd love to, thanks very much.'

She really has gone a bit bolshie. 'Fuck off!'

'I *am* fucking off. They're letting me out today. I came to say goodbye.'

'Goodbye.'

There is silence. Then she says, 'OK, goodbye, asshole.'

I hear her walk away. I lie and stare at the ceiling.

Knock. Knock. Knock.

'I said fuck off.'

'Charming.'

It's Sandy. Shit. I'd forgotten about her until right now. Is that weird? I glance around my room. 'Just a second.'

I hop off the bed and start cramming stuff into the wardrobe. It won't fit. I push a chair up against it. Another glance around. Everything looks cool. I open the door for her.

'I thought you'd be in the canteen,' she says.

The wardrobe door heaves and my clothes and stuff spill onto the floor.

'Jesus!' Sandy says, and hops over the clothes to pull open the curtains and window. 'What happened you?' Before I can answer, she makes a face. 'This room stinks. You stink.'

'Ah, the subtle way with words. I feel better already.'

She stares at my rumpled bedclothes, at my bare feet, at my T-shirt which reads 'Taking it to the Max'.

'Have you been holed up here for days?'

'Nah.'

'Did something happen?'

'Nope.' I start to pull on my socks. I can't look at her. 'Will you head on to the canteen and bring me back a coffee. Here.' I hold out a twenty. While she's gone I'll spray myself with deodorant. If I can find it.

'I am not drinking coffee with you in this room,' Sandy says. 'The place is rank.'

'You drank coffee under a hedge, don't be such a prude.'

'The hedge was cleaner. Less smelly.'

I don't want to leave the room. If I stay here, I can avoid stuff for another while. Sandy eyeballs me and then turns and walks out. I expect her to poke her head back in but she doesn't. I have a mind to leave her sitting in the canteen on her own, but she sat on her own in the middle of a town for days on end, so it probably wouldn't bother her the way it would a normal person.

In the end, I venture out of my room. No one says anything as I make my way up the corridor, it's like I've never been away. Like a fish re-joining his shoal. Only I have no clue what my shoal is.

Sandy is in the canteen nursing a cappuccino. I queue up and buy myself one and join her.

'You could have put on deodorant,' she says.

'I only do that when I'm trying to impress someone.'

'Hate to tell you, but you'd need more than deodorant.'

I laugh and she smiles back. Then she says, 'People on the outside wear it all the time. When you get out, think of the horror of that.'

When I get out. *When.* If.

Evie is over in a corner talking to one of the other losers. Without saying anything to Sandy, I hop up and stride over to her, barging into the group.

'Watch it,' she says.

'Can I ask you something?' My voice is urgent.

She flicks me a glance. 'Did your little girlfriend coax you out of your self-pity, then?'

I ignore that. 'Bit of privacy,' I say to the other people wishing her well, and they move off. No one really likes me in here except Vic. Most of them are scared of me, except Evie.

'You're so rude,' she says.

'What do you have to do to get out?' I ask.

'Not be an asshole, for one.'

'I'm being serious.'

She cocks an eyebrow. 'So am I.'

'Fuck off.' I turn away from her.

'I mean it,' she snaps. 'If you continue like this, you won't get out.'

Turning back, I see she is actually serious. 'So I have to lick ass, is that what you're saying?'

'Nope.' A hesitation before she shrugs. 'You have to co-operate. You have to really want it. I did all I could. I answered what I was asked, that sort of thing.' A pause. 'I'm not sure I'm better, though, I don't know if you actually get better. Just, you know, stronger.'

'You certainly have got stronger.' I think my tone could be nicer.

'Yep. Thanks to you,' she says, and I guess I must look surprised, because she adds, 'Don't look so surprised.' She cocks her head to the side and absently fiddles with her scarf. 'I mean, you really are obnoxious.'

Am I to agree? I say nothing.

'Poor Norm, who is the softest guy going, was terrified of you. I was too, you were so dismissive. But I guess my feeling sorry for Norm was stronger than my terror.'

I feel momentarily ashamed.

'And the first time I stood up to you, well, it just came out of my mouth, those words just popped out and you seemed to recoil and I couldn't believe what I'd said and it made me think that if I could say that stuff to you I could say it to anyone.' She beams up at me.

'Oh, well,' I say, a tad sarcastically, 'so glad I could help out. I should get brownie points for that.'

'The point is,' she over-rides me, 'that I had never in my life stood up to anyone, never. And I came here and stood up to you. Max freaking Coyle, PR man supreme. Or whatever it is you do.'

'You know who I am?' That's all I bloody need.

'Well, yeah,' she says as if it's obvious. 'Just before I came here, you were all over the papers.'

'I was?' That shocks me. I have no memory of that.

'Yeah.' She doesn't bother to explain and I don't ask her to as I'm pretty sure I won't like it. 'Anyway, good luck, Max.' She stands up and holds out a slim hand, which I take in mine. 'And a word of advice?'

'Yeah?'

'Let your folks in to see you.'

I say nothing to that. I just wish her well again and walk back to Sandy. 'I just had to say goodbye to that girl,' I explain. 'She's getting out today.'

'That'll be you soon,' she says, and I like that she seems so certain.

'She says I should let my dad in to see me.'

'You're going to have to face him sometime.'

I think about that.

Then Sandy says cautiously, 'You were sick, Max. You know you were.'

'OK, enough.' And she has the sense to say nothing more.

6

Imelda fucked me in every sense of the word. Thinking back on it now, I don't know why she did it. I feel pretty sure she liked Shane the best, she really did light up when he was there, but maybe she did it because she could. Which is a pretty shitty thing to do when you think about it. But then again, it wasn't just her fault.

She walked all over me. I let her. To be honest, I would have been happy spending the day just staring at her, watching her move, watching her laugh. She knew it and gave me more than I dreamed of. Or she gave me *exactly* what I dreamed of.

The day after we kissed was a Sunday. I got up early and tried to sneak out of the house. I wanted to go to the beach in the hope she'd be hanging around. Shane spent Sunday afternoons buried in his books. I was determined I'd fill in for him.

My dad was already up and eating. 'D'you not think a bit of study would go down well?' he asked me. 'You were down on that beach all day yesterday.'

'It was my birthday.' Outside the kitchen window, which was at the front of our house, I could see the grey waves in the distance. I could picture the sand dunes in my head, I could see the places I'd take Imelda so no one would see us. I was pretty sure she'd be as keen as me. 'I'll come back later.'

My dad looked at me. 'See you do.'

I just walked out.

She didn't come. I spent the day on the beach alone and she didn't come. I waited until eight that night and finally I packed it in.

My dad rowed with me.

I could barely look at Shane in school the following week.

Imelda chose when to spend time with me. It was sporadic, doled out like bread in a poorhouse, but always hungrily devoured. She'd communicate with me via notes through my letterbox. Or shoved through a gap in my school locker. They were always slightly cryptic. I can't recall them but they laid out a time and a place to meet and, while I'd be on time, she was always at least an hour late.

And just as the guilt was killing me and I was about to call a halt, we had sex. In her parents' bed. When they were shopping in the village. She'd told me to come over and I had, full of determination and feeling quite good about doing the right thing. She'd met me at the door dressed in pyjamas with a big picture of Daffy Duck.

'Are you sick?' I remember asking, and she'd laughed and I'd felt like a complete twit. She made me feel like that a lot of the time.

Instead, as I flushed and stammered and had no clue what gaffe I'd just committed, she took me by the hand and led me upstairs. Then, as I looked, she stepped out of her pyjamas and stood in front of me. I thought I was dreaming. I thought I was going mad.

I think she said, 'Well?' and all I could manage was, 'But they're only in the village, shopping.'

And like someone from a film, she said, 'Well, you better be quick, so.'

I don't think sex has ever happened as fast anywhere in the world. It was over before it began. But God, I was delirious.

I didn't see her again for another month or so. The memory kept me going. I couldn't bear to look at Shane, though. I started to find excuses not to be around him. Not that he noticed, he was studying so bloody hard.

I google myself. I haven't done that in such a long time. I never needed to, I always knew what I was up to. That's a joke, right there.

Anyway, Evie's comment alarmed me. I realise that I have very little recollection of the time just before I was admitted. In fact, bizarre as it may seem, I hadn't even thought about it, just an odd flashback now and again. Mostly, all I can remember is that I was consumed by the thought of Imelda following me.

And the fact that she was looking for payback, the fact that she might *know*.

It takes a while to pluck up the courage because I have no idea what I might read, but eventually, the following day, after I manage to eat some breakfast, I psych myself up and log onto Google. They let me use it now, which is progress, I guess. I key in my name and a rough date. The screen fills with data.

Max Coyle in Public Brawl with Adam Brown is the first headline. Adam? I had fought with Adam? Vaguely, like a shimmer on a hot road, I can recall one night when … what? What had I done? Adam was, or had been, one of my clients. He was young, an incredibly talented actor. Nice too, easy to get on with. A big hit with the women because he was very good-looking. Somehow, I had fallen out with him. With every one of my clients apparently.

My finger shakes as I log onto the newspaper site. There is a picture of me looking pretty shit, it has to be said, sitting down on a kerb, head in my hands, and someone in the background walking off, surrounded by people. As a photo, it's a pretty impressive shot and the PR man in me wonders if the guy who has taken it has an agent. Underneath the picture it says, 'Max Coyle in brawl with his star client.' The article is a little bit of nothing that manages to say fuck all. I can only admire the journalist who put it together. It's watertight: I couldn't sue even if I had the appetite for it.

Reading between the lines, apparently I verbally attacked Adam outside a well-known restaurant and accused him of trying to go with another agency. I wonder if I did. I wonder if he was. And if he was, why? No one ever left me.

I log out of that and into another newspaper article that says I was ferociously drunk at a film premiere and had to be hauled out of the cinema for shouting up at the screen. This piece is accompanied by an old file picture of me, which is a relief. But a 'source close to Max Coyle' says that 'Max has been under pressure for some time now. It appears he is unravelling.'

In yet another report, I'm accused of harassing my neighbours with my loud music and street brawls. Holy sweet Jesus!

All these pieces date from around the time I met Paddy. It's like meeting him pulled a string in my brain and the whole ball of wool started to unravel.

I read and re-read the reports. To be honest, because I'm in the media game, I know how it's played. I feel I need to get to the whole truth of them, to see what I was like, to see if I can remember anything that might spark a memory. I can remember being told Imelda was in Australia, but surely that wasn't enough to set me off.

I have to find out. I take a deep breath and look up my phone contacts. Adam's number is still there. More deep breaths. I dial and his phone rings at the other end. And rings and rings. No one picks up. I wonder if he's busy or if he's just not answering to my number. I know for sure if I block my number he won't answer either. He's been warned against that. By me. I think about it for all of one second and know that I have no option but to borrow a phone from someone. And a story.

In the end, I go out and talk nicely to the nurses or receptionists or whatever they're called and ask if I can make a call. 'I think my phone is on the blink.' I shake it about.

'Go on,' the pretty one says. 'Don't be on too long or I'll have to charge you.'

I could make some totally inappropriate comment here, but I don't. Instead I grin a 'thanks' and dial Adam's number. He picks up.

'Don't hang up,' I blab out. I wait. He doesn't. 'Adam,' I say then.

'Who is this?'

'Don't hang up, it's Max.'

'I should hang up, you bastard,' he says, and he sounds pretty angry.

'Well, thanks for not doing it,' I say hastily. 'I … eh … just rang to apologise.'

Silence. I turn away from the receptionists because the ugly one is looking at me.

'It's OK,' Adam says. 'I know you weren't …' he hesitates, 'quite yourself.'

'I was so not myself that I don't remember what I did.' I scoff out a 'can-you-believe-it' laugh.

Adam says nothing.

'So … eh … what did I do?' I say.

In the background I hear someone calling Adam's name. I think he's on a film set.

'Max, I have to go,' he says.

'Can you just tell me?' I say quickly.

Another small hesitation. 'You told everyone that I'd had a fling with that stripper during the time I was engaged to Chloe.'

I scramble to remember who Chloe was. His fiancée. Shit.

'You came into the restaurant I was having dinner in and you shouted it out. That's what you did, Max.'

I don't know what to say.

'There was a hate campaign on Twitter.'

'Really? Sorry.'

'The stripper is writing a book.'

'Sorry.' I want to dig a hole and bury myself.

'Chloe is no longer my fiancée.'

'Sorry.'

'Yeah, well …' His voice trails off. 'When I get pissed at you, I tell myself it was minor compared to what you did to Frank Daly.'

'Really?' Vaguely, like a car coming out of fog, I have a sudden snapshot of me at the races or a horse fair. 'What did I do?'

Someone calls Adam's name again and he tells me he has to go. 'Don't call me again,' he warns. 'I was told not to talk to you.'

'But, Adam—'

The line goes dead. I wonder what I did to Frank. I glance over and see that the two receptionists are not looking at me. I keep talking into the phone as I dial Frank's number. He picks up.

'Don't hang up,' I say, same as before.

'Who is this?' Frank's gravelly tone is the same. He's an actor too, only older than Adam. The joke in acting circles is that when Frank gets a gig, you've to pay for two, him and his ego.

'Don't hang up, I'm apologising. It's Max.'

He laughs, quite nastily, I think. 'Hey, Max,' he says, 'is this some sort of shit therapy thing you've been asked to do? Apologise to all those you've offended. Or is that for addicts? Are you an addict as well as an asshole?'

I let the insult hang there for a fraction before I say, 'I just heard I'd done something terrible to you and I wanted to say sorry.'

'I could have sued your ass only for what you said was true.'

A sort of slow horror takes me over. I hardly told people about Frank's past as a soft porn star. I'd spent years wiping that particular trail clean.

'I can only guess you weren't well at the time,' Frank says, and his voice is a little softer. 'I hope you're doing better now.'

'Did I tell people about—'

'*Big Willie Hangs*? Yep.'

'Oh, shit. Fuck. I can't believe I did that.'

'Well, you did.' He doesn't sound too mad, which is surprising. 'But, hey, everyone knows now, so no more watching my back. No pun intended. You probably did me a favour.'

Taken aback, I blabber out, 'That's great. Fantastic.'

'But you do understand I can't go back to you. I can't trust you. You know that, right?'

'I know that. I wouldn't dream of asking you back.'

'Would you not?' He sounds a bit miffed.

'Only because I've been such a thick,' I say.

'You have,' he agrees. Then, 'Take care, buddy.' The line goes dead.

I thank the pretty receptionist for the use of the phone and walk back to my room. I have the horrible feeling that I now know what happened all my clients. They ran for the hills. Max was in meltdown and they ran. I only hope I didn't blab anyone else's secrets.

'Hey,' Victor spots me, 'you're out of your room.'

He actually sounds happy to see me.

'Yep.' I wait for Victor to catch up. He's become my ally. I reckon he's about twenty-five, though he could be older. He's one of those people that are so self-conscious, they make you uncomfortable. It's like his limbs are borrowed from someone else and he has to seek permission to use them and when he does, it's as if someone else has the controls. Right now, he scratches his arm but in an apologetic way. I feel sorry for him. I wonder how he got so screwed up.

'You've been hiding away, man,' he says.

'Sorting my head out a bit,' I say. 'Seems I did a whole lot of damage before I came in here. A whole lot worse than I thought.'

Victor nods like it's no big deal. 'Once no one died,' he says, 'that's the main thing.'

Ironic.

SANDY

1

Molly is paying rapt attention as I read aloud *The Selfish Giant*. Her eyes are closed and she looks peaceful, yet I know she's not asleep. The story is so beautifully written, I get pleasure out of the sound of the words on the page. I'm at the part where the giant has thrown the children out of his garden and nothing grows there anymore. The two hours are up, but I want to keep going, to get to the end to see what happens. I've never heard the story and Molly seems unaware of the time, and so I continue.

There is a knock at the door. Molly's eyes pop open. Charles pokes his head in. 'Sandy, you can go if you like.'

It's as if he's broken some kind of a spell.

Molly sighs. 'That was beautiful, Sandy.'

'I'll read to the end,' I say. 'Sure it won't take long.'

'I'll pay you extra.'

'No, I want to find out what happens.'

Molly smiles at me and pats the bed for Charles to sit down. 'Come. Listen.'

I've discovered that Charles is unable to refuse his mother anything and so he sits beside her on the bed and takes her hand, clasping it gently in his own. Molly smiles up at him, her face grimacing with effort. He wipes a stray hair from her face. It's sad to see, but lovely too. I continue the story.

I read on and on, the words weaving a spell about us. As I come towards the end, my voice falters. 'OK, that's it.' I shut the book, leaving the story unfinished. 'I'm done with this.'

Charles splutters out a laugh.

'I am,' I say. I feel almost angry.

'Here.' Charles holds out his hand for the book and I give it to him. He finishes the story, only I try not to hear him. As he utters the final sentence, I say to Molly, 'I'm not reading you any more of those. That guy must have been a sadist; every time something in the story looks like it's panning out right, he shoves in a sentence at the end to ruin it for everyone.'

Charles laughs again.

'I like his endings,' Molly protests. 'The giant opened up his garden and his heart and was chosen to go to heaven.' A pause. 'Everyone dies, honey, best to die well. You should read *The Happy Prince* next.'

'Is that another sad one?'

'Yes.'

'Great.' I roll my eyes.

'You're a softie,' Molly teases. 'What good is a reader that can't finish a story?'

'A very good reader.' Charles winks at me. 'She gets involved.'

I'm not a softie. I just hate gratuitous misery. And yet, I hated other fiction because it always ended happily. Maybe Oscar Wilde was just being realistic. But he had the power, I think, he could have changed the endings.

'After *The Happy Prince* we'll read a funny one,' Molly promises.

Her idea of funny and mine are poles apart, but I just grin.

Downstairs, the bell rings. Charles hops from the bed to answer it. I'm pulling on my coat and wishing Molly goodbye when Charles leads Julian and Patricia into the room. I have to turn my face away.

'Visitors for you,' he says to his mother. 'A lovely surprise, Julian and Patricia.'

Molly looks a little taken aback.

Julian, I'm sure, pretends not to notice. 'Molly, lovely,' he says, 'how are you!' Without waiting for an answer, he bends down and kisses her soundly on the cheek.

'Hello, Molly,' Patricia says. She's a little older than Molly and as thin as a ruler. She's dressed in jeans and runners and bright pink sweatshirt. 'I decided to forgive your rudeness and visit you.'

'Did you buy a new pair of glasses?' Molly asks.

'Contacts.'

'Then I forgive you too. Sandy,' Molly says, 'this is Patricia. She used to read to me. You're better, though.'

'Hi.' I hold out my hand.

Patricia shakes my hand, staring hard at me.

'What?' I cringe inwardly, wondering if she'll give the game away. I had dropped hints to Julian about visiting Molly and he had said that he'd ask Patricia along too.

'You don't seem to have a thicker skin than me,' she says.

Charles, Julian and Molly laugh. I don't quite get the joke.

'So why have you both come?' Molly asks. 'Am I dying and no one told me?'

'We're all dying.' Charles grins. Turning to Julian and Patricia, he says, 'This is great,' and to me, 'You'll stay, will you? I'll run down and shove on the kettle.'

Julian taps a plastic carrier bag. 'Do stay, Sandy,' he says. 'I have something for you.'

'For me?'

'Yes, indeed. Sit back down. I'm so glad I caught you.'

Surprised, I take a seat and watch as he takes out a box of chocolates for Molly. 'I hope I remembered your favourites,' he says.

'All chocolates are my favourite,' she says, and I'm relieved to see she's smiling a little. 'Open them there and share them out.' He does as he is told and we all take one.

'I've been meaning to call up for ages,' Julian leans against Molly's windowsill, 'but between one thing and another, I haven't had much time. New boss in the library and quite frankly it'd be easier to get on with a rabid hyena. And then,' he pauses and nods in my direction, 'I got a book in and I thought you would love it.'

'Well, let's hope for all our sakes it's not a sad book.' Molly throws me a look. 'The poor girl will need therapy.'

Julian looks a little aghast. 'It's not happy,' he says, 'it's a volume of poetry by Melanie Fairbrother and I thought I'd get it to you, Sandy, before it was borrowed.'

He pulls the book from the bag and holds it out to me. 'We didn't have it in the last time and, not counting *Ruby Slippers*, this is the best.'

I'm stunned, first by his thoughtfulness – I'm always surprised by that because I'd spent years hearing about how people let you down – and second at my mother's name being brought up so unexpectedly. 'Thanks,' I say, taking the slim white volume from him and turning it over in my hands.

'I checked it out in your name, is that OK?' Julian says to Molly.

'I didn't know you were interested in poetry,' Molly says to me, by way of reply.

'Oh, yes,' Julian answers, 'she loves it. And Melanie Fairbrother is a particular favourite, isn't she?' he says to me.

I can only nod. The title of the book is *All Is Gone* and, because everyone is looking at me, I feel I have to show interest. I flick to the dedication page. It reads, *To My Daughter, By Way of Apology.* I flinch. A picture of my mother, this time more recent, is on the inside. She looks a lot older than I remember. I have missed her going grey, getting wrinkles. I have missed a great chunk of her life when once she was all my life. I push the thought away.

'You'll have to read me some of that poetry,' Molly says. She turns to Julian. 'She reads so beautifully, I'm thinking of taping her so I can listen to her as I die.'

'Stop it!' Patricia is horrified.

Molly sniggers as Julian laughs.

'That's typical.' Patricia folds her arms and glares. 'Make fun.'

'That dedication there,' Julian leans over me and I feel his coat brush against my cheek, releasing a perfume of cigarette smoke, 'caused a lot of interest at the time. What was she apologising for? People bought the book to decode it.'

'And did they find out?' My voice shakes but no one notices.

'Not at all.' Julian stands back up. 'Melanie is too private to be so public. Great poetry, though. Heartfelt.'

'Thanks, Julian.' I am touched. 'I'll read this and get it back to you.'

'No rush,' Julian says. 'Enjoy it now.'

By way of apology? What does that mean? I turn the book over. It was published two years ago.

'I've never heard of her,' Patricia says. 'Melanie who?'

'Fairbrother.' Julian says. 'She's notoriously private. Keeps herself locked away in a cottage in Wexford.'

'Poets are odd,' Molly agrees. 'I knew one once who used to bark like a dog before going to work in the morning.'

'Who was that?' Julian looks sceptical.

Molly says she can't remember. Patricia accuses her of making it up. They bicker a little. I can't leave, as it would look a bit weird, but I so want to go now. I pretend to examine the book, afraid something in my face will give me away.

Charles bustles in with tea and biscuits and after we all take a cup, instead of moving onto another subject, Julian starts on about my mother.

'Melanie had a lot of tragedy in her life,' he says. 'Though, again, we only have what she is prepared to tell us. But apparently, before she was well known, she had a lot of family troubles. Some tragic deaths, apparently. It caused her severe anxiety. I suppose it'd be post-traumatic stress nowadays or something.'

'Is she the one whose daughter ran away? Or got murdered or whatever?' That's Charles.

My head snaps up. Oh God …

'That's right,' Patricia says. 'I know who it is now. She's a skinny woman with a big forehead.'

'That's her.' Julian nods.

'I remember the daughter was a few years younger than me at the time and it was all over the papers,' Charles says.

'It was around this time of year,' Julian agrees.

How has the man such a good memory? I feel that the words 'It's me' are branded on my forehead.

'She was only seventeen,' he continues. 'Personally, I think she was murdered.'

'Murdered?' The word pops out.

'Yes, the police questioned people at the time but didn't file charges. She has to be dead. They say she rowed with her mother, but why would she stay away? And she was leading a weird life, people used to see her around the village on her own.'

'How awful.' Patricia shakes her head. 'It must break the poor woman's heart. My girl is in Australia—'

'We know,' Molly chimes in.

'She barely ever contacts me,' Patricia goes on, ignoring Molly, 'but at least I know where she is and that she's well. I couldn't begin to imagine the horror of not knowing.'

They all agree that this would be terrible.

What would they think of me if they knew? 'I better go.' I stand up hastily. 'I'll see you tomorrow, Molly.'

'OK, darling. Bring a poem with you to read. It's a long time since I heard a poem.'

'A poetry reading,' I hear Julian say as I leave, 'now there's an idea for the library. Maybe the hyena would go for that.'

Charles accompanies me to the front door.

'It was you, wasn't it?' he says in an undertone.

'Me?' My heart hammers in my chest. 'What?'

'You told them to come, didn't you?'

Of course that's what he's talking about. I feel I'm collapsing inward. 'He wanted to,' I say, my voice only a little breathless. 'Kept telling me how she ran the book club, organised library nights out.' I pause. 'It's good for her to see people.'

'Thanks.'

'You don't mind me interfering?'

'I welcome it.'

We grin at each other.

2

Facebook, social media, YouTube, they all became my way into the world. At night, when my mother was convinced I was studying, I hooked up my headphones and watched videos starring people I would never meet and read all about things I would never do. I started to read my mother's daily newspaper, the affairs of the wider world catching me in their grip. War, famine, pop concerts all going on while my mother and I stayed holed up in our little capsule of timelessness. I grew increasingly frustrated as our lives became as predictable as the tides. As time went by, Nana and Susan didn't call as much. I saw the Casey man go grey through the window. Every so often a woman, who I guess must have been a social worker, would show up and then disappear. I studied my school books and I learned. And all the while, the life that was going on beyond the lane that led to our house called to me.

It crept up on me slowly. It wasn't that I woke one morning and decided that I was going to lead my own life. At first, it was just a desire to creep out of the house after my mother fell asleep. Just to stand with my feet on the cold night grass and breathe in the night air and know that I was a little bit free. That I could escape if I wanted.

One thing about living so closely with another person is

that you get to know their habits and I knew that my mother was always asleep by ten fifteen. I planned my mini-escape carefully, dressing in old jeans and tattered trainers, things that were easy to move in. I wore a dark hoodie over a grey t-shirt that had once been white. At ten thirty, I pushed open my bedroom window, leaned across to the oak tree that grew just outside and climbed down. It was just as much a buzz as I thought it would be.

The following night, I ventured down the lane.

On the third night, dizzy with the illicit freedom, I took ten euros from behind the wall in the bathroom, where my mother stored her cash. It was the first time I ever stole. It wasn't real stealing, though, as I had no intention of spending the money if I could get away with it and then, following a map I'd drawn from Google, I started to run in the direction of Rossclare. It was two miles away and by the time I arrived, my legs ached. I didn't get much exercise normally.

I can remember it clearly. The night was calm and dry, the moon high in a sky that still held a lot of light. I ran on tired feet around a bend and into the main street of Rossclare. It was barely a road that would fit two cars. I stood at the top of the street, taking in the view of the village that formed part of my home address. An ice-cream parlour stood on the opposite side of the road, pink and blue with a picture of an elephant holding a cone. It was closed. All the little shops along the street were closed except for a chipper and a few pubs. I walked down the street, taking in the brightly coloured shops of a seaside village. There was a laneway between a gift shop and a clothes shop. At the top a sign said 'Beach' and I could hear the sea and smell the tang of seaweed, only at the time I didn't know that's what the smell was.

I didn't go down to the beach that night, I was drawn instead to a pub right at the very end: McMahon's. People, holding pints, spilled out onto the pavement. There was talk and laughter and the smell of smoke. Music belted out from inside and I was drawn to it. The male singer had a husky, raw voice and, for someone who'd never heard live music before, it sounded exciting. Not caring that I was rude, I pushed my way inside. Eventually, I made my way to the top of the room and found myself in front of a stage. Four lads were making music, the name 'The Unconventionals' emblazoned across the drum kit. I stood mesmerised, not by the music but by the way the lead singer, a skinny guy in a white vest and tight black jeans, strode sexily about the stage, a guitar slung casually across his body. His hair was long and dark and a little bit sweaty, his face was handsome in a bad boy way, his smile a cheeky leer. He wore enormous trainers which made his legs look even skinnier. I was enthralled by his maleness, his confidence, his swagger. I sat down on the floor in front of the stage and worshipped. His name, I learned that night, was Louis.

3

Max is in a bad mood when I see him. Apparently, he has a client called Laura who won't do what she's told. I think he's lucky to have a client, but I don't say it.

'Do you know what she did?' Max asks me.

I don't really want to get involved. 'Max, this is between you and Laura. She's your client.'

He ignores me. 'She only went and turned down an appearance on *Morning Live* because it clashed with her nan's birthday. Her fucking nan's birthday.' He gives a despairing laugh and buries his head in his hands.

I desperately want to laugh but think I better not. Good for you, Laura, I want to say. And it's brilliant to see Max so fired up.

'I can't wait to get out of here, she won't know what hit her when I get out of here.' A groan. 'Who cancels an appearance on *Morning Live* for their nan?'

'Well, obviously—'

'They owed me a favour on that programme. I saved the ass of that presenter once and now ... now ... that's it, my favour called in. Bloody great. I'm going to kill that girl.'

'Is he still on about that girl who didn't appear on the telly?' this guy asks as he passes our table. He looks weird, all angles and elbows. He bends down to Max and hisses, 'Let it go, this is the voice of your counsellor, let it goooo.'

'Vic, I will thump you,' Max says, without rancour.

Vic straightens up. 'He had us all glued to the telly,' he gives this weird high laugh, 'and his client was a no-show. We all cracked up.'

'Glad me and my sinking career is fodder for the well-being of all the nutters in here,' Max says dryly.

'Oh, it is, best laugh I've had in ages.' Vic winks at me and moves on.

'Don't know why you're smiling,' Max says sourly. He puffs out a sigh.

'So, any other news?' I change the subject.

'Not a particularly good steer.' He manages a grin.

'In that case, I'll go.' I stand up and pull on my jacket. 'It's one now, isn't it time for you and the nutters to do some art or something?'

'You're gone very cheeky,' he says. His eyes glitter and he adds, 'I like it.'

I like it too. Especially because he laughs at what I say and he has a nice laugh. 'See you next time,' I tell him, 'and you better be in better form or I'll start visiting that nice Vic fella instead.'

'He'd love that,' Max says. 'I'd miss you, though.'

'Awww.'

He grins and my heart flips. I'm not sure if the jolt of unexpected emotion shows on my face, but he turns away quite suddenly and when he turns back, I've got it under control.

I don't know what just happened, only that I feel like

reaching across the table and touching him, on his arm or shoulder. Even the thought of it sends a little shiver up my spine. I'm afraid to meet his eyes now in case he sees the longing in my own. Get a grip, I tell myself, he'd never look at you like that. But it's been such a long time since anyone has just held me. In any sort of a tender way. Remembering it makes me long for it. But I won't let myself get caught like that again.

'Can I ask you something?' he says, as he walks me to the nurses' station.

'Sure.'

'I was thinking of telling my dad he could visit next week, what do you think?'

He doesn't look at me as he asks, just keeps walking. I want to tell him I think it's brilliant. Max's dad is a lovely man, he's been up at the house twice since that first time, helping me with the garden. But I know Max, he doesn't want a pat on the back. He doesn't want to think he's been in the wrong the whole time. So I say, 'You think you'll be OK with him there?'

He shrugs.

'I know he'd be very happy.'

'Him and Ian both,' Max mutters.

I have no clue who Ian is. 'For what it's worth, I think you should.' We're at the exit. He stops and faces me. Impulsively, I touch his arm. A tiny smile lights his lips. 'Good luck with it.'

'Thanks.' He smiles at me and, even though I fight it, my heart whumps.

4

Snapshots of my time with Louis surface, mostly when I'm lonely. Throughout the long days in the cottage when time was treacle trickling off a spoon, Louis would break into my mind, all bright and dazzling and colourful. As I sat at our table or watched my mother labelling newspapers, I'd see him in my mind's eye, guitar in hand, eyes half-closed, playing hard rock music, sending my teenage hormones into overdrive. Images of him smiling at me, his lip lifted in a sexy curl, his t-shirt riding up and exposing belly made me hot and flustered. Every night he dedicated a song to me because I was always there, cheering his band on. I was in love with him before he noticed me. I fell for his energy, his enthusiasm, the life and fearlessness that poured out of him.

He told me he fell for my stillness, my air of calm. The cool way I was so Zen in the midst of everything. He said he'd never had anyone look at him the way I did. He said I was his mystery girl, appearing every night to hear him sing and disappearing by twelve. I said that was a coincidence because my name was Cinderella. From then on he called me Ella. I saw no need to correct him. He loved my eyes, the smudge of blue in them. He traced his finger over the scar on my lip that I got when I fell as a kid. He ran his fingers down my arms and I gasped. He pulled me to him and I closed my eyes. He laid his lips on mine and I thought my body could know no greater pleasure.

He was a dreamer and he dreamed big. There was nothing he and his band would not accomplish. He said, as a child, once he mastered an instrument, he discarded it. The only thing he'd stuck with was the electric guitar. He laid his electric-guitar-playing future out for me like a carpet of dazzling colour. I was blinded by it. He made me think that I had such a future too.

He never asked me about myself; he liked the mystery, he said. I was fine with that. For once in my life, the clothes I wore seemed fine. The worn-out jeans, the battered Converse, the shapeless T-shirts. My unkempt hair was cool. Girls should be natural, he said, nothing worse than kissing a faceful of make-up.

Louis filled my head and filled my life for a few months.

'How did you meet Dad?' I asked my mother one day. It puzzled me. It made me think that at one time she must have had a life.

'When the time is right, you meet the person who is right,' she told me.

She was full of little sayings like that. Things that actually meant nothing. Each time she trotted one out, I'd clench my teeth. 'How will I meet anyone if I stay here all the time?'

'Stop wishing your life away.'

Maybe I should have told her that I was going out, whether she liked it or not, but by then, the thrill of sneaking

out had me in its thrall. I was as quiet as a panther and as fit
as one too by then. Escaping at night was a drug that shot
through my system and took the edge off reality. It helped
me survive the cluttered cottage, the foul-smelling kitchen
and the mother who taught me everything she wanted me to
know and nothing that I actually needed to know.

Each night after his gig, Louis and I would take a walk along
the beach, his arm loped around my shoulders, my arm
around his skinny waist. Hip to hip, sometimes barefoot,
we'd stroll up the beach, turn and come back. It took a while
because we'd stop for a kiss and there was no better feeling
than being in his arms as he caressed my neck while the tide
caressed our feet.

One night, when the moon was huge and yellow, we
paused, kissed, and then Louis pulled me towards the dunes.
There was a look on his face, a mischievous grin that made
my heart beat fast. I ran with him. When we found a spot, he
pulled me down and lay on top of me. His palm caressed my
face. I moaned. His forehead touched mine. 'Would you?'
he said. His voice was a rasp. I knew the facts of life in a
sort of magical way. I'd read books where the whole universe
celebrates the union of two people, the stars spin, music
starts up, small animals come for a peek. In all my reading,
no one had ever said, 'Would you?' But somehow, it was the
sexiest line of all.

'I would,' I said.

Louis seemed to know what he was doing and I let him.
I didn't know it was finished at first, but as he rolled off me,

panting, I figured I'd better explain my ignorance. 'I never did that before.'

'I don't know whether to be appalled or charmed,' he said, but he was grinning.

'You can teach me,' I told him.

And he did.

5

I'm just about to round the corner by the library, on my way to get milk, when I spot the poster.

It's massive, a huge black and white picture of four guys standing on a beach, wind tossing their hair. 'The Unconventionals', it says. That was the name of Louis' band. It *is* Louis' band. I spot him, second to right, still skinny, still wearing the white vest and the tight jeans. He has a straggly beard now, covering the strong jaw that I remember. He looks as sexy as he did when he was my boyfriend. I can't take my eyes off him. I remember the dizzy way he made me feel, the way my skin tingled under his fingertips, how my legs shook when he smiled across the room at me.

The Unconventionals perform songs from their new album in Gratton's Music – 5 pm Saturday, 5th July

That's today!

I know where Gratton's Music is. Though I'm sure I should steer clear of any reminders of home, it's like a tidal pull. I can't even think about it, it's as if the decision isn't even in my hands. I hop on the next bus into the city.

The idea of a connection with home after all this time is like a drug to my system. And to see Louis is something I feel I have to do. Was the way I felt about him real? I'd thought it was love. Was it? How would I ever know? How will I know in the future? I knew nothing about life at all then and very little even now. He hadn't loved me back, though, that much he made perfectly clear. I still cringe when I think about it.

When I get to Gratton's, people are queueing all along the street. Some are holding bundles of CDs. A security guard pushes us all into a line. I don't want to be in a line as I have nothing to be signed and I can't afford a CD. I move out of the queue and stand opposite the shop, wondering if I'll see Louis when he goes in. It looks like the band is pretty famous.

The queue starts moving real slow and I jump as a voice from a speaker blares, 'Hi, folks, have patience, all your CDs will be signed after The Unconventionals perform. Take it away, guys.'

A cheer goes up. People stand alongside me. The band must be inside already, I think, feeling a bit disappointed. But what had I expected? Next thing, amid cheering, music begins to play. The louder it plays, the louder the cheers. I join in, feeling like a fraud. Against the backdrop of the music, Pete, the bass guitarist, starts to explain the origin of the first song before the band launches into it. It's good, I think, though I don't know much about music. It sounds different to the stuff they used to do in the pub down home. Edgier, as if they actually have something to say. More people come to listen and soon I'm in the middle of a crowd. Each time a song comes on, Pete talks about it first. It suddenly doesn't matter that I can't see Louis, I'm still connecting with something from before.

And then Pete says, 'We're going to sing the third track

from the new album, a song called "That Day in June",
and it's about a girl we all knew as teenagers and how she
disappeared one day in June.'

Something like an electric shock runs through me.
Maybe I gasp, I don't know, but the people around look at
me. I dip my head. Pete is still talking by the time I tune
back in again. 'She was Louis' girl,' he has to stop for the
whoops and cheers, 'but she disappeared. We think she's
still alive somewhere. This is a plea for her to come home.
OK, lads.'

'That is so sad,' a girl beside me says.

'I wonder who that was,' someone else asks.

'Melanie Fairbrother's daughter, you know, that weirdo
poet we had to study for the Leaving. Louis was going out
with her and she lied about who she was. Weirdo.'

'I'd lie about who I was if I was a weirdo poet's daughter.'

They laugh. I glare at them but they don't notice.

'That's right,' someone else chimes in, 'I remember it
being in the papers.'

'No way! And Louis went out with her?'

I move away. I can't listen to them.

I hear another person say, 'Ruby Fairbrother, it was. Her
mother was a weirdo. Her poetry is on the Leaving Cert and
it's shite.'

The conversation whirls around me. The words of the
song weave themselves in and out. By the time it ends,
everyone is singing the chorus:

Ruby, will you come home/we're missing you/we feel alone/
Ruby, will you please call/we're missing you/now that is

all/Ruby, will you get in touch/we're missing you/so very much/Ruby, Ruby, Ruby/come home.

I get away as fast as I can.

From the top deck of the bus I spot the girl sitting alone on a bench, head down, hands jammed into pockets of a black jacket. At first I take no notice, but then as our bus stops in traffic lights and the girl hops up off the bench and joins the queue of people waiting to cross the road, I jump out of my seat, run down the stairs and ask the bus driver to let me off.

'Can't, not an official stop.'

'I'm going to puke.'

The door swings open and I jump off. At that moment the lights go green and the bus drives away. I look around for the girl I saw and grin as I spot her walking rapidly in the opposite direction.

'Clara!'

She seems to freeze before breaking into a run.

I start to chase after her. 'Clara! It's me. Sandy.'

It stops her cold and she whirls about. I stop running too.

Two feet of pavement separate us. She looks the same, punk rocker with an emo twist. She regards me warily. 'Where did you spring from?'

I flap my hand at the retreating bus.

'What d'you want?' Hostile.

I don't actually know what I want. I'd just seen her and jumped off the bus. It had seemed a good idea five seconds ago. I shrug. 'I guess I want to apologise.'

'Is it not a bit late?'

'Maybe, but I'm still sorry.'

'No, you're not.' Clara sticks her face into mine. I stand my ground. She smells surprisingly of mint. 'If you had to do it again, you would, wouldn't you? You'd save that bloody house.'

She sounds hurt. My first ever friend and I'd betrayed her. 'If I'd known how it would all turn out, I wouldn't have.'

She pulls away, slides her head sideways and regards me through slitted eyes. 'Yeah?'

'You were my friend.'

There is a long silence.

I break it. 'I wasn't used to being a friend. I just thought if I did the right thing, it'd turn out good.'

'Like we were in some movie?'

'Or book. Yep.'

Clara scoffs, though there is a hint of a smile on her face. 'You lost me my job, you dickhead.'

'I know. I'm really sorry.'

'You were always a bit weird.' She starts to walk and I take it as my cue to fall into step with her. Neither of us says anything for a bit. Finally, I pull some cash from my pocket. 'Dinner?'

'Did you rob that?'

'Earned it.'

'I am ashamed of you,' she says, but she's grinning wider now.

'And I'm ashamed of you. You're losing your touch because I saw what you did at the traffic lights.'

She bumps my arm with hers.

I lead her to a restaurant and we take a table. The waiter looks at us funny and we look back at him. Clara asks if he's on the menu and he flushes. I'd forgotten what a buzz being with Clara is. She brings out the cockiness in me.

'How did you earn your money?' Clara asks.

I fill her in on Max and Molly. I give Clara Max's address on a paper napkin, just in case she ever feels like calling, though I think we both know she won't. 'I won't be there forever,' I tell her.

She tucks the address in her pocket. 'Did you not think it weird, this guy buying you coffee every day?'

'Maybe I should have,' I say, 'but there was something about him that was just …' I flounder a bit, trying to find the word, 'real,' I finally say, though it's not quite right.

'And then he lets you mind his house?'

'Yep.' I fiddle with my fork. The words Max's dad had said to me a few weeks ago keep knocking about in my brain and I can't get rid of them. Maybe it was Max's illness that had allowed him to be so kind to me. I fear sometimes that when Max gets better, I won't actually know him. That his normal self will be someone I don't like. Or that his normal self will allow him to see me for what I am.

'Weird,' Clara says.

'And you?' I ask, not wanting to hear how weird she thinks it is because maybe it *is* weird. What do I know?

'I'm at home and working in a shop now.'

'You went home? Were your folks surprised when you came back?'

She flushes. 'I wasn't a runaway,' she mutters.

'I thought—'

'I got thrown out.' She looks at me defiantly. 'I told you I ran away because, well, it sounded better, I wanted to impress you.' She pulls her napkin apart. 'Getting turfed out is kind of loserish.'

I laugh.

'Don't laugh at me,' she snaps.

'I'm not. It's just, you're the first person who ever wanted to impress me.' I feel all warm and delighted.

Clara makes a face. 'You *are* weird,' she pronounces, but not in a nasty way. Then she says, 'In homeless cool, you are at the top. Ran away, never went back. Respect.' She lifts up her fork and I lift mine and we clink.

'Why did you get thrown out?'

She makes a face.

'Stealing?'

'Yep.' A pause. 'I stole for my ma, food, medicines, clothes. We had nothing.' She shrugs. 'Then she met this prick and it was like, all of a sudden, she didn't want to know me. And every time he found out I stole stuff, he told the Guards, can you imagine? So I stole more and more stuff and hid it in the house and reported him.'

I laugh bigger this time.

'He got off but he threw me out. At Christmas time and all.'

'Fecker.'

'I know I shouldn't of done it. Couldn't help myself, though. What gets to me most is that she let him throw me out.'

'And you're still stealing?' I nod toward the wallet she has in her coat.

'Just for a birthday present for me ma, it's her birthday. Most times I don't.'

'So you get on well with your mother now?'

'Yeah. We get on OK.'

'Good,' I say. 'That's good.'

'Yeah?' It's like she's looking for approval.

'Yeah.'

We part outside the restaurant a couple of hours later. There is so much I still want to say to her but I can't find the words or the moment or a way that won't sound all crappy and mawkish.

In the end, I just tell her that I'm glad I met her. She says she feels the same.

It's only as I walk home, having blown all my money on the meal, that I realise why I'd jumped off the bus. Clara was something in my life I'd felt I could put right.

6

I stole money from my mother and gave it to Louis to buy me a mobile phone. 'I wouldn't have time during the day,' I told him. Then I added, 'And my mother would kill me.'

He thought this was cool. He thought everything I did was cool. When I got my phone, I hid it in my room and put it on silent. I checked it twice a day and each time there'd be a text from Louis telling me how much he missed me and wanted to meet me.

One night, after we made love behind the sand dunes, I told him I loved him. I said it after he'd pulled up his jeans and had rolled himself a joint. He sat on the sand, bare-backed, staring out to sea.

I pulled on my tatty sweatshirt and shook out my hair. 'I love you,' I said. He didn't reply. I assumed, like in the books, he was overcome. I would have been. Love meant sharing. So as I pulled up my socks and zipped up my jeans, I told him about my mother, how she wouldn't let me out. How I really wanted to see him all the time but that I couldn't. All he had to do, I told him, was to say the word and I'd walk out of the cottage and go to him. I told him all this in a stumbling, inarticulate flow of words.

He stood up, flicking away his joint. 'Come on, I'll walk you back down the beach.'

I caught his hand and for the first time ever, I was the one who did most of the talking.

The next day, there was only one message from him. He told me he was sick and couldn't meet me. I texted him back, wishing him a speedy recovery. The following day there was nothing, so I texted him a good few times. On the third day he texted me to say that it was over. That it was better if we went our different ways.

My first thought was that he had a terminal disease and was being brave about it. My knowledge of life was confined to the drama in books I'd read. I went that night to see him play. Armed with resolve, I was determined to tell him that I'd nurse him through his last days and love him forever. As I walked into the bar, his face took on a haunted look. His fingers faltered on the guitar. I thought how brave he was being.

At the end of the set, he came down to me, took me by the arm and marched me out of the pub. 'What are you doing here?' he hissed into my face. There was anger and something else in his voice that I couldn't identify. A few people stared at us.

'Your text. I just …' I paused. This was not right; for one thing, he was squeezing my arm too tight. 'You said it was over.'

'Yeah.'

'Why?'

'I'm not looking for love, OK? I don't want your neediness.' He let go my arm and stared over my shoulder. 'I thought you were cool.'

The hurt was like a knife going in, instant, so incredibly painful, yet numbing my senses. I waited a second or two, just to compose myself, then I turned and walked off.

'I'm sorry, right?' he called after me.

I was proud when I didn't look back. I wasn't that needy.

MAX

1

They walk towards me and my initial reaction is to run, run as far away as I can go. Run away from them like I've been running my whole life. But I asked them to come, in a moment maybe of madness, of regret, of trying to show Ian that I'm stable. I asked them to come here and they did. So I owe it to them to remain strong by staying where I am.

I tell myself that they came because they care, that despite everything I've put them through, they still care.

I've made an effort. I've shaved and Vic has cut my hair. He offered; I thought he knew what he was doing. He didn't. My hair is like a badly peeled potato. I'm wearing jeans and a shirt.

Ian did ask if I wanted him to be there, but I said no. I can handle this, I think. They're just visitors, after all. Just come by to say hi. There will be no major soul-searching in the centre of the canteen. I'm not sure what prompted my invitation – Sandy, Evie and the fact that, in the last while, I've been thinking a lot about what I put my dad through, not just lately but since I was eighteen. I've also felt lucky that they care because when I look at Sandy, I feel desperately sorry for her. Though she never says it, she is so alone.

Across the way, Vic gives me a thumbs up. He's drinking

orange through a straw and the noise carries. The person sitting down from him looks at him in irritation but Vic is oblivious. It makes me smile and my dad and sister think the smile is for them.

Which is good, I guess.

'Nice to see you smile,' my dad says, sliding into the seat opposite. A pause. 'You look good, Max.'

He doesn't. He looks thin and pale and ghostly. His shirt is too big, his trousers are slightly creased. I wonder if I'm responsible.

Maya on the other hand has never looked better. Her hair, once wild and curly, has been tamed into a sleek shine. I guess she's wearing make-up because her face looks brown while her neck is white. She wears a white T-shirt that says 'I Love Spain' and a pair of tight jeans and high shoes. I wonder how long she has had that hairstyle and regret swells in me that I don't know. I clamp it down. 'Hey,' I say to her.

'Your hair looks shite,' she says.

'I know.' I try out a smile.

She looks away from me and folds her arms. 'Any coffee in this place?' she asks Dad.

'I'll get it.' I hop up, eager to please. Also, I want to escape. My chair tips over. Mortified, I bend down to pick it back up again. I think I see a smile in Maya's eyes but as soon as I think this, the smile vanishes. 'What sort of coffee do you want?' I ask them.

'None of your fancy shit,' she says. 'Just a plain coffee with milk.'

I'd forgotten that Maya hates anything that reeks of pretension. She has this thing about coffee especially. I used to tease her over it and she used to laugh. I have to cough to rid myself of the memory. 'Dad?' I say, my voice hoarse.

'I'll have ...' he thinks for a second, 'a hazelnut mocha.'

Maya glares at him and I can't help a chortle.

'Fuck off, Dad,' she says.

He smiles, unconcerned.

I take my time at the counter. Vic slides in behind me. 'You're doing good,' he hisses, totally invading my space. He shuffles about awkwardly and, nudging me unintentionally with his elbow, adds, 'That chair falling was a bit shit but other than that, it's all good.'

'Thanks, Vic.'

'That sister of your looks a bit scary now, I don't mind admitting that. I'd be afraid of her. And what's with the T-shirt?'

'T-shirt?'

'"I Love Pain". Fucking hell.'

'"Spain", Vic. "I Love Spain".'

He looks blankly at me before suddenly understanding his mistake. Then he laughs like a sea lion.

I grin.

'Sorry. I'm an idiot.' Then he shuffles back to finish his orange.

I carry three coffees and three muffins down to the table. The muffins are great, massive chocolate ones. Maya liked chocolate.

'This is great,' my dad says. 'Thanks, Max.'

'Great?' Maya raises her eyebrows. 'How is this great, Dad?'

'Now, Maya,' my dad attempts to say.

'No, someone has got to lay it on the line here.' She looks across the table at me. 'This is not great.'

'D'you not like chocolate anymore?' It's a terrible joke, but I really just want to tell her, not here, not now, Maya, *please*.

Her brown eyes burn into my face. 'Actually, I'm on a diet, but you wouldn't know that because I haven't seen you in about four years.'

'Three.'

'Four, you tool. And you know, visiting you here is not great. In fact it's shit. My brother having a very public meltdown is shit. My brother not letting his own dad, his own dad who saved his life, visit him is shit. My brother sipping cappuccinos while our lives fall apart is shit.' She seems to be searching for more shit stuff but finally decides to end it. 'Now. There,' she finishes off, before leaning back in her chair and glaring at me. She looks for a millisecond as if she could cry.

The silence stretches. My dad stares into his coffee.

'It *is* shit,' I agree eventually, the words ambushing me. 'I'm sorry.' I have to take a bite of muffin, just for something to do.

'It's OK, son,' my dad says.

'It fucking isn't,' Maya snaps.

'Maya, I thought we agreed—'

'I didn't agree,' she says to him. 'You,' she points at me, in case I'm in any doubt, 'you put our whole lives on hold with the way you carried on.'

'I was just so angry with Dad putting me in here.' I swallow so I won't cry. I wish I hadn't eaten a big chunk of muffin now. It's like lead in my stomach. 'I didn't realise how bad I was. It was only when I read about myself on the internet that I thought what you did was OK.'

I think maybe the canteen is a bad place for this. I just thought they'd visit me. I should have known Maya wouldn't come quietly, though. She's always been a firebrand.

'Once you're OK, Max,' Dad says.

'Once *he's* OK?' Maya says. 'What about *us*?'

'Maya,' Dad says, 'Max is sick. You, very thankfully, are well.'

If looks could kill, Dad would have died roaring.

'I'm sorry, Maya,' I say. 'I really am. I know I treated you badly when you called up that time.'

'I adored you, Max,' she says, and her voice cracks but she reins it in. When she speaks again, it's harder. 'I looked up to you. You were my hero.'

The word 'hero' gut-punches me. 'Don't.' I try to fend the word off. 'Please.'

'You were,' she insists. 'I thought you knew everything.'

'Yeah, well, I didn't.'

'Then you ran off to Dublin and hardly ever returned our phone calls. We thought you were real busy and important. We thought they knew they had a really great guy on their hands up there.'

'Maya, stop,' my dad says, laying a hand on her arm.

I bite my lip. I taste blood.

'And you did so well.' Maya shakes dad off. 'We were so proud of you.'

'I lied for a living,' I say.

The canteen noises whirl around us.

'You were a PR man,' my dad says. 'You had to look out for your clients. Keep them out of trouble.'

'Yeah. I got good at keeping people out of trouble.' My words are bitter. I think I've been wanting to say them a long time. Maybe I should say them to Ian or someone, but the thing about Ian is he's not here to judge. I need to be judged. I need the harsh axe to fall. 'I kept myself out of trouble, I kept others out of trouble. I dragged everyone down with my lies.'

'Oh, less of the angst.' Maya snorts. 'Christ, can you not get it into your thick head, you chose to work at that. Accept it.'

Her misconception drags me back from the brink. I am shaking from almost going there. 'When did you become so bloody-minded?' I say instead.

'When you left me alone in your house for two days with no food. I thought you were dead.'

I have no answer to that. 'Sorry.'

'Look,' Dad says quite sharply, making both of us jump, 'it's great you asked us to visit, Max. Let's just be happy with that for now. We can't sort everything out in one visit. I am glad to see you, son. And I know Maya is too. Aren't you, Maya?'

'Yes,' she says. 'Of course.' Her voice wobbles. Then she says, 'What's the story with your house guest?'

'Sandy?' Has she met her?

'Is she a girlfriend?'

'Maya, can we just leave it for now?' Dad asks.

'It's just a question,' Maya says, innocently.

'She's just a friend,' I say, 'just a girl I met on the street one day.' I can't lie but I don't know how they'll react to the truth. That I thought she was an angel.

'On the street? Like outside a pub smoking or what?'

'No. She was sitting on a bench.'

'What? You sat beside her and suddenly she's in your house?'

'Maya—' my dad says.

'Something like that,' I say.

'Jesus! How long do you know her?'

'She seems like a very nice girl.' Dad unexpectedly sticks up for Sandy. 'She reads to Molly and Molly loves her.'

Maya shrugs. 'Still tells us nothing.'

'Dad is right, Sandy is sound.' I know it'll look bad if I explain how we met. And that wouldn't be fair to Sandy. I try to change the subject. 'I still have a client left. One I'm very excited about.' I hope that sounds convincing. Laura is not going as well as I'd hoped. For one thing, she's too bloody nice. One more chance, that's all she's got. I managed to get her an invite to the People of the Year Awards and if she doesn't get her mug into the paper, she's gone. 'She'll go far,' I say.

'Max?' Maya is peering at me, dipping her head so she can look into my face. Her hair smells of apples. 'How long do you know this Sandy person?'

I heave a sigh. 'A few months.'

'Great.' She plonks back in her seat.

'Shut up, Maya,' I snap. 'If all you came for was to have a go, you've done that really well. Thanks.'

She stands up and walks out. Aw, shit! Now it's just me and Dad. 'She's trying to look out for you, Max,' he says. 'She feels so guilty that she hasn't been in contact.'

'Well, you can tell her that she shouldn't. I wouldn't have contacted me.'

'Don't be so hard on yourself,' Dad says. He smiles a bit. 'Ever since you were a kid, you were hard on yourself. No matter what you did, you had to be the best at it. The best swimmer, the best runner, the best in school. Well, until it counted, that is.'

I had not done that great in the Leaving, way too many distractions.

'What happened to you, Max, eh?'

I dip my head. Shrug. 'I'm sorry, Dad. I just, well, I couldn't cope anymore.'

'With what? You have everything. A good job, nice house, a friend called Sandy.' He smiles at the last bit.

I shrug again. I couldn't cope with what I know. With what I did. I still can't. Lies kill, really. Instead of killing me, I've turned lying into an art form. Convinced myself it's OK.

'I love you,' my dad says. 'No matter what is bothering you, we'll sort it, OK?'

I'm a thirty-five-year-old guy but hearing my dad say that makes me feel about two. Tears gather in the back of my eyes and in slow motion horror I watch one fall and splash onto the table. My dad either pretends not to see it or doesn't. Instead, he squeezes my hands, but I pull away and walk off.

2

Once we slept together, I was on the slippery slope. They say when you first kill, it's traumatic, but that the next time, somehow, you rationalise it and it becomes easier. Maybe you feel that killing one person is just as bad as killing two. There is no lower you can go. Well, that's what sex with Imelda was like. After the first time, I was guilt-ridden. I couldn't look at Shane, I found excuses not to meet up with him and I gradually dissociated myself from anywhere he was likely to be.

So, the second time I slept with Imelda, which was a few weeks later, I told myself that it was fine. She obviously wanted me and it was a free country and if Shane was going to spend all his spare time studying, tough luck on him. I wasn't going to be that stupid. The third time, I began to despise Shane; after all, he couldn't keep his girlfriend satisfied.

I remember lying in bed one afternoon with her. She was on her back, her hair spread out over the pillow and her skin was so soft, all I wanted to do was run my hands over her. Her gaze was fixed on the ceiling and the late afternoon sun was slanting across our bodies, making a glamorous splash of bright across her face. I decided to go for it. I hoisted myself up on my elbow and looked down at her.

'What?' she asked.

'Would you not just ditch Shane?' I said. As soon as the words were out, I knew they were wrong, as if I'd just struck the wrong note while singing in harmony with a group.

'Would I not just ditch Shane?' Imelda mimicked, and I recoiled. 'No,' she said.

I didn't know quite how to cope with her blunt rejection. With the mocking tone. But I figured, I'd blundered once, I wasn't going to do it again. 'OK.'

I lay back down and there was silence. I wanted to go home all of a sudden. Back to where my life was uncomplicated. To where people thought I was great. I felt angry with her for making me feel bad. I made to get up.

'I can't choose, you see,' Imelda said, the palm of her hand on my spotty teenage back. 'I'm mad about you both, and it wouldn't be fair on Shane, it might wreck his exams on him.'

That was thoughtful of her. I took it as a hopeful sign. I told myself that when the exams were over, she'd choose me. I was prepared to do that much for my friend.

SANDY

1

Someone hammers on the door. I'm pouring milk into a cup of tea and it splashes out onto my mother's book of poetry. I wipe it down as the person at the door presses the doorbell so hard, it jams and keeps ringing.

'I know you're in there, I can see you through the glass,' a woman shouts.

'Maya,' someone else says. A man. It sounds like Max's dad.

The bell stops. Then starts up again. I close the poetry book and make my way to the door.

It is Max's dad and he's with a girl that I'm guessing must be Max's sister. She looks so like him, the dark hair and eyes. The look in her eyes is not friendly.

'Can I come in to my brother's house?' she asks. 'I'm Maya.'

'Sure.' I pull the door wider and she walks into the hall. Pierce is behind and he shrugs at me in what seems like an apology.

'Making tea for yourself, that's very nice.' The girl eyes up my cup.

'I thought so,' I say back. It takes a lot to intimidate me. 'Would you like one?'

'Yeah, seeing as it is my brother's tea.'

'Maya,' Pierce says, like a warning.

'It's mine, I bought it,' I say.

She ignores that and struts into the kitchen on high heels. She plonks into a chair and looks at me expectantly, as if I'm her slave.

'Pierce?' I ask.

'Thanks,' he says. He looks tired, I think.

'How did the visit go?' I ask.

'You told her we were visiting?' Maya says.

'Max told me,' I say.

'He looked good,' Pierce interjects hastily. 'And less agitated.'

'He does look good.' I pull two cups from the press and dunk a tea bag in each.

'So, what's the story between you and Max?' the girl asks. 'He says he met you on a bench.'

I pour hot water into the cups and hand her one, holding her gaze. She stares back unflinchingly. 'Well?' she asks.

Pierce sighs a little. 'Maya, come on, your brother is entitled to befriend who he likes. Thanks,' he adds, as he takes the cup from me.

'I'm only asking, out of interest.' Maya makes an innocent face.

'He did meet me on a bench,' I say, thinking, damn it, I'm going to tell them. Max deserves some credit for what he did. And what's the point in holding back? What can possibly happen to me? 'I was cold and wet and he bought me a coffee.' The memory stirs something in me. I wish I'd known how sad Max was.

'Just like that, out of the blue, he bought you a coffee?' Maya's lip curls.

'Yes.' I eyeball her again. I pause, say softly, 'Then the next day he did the same and the day after that. Every day at eleven, he bought me coffee and a cake or a sandwich.'

'Why?' Maya's hostility has been overtaken by curiosity.

Here it goes. 'I was homeless,' I say, watching their reactions, which I find I can't quite gauge. Pierce jerks and stares hard at me. Maya looks a little shocked. Serves her right, she did ask. 'I had nowhere to go,' I continue, 'or be. I liked sitting on the bench and watching people go by.' I take a sip from my mug so I have an excuse to lower my gaze. I don't want their pity, I'd rather their suspicion.

'You were homeless?' Maya repeats.

'Yes. And then one day, Max didn't turn up. And for the next few days I waited for him and he never came and I got worried and so I went looking for him. I missed him because he was one of the few good things I had to look forward to in my day.' It seems so long ago now.

'Fuck's sake,' Maya says. 'He let you move in here?'

'Yes, he did.'

'Obviously he wasn't thinking straight,' she says.

That again. 'Maybe not,' I concede. I look at Pierce. 'But I won't take advantage of him. I'll leave when he comes back.'

Neither of them knows what to say, which is a little gratifying.

'All I know,' I go on, 'is that he brightened up my day.'

Maya looks at her dad. 'Fucking hell,' she says. She might as well have said, 'Max was more unstable than I thought.'

'I'm sorry, Sandy,' Pierce says after a beat. 'I don't know what to say, I was not expecting that.'

'Were you homeless for long?' Maya asks.

'Nope, just a few months. I'd lost my job and couldn't pay rent.'

'Lucky Max lets you stay here for free then.'

'Stop,' Pierce says firmly, and Maya does. In fact she looks a little ashamed.

'I came looking for Max because I was worried. That's all. And I won't rip him off.'

'I know you won't.' Pierce says it like he believes me.

After a bit, Maya mutters, 'It's nice to know that he could still be kind among everything. Isn't it, Dad?'

'Yes.' His voice breaks.

'Aw, Dad.' Maya hops up and wraps her arms about him. 'Jaysus, stop, will ya.' He hugs her to him and I'm left in a place I've had to become used to in the last few years, standing on the outside, looking in.

I pick up my mother's poetry book and leave the house and wander around until it's time to go to Molly's.

Molly has put off reading *The Happy Prince* because she wants me to read her some poetry. I've read her some from books she had herself but she keeps pressing me to read my mother's poems. 'If you like a poet, you'll really do justice to the poetry,' she keeps telling me.

I keep 'forgetting' where I've left the book. Today, though, I have to give in because she's started asking me if there's a reason I don't want to read aloud those poems.

'Let's hear this Melanie Fairbrother person,' she says as she closes her eyes. 'Pick out your favourite poems.'

I pick out my least favourite because the nicest ones upset me. But there is something about reading poems aloud that makes them grow and live anyway. You can suddenly hear the hidden rhythms and rhymes. The meaning of the poem shakes off its words and becomes clear. The last poem I pick, entitled 'Loose Change', was one I hadn't understood until I started to read it. It was, I thought, about the sound money makes in your pocket, but it's really about money not spent. Money saved and stored and never used and then by the time you decide to spend it, it's too late. And the thing is, you never actually know it's too late until it is. You never know it's the last time until it never comes again.

'Are you OK?' Molly's eyes pop open as my voice falters.

'It's just a sad poem.'

'Softie.'

It's now or never. 'One day it'll be too late for you to get out of this bed.'

I fancy that my words change the air in the room. A hush falls and I hold Molly's gaze. I expect her to order me out because I know how cross she can get, though she's never lost it with me. Not yet. But maybe the poem touched her too because after a few tense seconds, she says, 'Tell you what, when Max's garden looks presentable, I'll get up.'

I think of the wilderness it is at the moment, despite my best efforts, and I groan. 'Define "presentable".'

Molly cackles. 'Clever girl. Presentable is nice grass, no stones, neat flowerbeds.'

It sounds do-able if Pierce continues to work at it. My skinny arms are next to useless. 'Deal,' I say, and shove out my hand. We shake on it.

'If Max comes back, will you still be around?' Molly asks then.

'I don't know.' I push the dread of leaving down deep and try not to think about it. 'But if I'm gone, you still need to keep our deal.'

'Hopefully you will,' Molly says. 'I enjoy you coming here.'

'Thank you.' It's nice to be wanted somewhere.

'I'll miss you if you go.'

'You have Charles. You're very close.'

'We are.' She give me a large smile, a little sad mixed through, though. 'There was only ever the two of us against the world.'

I want to ask if her husband died but it seems a bit personal. Then she tosses out, 'Charles' dad ran off when he found out I was pregnant. I never missed him.'

'Did Charles miss him?'

'I don't think so. He never said. It was tough, though, bringing up a boy alone and unmarried in those years.'

'You were a bit of a radical, then?' That fits, I think.

'I was as tough as nails.' She half-laughs. 'It was good because I managed to keep Charles but bad because I was afraid Charles would be bullied in school for having no dad so I headed it all off at the pass.'

'Yeah?'

'I was up at the school day and night, fighting his corner. It was only when he told me to lay off that I realised how mortified he was by me.'

I smile. Poor Charles.

'Still, I was only doing my best. That's all we can do, eh?'

'Yes.'

'And no matter what a mother does, her child will think it's wrong,' she laughs.

'Unless of course it *is* wrong.' The words pop out unexpectedly.

She shoots me a look. I dip my head, cursing my tongue, which seems to loosen up whenever I'm here now.

'I think most people do their best, some just don't have as many tools to cope as others.' Her words sound carefully chosen and when I look up, she's staring keenly at me.

I can't speak for a second or two. Finally, I give what I hope is a smile. 'I'm off to do Max's garden.'

Her laugh follows me out of the house. Her words keep me awake that night.

2

It was only when it ended with Louis that I realised how alone I actually was. I had no experience of having my heart broken, and besides the internet, there was no comfort to be found anywhere. I hated that I couldn't tell my mother. I resented that I had no friends to confide in. My life, in the space of a few hours, had gone from bright nights to dull, grey days. It was as if someone had hollowed out my inside and there was nothing left.

'Are you OK?' my mother asked on day three. She ran her fingers through my hair. 'You're not sick?' She lived in fear of me being sick.

I pulled my head away from her touch. 'Our lives are abnormal,' I said. It was a statement, my voice flat.

There was a beat, before she began to wipe down the table.

'Why are you like this?' I asked.

'Like what?'

'Like this!' I spread my arms wide. 'Why don't you go out?'

'I have nowhere I want to go.'

Her implacable manner and soft voice infuriated me. 'I want to go places. I want to meet people.'

Her shoulders hitched a bit. She wiped the table harder.

That's what she was doing to me, I suddenly thought, wiping my life away. 'Staying in this house isn't normal.'

She lifted her eyes to me. 'There is no normal.'

'We are not like other people!' My voice was rising.

'Other people aren't so great.' She froze suddenly, her ears always attuned to the sounds outside. I heard it then, the squeak of the postman's bike as he cycled up the potholed drive. She abandoned her cloth and darted to her position at the door, burying herself in the shadows.

I watched how she cowered and it galvanised me. This would go on forever if I didn't do something, so before she could react, I strode over to the front door, unlocked it and flung it open.

'Jesus, Mary and Joseph!' the postman said as he wobbled dangerously. 'Holy mother of God.'

'Sorry.' I tried out a bright smile. 'Sorry if I scared you.'

He paled. I think my smile unnerved him. Or maybe it was seeing my face for the first time in seventeen years.

Behind me my mother's breathing picked up pace.

'No harm done. No harm done.' He hopped off his bike and searched through his postbag, finally handing me two envelopes. One of them, the pink one that came most days, and another fat padded envelope. With a slight shock, I noticed that the pink one was addressed to me. 'I'm Seamus,' the postman cut through my surprise. 'Nice to put a face to the letters.'

'I'm Ruby. Hiya.'

'Nice meeting you, Ruby.' And he hopped back up on his bike and was gone.

'Give me those.' My mother's voice was as hard as flint from behind. 'How dare you do that!'

'I opened a door,' I told her. I could feel it, the gathering tension in the air. It had been years coming, but I sensed that today would change both of us, only I had no idea what I was getting myself into.

'You had no right. Now give me those letters.'

I looked at her, really looked at her, and I saw genuine terror in her eyes. Slowly I shut the door and said, 'The pink letter is addressed to me.'

'That always comes, it's nothing.' She came towards me, hand outstretched.

'Why did you never give it to me?'

'It's nothing. Give it to me.'

I ripped open the top and she sucked in her breath. Her shoulders tensed. 'No, don't,' she said, backing away a little. 'Please. No.'

Inside was a small, slim sheet of paper. I kept my eyes on her as I pulled it out. Unfolded it. She watched me and moaned. It was an address and a phone number. Somewhere in England. I remember my eyes slid over it to the text beneath.

Still writing to you, Ruby. This is my address now and maybe you have decided not to talk to me but until I get a reply, I'll keep trying. He would have wanted it that way. Hoping to hear from you one day.

Ivy

The name rang a bell. All those years ago, in my grandmother's house. A photograph of a girl.

I read the letter out loud. 'What does it mean?'

My mother groped for a chair and sat down. 'I don't usually open them,' she said.

'Do you know what it means?' I advanced on her.

She turned away.

'I've seen these envelopes arrive every day practically since I can remember,' I said to her back. 'It must be important.'

Still she said nothing, though she had begun to shake.

It was one of those moments, when you could almost sense the change of direction your life was taking. It was as if the air in the room was humming. I'd learned my lesson when Susan and my nana had come calling that time; never again would I bend to her will. I walked to the phone and picked up the receiver. 'I'm calling this Ivy person.'

'No!' She hopped up and darted towards me. 'Put down the phone.'

I held it aloft. 'Tell me.'

'Please put down the phone.'

I began to dial.

'I can't,' she said. 'Please, I can't. It's been so long.'

'I think you have to. This is my letter.'

'Don't do this, Ruby, please.' Her eyes filled with tears. She held her hands out in supplication. 'Please. I don't want to remember.'

I almost gave in. Almost. I hated to see her like this, but there was no going back. Even if I put the phone down, this secret would always lie between us. I knew, instinctively, that this was the thing that had undermined the foundations of both our lives.

'Tell me or I will ring.'

'I can't.' She shook her head.

And so I finished dialling as she moaned. It was as if by punching in the numbers, I was hitting her.

'It will ruin everything,' she said, and I almost stopped.

But then I continued. I didn't breathe as the phone at the other end of the line rang and rang. My mother stood up and went outside to the garden. Finally, someone picked up and a woman's voice chirruped, 'Hello.'

'Is that Ivy?'

'Yes. Who is this?'

I hesitated, my mother's warnings ringing in my ears. But if I'd listened to her I'd never have got out of the house. 'This is Ruby. Ruby Fairbrother.'

I heard a sound that I took for a sob. 'Oh my God.' Then a yell, 'It's her! It's Ruby.' I heard more people enter the room. 'Can I put you on speaker? We're all so excited.'

'Who are you?' I asked.

A pause. 'She didn't tell you?'

I said nothing.

'I'm your sister.'

I heard nothing else. Just a great roaring in my ears. I had to hang up. It was automatic. Whatever this was, it was too big. Too overwhelming to be taken in right at that moment. My mind singing with betrayal, I turned and went back to my room.

A couple of hours later, I found my mother still in the garden. She was staring into space. I was going to give her one more chance, I decided. One more chance to make it right. To see if there was even a small possibility of getting the truth from her.

'Tell me,' I said, 'who is Ivy?'

'You didn't ring?'

I shook my head.

She looked at her hands. 'Ivy is,' she hesitated for the longest time, 'my past and I want to keep it there.'

'You won't tell me?'

'I need,' she hesitated, 'time.'

'Is Ivy the reason you lock yourself away in this house?'

She moaned a bit, doubled over.

'Just tell me the truth.'

'I don't know the truth anymore,' she said. 'I've spent so long trying to forget. Please understand.'

I told her I didn't.

We looked at each other for a long moment before she turned away. I had wasted my life listening to lies. I was getting out before it was too late. That night, I packed a haversack, stole some money and left.

MAX

1

Laura arrives in, all perky and smiling and hopeful, like she hasn't just fucked away two hundred and fifty euros that I spent on getting her that ticket for the awards the other night. One look at my face and her smile dies a bit.

Sandy arrives in at the same time. She walks towards me and stops just short of our table, looking a little confused to see my visitor.

Laura, her back to Sandy, gives a nervous giggle which instantly grates. 'Is this about the awards night you sent me to? I'm sorry, Max, I can explain.'

I ignore her and say, 'Sandy, this is Laura, my client.'

Laura turns. Sandy smiles. She holds out her hand to Laura, which is progress. 'You're the girl with the nana who's one hundred years old,' she says to Laura, while grinning at me.

I don't grin back.

'Yes.' Laura shakes Sandy's hand and I see Sandy wince at the strength of Laura's grip.

'Good party?'

'Brilliant.'

If I was a dog, my hackles would be up and I'd be growling. 'We've got a bit of business to discuss, d'you mind hanging on?' I ask Sandy with a bit of a glare.

'No. I'll be over here.' Sandy takes a seat a table away.

'Now,' I turn back to Laura, 'dazzle me with your explanation.'

Laura swallows and I'm glad she's nervous; at least she takes me seriously.

Before she can start, I say, 'Waving at photographers as you come out of a night club is bad enough, being seen with the weirdest guy in town is not so good either.'

'He's my boyfriend.'

'Oh, even fucking better!'

'You told me to ask a guy to the nightclub.'

'I wasn't expecting you to ask Nerd Man.'

'That's horrible.' Laura glares at me but I ignore her.

'Falling asleep at a concert and being photographed with your mouth open and your eyes shut is even shittier, cancelling *Morning Live*—'

'My nan's one hundredth birthday, even your girlfriend asked about that. It's a big deal.'

'She's not my girlfriend and *Morning Live* is a big deal.'

Laura bites her lip.

'But fucking up an awards ceremony when you are sitting at the best table with the best DJs and the top TV presenters in the country is in a league of its own. Congratulations, you win top prize.'

'Cop on, Max!' Sandy butts in. She sounds a little cross.

'My business,' I say to Sandy. 'You go get coffee.'

She looks a bit pissed off at that and she doesn't even go to get the coffee.

'I can explain!' Laura bleats.

'Do.' I hold out my hand. 'You tell me why there is not

one single picture of you in any paper or on any TV set that I've seen. Tell me why there is nothing on the internet. Why not one DJ or TV person rang me about you. Tell me that, Laura.' I sit back and fold my arms. This better be good. Already I feel my stress rising.

'Well,' Laura licks her lips, 'I did go.'

'I should bloody well hope so!'

'Max, keep your voice down,' Sandy says. She moves to sit beside me.

'And as for you,' I turn on Sandy, 'telling Maya and my dad how we met, Jesus!'

'I thought it was time for some honesty.'

The word 'honesty' gets me every time. I have no comeback.

'How did you meet?' Laura asks.

Sandy flinches. Shit!

'You will not change the subject.' I find my footing again. 'Go on, I'm waiting.'

A pause, then she launches into her story, sounding quite defensive, I think. 'Well, this girl I was at the table with, some model or other—'

'Amanda Ryan?'

'No, don't think that was it.'

'Lucy Kilfeather?'

'No.'

'June Anderson?'

'Jesus! You sure know a lot about models for a guy,' Laura says.

'It's my business to know people, Laura,' I snap. I eyeball her. I want her to squirm. I am really annoyed about this.

It was her biggest opportunity and she blew it. 'You were sitting beside a model whom you never got the name of, which is wonderful, by the way. Then what?'

'Then, eh, well, I go outside for some air.'

'Air?' I glare at her.

'Smoke,' she admits.

'For fuck's sake, you shouldn't be smoking, haven't I told you that?'

'I'm cutting down, honestly, I am. But I was nervous, I needed something to calm me.'

I say nothing.

'And when I get outside to the smoking area this model girl is there and she's crying.'

'Oh?' This could be promising.

'And, well, at first I didn't want to go over to her and then I did.'

'And?' This is good.

'She told me to fuck off.'

'Great.' Bloody hell.

'So I told her to fuck off.'

'I hope she wasn't too famous.'

'And then she cried some more and I couldn't leave her, so I sat with her for a bit and when she saw that I wasn't leaving, she said that she'd been diagnosed with cancer and that she thought she might die.'

'Oh great!' Wow, there's a scoop. 'And?'

Laura is looking at me funny. 'And I took her home and asked her was she mad turning up at a bash like that when she was so sick, that's what I did.'

'And did you ask her name?'

'No.'

I rattle my brains. 'If I showed you a list of pictures, could you identify her?'

Now she's really gawking at me. 'Probably. Why?'

'Because it's a scoop, we could get a headline saying that you were the confidant of this model and that—'

'That poor model was ill.' Sandy sounds appalled.

I open my mouth to answer and Laura gets in there first.

'I'm not exploiting that,' Laura says. 'No way.'

'You want her to use that?' Sandy gawks at me.

And I think, yeah, yeah I do. And the other part of me thinks, Jesus, no. Only a monster would use that. Only a monster. I wonder if that is what I am. Or was I always one. I stare at them, hating their goodness, knowing that I gave mine away, once upon a time.

'I think I'll go.' Laura stands up, her nervousness all but gone. 'And I think, well, Max, thanks for taking me on and all, but, like, I don't think this is for me. I don't mind all the other stuff, well I do … I just want to sing. I thought I would like to pretend to be in places and stuff like that. And I thought it was OK to change my clothes but, well, I like the way I dress and so docs my boyfriend, so I'm not wearing the stuff you want me to anymore.'

She is firing me?

'It's just not me,' she goes on. 'I'm a fish and chips girl. Maybe I'll never make it in the big time, but at least I know that now.'

Sandy glances in alarm at me and hops up to try to stop her. 'Don't be hasty. Max is great.'

Laura looks at me and I look back. I think my heart is

breaking a bit. 'You can get some coverage by telling the media that you sacked Max Coyle.' I attempt a grin.

'I don't think that makes me unique.' She half-grins back.

Ouch. I know she meant it as a joke, but it hurts. 'Yeah, you'd have to join the queue.' I pause. I try to tell her that the decent part of me hates what I just tried to make her do. 'Sorry,' I say instead. Only I don't mean just her. I mean every stinking lie I made every client of mine tell.

'You were right in the beginning,' Laura nods, 'it's not just my voice that's me, it's everything. And I like it and I want to hold onto it.'

How nice to like yourself. How nice not to want to lie.

She leans over the table and I can see down her top. I'm ashamed to admit that it's a bit of a turn-on. 'I want you on my side but I can't be someone I'm not. Andrea was upset—'

'Oh, so you *did* know her name.' And it must have been Andrea Harte. That would have been a massive scoop. Bloody massive.

Laura ignores this. 'And I helped her out and I did it with no agenda.'

'I was just exploiting all possibilities to help you.' How shit that sounds.

'Yeah, well,' she shrugs and picks up her bag, 'I don't need that kind of help. Sorry.' She does look sorry. A pause. 'See you.'

Sandy and I watch her leave. 'Well, you blew that,' Sandy says.

'Nah, she's made the right decision. She might not have a music career, but she might have a soul.'

'Don't be so dramatic.' She smiles at me and instantly I
feel better. 'You're a good man.'

Bang. Wallop. I wish it was true. I'd done the same for
all my clients and had success after success. They'd been
papped, primed, sold their life stories, sold their secret fears
and desires and made loads of cash. But maybe it had only
worked because of who I was. Because of what I made them
do. And maybe it had worked because of who they were too.
'Would you have done it?' I ask Sandy. 'Told of your night
with the distraught model?'

'No.' She says it without hesitation.

'Even if it meant front-page coverage?'

'No. I'd want to be on the front page because I had talent,
not because I was spilling a confidence or pretending to be
someone I wasn't.'

And I think of the time I was on the front page, long
ago, when I'd told that lie and Paddy had told that lie and
I'd been hailed as a hero. I put my face in my hands and my
shoulders start to shake and I cry and cry and I think I might
never stop.

2

I'd been nervous when Shane had rung. He'd sounded upset, on the edge almost. I'd tried to act cool, be normal. Shane never really rang me, it was always just a case of meeting up, of having a laugh. That morning, the sixth of August, he'd called and he'd asked to see me. He didn't sound too good. I asked him if everything was OK and he'd hung up.

Of course, I didn't have to go, I could have avoided it, but part of me wanted my deception to be out in the open. I know I justified it to myself time and again, but when I really thought about it, I hated what I was doing. I had never seen myself as a girlfriend stealer, but then again, most of the girls my mates went out with were not that great. They weren't Imelda.

I told Dad I was heading out to meet Shane and before he could say anything, I was gone. Me and my dad had grown apart that summer. I think it was because we'd fought a lot over my exams. He'd never been a pushy parent before, but I think my total lack of study had freaked him. I simply didn't care. I was having sex with a girl I was mad about: everything else paled into nothing.

As I made my way to the harbour, I wondered if Imelda had told Shane, I wondered if now Imelda and I could be together for real. Yes, it was bound to fracture all my friendships with the lads, but I didn't care. Shane would probably hit me but I deserved it, I would let him hit me. I wouldn't hit back. I wouldn't.

Shane had asked to meet me on the pier. To my surprise, Paddy was there too. Both of us were early and I asked Paddy if Shane had rung him.

'Yeah, really weird or what?' Paddy lit a cigarette and leaned against the wall, blowing smoke out to sea, where it was blown back into our faces again.

'So, what d'you think it's about?' I was wrong-footed totally. This was no private discussion.

Paddy shrugged. 'Beats me.' He seemed unconcerned.

We sat on the pier wall. There weren't many people about as it was a wild sort of day. Gulls screeched overhead and I watched as they wheeled and dived about each other without ever crashing. The tinkle of moored boats was only beaten in volume by the smashing of waves against the bulwark.

Shane arrived a few minutes later and he appeared agitated. I looked at his pale face and unwashed hair and realised that I hadn't seen him in weeks. He looked thinner too. He flashed us both a brief grin and sat in between us. 'Thanks for coming, lads,' he said. 'I rang the others too but they were busy. Thanks for coming.'

My heart sank; this did not sound like he was angry with me. Imelda still hadn't told him.

'So, what's the story?' I asked, and I know I sounded a bit pissed at him.

'Aw, it's terrible.' He ran a hand through his hair and then put his hands over his face and groaned. 'Imelda is pregnant.'

The world stopped turning for me right then. It was like

all the sounds disappeared, as if I was being swallowed up in a huge vacuum and squeezed tight.

'What?' I remember Paddy saying from the void. 'Imelda is pregnant?'

Shane nodded, his head in his hands.

'I thought all girls were on the pill now,' Paddy said.

'I dunno.' Shane lifted his head and I saw devastation on his face. 'I mean, we used protection. Jaysus, my parents are going to kill me.'

Of course they were. They'd never let him forget it. They expected their kids to achieve big and Shane was a bright light.

'They'll go mad,' Shane said. 'You've no fucking idea.'

Paddy and I couldn't argue with that.

'I sacrificed her this summer to keep them happy,' he said. 'I only saw her once a week to shut them up. I hated it but I did it and now this. Oh, fuck.' It sounded like he might cry.

I found courage from somewhere. 'Is it yours?' I stumbled out.

'Of course it bloody is,' Shane snapped. 'Jesus, that's great, thanks for that, Max. Appreciate that.'

I'd done my bit. I felt a bit better.

Paddy flashed me a look. Then he said, 'So, what are you going to do?'

'I don't know.' He sounded really young all of a sudden. 'I have to stand by her, don't I?'

'No,' Paddy said. 'You don't.'

'My folks will kill me. Like, I love her and all but I can't be a dad.'

'Can she, would she, get rid of it?' Paddy winced at the question.

'I dunno if she would. I think she's going to have it.'

I wish one of us had told him that it wasn't so bad. That we'd be there for him. But we didn't. I wish I'd told him the truth, that it could be mine, but I didn't. We just stood there, thick eighteen-year-old lads with no clue, and watched as he crumbled. Inside I was crumbling too. Maybe it was my child. But Jesus, I couldn't be a dad either. There was no way. And maybe I should have told Shane but the truth was, I didn't want to now. I wanted to walk away, tiptoe away like a kid that has broken something and does not want to be found out. So I said nothing. I told him it'd sort itself out and asked him if he wanted a pint.

He said no. He said he was grand. He said he loved us. And he thumped us on the back and we thumped him too. And because I couldn't look at him anymore, I told him I had to go. Paddy said he had to go too. We said we'd help him out babysitting. We joked a bit and then Shane turned around and stood up on the wall. We thought he was going to walk back with us – we often messed about on the wall – and he did for a second, but then he leapt. He just jumped off. There in front of us one second and gone the next.

The shock of it stilled our reaction, before I jumped in after him. I remember thinking that this could not be happening. That my friend could not be killing himself over this. I swam hard, knowing that if I let him go, I'd never live with myself. I swore I'd tell him the truth if I could just save him. He was being pulled along and my mind was numb and my arms were tired.

'Shane,' I yelled, as water poured into my mouth, 'come on, hold me. I swear I'll bring you back.'

A wave carried him further out.

'Shane!'

He shook his head. Like, I think he shook his head.

I wish I had told him then that I could be the father of that baby. I wish I had yelled it out. But I was too scared and it was too late. He was drowning and I didn't want him to go with his girlfriend's betrayal ringing in his ears.

'We'll sort it. I swear!' I tried one more time to reach him but the undertow was too strong and I began to fear that I would drown too.

I was picked up by a boat a few minutes later. They didn't find Shane for a few days. And at that stage Paddy had told the lie. Shane had fallen in. I was a hero.

I've lived the lie ever since.

3

I'm not sure how much of my blubbering made sense to Sandy, I'm not sure how coherent I was. All I know, when the storm passes, is that she is rubbing my back and forcing water on me and telling me that it's OK. It's all fine. I've blown it out of proportion. I was young. I was stupid. I was scared. Ian is here too. I don't remember him arriving, but he's in my room and his presence is solid. It anchors me.

I feel utterly stupid. And strangely, I feel about a million times lighter. As if I've dropped some burden I was carrying. The deepest part of me, the part I despised, I've let out into the light. And yes, I can see that at the time I was just a kid. We were all just kids. And when you're a kid, you don't expect your friend to jump off a pier.

'If Shane hadn't jumped,' Ian says, 'you might have told him. Imelda might have. He didn't give either of you a chance.'

I hadn't thought of that. 'Maybe I would never have told him, though,' I say.

'But the point is, you don't know that,' Ian says. 'That's the thing with suicide, the ones left behind haven't been given a proper chance to prove their love for the dead person. That's one reason why people get so angry later on. The ones left behind feel like failures, because they have been denied the chance to step up to the mark.'

'He must have been in a lot of pain,' Sandy offers.

Ian nods. 'No doubt about it, but look at the pain Max has been in over it.'

I bow my head. 'If I'd told him,' I swallow hard, 'I might have stopped him jumping, I might have saved Paddy from having to lie. He's lived with that lie too.'

'Have you ever talked to him about it?' Ian asks.

'Will I go?' Sandy interrupts, gesturing to the door.

Ian looks at me. I shake my head. Sometimes it's good to have someone who knows everything about you. 'Well,' Ian asks, as Sandy sits back down, 'have you and Paddy ever talked about it?'

'Nope. Never. When I heard what Paddy had said, I just went along with it. What would be the point of telling Shane's parents the truth? Of course questions were asked but there were no witnesses.'

'And Imelda?' Sandy asks.

'She had the baby and Shane's parents loved it, I guess because it was part of Shane or something.' My eyes fill up again.

'Did you ever talk to her?'

'No.' I heave a sigh. 'I wanted to, but, well, she was Shane's girl. As far as everyone was concerned, she was Shane's girl. She was up at the top of the church at his funeral, she did a reading. How could I have told everyone? How could she have? And there was no proof.'

'And now?'

'Now she's out of the country, married to some Australian guy.'

There is silence in my room; it's a peaceful room, probably decorated to calm people down.

'You need closure on this,' Ian finally says, firmly. 'If you sort this out, if you come clean, then you'll move on, Max. You really will.'

'Closure? How? I can't go telling Shane's parents what happened, not now.'

'No.' He looks at me, waiting.

The word forms slowly. 'Imelda?'

'I think so. I think you've wanted to do it for a long time. You need to contact her and find out if the baby was yours. Or tell her you'd like to help with it if it is. You need to stop the lie right now, Max. And I think you need to talk to Paddy.'

I bow my head. It was talking to Paddy that had put me in here in the first place.

'Look at it like this,' Ian says. 'Would it have been such a big deal if nothing had ever happened? If Shane had found out at the time. All these years later, would it have been such a big deal in the pattern of your life?'

'I dunno.' I think that I might have stayed at home if nothing had happened, I might have fished and swam and repeated my Leaving.

'It wouldn't,' Sandy pipes up shyly. 'It was just you being a bit of a wanker, Max. You were only a kid. And so was Imelda. You're not responsible for what Shane did.'

'She's right.' Ian half-smiles at Sandy. 'We'll make a counsellor out of you yet.'

Sandy laughs.

And though some of the guilt lingers, like wisps of fog on early mornings, I have confessed. And the harshest judge all along was me.

SANDY

1

I'm shaky after all that emotion. Poor Max. I'd wanted to hug him when he started crying, those horrible jagged sobs. It was as if he was vomiting tears. Everyone in the canteen had looked at us; some of them I'm sure thought I was to blame. Then Vic had come over and told me to bring Max back to his room and he'd go and find Max's counsellor.

I don't think Max registered when I touched his elbow to lead him back to his room. It was as if he was buried under mountains of tears. It freaked me a little because even though Max was in here, I'd always assumed that underneath the jitteriness he was a pretty cool customer. Strong. Confident. Or maybe it was just that my first impressions of him would never change. And seeing him cry, it was like he was behind glass all of a sudden. Still, I kept my hand on his arm until eventually he stood up and I led him back. I told him it would be fine; I don't know if he heard me. We sat in Max's room, me telling him that I was his friend, that whatever it was, I didn't care and he held me and I held him. I don't know if he remembers. He smelt nice.

Then Ian, his counsellor, arrived. And though it has no

bearing on anything, Ian was the best-looking man I have ever seen in my entire life. Tall, dark, stubble-faced, with the bluest eyes. I know it's probably a bit weird to notice a great-looking man when your friend is breaking down, but Ian's looks are too obvious to ignore.

He was great at his job too. The minute he came into the room, I felt calmer. I'm sure Max did too. Ian told Max that he was there if he wanted to talk. At first, what Ian was saying barely registered; all Max did was cry and apologise. I began to think he'd never stop, that something had been turned on inside him that couldn't be turned off.

'Please, Max,' I said.

And Max had looked at me and the whole story had poured out, a river of words, jumbled, like stuff being tossed up by the tide. I swear, my heart kind of broke for him. I felt gutted because in a way he reminded me of my mother. Both of them keeping secrets locked inside them for years. Except while my mother had run from life, Max had run into it. Only he had never stopped running. And it reminded me of myself too.

'Sometimes,' Ian said to Max, 'you have to break down to build yourself back up.' And though it was like something you'd hear on *Oprah*, it sounded real coming from him.

I left Max once he'd calmed right down and Ian had assured me that he'd be OK. 'He'll be more than OK,' he'd said. 'You take care now.' I am startled to see that the clock in the hospital foyer reads three fifty. How could so much time have passed? I'm late for Molly. The days, which were slow once as I sat on benches or walked streets, have speeded up.

Soon my life will have moved on and where will I be? The thought makes me shiver.

'Pierce tells me you were homeless when Max met you,' Molly says the minute I walk in the door.

Charles makes a hasty exit, though I can imagine him rolling his eyes and mouthing 'Shut up' at his mother behind my back.

'I was only homeless because I had no job. I have a job now.' I take a seat and find the book we're reading.

'It's hardly a job.'

'Can we get started?'

'Living on the streets is not a nice place for a young girl.'

'It was only for a couple of months.' I open the book. 'Now, where were we?'

'Could you not have gone home?'

'No.' I hope my snappy tone will cut the conversation off.

'Why?'

'Please don't, Molly.'

'Have you no family? Are the family you have not great?'

'Molly …'

'Indulge a dying woman.'

'That's blackmail.'

'I am dying, though,' she says a little urgently. 'Soon, my voice will go and I won't be able to ask those questions and God knows Charles won't ask them for me. He's says I'm too interfering by half.'

'You are.'

'Well?'

Grudgingly, I say, 'I did have a mother.'

'I thought so. Did she do something terribly wrong?'

'She lied to me.' Despite my best efforts, my voice hitches up a little, a mix of anger and upset.

'Why?'

'I don't know. In the end, I had to leave.'

'And did you write to her to tell her you were OK or does she know what happened to you?'

She actually sounds sorry for my mother. 'I was angry,' I admit, getting angry again. 'In the beginning I wanted her to suffer, not knowing about me.'

'And now?'

'I did try to write a few times but ...' How can I explain that weird mixture of terror and longing that coexist inside me? Terror because if I make contact, it'll be front-page news, they'll track me down, she'll be in my life again whether I want her to be or not and I don't know if I can live with more hurt. And yet, when I think of going home, sometimes the longing to be there is so bad that I can't function for a few days. So I bury it.

'Just tell her you're safe or go back home and sort it out.'

'I can't,' I say to Molly.

'Charles went missing once, in a supermarket when he was five. I'll never forget the terror, Sandy.'

'I just can't.'

'Did she not love you?'

I think about the way we lived. I've never told anyone except Louis before. But Molly wants to know, that's the difference. 'She loved me too much,' I say, striving to sound matter-of-fact when in fact I feel I could choke on the words. 'We spent all our time inside, avoiding life. I spent years terrified of being outside.'

Molly says nothing for a few seconds. The road outside is quiet. 'Do you think,' she says after a bit, 'that it would help if you found out why she did it?'

'I know why she did it. She was crazy.'

'So was Max and yet there is a good man there.'

I can't answer that.

'Put another way,' Molly presses on, 'do you want to live like this forever?'

'I like reading to you.'

'I'm talking about wasting your potential. Only someone avoiding the taxman would take a job like this and call it their work.'

I flush.

'But if you contacted your mother, you would have a PPS number and be able to get decent work. It's not just about her, it's about you, Sandy.'

That she's worried about me touches me. But the thought of making contact hammers me to the seat. 'Thanks for caring,' is all I can say.

'Think about it.'

I nod.

'Good girl.'

Two words. So lovely to hear.

2

My plan when I left home was simple. I wanted to get as far away as possible and I wanted to meet Ivy. After that I had no idea. There was no one I could call to ask for help. Nan hadn't talked to me on Facebook in years and Susan and my nana hadn't been down to the cottage in a long time. I didn't even know their addresses in Galway.

So, my plan was that once I got to Dublin, I would ring Ivy and ask to meet her. Maybe I'd have to go to England, but as I had no ID on me, I wasn't sure how that would work out. I didn't care, it was nice just to have a plan, a future, somewhere to go.

I don't know how long it took me to get to Dublin, but when I walked onto the south quays during rush hour, I knew I'd arrived. It was as if I'd smashed into a wall of noise and colour. Cars in endless streams snaked down the road; there were horns blasting, engines chugging. And so many different voices, arching over the clamour. I felt like a rock in a stream as reams of busy people passed me by. I took my time, savouring the city chaos, looking left and right, taking it all in, afraid I'd miss a thing. Step by step towards the city, feeling a little lighter the nearer I got. I couldn't wait to see O'Connell Street and Grafton Street, places I'd read about on the net. In the end, a little overwhelmed, I had to sit down. I found a bench, peeled off my haversack and put it at my feet. My legs and back ached.

Someone sat beside me and I moved up to give him some room. He smiled his thanks and offered me a cigarette.

'No, thanks, I don't smoke.' I dipped my head, afraid I'd be recognised.

'Good decision.' His voice was friendly. He stuck a fag between his lips and bent over as he struck a match. His cigarette pack was still open and his cigarettes fell out, scattering over the path. I helped him pick them up. He smiled his thanks again and moved on.

And I discovered that while I'd been distracted with him, someone had stolen my haversack. I had no phone, no address for Ivy and no money. And there was no way I was going home. Not ever.

3

I hang in the doorway of the canteen and watch Max. He's at a table with some of the nutters and he's entertaining them with a story. When he delivers the punchline, a loud laugh goes up and Max grins. He looks so relaxed and at ease that my heart flips over and over. His smile is slow and easy, like he's expecting people to smile with him. I think I love this man and that knowledge is horrible because I know it can never be.

He turns and catches sight of me and excuses himself from his new-found friends.

'Hey, were you there long?'

'Just a couple of seconds. Hanging with the nutters now, eh?'

'If you can't beat them, join them.'

'Coffee? Muffin?'

'I'll buy.'

'No, Molly has upped my wages. Your dad told her I was homeless. I feel a bit bad about it.'

'Glad you're getting something out of the old bat.'

'She's a lovely woman. You were just an obnoxious neighbour.'

'I know.' He follows me up to the counter and I ask the woman for two cappuccinos and a chocolate muffin and a raspberry one.

'I don't eat raspberry.'

'I do. I hate the chocolate.'

'You should have said.'

'I *am* saying.'

'I mean you should have said from the beginning, stupid.' Max tugs my hair gently.

'I didn't know you well enough.'

'And you do now?'

I shrug.

'Good.' His smile dazzles me.

I hand him his coffee and muffin and take mine and follow him to a table. He sits across from me and we smile at each other. And smile some more and then it gets a bit uncomfortable so we both look down at our coffees.

'I'm sorry about the other day,' Max says. 'The whole meltdown thing.'

'Why?'

'I'm embarrassed.'

'Why?'

'Jesus, Sandy, in front of you? It was the last thing I wanted to do.'

It hurts that he feels like that and I can't focus for the rest of the visit.

When I get back, there is a yellow skip in the front garden. Pierce is chatting to Charles over the low wall that divides their garden from Max's.

'Hi.' Pierce smiles more warmly at me than he ever has before. 'I thought I'd make a stab at finishing the back garden. I'll pile this with rubbish. After that, I'll do some digging, I've hired a rotavator and bought some grass seed. Is that OK?'

He always asks me that. I always say, 'It's your son's house, of course it's OK.' I smile at Charles and unlock the front door. Pierce follows me inside. 'I'll give you a hand.'

'It'll be a lot of heavy work today, worse than before.' Pierce eyes me up.

'If it gets too much, I'll just disappear.'

He grins. 'You're on.'

We work in silence, him occasionally telling me what to do. By tea time, despite the break I had when reading for Molly, my muscles are aching. Pierce rings for chips and we sit eating them on the back step of the house.

'I'll buy the next time,' I say.

'Grand. I'll be sure to order a lot more then.'

It takes a second to realise he's joking.

'Do you mind me asking,' Pierce says, 'if your parents know you're alive?'

I shoot him a look. Not him too.

'It's fine.' He holds up his hands. 'You don't have to answer.'

My chips are finished and I ball the paper up in my hands, squeezing it hard.

'It's just …' Pierce says, then stops.

I wave him to go ahead.

'The night I found Max unconscious, I only came up because Charles had rung to say that Max had music blaring all over the street for three days. I drove up here like a lunatic. And I'll never forget the dread of thinking he was dead.' He closes his eyes. 'I still feel sick when I think about it.' He brings his gaze to mine. 'You should at least let your parents know you're alive.' Hauling himself to his feet, he thumbs towards the kitchen. 'Cuppa?'

I know it's his way of saying the subject is closed but, funnily enough, I don't want him thinking badly of me. 'I'll think about it. My mother hurt me a lot.'

He looks at me. 'So don't hurt her back.'

He leaves it at that.

The ringing of the phone shatters the silence of Max's house after his dad leaves. Caller display shows Max's mobile. He must be ringing from the hospital.

'Hey,' I answer.

'I want you to be the first to know,' he says, and there is a grin in his voice. 'I'm out for the weekend next week.'

'Brilliant.' Whatever happens with me, I mean it. He sounds so happy, it's worth sleeping under a hedge for.

'It is, yeah,' he says. And then goes on, 'My dad will be with me but you have to stay.'

'We'll see,' I say. 'But congratulations, that is brilliant news.'

'There's no "we'll see",' Max says, and he sounds quite firm. 'We'll have a celebration pizza on Saturday, right?'

'OK.'

'That's my girl.'

He rings off.

MAX

Sandy comes in to visit. Something is wrong because, as far as I can remember, she never visits on a Friday. She looks a bit shook, which is a surprise. In the last few weeks, she has come out of her shell, no longer the reclusive girl that I once thought was an angel.

'Hey,' she says as she sits down. She's wearing that white coat today, the fluffy one. She pushes her hair behind her ears and says, 'I came to tell you that I have somewhere else to stay the weekend you get out.'

'You have? Why?'

'You need your privacy.'

'No, I don't.' I jump in like a suicidal diver. 'Not at all. I'm not a private guy.'

Sandy looks oddly at me. 'Maybe you don't think you do, but I'm sure your dad would prefer if I wasn't there.'

'Tough luck on him.' My dad had asked actually and I'd told him that Sandy was sleeping in the spare room and he could have the sofa, take it or leave it. I don't want Sandy to leave. She's like my good luck charm.

'No, Max,' Sandy swallows hard, 'it's better that way. And anyway, I'll have to move on when you come back.'

I'm not good with emotion, especially the negative types, but surprising myself, I reach out and touch her, just on her hand. 'No. Not true.' I like touching her. Not that I spend all day thinking about it or anything. 'You can stay as long as you like.' She can't go.

'I can't stay that long,' a small laugh, 'otherwise it'll be forever.'

'That's OK.' There's a silence. One in which I squirm because I feel I've said too much, so to save face at her lack of response, I blurt out, 'Well, until I throw you out, that is.'

She laughs a bit, though it's so not funny.

We look at each other. I flounder about for something to persuade her to stay. 'I told my dad I didn't need him babysitting me. I could tell him to go.'

'But it's your house, your space.'

I so don't want space. I'm afraid my brain will take off on its own again. 'Please, just stay this weekend. You can be a buffer between me and my dad.'

'I don't want to be a buffer, Max.'

'Then don't be.' My hand involuntarily squeezes hers. 'Just stay.'

She shakes her head.

'Please.'

She looks at me as if trying to gauge my motivation. I don't know what it is only that I don't believe for one second she has a place to stay.

'Please,' I say again.

'Why?'

Oh God. Why? I hate that question. Everything in here begins with a 'why'. I don't know why with Sandy. 'Can I confess something?' I say.

'You haven't answered my question,' she half smiles, 'but go on.'

'This might,' I tell her. 'Now, you'll think I'm a freak, but just remember, I was mental.' She smiles at me, at my ham-fisted attempt to find humour in mental illness. 'The first time I bought you coffee, I thought,' my voice hitches up a notch as I blurt out, 'that you were an angel.'

Her reaction is pretty much the wide-eyed and amused one I expected. 'Me?' She giggles. 'Why would you think I was an angel?'

'You had that white coat on, for starters.'

'No, I didn't.'

'You did, you were in white.'

'It was snowing, Max.'

Holy crap, was it? 'Anyway,' I brush off her comment, because there is so much about that time I don't remember, 'it doesn't matter. I thought you were an angel and while this might make you run for the hills, sometimes I think you still are.' I give her what I hope is a glum grin. A sort of *See what a basket case I am, can you not just stay, for fuck's sake?*

She looks upset.

Oh, shit.

'That's the nicest thing anyone has ever said to me.'

Oh, so she's not upset, just pleased. 'So? Will you stay?' I press home my advantage. 'Just for the weekend? I'll feel better with you there.'

'I told your dad I'd go when you got out of hospital.'

'I told him you were staying. He didn't seem to mind. Please.'

A pause. Then a nod. 'Yeah. OK.'

'Excellent.'

'I think I'm the one who should be saying that,' she says. 'I like being there.'

I bloody well don't. I lived on that road for four years and the only people I knew were Patricia – because she baked some cakes for me the week I moved in – and the small, bald guy. I can't remember his name but he keeps pigeons who insisted on shit-bombing my garden every chance they got. And Molly, because she rowed with me about my bonfire. Maybe I should make more of an effort when I go back. No one bar Paddy has bothered to ask after me. It makes me feel a bit crap, to be honest.

'You have a lovely road.'

'Thank you,' I say, then feel ridiculous.

She smiles. 'Anyway, I better go. Clean up your house for you. See you when you come home.'

I want to tell her to not go, but it'll sound a bit desperate. She pulls on her fluffy coat, pauses, hesitates, comes around the table and, to my surprise, wraps her arms around me. 'Thanks, Max, you're a legend.'

I reach up and clasp her arm. 'Thanks for the reminder.'

We stay like that for maybe a fraction too long. In the end she pulls away. It's a bit awkward.

'I'm glad you're OK. I'm looking forward to seeing you out of this place again.'

'Ta.' I watch her leave.

I'm in my room watching some rubbish show featuring Z-listers who are eating snakes. It relaxes me as, earlier, I'd been forced to attend some drama therapy session and if anyone I knew saw me, they'd have cracked up laughing.

Vic, it turns out, was an actor. *Is* an actor, I suppose … well, before he had the meltdown. He made us all laugh and it was good to see him actually being the best at something, though the counsellors would tell us it's not about being the best. That's something I've learned. The more you feel you have to be the best, the less you actually like yourself. I've wanted to be the best since I could remember. I don't know why.

I'm about to witness someone munching on a snake's head when Vic walks in. He doesn't even knock on my door, he's that agitated. 'Thanks a bunch,' he says, followed by, 'I hate that fucking show.'

'Thanks a bunch for what?'

'You never told me you were getting out for the weekend. I had to hear it from one of the nurses.'

'It wasn't a secret, I would have told you.' I can't believe he's upset. 'What's the problem?'

'How did you manage it?' he asks. He sits on the chair and leans forward, bony elbows resting on his bony knees. 'What magic words did you say?' Then before I can answer, he adds, 'I thought you'd be here for ages more.'

Now it's my turn to thank him.

'Sorry,' he winces, 'that came out wrong. So, how'd you manage it? I was committed too,' he admits, flushing.

How does he know I was committed? Does everyone know? Then I think about his question. How did I manage it? I remember asking Evie the same question. I don't know how I did it. I still feel like the snivelling wreck who got drunk and fell down the stairs and lost all his clients, and yet, in another way, I don't feel like getting drunk and falling down stairs anymore. 'I don't know,' I tell Vic. 'I think I just gave up fighting the crap that I was fighting. I just put it out there.'

Vic studies me. 'You were fighting crap? Like what?'

'Stuff I …' I pause. 'Stuff I couldn't face, I just faced it. I never knew it was killing me until that moment.'

'How did you find out?'

I shrug. 'When I faced it, I felt better, that's all.'

'Oh, man.' Vic groans. 'That does not help me. I am a mess, I don't know why. And the drugs aren't working.'

I'd like to tell him I'll keep in contact, I'd like to tell him I'll visit, but the truth is, though I like Vic, I don't want to be reminded of this place. This is a phase, a moment in my life, not my actual life. I want to leave and rebuild the good stuff. I want to talk to my dad, to my sister. I want to do my job with a new integrity. I don't want to encourage my clients to spill their secrets to the media just because I'm unable to spill mine. I want to publicise any new clients the way they need to be publicised. It'll be a fucking nightmare in the beginning, I suppose.

'You'll get out, Vic,' I say with conviction, because he will. 'You'll get out and d'you know what? You'll be a better actor than ever because of it.'

He nods. 'Yeah, I can really use this stuff, if anyone will ever cast me again.'

'Of course they will.'

He makes a face. 'My last show, d'you know what I did?'

'What?'

'I was in a play by this brand-new playwright. A lovely guy. Big future ahead of him. He'd actually seen me in something and written the part for me and for some, yes, insane reason I got it into my head that this play was my real life and so on opening night, when the time came for me to drink poison, I swallowed a load of floor cleaner.'

'Shit!'

'Yeah.'

It's the way he says 'yeah', like as if it's par for the course that someone should drink a load of floor cleaner onstage, that cracks me up. I start to laugh.

'Hurt like hell,' he says a little indignantly, before grinning.

'I bet it did. Bet you polished the floor with the other actors, though.'

That cracks him up.

'The other actors had to make up the end of the play as I was hauled off by a doctor.'

'Make it up?'

'And apparently it was really confusing and no one had a clue what had happened.'

'Jaysus, stop!'

'And I nearly died, apparently.'

We laugh and then realise we shouldn't actually laugh at that but we do anyway.

'Nothing like nearly dying to get you some attention,' I say, and I'm not just talking about him.

We sit in silence for a little while after that. Every so often Vic goes 'glug' and that makes us chuckle but eventually he stops and the evening light drains from the room. Vic stands up and holds out a hand. 'Good luck out there,' he says, nodding towards the window. 'I hope it goes great for you.'

'Thanks, Vic.' We shake. His grip is strong and firm.

After Vic goes, feeling only a little guilty, I google Sandy. I do it now and again, hoping to find out about her. This girl, with her fluffy coat, tiny facial scar and brown hair that looks as if it hasn't been styled in a while, has me more curious than if I'd just discovered some amazing new talent. 'Sandy Fairbrother Wexford' I key in and, just like every other time, nothing comes up. I wonder if she's lied about her surname but I don't think so. It takes a moment, but then I wonder if her first name is correct. Drumming my fingers on the keyboard, I type 'Fairbrother Wexford' and reams and reams of stuff pop up. Only it's about Melanie Fairbrother, who's a poet. I know her, actually. She's terribly private; she's the one person in this whole dumbass world of fame where not speaking to the press actually got her somewhere. As I scroll down the page looking for anything that might help discover more about Sandy, I see a piece from last June: *Ruby, Ruby, Ruby Come Home, Pleads Distraught Melanie.*

That's the title of the new Unconventionals song. Big hit. Something taps at my brain. From a while ago. Sandy liked The Unconventionals. So I click.

On the eve of the eighth anniversary of her daughter's disappearance, Melanie Fairbrother issued an appeal for her daughter to contact her. 'It's been eight years since my darling Ruby ran away. I hope wherever she is that she has finally forgiven me. That she will allow me to explain what happened the night before she went missing. To be left without any closure, any note, is a horrible place to be. All I ask for, Ruby, is a chance to explain. And if you can't give me that, just a letter to let me know you're alive. I love you.'

If anyone has any information on Ruby Fairbrother's whereabouts, please contact Rossclare Garda Station.

There is a black and white picture of Ruby Fairbrother that I blow up until it fills the screen. It's of a child. One who smiles a little too brightly. There is a tiny facial scar just about where Sandy has one. It looks like Sandy and yet it doesn't.

I click on another article and stare at another picture. And sit back and think, *Sweet Holy Jesus!*

SANDY

Max arrives home at ten. I watch from the front bedroom as he climbs out of his dad's car. His father hops out and runs around to the boot. Popping it open, he pulls out a wheelie case and starts up the driveway. Max calls him back.

I watch as his dad ignores him and Max, in frustration, strides up after him. They enter the hall and I run lightly downstairs, ready to greet them. I'm dressed in red jeans and a yellow top. It's all I have that looks decent.

I'm not sure of the protocol in any situation, never mind one like this. All I know is that something inside me is happy to have Max in the world again. I feel good when he's around, simple as that.

'Hi,' both Max and his dad say together. Pierce looks a little hassled.

'Hi.' I beam at Max.

He beams back. His dad coughs. I suddenly realise we're beaming at each other. So does Max. We both move away at the same time, he into the house, me out of it. 'I'm off to read to Molly.'

'Now?' Max looks disappointed.

'Yeah, sure you've got your dad.'

'He's going now.'

I feel sorry for Pierce, who looks a little conflicted. 'I'm not. I need to see that you're OK here,' he says.

'Dad, I'm grand.' Max sounds cross. 'Sandy's here.'

'She's going next door,' Pierce says. Then adds, 'Look,

Max, I'm your dad, and sorry, but I'm hanging on for the weekend.'

'Jesus! I'm not a kid.' Max rolls his eyes and stomps into the kitchen.

Pierce looks a bit sad. 'I'm sorry,' I whisper to him. 'He asked me to stay on. I was going to leave.'

'Not your fault,' Pierce says flatly, before he follows Max.

I had decided to give father and son a bit of space when they came back. Looks like it was a good idea. I really do not want to be caught in the crossfire. I feel a bit sorry for Pierce, though.

Charles opens the door before I even knock. 'How is the homecoming going?' he asks as I follow him down the hall.

'Great,' I lie.

'My mother got him this.' He points to a hamper sitting by the side of the stairs. It seems to be filled with food and candles. 'Don't forget to bring it in to him when you go.'

'You should bring it in to him yourself, I know he'd really appreciate it.'

'No.' He grins. 'Better if it was you.' He points upstairs. 'Go on up. Patricia is there at the moment, so brace yourself for fireworks.'

Molly is sitting in the bed, propped up by pillows, and Patricia is knitting what looks like the longest scarf ever. Both of them greet me with way more enthusiasm than I merit and I'm pretty sure it's because they're just relieved that their time together making fractious small talk has ended.

'How's the homecoming?' Patricia asks, her needles click-clacking in and out. 'I saw Pierce yesterday, he looks as if he's aged about a hundred years.'

'Well, he must have used some fantastic face cream because when I saw him, he looked great,' Molly says.

'The homecoming is going well,' I interrupt, before a spat can break out.

'Max must be thrilled with his back garden,' Patricia says. 'Have you seen it, Molly?'

'No.'

'Oh, you should,' Patricia says. 'It's all dug up and flattened and there's grass seed down, though really, it's a little early for grass seed. And I see Pierce dug up some flower beds?'

'He did,' I say.

'Such a lovely man.' Patricia loops some different-coloured wool onto her needle.

'Molly is getting out of that bed once the garden is finished,' I say. 'Aren't you?'

Molly doesn't answer.

'You don't have long now, better get your wheelchair on standby,' I tease.

'Stop!' Molly says.

'Cold feet, eh?' Patricia quips.

'I won't be getting out of this bed.'

The words and the way she says them are like a slap of a ruler on a desk.

'We shook on it.' I strive to keep it light.

'It was a joke.' Molly eyeballs me, pulling her covers up to her chin. 'Now, can you just read to me, please.'

'It wasn't a joke.' I can't let it go. I don't want Molly to have lied to me.

'Are you going to read to me or not? That is why I'm paying you.'

'Don't speak to me like that.' Hurt seeps into my voice.

Patricia, sensing tension, starts to hum.

'I only asked you to read.'

'You told me you'd get out of bed when Max's garden was done. I helped do that garden.'

'I was joking.' Each word a nail.

I want to shake her. I want to yank her out of bed and down the stairs. 'You're great at giving me advice on life.' I can't help the anger. 'It'd be better if you sorted out your own.'

'My life is sorted, thank you. I'm dying.'

'You're not dead yet but you might as well be, buried alive in this room.'

'I have my music. My books, if you'll read. I have visitors.'

'You have four walls, make-believe stories. You'd have a lot more if you went outside. You're going to die anyway, might as well be happy doing it.' I fling her own words back at her.

'How dare you!'

'I dare because you're wrong, what you're doing. And you're making your son a prisoner with you.'

'Let's calm down,' Patricia says, in a bright, false voice that would be funny if we wanted to laugh.

We both ignore her.

'Charles chose to mind me,' Molly grinds out.

'He thought you'd go out at least.' I eyeball her and she meets my gaze. I try one last time. 'Are you coming into Max's garden or not?'

The air hums. I hear Patricia inhale in what sounds like fear.

'No.'

'Then I am done.' I put the book down and walk out of the room.

Patricia calls after me, but I don't stop. I hear her berate Molly but I'm out that door with the hamper and gone.

MAX

I hear Sandy come back after hours and hours. I don't know how she could have spent so long drinking tea next door. It's almost eight o'clock, so that means she has spent a whole day drinking tea.

For some reason, which is a bit selfish, I admit, I thought she'd be with me when I came out. I thought we'd have a proper chat about stuff. Instead, I had to endure a day with my dad. It's like the title of a horror movie: *A Day With Dad*. He watched me, all the time. When I automatically reached for a beer during the soccer matches, he said that with my meds I wasn't meant to be drinking. Of course he was right and of course I should have remembered, but I hadn't and I was annoyed that he did. I slammed the beer bottle down. He said nothing,

There was other stuff too. If I went to the jacks, I think he thought I was going to top myself. When I wanted to walk to the shops to get the papers, he told me not to stress myself out by reading them.

Though it's all tempered with the delight of being at home, in my own space. I remember now that I'd bought the house because it was just the right size for me. And it was on a nice, quiet street. And though it's on the small side, it seems so big after being confined to one hospital room and I spend ages just thumbing through my CDs and DVDs and I see that Sandy has put them all in order. Some things are in the house too that I never bought – little ornaments and lots of strange metal things in the kitchen drawers that

I don't have a clue what they're for. I think they're used in cooking. I think Sandy must have bought them for me as a thank you or something. A picture stands in the upstairs landing. It shows men launching a currach on a beach. That was thoughtful. I'm going to hang it up. And packets and packets of marrowfat peas, which is weird.

When Sandy arrives back, my dad and I are watching an arts show, both of us gritting our teeth to stay calm.

'Only me,' Sandy calls.

I get up and go out to her.

'You were ages.' I lean in the doorway observing her as she takes off her fluffy coat.

A smile. 'Just thought I'd give you both time together,' she says. 'Charles and Molly sent that in as a welcome home present.'

It's a hamper full of biscuits and cooking oils and, weirdly, a scented candle. 'That was nice.'

'You should call in and thank her,' my dad says from behind. 'She'd like that, wouldn't she, Sandy?'

'Yep.'

'Thank her in the morning,' my dad goes on.

'I do know about manners, Dad,' I say, without looking at him.

Sandy's eyes flicker from me to him. Behind me, I hear Dad inhale sharply. 'I'll go to bed,' he says.

I hear him turn and then his footsteps on the stairs. I've given him my room; it's only fair, I guess.

'That was a bit harsh.' Sandy eyeballs me.

I pull a milkshake out of the fridge. Ripping off the top, I down it in three gulps. 'He won't let me breathe.'

'He's worried about you,' Sandy says mildly.

I don't answer. I know she's right.

'And you *should* thank Charles for the hamper. Tomorrow.'

I heave a sigh. 'I will, but right now, I just want to watch TV. You coming?'

'Go on.' She follows me into the TV room and sits down. 'Can we change over?' she asks. 'I hate chat shows.'

'Sure.' I toss her the remote control. 'I was just watching because Julie Winterson was on. You know the writer who fired me? Well, she's got a new agent and I wanted to see what he'd done with her.'

Sandy couldn't be less interested. She doesn't even reply, just switches to some awful reality TV show. I don't care. Just sitting in the room with her is pretty cool. Probably because it's normal.

I have missed normal.

The next day, the last day of my freedom, I get up early, before anyone else, and I sneak out of the house. I am not missing the newspapers for two days running. Plus, the act of leaving my house and walking to the shops, perhaps stopping for a coffee in High Hills, makes me feel free.

Charles is heading towards me, at least I think it's him. He has a red sports jacket on, which looks a little daring for him. From what I can remember, he usually flittered about in baggy trousers and dull polo shirts. I know he spots me because he pretends that something across the other side of the road catches his interest and crosses over. He's a weird guy. He's younger than me but appears way older.

'Charles?' I call.

He freezes, before turning around comically. 'Yes?' Anxious.

He is scared of me, I realise with something akin to shame. Scared. Of. Me. I cross towards him and he straightens up.

'I thought it was you,' I say, 'I just want to reiterate my apology for the night of the bonfire.'

'I'm glad you're OK.' He smiles a bit. 'And thank you for allowing your garden to be done, it meant a lot to my mother and Tar.'

'I should have done it a long time ago,' I say. 'I was just being a prick.'

'You were, I suppose.'

'And I'm sorry for yelling at your mother and for playing loud music and for shouting at some of your relations when they visited you.'

'Yes, they've never come back,' he manages a smile, 'so you did us a favour.'

I smile too. 'And whatever else I did that I can't remember, sorry about that too.'

'Forgotten.' We smile briefly and I turn to go.

'Is Sandy OK?' he asks.

'Sandy? What happened Sandy?' It's like his question chokeholds me.

'Nothing.' He flaps a hand. 'My mother was a bit sharp with her yesterday.'

'How?' I want to kill the old bat again now.

'I think she was trying to coax my mother out of bed and my mother lost it with her. Honestly, I could kill that woman sometimes but the MND got there first.' He smiles bleakly at me and I feel sorry for him. 'Tell Sandy my mother feels bad about it.'

'Will do.' I turn to go.

'Thanks for the apology,' he calls after me.

We move on.

SANDY

I hardly slept all night. It's hard putting on a show for Max and his dad while all the time I feel like crying over Molly. I had no idea how important it had become for me to see her out and about. I can't just go back today as if nothing happened. It took so much for me to talk to her, debate with her, open up to her about my life and then, suddenly, when it didn't suit her, without any warning, she just shuts me down as if I'm nothing. There's an ache in the middle of my chest now, though it's an ache that's been growing steadily since I got here. For years my anger pushed all my other feelings aside, the ache of loss only surfacing briefly when Clara and I would stay in our favourite family homes, but living here softened me around the edges again, which makes it easier to get hurt.

I sit on the couch nursing some tea, trying not to wince at the pain in my arm. That bloody hamper was pretty heavy yesterday. I must have carted it about for hours before I went back to Max's.

Pierce paces anxiously between kitchen and hall, his mobile phone clamped to his ear. I don't think he's even aware he's doing it. He wouldn't sit and have lunch with me. He's worried because Max is gone. I've tried telling him that I didn't think Max would do anything silly, but it was no use. He is distraught. He'd woken up and found Max had left the house. There had been no note from him.

'He could have left a note,' he keeps saying.

'He probably just didn't think.'

'When his mother died, I swore to her that I'd mind the kids. I haven't done a great job. Max is sick and his sister barely talks to him. Where is he?' He jabs the phone again.

'Max is great.' I say. 'This is just a glitch.' It barely registers.

Finally, I go and sit in the kitchen away from him, leave him to his slowly growing panic. If Max doesn't come back soon, Pierce will fall apart, I think. I wonder if my mother was like that when I left and I banish the thought. 'Will I go and look for him?' I call out.

'That's an idea.' He joins me in the kitchen. His eyes flit across me. 'I'll go, though. I have a car. You'll give me a ring if he comes back, yeah?'

'OK.' I watch as the man frantically searches for his jacket before putting it on upside down. He's in the middle of righting it when the door opens and Max enters, beaming.

'How's things?' He smiles at me.

Anger tempered with enormous relief floods through me. I thumb to his father, who has paused, his jacket half on.

'Max,' he breathes, and his voice is a whisper. Then he sits down.

'Hi.' Max barely looks at him. 'I got the papers, if anyone wants a read.' He passes me to throw the papers on the table. Then he takes bread from a press and, folding a slice in half, he starts to eat it. 'Oh, and I was talking to—. What?' he asks, suddenly aware of our silence.

'Your dad was worried, Max.'

'Not at all,' his dad says hastily.

'You were,' I say firmly. Turning to Max, I add, 'You could have answered your phone.'

Max throws me a funny look. 'There is no need for worry,' he says. 'And my phone is dead.'

He's lying. I know by the way his eyes don't meet mine.

'I was just concerned,' Pierce says. 'That's all. You left no note.'

'I wasn't aware I had to leave notes lying around.' Max is belligerent. 'I told you already, Dad, stop babying me. Jesus!'

'You could have left a note,' I say. 'It would have saved a lot of stress.'

'I am not a kid,' Max grinds out.

'No, you're an adult, act like one.' I don't even know why I'm saying this. I think it's because I want him to be the Max I want him to be.

'At least I came home, not like you. Did you leave a note?' His words sting like a whip.

'Did you?' Then he says, almost maliciously, 'Ruby?'

I can't speak.

'Did you really think I wouldn't find out? Do you think I'm that stupid? Well, did you leave a note?'

'What's going on?' That's Pierce.

'Arsehole.' My voice cracks.

'Let's not argue.' Pierce positions himself between us. 'You're back and you're safe and that's good.'

'You know nothing about me.' I ignore Pierce.

'I know who you are.'

'Which means nothing.' We glare at each other. He looks suddenly upset. I wonder how I look. 'Nothing.' My voice wobbles.

'This is all my fault, Max,' his dad butts in.

'Well, yeah, that goes without saying,' Max says. 'All of this is your fault.'

I watch as Pierce recoils under the words. It's like he's trying to reach Max and he just can't.

'You are a selfish bastard, Max,' I gulp out.

Both men turn to look at me. I push by them and walk out of the house.

The street is deserted. It's cold but I can't go back in for my coat. I duck my head and start to walk, my arms wrapped around me. I try to put as much distance between Max and me as I can. How could he have known who I was and said nothing, only to bring it up to taunt me? I thought we were friends. I liked him. Maybe Molly was right. Maybe he is nothing but a horrible man. Maybe the coffee-buying and the moments of gentleness belong to the crazy part of him. Maybe my fears are right. Maybe I liked him because he too shrugged off his home and his parent. Maybe—

'Hey!' I hear him behind me, running to catch up with me.

I start to walk faster.

'Aw, Jaysus, Sandy, come on,' he calls.

'Ruby,' I snap.

'You'll always be Sandy to me. Come on, please. I was a shit, I know. Please.'

'Go away.' My voice cracks.

I hear him closing in. I start to run.

He catches up, runs past and comes to stand in front of me. We face each other, panting. His face changes. 'Hey,' he says softly, reaching out a hand. 'Hey, don't cry.'

I step away. 'I'm not crying.'

He says nothing.

And I realise that I am. I have not cried in years, but now tears are running down my face like water from a burst pipe. I scrub my eyes. 'All you had to do was leave a note, one fucking note, and you didn't. And all you do is …' I am blabbering and not making sense and half-sentences are falling from my lips. I don't know what's happening to me. And then, something inside me breaks. I stumble away from Max but he catches me. 'I've got you.' He pulls me in close, to the front of his body. 'Come on.'

'No, leave me!' I try to push him.

'I can't,' he says into my hair. 'I can't leave you. I'm sorry, OK? I'm sorry.'

Somehow, Max leads me to his dad's car. I'm vaguely aware of his dad handing over the keys. Max straps me in and wraps a smelly rug about my shoulders. He fires the ignition and drives away.

He ignores me and my tears and, after a bit, I stop crying, not because I want to but because I can't cry anymore. I feel washed out. I wonder where we are going. At first I think that he's driving aimlessly. But after a bit, he parks the car facing a beach and, though the sky has greyed over, people are still splashing around and walking dogs and throwing frisbees.

I risk a glance at him. He doesn't seem aware that I've stopped crying.

'Welcome home, Max,' he says wryly.

I hiccup out a half-laugh, half-sob.

He turns to me. 'I'm sorry,' he says. 'That was not the way I planned on telling you that I knew who you were.'

'You were right, though. I can't lecture you. I'm as bad.' I blink hard.

'I just lost it with my dad. I'm embarrassed to be treated like a baby by him, especially in front of you.'

'He cares about you. You're so lucky.'

He pulls a packet of mints from his pocket and offers me one. I shake my head and he pops one in his mouth. After a bit, he says softly, 'Did no one care about you?'

I turn away. He crunches the mint and swallows before saying, 'You crying just now reminded me of me when I cried that day in the hospital.' His voice catches and I'm forced to look at him. He's staring at the view of the sea out the window. 'Whatever it is,' he goes on quietly, 'it can't be worse than what happened me.'

His profile is beautiful, but I know now why Molly called him sad. 'Like you,' I say softly, 'I left because of a lie.' As he turns to me, I add, 'And now the guilt is killing me. I saw your dad, how upset he was, and thought of my mother.'

'The poet.'

'Yep.'

His smile is crooked. 'You can burden me with it. I'm much better now.' A sardonic lift of an eyebrow. 'Can't you tell?'

I love this man's dark humour. And he does have a calmness in him that wasn't there when I visited him first. It wasn't there when he brought me the coffees. His gaze is steady. I want to be like that. I might appear calm – you get like that when you sit all day – but inside, everything churns. Even though I'm safe in Max's at night, my shoulders ache sometimes, just from squeezing them up hard. My stomach cramps. Maybe if I tell him, all that will go.

'You were right earlier,' I say, my voice not quite steady, 'I wasn't concerned about anyone when I left home.'

He says nothing.

'I was angry and hurt and I just wanted to get back at her.'

'Back at your mother?'

'Yep.'

'What did she do?'

And with that question, images pop. Like a flash in my brain. All the things she did. Her arms around me as she read me stories when I was young, the songs, the games, the funny little poems. The way she educated me, giving me broad knowledge threaded through with dire warnings, her awful cooking, the concern for me when I was sick, treasure hunts, all the books she bought me. The bizarre hiding games, the tests, the way she told me she loved me every day.

I tell him everything, the revelations pouring from me like my tears earlier. Only I don't cry. My voice is flat. But I'm crying inside. 'She did care but it was all wrong.'

'*She* was all wrong,' Max says.

'But I've destroyed her.' I stumble to a stop.

Max looks a little battered. 'Her lies destroyed her, not you.'

'I should have thought things through.'

'You were a kid,' he says, and the parallels between us are not lost on either of us. Something shifts inside me. Tiny. But it allows some lightness to penetrate.

'I think,' Max says eventually, 'you need to go back, tell her you're alive and confront her. Just like I have to.'

Maybe I do, I think. First Molly said it, then Pierce and now Max. And I trust Max the most.

'You need to find out what the story is with this Ivy person. With your dad. You're an adult now, your mother is out and about. Maybe the time is right.'

Part of me wants to believe that. Part of me is terrified. 'What if knowing is worse than not knowing?'

He quirks an eyebrow and I have to smile a bit. 'OK, not knowing is pretty shit,' I admit, and he smiles. Then I add, 'I might get trapped down there again.'

'As opposed to what? Sleeping under a hedge and seeing no one?' He offers a grin. 'I hate to break it to you but you didn't change much about your life when you ran away.' He opens his door. 'Let's walk.'

'My eyes—'

'Are grand, come on.'

Side by side we walk along the promenade. The breeze is strong and it blows my hair back. Max and I dip our heads against the wind. He takes his jacket off and wraps it around me. It smells of him and I breathe in his scent. It's impossible to talk so we just walk in the clear, bracing air. By the time we've reached the end and turn back, I feel better. The breeze is at our backs and the change in direction makes the air feel warmer.

'So what now?' Max asks. He makes a face. 'I have to write to Imelda, I have to talk to Paddy. I'm dreading it but I'll do it because I reckon it'll make me feel better. What about you?'

His comment about my life under a hedge being pretty much the same as my life before I ran away has hit home. 'I've made a mess of everything.'

'So do something,' Max says. 'Your choice.'

And bizarrely, I think of Oscar Wilde. My choice how I continue my story. 'Yeah, maybe,' I say.

Max winks. 'I'm indebted to you,' he says.

'Why?'

'Because,' he lopes a companionable arm about my shoulder, 'you've made me think I'm a really nice guy.'

'I have?'

'Me finding Ruby Fairbrother? This would be a fucking scoop,' he grins down at me, 'and I don't want to sell it to a newspaper.'

I love that he can make us both laugh. I love his arm on my shoulders.

MAX

When we get back, my dad has left a note: *Gone to see a friend. I'll collect the car in the morning to bring you back. I hope Sandy is OK.*

That makes things a whole lot easier. On the way home in the car, I'd promised Sandy that I would google her mother for her, that I would find out what I could from all the news sites I had access to. I've told her I will help her in any way I can. I have no fucking clue what I'm doing. My head is reeling. I only hope I don't give her a bum steer, though she seems a lot calmer and I like the way she smiles at me. As if I've saved her, like she saved me. I think I love her. I must, because I haven't run a mile. I am doing all the right things. I can't tell her that I love her, though. I'm not exactly a good bet for anyone.

And she's not Sandy. She's Ruby. This is not good for my head.

Though I like that I can help her. I like that a lot.

We head into the office and I see that my laptop is on. Sandy says it's been on since I left. I let her sit in the chair and I pull up another one.

The only pictures of Melanie online are ones of her when she was younger. Site after site shows the same picture over and over. And then, after about an hour, just when I've given up, I find a tiny autobiographical note on a site of poets. Sandy leans over my shoulder as I click onto it and my body tenses, hyper-aware of her proximity. She smells of the sea and salt and warmth.

'Here we go.' My voice trembles a little. 'Melanie Fairbrother, Irish poet, was born in Galway. The second eldest of three children, she was brought up by her mother when her father drowned in a fishing accident when she was nine. At twelve years old, she lost her brother, when he fell from a roof. She has famously said that the randomness of life and the way it can change is what informs her poetry. She is married with one child.'

'I know more about her from that than I ever did,' Sandy says wryly.

'I can keep looking, you go and watch TV or whatever,' I offer.

'You don't mind?'

'This is my life, baby. This is what I love.' I'm not sure that reassures her but she goes and I keep looking. I scroll through pages and pages of newsprint regarding Sandy's disappearance. I look again at a picture of Sandy that was used at the time. She was a pretty girl. The last few years have robbed her of that attractiveness, but to me she's even more beautiful now.

There is a photo of Sandy's mother with her sister, who has her arm around her, pleading for news of her niece. Sandy's mother has her face half-hidden while her Aunt Susan, that's the name on the picture, is boldly staring forward. It looks like they made up.

I search for reports of Sandy's grandfather's death, but it was so long ago, there is nothing on it. There is nothing about her uncle's death either.

I go into the TV room and tell Sandy that her mother must be the most private person in Ireland. I tell her I'll help her whatever way I can.

'Thanks,' she says. 'You're such a good man.'

I smile, and she bends toward me and kisses my cheek. I catch her hand and stare into her eyes. My heart is rocketing. She gives my hand a squeeze and pulls away.

'Anything,' I say, as she moves off.

Much, much later, just as dawn in peeping in, she peers around the door of the office. Her hair is messed up and she's wearing a long T-shirt. Her legs go on forever. 'I don't want to be on my own,' she says.

I think I'm dreaming, but I'm not. I let her in beside me and she curls up, her back to my front. My chin rests on her head. We stay like that for ages. I have to battle the urge to kiss her. I remember something I should have told her earlier. 'Charles says you had a bit of a spat with his mother?'

'Yep.' She sounds sad. 'It's another reason I can't sleep.'

'What happened?'

'She promised she'd get out of bed when your garden was finished and then she reneged on it.'

I say nothing. I think she's better off in bed, the old bat.

'And she was horrible about it. And I was horrible back.'

'You, horrible? Never!'

Sandy says nothing to that.

'Charles says to call in, if you like.'

She shrugs.

'Is that the best you can do for a job, Sandy? Is there nothing else?'

She is quiet for ages before finally whispering, 'I had a few jobs before this. None as good.'

'Like?'

'I delivered leaflets, which I hated, and then I worked as a sandwich board.'

I stifle a chuckle. 'What did you advertise?'

'Fortune telling.'

'Did you leave when you discovered there was no future in it?'

I feel her shake with a laugh. After a bit, she goes on, 'I became a cleaner and I met Clara, she was my friend.' She pauses and inhales and says in a rush, 'We stole, Max. From shops. We stole things and sold them on. It kept us alive.'

'Did you steal the picture on the landing, the fisherman one?'

'No, that was there when I came. I haven't stolen in ages.'

Shit. I obviously bought that picture so. 'Is that why you lost your job?'

Then she tells me about their scheme of living in vacant houses. How her and Clara slept in kids' bedrooms on the floor and pretended that it was their house. My heart kind of breaks for her.

'Do you think I'm a bad person?' she asks.

'Nope, I think you're great.' I can't help it, I kiss the top of her head.

She says nothing after that and then she falls asleep.

SANDY

Max is up before me the next morning. He was the perfect gentleman the previous night when I couldn't sleep, his arms about me, his breath on my neck, anchoring me in the present. It's funny the things you tell people in the dark. I'm glad he knows about my past and still likes me.

I hear him upstairs and, as I walk into the hall, he comes down, taking the steps two at a time.

'You'll fall.' I smile. I could look at him all day.

'Nah, it's only when I drink that I do that.' He laughs.

'That's not funny.'

'How do you know? You weren't here.' He smiles and I think how great he is. What's more, he doesn't even realise it. Despite his successes, he's got this inferiority complex going on. Lying beside him on the sofa last night was my best night away from home.

'I'm making coffee.' He strides before me into the kitchen and switches on the kettle. 'Want one?'

'Thanks.' I sit at the table and watch as he fills two cups with instant and pours hot water into each. He puts milk on the table and hands me a mug. Then he sits down beside me.

'You OK?' He nudges me with his elbow.

'Yeah.'

'You know I won't tell anyone?'

'I do.'

'Because I'm not that unscrupulous. I'm not. I'd never—'

'I know,' I say, cutting him off.

He smiles at me again and I feel like a cat in the sun. Then the look in his eyes changes. I squirm a little, uncomfortable with the scrutiny. 'What?'

'I'll go with you to meet her,' he says then. 'If you want.'

'My mother?'

He nods.

'You would do that?'

'I have to guard my guardian angel, don't I?'

It's a joke but it touches me something rotten. And without thinking, I lean in and kiss him, very softly, on the lips. I zing at the contact. It's as if he senses it. He cups my head in his hands and kisses me harder. Oh God, I want him. I think I've wanted him from the very first 'hi'.

His hand snakes down my body and we stand up, still kissing. The palm of his hand rubs my lower back, pressing me into him.

He pulls me closer, one hand cupping my head. I slide my hands into the back pocket of his jeans. It feels so right.

He pulls away and looks down at me. His eyes burn into mine. He's just about to say something when his dad arrives back.

He gives me a wink that turns my knees to jelly and lets me go.

Ten minutes after Max leaves, the bell rings. I have the radio on and some guy is singing about forever love and I'm smiling and humming, trying to catch the tune as I walk to the front door. Without thinking, I pull it open and it's Molly, looking nervous, Charles grinning widely behind her.

Molly and I stare at each other for what seems like an age. She's heavily made-up, like she's wearing a mask against the world. I wonder if Charles put the make-up on for her. Her hair is in a bun. She's wearing a bright blue jacket. Finally, she speaks, her words coming with difficulty, her eyes alive with determination to say them. 'I'm sorry.'

And that's all it takes.

With a half-sob, I fling my arms about her.

'It's OK,' she says. 'It's OK.'

I bring her into Max's garden and wheel her to the centre. She takes a great gulp of air, sucking it deep into her lungs. I touch her shoulder. 'Guess it's my turn to make the coffee now.'

Molly smiles, reaches back and clasps my hand. I dip my head and hug her briefly, and she closes her eyes. After a second, I turn and make for the kitchen.

Charles follows me. 'It took a lot of courage for her to get out of that bed.'

'I know.'

'She thinks a lot of you.' He sounds so emotional that I have to turn away. 'She said that apologising to you was more important to her than hiding away.'

I think of my mother. Trying to find me must have taken massive courage too. And suddenly my decision to go home is made.

MAX

When I get back to the hospital, Ian asks me how my time away went. I tell him it was good.

The doctors ask me. I say the same.

If I tell them that my world has suddenly gone from the chalky grey of the sea on a bad day to all the dazzle of the Med, they'd probably lock me up. So I just say it went well, thanks very much. And they believe me, because they tell me that I'm free to go in a week. They think I'm ready.

And I am. I'm ready to take on the world. Take on Sandy's mother if I have to, though, I admit, the thought panics me. I probably shouldn't have suggested it. It had seemed perfectly sensible at the time but what do I know? I have to repeatedly tell myself that I am not Ian. That despite a few months' counselling, I do not have a clue how to solve other people's problems. But there is no other solution that I can see for Sandy. Mind you, is it about what I see or what she sees? Should I even tell her what to do? I am not her. And she is not me.

Fuck. If I keep thinking like this, I'll go mad again. But I will do it for her. I'll do it because that kiss we shared told me everything I need to know about us. No matter how hard I try, I can't help smiling. I talk to her on the phone and we make each other laugh.

She comes in to visit me on Wednesday. I watch her as her eyes search me out in the canteen, that turn of her head, the way our eyes lock and the smooth way she zig-zags in and out between the tables. I watch with a grin that I think might split my face as she sits opposite me and asks how I'm doing.

'Fine,' I say. 'I'll be out this time next week, ready to terrorise my neighbours.'

She smiles, though I thought it was a funnier joke than that. Something in me tenses, like a cat on high alert. We're not smooth the way we were. I throw out a line, she picks it up, but today, she's not biting. Her smile comes a fraction too late. She didn't try to kiss me. Her eyes look like they've left her already. Finally she catches my hand. My poor heart doesn't know whether to celebrate or mourn. I can't fathom her expression. 'Max,' she goes all serious, 'I can't thank you enough for everything. I'd no idea when you bought me that first coffee that we'd end up such ...' she pauses, 'good friends.'

My heart decides to sink. 'Yeah. Me neither.' I cover her hand with my other one.

She studies me, head to one side, but she says nothing. A hole opens up inside me.

'What?'

'I've decided to go back to Wexford.'

That's not so bad. I gather myself. 'I'll drive you down at the weekend.'

She looks suddenly awkward. 'Thanks, but no.'

'It's no bother. I—'

'You have to look after you,' she says, and she sounds firm, as if she's thought it all out. 'I can sort myself out.'

'But—'

'You are going to stay here and get better and write to Imelda and do everything you have to.'

What is going on here? Is she leaving me? 'I can do that anytime.'

'No. Your dad worries about you and—'

'Fuck my dad.'

'He's not my type.'

The quick wit makes me smile despite my scrabbling around for something to say. 'He doesn't matter. I want—'

'He *does* matter.' She squeezes my hand. 'You owe it to him to sort yourself out. And when you do, you might think differently about stuff.'

'About what stuff?'

An age. Finally she says, 'Us.'

And there it is. She's had a think, she doesn't want someone like me in her life. The hurt slides in. 'I don't have to think about us.'

'That's what you say now.'

I'd thought more of her. 'I know what I want. Do you?'

She pauses for the longest time. 'When you get back, I'll be gone. I'm leaving Saturday morning.'

'No!' My shout makes people look. I lower my voice. 'Please.'

'I'll ring you. I promise.'

'Don't go.'

'I have to. It's thanks to you and your dad that I'm doing this. I promise I'll ring.' Then she lets my hand go and we look at each other and I turn away.

SANDY

I've hurt Max but there was no other way. I'd turned it over and over in my head and even though he might have accepted me going alone to Wexford, the fact that I'm leaving without him being around to say goodbye probably strikes him as cold. Truth is, if he'd been around, I couldn't have refused his help and I have to. I know that now.

I know because Pierce is up the wall over him. He'd come over on Tuesday to plant some flowers and, as I'd scooped out the holes in the soil, he'd asked me if I was OK now.

'I'm getting there.'

'Good.' He smiled and popped a blue flower into one of the holes I'd dug.

'I'm going home.'

He nodded, didn't seem surprised. 'It's the right thing to do.'

'Max said he'd come with me.'

The silence went on a little too long and when I glanced over at Pierce, I saw that he'd frozen just as he was planting another flower. His head was dipped and for a moment I thought he'd hurt himself. He turned to me, made to say something, then stopped and turned back to his planting.

'What?' I asked.

He sighed. 'Sandy, Max has a lot of stuff going on too.' He sounded wretched.

'I know,' I said.

'He can't help you and help himself.'

His words sank in, stinging, like salt on an open wound.

'Do you know what I mean?'

'Yes.'

'Max isn't fully right yet,' Pierce said. 'He doesn't need stress.' His voice cracked. 'He was in a really bad way, Sandy.'

'I get it.'

'Good.' He flashed me a bleak smile. 'I'm sorry. But I had to say it.'

'You did. I know.'

And we left it at that.

On Friday, I pack my haversack, feeling sad with each little item I stow away. It's as if I'm leaving Max's place bit by little bit. Tonight will be my last night under this roof, in this bare, unloved spare room. I peek in at Max's room and am caught by a faint whiff of his aftershave. I hope he likes the fact that I've rearranged all his CDs and DVDs. I stand in the kitchen and remember our kiss, which we never managed to talk about afterwards. I suppose we both thought we'd have time when he got out.

Tomorrow, I will get up and walk out the door. I won't look back. I will miss this house and its cosy rooms and bright kitchen. I'll miss the lovely garden Pierce has created. I'll miss the sounds of the street and the way I can look across into the window of the house on the opposite side of the road. I wonder if coming into Rossclare tomorrow will feel like I'm coming home. I hope it does, to help fill the ache I already feel at leaving this place.

The only thing left is to read for Molly for the last time. I owe her so much. I have money now to go home. I have fallen in love with fairy tales again. I've learned that my opinion matters. She has taught me that. Today, because it's sunny, I'll read to her in her back garden.

Charles answers the door. He smiles at me. 'Last day, eh?'

I nod.

'How are you feeling?'

I don't have the words to describe it but something in my expression causes him to pull me into an embrace. He smells of coffee and smoke. 'I wish you the best.' He holds me at arm's length. 'Is Pierce bringing you down?'

'Pierce has enough to worry about.'

'D'you want a lift? Save you the bus fare? I can bring you?'

'But Molly?'

'Patricia will stay with me for the couple of hours,' Molly says, wheeling herself up behind him. 'Charles is a free man now I'm up and about.'

'You sure?'

'Yes.' Molly nods. 'I'll pop up now and ask her. She's so delighted I'm out of the bed, she'll agree to anything.'

Charles smiles and turns back to me. 'Well?'

'Then that'd be great, Charles.'

'Come over later for some dinner,' Molly says. 'No reading today, just a nice evening.' She doesn't say it, but it'll be our last.

'I'll ask Patricia now,' Molly says, and Charles, with a

smile at me, manoeuvres her chair onto the ramp, locks their front door and begins pushing her up the driveway.

I follow them out and watch as they move up the road. One of the neighbours I haven't met gives a shriek of delight as she sees Molly and exclaims how it's been too long.

I wonder what my mother will do when she sees me.

Part Three

RUBY

Charles drives me to the outskirts of Wexford. He plays easy jazz music all the way, tapping his finger on the steering wheel in time to it. We barely talk, but it doesn't feel strained or anything. I really do think he's enjoying his new freedom from the house. It's only when I instruct him to pull into a garage on the edge of my old hometown that I angle myself towards him on the seat. 'I have a confession to make.'

'Go on.'

'I'm Ruby Fairbrother.'

For a second the name means nothing to him and then something sparks behind his eyes. 'The poet's daughter?'

'Yes.'

More memories. 'The one we were discussing that day—'

'Yes.'

An anguished face. 'I didn't say anything too awful, did I?'

'No. Julian said he thought I was murdered.'

'He'll be glad you're not.'

I laugh a little. 'As I am.'

He smiles back awkwardly, before shaking his head. 'Jesus, Sandy … Ruby.'

'It'll be on the news. Tell Molly for me.'

'Why didn't you tell her yourself?'

'I liked being Sandy.'

A small smile, sort of sad. 'You've been missing for eight years.'

'I know.'

'Do you need anyone with you?'

I'm taken aback by his kindness. In the last few years, it's been such a rare thing. I would love someone, but it wouldn't be fair to Max. 'Max already offered and I refused him too. I have to do this on my own.'

'OK.' He pulls a piece of crumpled-up paper from his pocket and scribbles on it before handing it to me. 'Here's my number. Call me about anything.'

'Charles—'

'Anything.'

'Thank you.' I pocket his number.

'D'you want me to drive you the rest of the way?'

'No, thanks.' I need the space to think, though I've done nothing but think since I made my decision. I hop out of the car and slam the door.

Charles raises his hand in a wave and then, as I start to walk, he drives off.

MAX

It's the emptiness that gets me. The minute I walk in the door that first Saturday of freedom, I know she's gone. Though she'd told me, I had somehow expected her to have changed her mind. My dad dumps my case in the hall and strolls into the kitchen to fill the kettle.

'I thought your friend Sandy would be here to say hi,' he calls. Then, he adds, 'There's a note on the table for you.' He comes back out and hands me a white sealed envelope. I know it's from her. For the first time I see what her writing is like. It's big and round, with generous loops and swirls. I stare at the envelope, afraid of opening it. I want to nurse my heart in private. I should never have kissed her. I know she's gone but I can't read it just yet.

I watch through a daze as my dad makes me tea. He doesn't seem to notice my sudden lack of interest in anything he has to say. He talks about his fishing and his boats, his friends, the fact that Maya is talking about getting married and of how it's about time. That fella of hers is dragging his feet over it all.

I drink my tea to please him, I eat a few biscuits. 'Dad,' I finally say, interrupting him mid-flow as he expounds on the lack of tact of his future son-in-law, 'I'm going upstairs for a rest. Set yourself up in the spare room if you're staying tonight.'

'I can stay longer if you like.' Then a thought hits him. 'Is Sandy not in that room?'

'No, she's gone.'

I don't hang about for his questions.

Dear Max

I started this letter about a million times. There is so much I want to say, all of it important, so I don't know which piece to put first. I suppose a 'thank you' is the best thing to go with. Thanks for your friendship, for your total lack of judgement, for your sense of humour, for your house, your life (for a bit) – you have a wonderful life – and for making me do something about my own life.

Your advice is spot on. Well, let's face it, you're the therapy king ☺ By the time you get this, like I said, I'll be in Wexford. It's time now for both of us to sort our lives out. Look after yourself. Write to Imelda, see your old friends, talk to your dad. Get your real life back.

Once, long ago, my granny told me that my mother made buns and put salt in instead of sugar. She baked them anyway because she couldn't find the salt among all the flour to take it out. I'm like that, Max. I have no clue what normal is, everything about me is all mixed up together and I only find out I've fucked up when I make mistakes. You don't need that right now. You don't need me right now.

You need your dad and all the people who know who you are.

I'll ring you, I promise. We'll talk.

It has been brilliant knowing you.

Your friend – Love Sandy

I have to read it a couple of times. I'm like that, it takes a bit for things to sink in. It sounds as if she's saying goodbye. As if she's saying that we're both too messed up to ever make each other happy. Thanks, Max, see you around. And I'm not sure I get all the baking stuff.

I read the letter again. I lie on my bed and close my eyes. I wouldn't mind a drink.

RUBY

I know that once I go back, everything will change. But I think that if I continue to stay away, I could end up like Max, full of so much regret that it'd follow me around.

Max. He's probably got my letter by now. I picture him reading it, hoping he'll understand I've done it because I want the best for him. If he hadn't been losing it, he might never have spotted me sitting so still on the bench that day. When he gets back to himself, he might not see me once more. Pierce is right, Max needs to find himself first. I'm not going to pressure him to stay with me because of a kiss. I'll remember his kiss as long as I live. The girl he falls for will be such a lucky girl, I only hope she treats him well.

It's late August and as I walk from the garage and into the town, no one gives me a second glance. I'm wearing tattered jeans and a green T-shirt. I washed my hair and it hangs shapelessly around my face like a veil. All the better to peer out at the world. I've got my white jacket on too, the one Max likes.

Max. He keeps popping into my head.

It is odd seeing the town in daylight. I only ever saw it after dark. In daytime, it's more colourful, though the shabbiness of some shops is more pronounced. And it has changed. Little restaurants have sprung up. On any other day, the aroma of food as I walk past would be delicious. Today, I have no appetite. I've barely eaten since last weekend. The sooner I do this, the better I'll be.

'Why don't you just do the easy thing and leave it?' The thought worms its way in, a little insidious whisper. But in the long run, it wouldn't be the easy thing.

I pass McMahon's pub, where Louis and his band played. That hasn't changed. Posters for bands are still plastered all over the doorway – new, upcoming bands, bands hoping to emulate The Unconventionals. Beside the pub is the newsagent's. No change there. And then, across the road, I spot the small laneway that leads to the beach and time peels back and I see Louis and me, hip to hip, strolling down it, stopping to kiss every now and again.

Someone bangs into me and moves on. I tear my gaze away. I walk on, past the bookshop and the library, past another restaurant, past the dry cleaners and the gift shop. Finally, just at the top of the town, I turn and start the two-mile walk towards home.

Forty minutes later, I arrive at the end of the lane. Someone has tarmacked the path up to the house and trees align the edge. It looks very … civilised.

Something inside me stills. My mind empties. I'm here now. I'm going to do this. There is no point in being afraid anymore. This is what is going to happen, and after that, I have no control. I start to walk towards the house, which comes into view once I turn the bend. It looks the same, a squat building with dormer windows. The walls are whitewashed and hard to look at in the bright afternoon sun. The door is still red. A large tabby cat sunbathes in a patch of sunlight. He looks up at me lazily as I approach. I wonder if my mother sees me. I wonder will she answer the door if I knock. Will she know who I am?

It's so quiet; I'd forgotten the utter hush of living out here.

I'm almost at the house when someone emerges from behind the cottage. I can't quite see who it is, but the person pauses and puts their hand to their forehead to block out the sun, all the better to peer at me. Then the woman – because it's a woman, judging by the slightness of her build – straightens up and drops her hand and stands staring at me as I approach.

It is *her*.

I stop walking. The two of us gaze at each other. She makes to take a step towards me and pauses, unsure. I remain quite still. It's weird, it's as if I'm poised on the point of a pin where all the force comes together. Seeing her, in the flesh, after all this time has passed, is numbing. Maybe too many emotions are vying to be heard. I try to say something but my voice won't work.

And I think she knows it's me. Or else she thinks she's going mad. She stares some more before turning away abruptly. I swallow hard. Then she turns back and stares some more before rapidly coming towards me. She's wearing a loose white dress and open-toed sandals. Her hair is long and grey. Her walk is urgent. She's panting. I couldn't move even if I wanted to.

She stops right in front of me. We stare at each other. Hazel eyes with a blue patch search mine. She sways a little on her feet. 'Ruby?'

I nod.

'Ruby?' she says again, moving a step closer. 'Ruby? My Ruby?'

I wish so much to be detached. To be above this emotion. But she's my mother. I see her once again playing with me, laughing with me. 'Yes,' I whisper. 'I came back.'

She doesn't do anything. Her face is white. Finally, 'Can I …' She reaches out and her hand paws the air. 'Can I touch you?'

I move a step closer and she catches hold of my arm. Tears spark her eyes. She bows over as if she's been punched.

'Mam?'

'Ruby,' she whispers. 'I can't …' Her mouth moves but nothing comes out.

I touch her hand, which still rests on my arm, and her eyes meet mine. Then she pulls me into her and holds me fiercely, without uttering a word.

MAX

The sense of powerlessness sweeps through me like wind in a valley. Sandy is gone and I have no way to find her. No way to contact her. And even if I could, how can I barge in on her now? Like Shane, she's moving away and I can't reach out and catch hold of her.

My dad calls up that he's going to get the paper and when the door slams after him, I sneak downstairs and try to source a bottle of wine. I know I have quite a large stash hidden away in the back of a cupboard in my office.

Opening up the press, I pull out a load of junk. Only it doesn't all look like junk, there are a few nice ornaments that I don't remember buying. That's a bit worrying. I decide not to worry though and, shoving my arm in, right to the back of the press, I try to locate some wine. It takes me longer than I expected to feel the neck of a bottle. Pulling it out, I see that it's been opened and that over half of it has been drunk. I unscrew the top and the stench of gone-off wine hits me like a hammer. I put the bottle aside and scrabble about again. There were way more bottles than this. Surely Sandy didn't drink them all. I can feel nothing else. No booze at all. Where did it go?

Bang! I see myself surrounded by booze, drinking it back like water, popping pills, music playing loudly. I see my descent into oblivion and then I see the woman, Imelda, standing at the top of the stairs and coming for me. And I run. And fall like a damaged kite.

I drank it. I drank everything that one night. And I was about to do it again. What kind of a thick am I? Stupid. Stupid. Stupid. If there is one thing I should know, it's that I should never drink again. I sit on the floor for a bit, shaking at the fact that I almost succumbed to the pull of oblivion. I can't let that happen. I remember what Ian said: the things I can't control, I can't control, so forget about them. The things I can, do something about them. Sandy's letter said that I need to get myself in order. I need to write to Imelda, make peace with Paddy, maybe go home for a bit, reconnect. Maybe if I do these things, and do them properly, I'll at least have a life. Maybe one without Sandy, but a life nonetheless. It's better than drinking and whinging about all the stuff I can't do. I rub my hands over my face and stand up. I feel like I've just avoided a car crash.

The front door bell goes, and then the bell rings again. Finally the letterbox gets a rattle and a high, girlish voice calls, 'Sandy, Sandy, it's me. Open up, would you?'

It's someone for Sandy? I almost run into the hall. I pull the door open and see an urchin on my doorstep. That's the word that best fits a girl skinnier than an Olympic marathon runner with spiky hair and a nose ring. Her face is spotty and she has a chin which juts out, looking for a fight. She's carrying a tattered haversack, with a rolled up sleeping bag. Her coat is cool though.

'Who the fuck are you?' she asks me as I poke my head out.

I have to laugh. 'Eh, more to the point, who the fuck are you?' I say.

'Where's Sandy?'

'Gone.' I almost choke on the word.

She winces. 'Are you Max?'

How does she know my name? 'Yes. And you?'

'Clara. Sandy probably told you all about me.'

'The girl who pick-pockets.'

'There's a bit more to me than that.'

I've offended her. 'Sorry. You're Sandy's friend from the cleaning job.'

The girl folds her arms. 'Yep. So where is she?'

I don't know what to tell her. 'Sandy's going back to see her family.'

'No way! Her family? Why?'

'I suppose she thought she had to.' I try to get off the subject as quick as I can. 'What do you want?'

'Nothing. I just wanted to see Sandy. She told me she was here and, well ...' her voice trails off and she turns to go.

The sleeping bag makes me think she was planning to stay here for a few days. This girl is my connection to Sandy, I can't let her leave. 'Have you anywhere to go?'

She turns back, shrugs. 'I'll find somewhere. It's cool.'

'You can stay if you like. I can offer you the sofa.'

She turns about and gawks at me. 'Wha'?'

I shrug. 'Any friend of Sandy's and all that.' Please stay, I want to beg, but I know that'll make her run.

'I can sleep on your sofa?' She looks disbelieving.

'Yes.'

'No funny business?'

'Jesus! No!'

'And you won't want paying or nothing?'

'Just keep the place tidy, don't steal and don't invite all your friends around.'

'I don't have friends,' she says with a withering look. 'Just Sandy.'

'So?'

'Do you take pity on homeless people or what?'

'You're a friend of Sandy's. I liked her.'

She thinks about it. I wouldn't have imagined that there was a lot to think about. 'OK, fine. Thanks.'

I open the door wider. 'I'll make you a sandwich, you look like you could do with one.'

'Thank you,' she says.

'Max,' my dad says later on, 'is this wise?'

Clara is up in the shower, singing loudly in a surprisingly nice voice about how she's gonna take over the world someday.

'Is what wise, Dad?'

'You know what. Having that girl here. You don't even know her.' He's looking at me in despair. I'm reminded of all those days when I was eighteen and he was trying to get me to study for the Leaving.

'She's Sandy's friend and I'm sure Sandy would hate to see her out on the street.'

'It is not your business to look after every …' Dad lowers his voice as the singing stops and the shower is turned off, 'homeless person on the street.'

'It's just one.' I'm being deliberately obtuse. Of course I know it's a risk, but I don't care. She's Sandy's friend.

'Max, think.' He taps his head. 'Look after yourself before you try to look after other people.'

'This is how I'm looking after myself, Dad,' I say. 'Now, can you drop it? What d'you want for dinner, I'm going to order in.'

To give him credit, he does drop it and when Clara emerges ten minutes later, he treats her like a lady, offering her his bed and making sure she has enough to eat. When he leaves the room, Clara turns and smiles at me. 'Top man, your da,' she says.

I guess he's not too bad.

RUBY

'Come,' my mother says to me and her voice wobbles. She keeps a hold of my arm all the way to the door. Then she pushes it open and I step inside, back in time.

Everything is the same. The blinds on the windows, the battered oak table with its four chairs, the flagstone floor, the huge fireplace and mantel. Pictures that I drew as a child still hang on the walls. The only things missing are the mounds and mounds of newspapers and the stench of sour milk.

The familiarity catches me around the throat and shakes me hard. Nothing has been painted or repaired, not even the crack in the plaster on the stairs. 'It's just like I remember.'

'So you'd know it was yours when you came back,' my mother says. She moves to close the door.

'Don't!'

So she leaves it open a crack and I sit down.

The silence builds. Neither of us knows what to say. Seeing her has affected me more than I thought. It's like the last eight years, in order to survive, I blocked out my best memories of her. Now, they seem to be rushing back in.

'Ruby,' my mother says after a bit. She makes no effort to touch me now. 'It's so good to see you.' She chokes out the words. 'More than good. I don't have the words. It's really you.'

'Yes.'

'I've missed you.'

I dip my head.

'I am sorry.'

That's all I want to hear. Tears drip from my eyes and she comes around the table and wraps her arms about me.

Max said that maybe the time was right. I take that chance. We are in the living room, at the table. She has made pasta and neither of us has been able to eat it. The unspoken is a barrier that we have to cross. The air around us stills and grows heavy. Finally, I say, 'Why did you tell me so many lies?'

She nods and I'm reminded of a film I saw where a prisoner is accepting his fate on a gallows. There is no surprise, no emotion, just a nod of recognition almost, as if this moment was always coming. After a few seconds she says, 'You might not believe it, but I never meant to.' A pause. 'That's the thing with lies. You spend so much time covering up, they become your life.'

'So why?' The words float into the air between us.

'Mainly to keep from the pain of remembering.' A second passes and she adds, 'Before I had you, I had another life. I spent all my time trying to forget it.'

'What was so bad about it?' We're whispering, as if the story is too big to let right out. It gives me chills.

'I made too many mistakes, have too many regrets.'

'Like?'

'So many.' A beat, before she admits, 'And it was all my fault.'

'What happened?'

'I wasn't normal,' she says. 'I was …' she looks at me,

'incredibly shy. Over the top shy. By the time I was twenty I was living at home like an old woman, writing my poems and seeing no one. Oh, I'd tried to go out but, well ... I couldn't hold down a job or hold a conversation so finally my mother agreed that if I was happy, I could stay at home. And I was. Happy.'

'That sounds OK.'

'It was until I met Joe.'

'My father?'

A nod. 'He came every Saturday to do my mother's garden. I used to watch him, because I liked the garden, and after a bit he started asking me about myself and my poems. At first I was hopeless but Joe didn't seem to notice – maybe he wasn't listening half the time, I don't know – but soon I was chatting away to him. It was like I was normal for the first time in my life and so I married him. I never should have done it. Would you like water?' She stands up abruptly.

'No. Thanks.' I watch her leave for the kitchen and then I hear the squeak of the tap and the splash of water as it hits a glass.

She returns, holding the glass tightly in her hands. Sitting back down, opposite me, she says, 'I promised myself that if you came back, I'd tell you this story, just bear with me.'

'If it's too hard—'

She waves me away. It's hard to ignore the shake in her hands as she lifts the glass to her lips. She drinks, puts the glass back down and offers me a smile. 'That's better.' A pause, 'Anyway, Joe.' Her voice chokes with something like regret. 'After we married, we moved to Dublin because he got a job in the Botanic Gardens. I didn't mind because I thought I'd be able to bury myself away in our house, just like I'd done at home. But Joe, he was such an optimist. He was convinced that all I needed was someone to push me into the world. He made me go out with him, he introduced me to people, normal things, I suppose, but I was having panic attacks and weird feelings that my life was this big pretence, like I was floating far away from what I was or needed or whatever.'

'Oh, Mam.'

'I was about to tell him that I couldn't take anymore when I got pregnant.' It's ages before she speaks again. 'I was a terrible mother.'

'You did your best.'

'Not with Ivy.' Her eyes spark tears, and though I'd been expecting her to mention Ivy, it still sends a shiver through me. She starts to cry, silently, her shoulders shaking.

I don't know whether to comfort her or not. I watch as she rubs her face with the heel of her hand. 'It's OK,' she sniffs, pulling some kitchen paper off the roll on the table. 'It's good to cry. I should have done it years ago. I'll be fine. I just get upset, that's all.'

'You don't have to—'

'I do,' she says firmly, and her red eyes look determined. 'I owe you this at least. If you want to walk away afterwards, you can.' She drinks some more water. 'Ivy is,' she swallows, 'she is your big sister. She was lovely. Beautiful. But when I had her, I went into freefall. I couldn't cope with my own life and now I had to look after her. And I didn't know how.' Her voice dips some more and I have to strain to hear her. 'People I barely knew admired her and I didn't know what to say to them. I wanted to scream out that I couldn't cope but it was as if I was behind glass. I wanted people to see my eyes, to look at me and see how I couldn't cope but no one did. When Joe went to work in the mornings, I spent the days crying. I had to drink to relax me. In the end, I was drinking all the time. They took her away from me.' More tears trek down her face. Then she whispers, 'I wanted them to take her.'

I can't disguise my shock.

'I know, it's terrible. Susan offered to mind her for me when she found me drunk one day, but I couldn't let my sister do what I was unable to. In the end, she told the social workers. I pretended that I hated her for it but I was desperately relieved that she had.'

The cat, who has padded inside, hops into her lap. She occupies herself rubbing it. 'They said I was depressed. And maybe I was but I knew I couldn't hack my life.'

'And Joe?' I can't call him Dad.

'He tried hard, but in the end he left me. I don't blame him, he wanted Ivy back. He might have taken me back in time but I never wanted it.' A pause before she adds quietly, 'You must think I'm a terrible person.'

'No.'

'I wouldn't blame you if you did. I was so ashamed.' She wipes her eyes with the kitchen roll. 'When Joe got Ivy back, he let me visit her. But each time I did, it hurt a little more. And at the end of the visit, she would cry for me to stay and hold onto me and I'd have to peel her little hands off me.' A silence that stretches before she says, 'One day, I just stole her. It wasn't about kidnapping or anything, I just wanted to be a normal mother for one day. I wanted to give her a day she would remember. A fun day. I brought her to the park, got her ice-cream and we sat looking at the ducks, until they found us. They got my mother to lift her out of my arms.'

She says nothing for ages, like she's back there. I don't say anything either.

'I didn't cry,' she goes on then, 'I just breathed in the smell of her hair that final time and I never went to see her again.'

'Oh, Mam.'

'It was for her own good. I thought she was young enough to forget me.'

I reach across and take my mother's hand. 'Nana kept in touch with her.'

'I know, but I couldn't bear to ask.'

'And how did you end up here? With me?'

'I got out of Dublin and came here. I just blanked it out. Didn't think about it. Then I found out I was pregnant with you. Can you imagine?'

'How did you cope with me?'

'I can cope when no one else is around. Other people make me nervous.' She looks at me. 'Though I messed up with you too.'

'I'm here now.'

'I was so scared. I had no idea what normal mothers did. I was afraid to let people in, in case they'd see how terrible I was. I was scared to lose you the way I'd lost your sister. But I swore to myself that I wouldn't drink.'

'That was good.'

'I did well for the first few years.' She sounds like a child. 'There was no pressure on me from outside. But when I won a prize for one of my volumes of poetry a picture of me was published in the paper along with a biography. You were just going on five. Even though I used my maiden name, your dad still saw it and read about you and wrote to me to see if you were his. I didn't answer his letter, which I suppose told him that you were.'

'So when did he meet me?'

Her look tells me that he never did. It's like grief. The lovely fisherman dad she conjured up for me was not real.

'I'm sorry,' she says.

'Where is he now?'

'He died when you were six. Jean, his wife, wrote to tell me.'

So much wasted time. 'Did you go to his funeral?'

She gives me such a look of despair that I reach across and clasp her hand. She holds mine tight. 'The only way I'd survived all these years was by not thinking about Ivy. As far as I was concerned there was only me and you.'

That's the way she'd brought me up. As if the outside world didn't exist.

'After the funeral, Jean started to write. To you. I don't know how she found out where we lived. Your dad wrote care of the publishers. That's when I started hiding from the postman. I wanted you to be scared of him so you would never open those letters. I shouldn't have done that. That was my chance to tell you.'

'Yes, it was.'

'I wrote and told Jean not to write, so then ...' she stumbles on the name, 'Ivy took over.'

'Did they know when I went missing?'

'Yes. When you …' she hesitates, 'ran away, I thought you'd go there so I rang them. When you didn't arrive over, they told me that they were coming here to help in the search.' Her voice wavers.

'You saw Ivy again.'

'She was only small when I left.' She makes a space with her hands. 'So small.'

'And is it OK now?'

'No.' She shakes her head. 'How can it be? I left her.'

'I left you.'

'That was different. I'm your mother.' She swallows hard. 'I'll always welcome you back.'

Her words are like balm. She pulls me towards her and we hug, closing our eyes and inhaling. We stay like that until the cat, feeling squashed, lets out a cross meow. It makes us laugh.

'Where did the cat come from?'

'Bill got him for me. To keep me company.'

'Bill?'

'Casey's man.'

And that's when I cry. Which is weird.

MAX

Task one. Compose a letter to Imelda. I'm handwriting it as it's more personal than typing it up or sending an email. So far, I've got:

Dear Imelda

Followed by a load of scribbled-out sentences and half-baked words. Letter-writing is not my forte. I mean, how do you write to a girl you last saw nearly twenty years ago and ask if the baby she had then was yours? How do you do that? There are no guidebooks for it. I don't even care if she hits me for years of child maintenance. I should have done it years ago.

Doing it takes my mind off the fact that I haven't heard from Sandy yet. It's been two days. And there has been nothing in the papers either. I hope she's OK. If I don't hear within a week, I'm going after her. I don't care how it looks, I don't care if she rejects me. I just want to make sure she's OK.

Dear Imelda, how are you? I hope you are keeping well. I know it'll be a surprise to hear from me.

'Surprise' sounds wrong. 'Total shock' makes more sense but might not be the thing to put down either. Shit.

I rub my eyes. It's nine in the morning and I'm wrecked from lack of sleep. I find, weirdly, that I'm a bit worried about being away from the hospital now. There is no structure on the outside; instead the real world is full of pitfalls and temptations and I have no way of knowing how I'll cope.

The most attractive idea for me is to lock myself away in the house and never go out, but I know I can't do that. It'll be just another way of escaping.

Plus, the neighbours will begin moaning about the garden again. It looks pretty cool now, it has to be said. Dad says he'll buy a garden seat for me and then it'll be finished.

I turn back to the letter and re-read what I've written and scribble out *I hope you are keeping well.* That sounds crummy.

'Sandy is on the telly!' Clara's shout makes me jump. That girl has a foghorn quality to her voice that is not immediately evident. 'Look, it's on the telly. Come on in.'

The relief that Sandy is still alive hits me like a steam train. I fall over my feet in my eagerness to have a look. A picture of Sandy, obviously posed, is on the screen. She looks good. More than good.

The newscaster is in the middle of the item.

... turned up two days ago outside her mother's house. No details have emerged yet about where she has been or what she has done. Her mother, the renowned poet Melanie Fairbrother, says that they have a lot of time to make up and will not be issuing any more statements.

Then the news anchor turns to the camera and smiles. 'Nice to end on a good news story,' she says, and the credits roll.

'I always knew she was posh,' Clara says, wonderingly. 'Her ma is a poet. Hey, Mr C, did you hear that?' She calls out to my dad as he passes by the room.

'Hear what?' He pokes his head in.

'Sandy is only Ruby fucking Fairbother!'

'Brother,' I correct. 'Fairbrother.'

My dad has stopped recoiling at Clara's liberal use of the F-word. 'Sandy?'

'Yes. Sandy,' I say, already hurting.

'Sandy that stayed here? Homeless Sandy?' My dad looks from one to the other of us.

'Her real name is Ruby Fairbrother,' Clara says. 'Some poet's missing daughter.'

'Melanie Fairbrother?' my dad says. 'Her daughter?'

'Yeah.' Clara nods. 'Mad or what?'

'Is that true?' my dad asks me.

'Yes,' I nod. 'It said so on the news.' I go upstairs. At least she's safe.

As the day goes on, more information is broadcast about Sandy. At six, I turn on the evening news and she and her mother have made the headlines. There's a picture of them standing together, both of them looking a little uncomfortable. Sandy is wearing red jeans and a white T-shirt.

She still hasn't rung.

'She looks great,' Clara says, without a hint of envy. 'I like them jeans.'

'Did you know all along, Max?' My dad turns to me.

'Not all along. Coffee, anyone?'

They both say they'll have some and I walk to the kitchen. I have to steady myself against the table and I stay there for a second or two until I'm shocked by my dad coming up behind me. 'Did you know she was going home?'

'Yep.'

'Did she ask you to go with her?'

'Nope. I offered, though.'

'Be sensible, Max. You have enough going on.'

'She was on her own, Dad.'

'I know. I know.' A beat before he pats my arm. 'So are you.'

'Not like her.'

'She'll be back.'

'Nah, why would she come back here?' I manage a grin. I'm too old and too cynical for a broken heart.

'Because she likes you,' my dad says, and his certainty is gratifying.

I hear Dad talking to Clara later on. I'm on the stairs, just about to come down for a glass of water, when I hear Clara telling my dad that her mother threw her out. 'I always robbed for her,' Clara says. 'Now she says it's wrong.'

'It *is* wrong, Clara, especially when you don't have to do it.'

'Me stealing stuff never bothered her before. Like, her fella wasn't even there when I gave her the coat. I said to her, there's your birthday present, and she asked me did I nick it. I said to her it's Brown Thomas, what do you think? And she threw me and the coat out and told me I could only come back if I stopped.'

'Sounds like she cares about you.'

Clara snorts.

'Sometimes parents have to do things that will make their kids hate them,' my dad says. 'They don't want to do it, but they do. 'Cause they love their kids.'

I have to turn and go back up. He is a top guy.

RUBY

I ring Max once the news breaks. It's a good excuse. I've wanted to ring him since I got here but he doesn't need me crowding him when he's trying to recover. I dial his mobile.

'Hello?' Max answers and he sounds as if he has a cold.

'It's me.' I feel suddenly shy.

A pause before a cautious, 'Sandy?'

'Yep.' My heart is hammering. I don't want to stress him out. But I need to hear his voice. 'Just checking in. How are you?'

'Sane.'

We both giggle a little at that.

'You?' he asks, and I fancy he is smiling.

'Great,' I tell him.

'Cool. I saw you on the news.'

'In my red jeans?'

'Yep. By the way, your friend called.'

'Clara?' That's a surprise.

'Yep. She's living here now for a bit. Her mother threw her out.'

'You took her in?'

'She's your friend.'

'Max—'

He interrupts my would-be emotional thank you. 'She's downstairs teaching my dad the art of pickpocketing.'

He wants me to laugh, so I do. 'No way. Candy pocket?'

'I think she just wants an excuse to feel my dad's arse.'

I laugh again. No one makes me laugh like he does.

'My dad is fascinated by her. She calls him Mr C. I think he secretly feels quite macho.'

I quash a sudden longing to be there with them. 'Anything else?'

'Don't tell your mother you know me.'

'Too late.'

'Fuck.'

'She likes the sound of you.'

'Good.' Then he says, 'You'd be very proud of me. I wrote the letter to Imelda. I just need her address now.'

'Big shiny halo for you.'

'And Charles said Molly said she'd write to you. What's your address?'

I give it to him and he scribbles it down. 'I'll drop it in,' he says. 'I'm chilling with the neighbours these days.'

'You'll be reading to Molly next.'

'My arse!'

'You do talk out of it so it should be no problem.' More laughter and I hold the phone closer to my ear. I can hear him breathe.

'Not funny,' he says.

'You laughed.'

'So I did. I'm obviously not as sane as I would have you believe.'

We laugh some more, then he says, 'I would have brought you down.'

'I know. But it wouldn't have been fair. You have a lot on.'

'I can cope.' He sounds suddenly irritated.

'Maybe, but—'

'You asked Charles.' There's a world of hurt in his voice.

'He offered.'

'So did I.'

'I know.' I think whatever else I say would be wrong so I leave it at that.

His voice, when it comes, is subdued. 'So, going home was the right thing?'

'Definitely.'

'You ever going to tell me about it?'

'I will.'

'When?'

'Soon … when we've all found our feet again. I'm meeting my aunt on Saturday.'

'OK. Good luck with that.' A pause. 'I'm meeting Paddy on Friday.'

'Good.'

Neither of us seems to know what to say after that. It's like his irritation has coloured the conversation. Then we both stumble out a 'goodbye' and I hang up, already batting away the ache of his absence.

MAX

I keep re-reading the letter I've written to Imelda. It's not ideal but, then again, give me the person who could write an ideal letter in circumstances like mine. I go over every word, tease out every phrase, but even now, I can't post it until I talk to Paddy. For one thing, I need the address, and for another, I need to talk to him about what happened. Badly. He's arriving at two and Clara and my dad have gone out. Together. Dad has finally agreed to leave tomorrow and he's treating Clara to a film in town. She's chosen one about a heist. Probably to get ideas.

I'm edgy. The last time I saw Paddy, I'd basically gone into meltdown in the middle of a restaurant. I can't eat lunch, all I can do is drink endless pints of water. I tell myself to calm down, that the stress isn't good for me, but my mind feels like a tumble dryer as it churns out possible outcomes to this meeting over and over.

Outside, the bell rings and unexpectedly a calm descends on me. There is nothing I can do except go with it now. I open the door and see that Paddy looks a little stressed too.

'Hey,' he says, managing to grin. 'You're looking good.'

'Thanks. I feel a lot better. Sorry about, you know …'

'No problem.'

I'm glad he knows what I'm apologising for because I don't. Not quite. Great chunks of those last couple of months are still hazy. Every so often a piece jumps up and bites me and I cringe. All I can remember about that last lunch with

Paddy was him telling me Imelda was in Australia and me searching for her all over the restaurant. That's enough to remember, actually.

'Come in,' I say, holding the door wide.

He follows me down the hall and sits down at the table while I make him coffee. My life revolves around making coffee. I'm really going to have to go back out into the world one of these days.

'Your visitor is gone?' Paddy asks. 'The last time I was here, a girl was living in the place. Don't mind telling you, I thought she'd chopped you up and put you in a suitcase.'

'There's another one here now,' I tell him. 'The one you saw,' I'm about to say it was Ruby Fairbrother, but for some reason, I don't, 'is gone.'

Paddy nods. He's fiddling with the sugar, spilling it from the spoon onto the table in neat little cocaine lines. He looks up as I place the coffee in front of him. 'Thanks.'

'No prob.'

We sip in silence for a few seconds and I wonder if I should have bought biscuits, but it's too late now. I go for it. 'You're probably wondering why I asked you to come here,' I say.

'It's not about the job?'

'No.'

We look across the table at each other. The truth lies between us like a fine spider's web, glistening with dew. Shining in the light.

'We've never talked about that day,' I say to him. My voice is quiet but steady.

He nods. He knows the day I mean.

'You told a lie, I told a lie. It's bugged me ever since.'

He dips his head. When he looks up, I'm a little shocked to see the pain in his eyes. 'It was a good thing to do,' he says, before swallowing hard. 'At least, that's what I thought. And, I guess, I wanted to believe that somehow he fell. That it was an accident. Otherwise ...' He bites his lip. 'He jumped. Right in front of us, Max.'

'I know.' I rub my hands over my face. 'But it wasn't an accident.'

We are silent.

Eventually I mumble, 'I always felt it was my fault.'

'Nah.' He pauses. 'No. Never.'

It comes out in a rush. 'I need Imelda's address in Australia from you, Paddy, I know you keep in touch with her.'

He jumps like I zapped him. 'You're not going to tell her, are you? Jesus, Max, she doesn't need to know that.'

'No, no, I'll never tell anyone that. I need to contact her, though, over ... over something different.'

He looks like he wants to know, but he doesn't ask. Instead he nods. 'OK. I'll email it to you. I don't have it on me.'

'Thanks, Paddy.'

''Sno bother.' He pauses, leans over towards me and says, a little urgently, 'She's not like what she was, you know. She grew up too, like the rest of us.'

I nod. 'Yeah, grand.'

He takes a sip of coffee. He looks so, I dunno, alone or sad or something that I blurt out, 'I was sleeping with her, that time. She was two-timing Shane.'

Paddy's mug clatters onto his saucer. Coffee splashes out.

'I need to know that her baby was Shane's and not mine. It's years too late, but still ...'

Paddy has gone pale.

'That's why I want to write to her,' I blunder on. 'To apologise for not being a man back then.'

'You—'

'But I couldn't, don't you see?' I'm desperate now to explain. Paddy was so sensible, how would he understand? 'I couldn't because it was all Shane this and Shane that and I couldn't say, "Oh by the way, me and Imelda, we were selfish shits, we didn't care about Shane." I couldn't go—'

'It's not yours,' Paddy says.

'It might be. That's what I want to—'

'It's mine.'

My mouth remains open but no words come. Did I hear right? Paddy said the baby was his. I can almost see the shapes of the words he spoke, hanging in the air, just in front of me. 'Yours?'

'Yes.' He looks at me. 'We were all sleeping with her, Max.'

So it wasn't just me. The relief hits me just as quickly as the sorrow.

'She was a strange girl, her family were weird, did you ever meet them?'

I shake my head. It wasn't just me.

'I told my folks about a year after Shane died, the guilt was eating away at me. They asked her to get a test and it confirmed that the baby was mine. I never told anyone, just tried as best I could to pay for her and the baby. I told her never to tell Shane's folks and she never has but she had to go away to live with the lie.'

'Jesus!'

'I don't regret it, he's a great kid. Imelda's a great girl.' A pause. 'You can rest easy; if there are any little Maxes out there, it's not Imelda's one.'

If I'd only faced it years ago, I'd have been free of it. But a tiny voice says, *You'd never have come to Dublin, you'd never have had a breakdown, you might never have met Sandy ... Ruby. Whatever.*

'I don't regret it either,' I tell him. Then I add, 'I wish we had talked about Shane, though. Just talked about him.'

'We can still do that.'

And we do. And in my head, I fling a silent apology to my friend, wherever he is. I apologise for being that awful young man who stole his girlfriend. Paddy does too, I'm sure.

I think about calling Sandy to update her. I have her number now and I look at it all the time. Sometimes my finger hovers over the call button but I always pull back. What if her mother answers? What if I have to talk to her? What exactly has Sandy told her about me? And even though I was made up when Sandy rang the other day, I got the hint. She thinks I can't cope. She won't say it out loud, because she's too nice, but the last thing she needs is a guy that can't cope. She will tread on eggshells all her life around me because she'll be afraid I'll get stressed out. I can't live like that. If I'm with someone, I want them to believe that I can be there for them.

Maybe friends is all we'll ever be now and I'm not sure I can live with that either.

RUBY

For a few days after I come home, all my mother and I do is talk. I stay in the house and sleep in my old room. We relive our shared past, her changing my view of it, like a landscaper on a tangled garden. Her ways of acting and reacting I can see now in a different light, one that makes more sense. I steer clear of talking about Ivy, not wanting to upset her. I tell her stories of my life. Of Clara. And Max. She likes the sound of Max. I tell her that he's from Wexford originally, that he's lovely. I don't tell her that he thought I was an angel.

On Friday she tells me that Nana is dead the past two years. I haven't asked about her because in my heart I knew she was gone and there was only so much sadness I could take in one go. Hearing that my dad had never met me and that I had a long-lost sister was enough. But finally, after breakfast on Friday, I say, 'She's dead, isn't she?'

My mother doesn't even have to ask who I mean. 'Yes,' she says.

Silence descends on us then. I'm not sure how to proceed. There are so many black holes in this life now. But there were before too only I hadn't realised it. Better to live with the truth than lies. 'When?'

'Two years ago. Cancer. Me and Susan were with her when she died.'

'I should have been there too.'

'If you hadn't run away, I would never have been there myself.'

Her admission doesn't make me feel any better.

'Just a second.' I watch my mother go upstairs and reappear a few minutes later with an envelope. Holding it towards me, she says, 'About a month before she died, she asked me to give you this when you came back.'

'When I came back?'

'She always believed that you would.'

I wish I could have come back sooner so she could have known how right she was, but it's too late for that. The knowledge is like a bereavement. The envelope has a big bright Ruby drawn on it instead of my name. My vision blurs as I picture her drawing it.

'I'm so glad I can give it to you,' my mother says.

I'm glad I'm here to receive it. Her last gift to me.

A while later, in the privacy of my room, I tear open the flap and a letter and a photograph fall out. The picture is of me on the day she'd brought me shopping. My smile is so big and so happy that my heart twists up. I'm wearing my new pink glittery sandals and a bright red winter coat. I look ridiculous as I stand in the doorway of my nana's house. Behind me, the shiny vastness of her kitchen. My hands are behind my back and my chest is puffed out. My hair is bouncy with artificial ringlets. I truly think that that was the happiest moment of my life. I touch the picture, running my finger down the image of this happy little girl and wondering where she went to, wondering if she'll ever come back. She's like a country I once visited.

I unfold the letter.

Darling Ruby,

I'm writing this because I know one day you'll see it. It's my last attempt to put my arms around you and assure you that it will all be OK, because despite her troubles, you have a magnificent mammy and that is all we need to survive in this world, believe it or not. One day you will come home and she will tell you her story and you will see how courageous she really was in all this. She won't tell you of the time Ivy was sick and she braved the nurses and doctors at the hospital to get treatment for her. How afterwards, she shook for a week from the trauma of engaging with the world. All the things she has done, the steps out into the world she has made since you went missing, have taken tremendous acts of courage on her part.

As for me, my darling, you will be the grandchild that remains special. The one who saved her own mammy despite being afraid of the world too. The one who blossomed like my flowers when she came to stay. And you will blossom again, with the right love and care.

I am dying. I want you to have this photograph as a reminder of how good life is. I want you to have some jewellery of mine too, which Susan has in a safe for you.

Take care, live well, be happy.

Nana

When my mother comes back, I wrap my arms about her and tell her I love her.

At the weekend, Susan, Dan and my three cousins arrive. I watch their car pull up and see them greet the lone reporter who is camping outside the house. He's a nice enough guy; I bring him out cups of tea, with a 'no comment' each time he tries to ask me a question. He's started telling me about himself now, which makes us both laugh.

Susan hugs my mother as she comes in and a brief flare of grief hits me, I don't know why. Maybe it's because of all the wasted years. Susan turns to me and smiles. I am embarrassed. I feel like a kid that had a tantrum and has now calmed down. My uncle and cousins crowd around Susan.

Susan is the first to speak. 'Ruby,' she says. I think she might cry.

'Hi, Susan.' I try out a smile and in two steps she has crossed the gap between us and is embracing me in a fierce hug. Then she holds me away from her before embracing me again. 'You look good,' she says, as if she's surprised. 'And you look well. Say "hi", girls.'

Her girls aren't girls anymore. Nan has turned into a glamorous woman, tall, glossy-haired, well dressed. She flushes and nods a hello. I nod one back. In her presence I am once more the gawky kid who didn't know what Friends Reunited was.

'We're hardly girls,' Nora says, and it's hard to make out if it's a dig at her mother or not. She follows it with a smile. Maybe not a dig, then.

Nelly looks sullenly at me. She folds her arms and slouches in the doorway. She is wearing an engagement ring. I seize on it, desperate to say something that might spark a conversation. 'You're getting married, Nelly?'

Sudden silence punctures the chatter.

'It was Nana Fairbrother's,' Nelly says flatly. Every word a wound.

'It's beautiful,' is all I can manage.

'She died of a broken heart over you,' Nelly says, standing straight, her hands balled. 'Do you know that? You broke her heart!'

'Nelly!' Dan snaps. 'That's enough of that!' He turns to me. 'She had cancer. Nothing to do with you.'

'Stress causes cancer, everyone knows that.'

'Nelly!'

Horrible, horrible silence.

No one knows what to say.

'Your nana always knew Ruby would be back,' my mother says firmly. 'If anyone broke her heart it was me.' I love that she has stuck up for me. She crosses over and lays a hand on my shoulder.

'I wish I had been here,' I interrupt, wanting this visit to go well. 'She was lovely to me.'

Susan nods. 'She was lovely to everyone.'

'And Nelly, you're right.'

Nelly looks at me and I see that, behind her eyes, she's just sad. Sad about Nana, sad about the worry I've caused them all.

'Running away and staying away was unforgivable. I see that now.'

'You put our lives on hold,' Nelly says, pinning me with her gaze.

'Nelly!' Susan snaps. 'Can't you see—'

'She's right,' I interrupt. 'I did.' I turn back to Nelly. 'All I can say is sorry.'

My mother squeezes my shoulder. Nelly turns away from me.

'I'm sorry too,' Nan says into the silence that follows.

'For what?'

'For the way I treated you on Facebook,' she says.

'What way?'

'I never replied to your friend request or to anything you asked me. My friends said you weren't cool, that you never went anywhere, so I just ignored you.' Now she looks like she might cry.

'I wasn't cool,' I agree. 'And I didn't even notice you were ignoring me. I just thought you were too busy living.'

'Really?'

'Yeah. How uncool is that?'

She laughs slightly. 'I felt so guilty about it when you disappeared. I kept thinking if only I'd kept in contact.'

'It wouldn't have made a difference.' We smile awkwardly at each other.

'I think we just need to accept that what happened, happened,' Susan says. 'And move on.'

'Get those photographs,' Dan says, his voice mock-cheery, 'we'll have a laugh.' He turns to me. 'They're pictures of you when you stayed in Galway that time.'

'Christ.'

They laugh.

'Nelly, take them out of my bag,' Susan orders.

Nelly stomps off, not quite ready to welcome me back. She brings a packet of pictures back into the room and flings them towards her mother. Susan pulls me down onto the sofa beside her and begins telling the stories behind the photos. Years of stories.

It's a start, I suppose. Across the room, my mother smiles.

MAX

I tell Clara she can have the house to herself for a bit. I ring my dad and tell him to expect me. Neither of them seems surprised, neither of them objects.

This is the next part of my sane campaign. The laying the past to rest part of the plan. And even though I try not to admit it to myself, I'll be near Sandy. Three miles away from her. Maybe I'll see her on the street or something. Or walking the beach …

I pack a small case, hop into my car and fire the engine. It's dead. Well, there's a surprise. I haul my cases back out and call a taxi. If I don't leave now, I could change my mind and I know that I shouldn't. Like medicine, this will be good for me. I stand at the side of the street waiting for the taxi.

'Going away?' the pigeon man says from next door. I keep forgetting his name.

'For a bit,' I tell him. Above our heads, his birds wheel and dive. I hope they don't shit on the new garden bench that my dad bought for me.

'Going to see that girl, Sandy or Ruby or whatever she's called?'

'No.'

'Oh, right.' He seems not to know what to say to that. 'Cause if you were, I was just going to tell you to say hello to her.'

'Right. Well, I'm not.'

'You said.'

'Sorry about that.'

'No problem. It was just if you were, I'd tell you to say sorry for being rude the day she gave me that very nice apology from you.'

'Yeah, well …'

This conversation is staggering like a guy having had too many pints. Where is my taxi? Because pigeon man is still looking at me, I say lamely, 'But if I *was* going, I would have done it for you.'

'That would have been great. Thanks.'

'Yeah. But I'm not, so …' Shut up, Max.

'Is your car not working?'

'No.'

'I suppose the battery is dead after it not being used.'

'Yeah.'

'I would have started it for you if I had known.'

'That would have been great, thanks.'

'But I didn't know, so I didn't.'

Jesus! 'Right.' Like Mecca, I spot my taxi and wave at it. After confirming to the driver that I'm Max Coyle, I hop in. Pigeon man waves me off.

'Where to?' the driver asks.

'Wexford,' I say. 'Rossclare beach.'

The driver turns to gawk at me. 'You for real? Wexford? You could have caught a bus.'

'I would have to wait for a bus.'

'D'you not have a car?'

'Battery is dead.'

'You should have jump-started it.'

'Do you want the gig or not?'

'Yep.' A pause. 'I'll need to see some cash in advance, no offence.'

I turn out my pockets. Show him my money.

'Then let's go.' He smiles.

He loosens up after a bit. We start talking about the weather, which is a sure-fire icebreaker. He likes hot weather, I like cold. He tells me about his kids, who are all grown up. 'I married early,' he says. 'Me and me missus are free now. Our youngest is twenty-two.'

If I had a kid right now, in twenty-two years I'd be fifty-seven. Fuck's sake.

His wife got pregnant so he had to marry her, he says. No one thought it would last but it did. Talk turns to me.

'I'm not married,' I tell him.

'Time enough,' he says, 'no point rushing into things.' Then he laughs. 'So, what do you do?' He looks me up and down. 'I'd say a ...' he screws up his face, 'some sort of a ...' another wince, 'no, don't tell me. Eh, you're a plumber or something.'

'Nope.' I'm amused at that. 'I was, am, an agent.'

'Yeah?'

'Then I had this massive breakdown, I mean massive. I ended up drinking piles of stuff and taking a load of tablets and jumping off the top step of the stairs.' I'm interested to see how he reacts. Step one of re-entering the world. What will people think?

'Jaysus. Sounds like a great night till you jumped off the stairs.'

I laugh.

'I had a breakdown once,' the driver admits then.

'Really? What happened?'

'Battery was flat.'

It keeps us laughing all the way to Wexford.

Just over an hour later, we arrive in Rossclare. I ask the driver to bring me to the strand. I want to walk it before I head to my dad's.

'D'you want me to hang around?' the driver asks. I think we've bonded.

'It's fine.'

He hesitates. 'You're not … eh, planning on drowning yourself or anything?'

'With what you just charged me, I might.'

He laughs. 'Jaysus.'

'No, I won't drown myself,' I say then.

He turns the car around and, with a bip of his horn, he's gone. I turn my face to the sea and inhale the freshness. I start to walk down to the strand and the smell of salt and sea and the sound of the gulls causes me to catch my breath. The sky is grey and the sea is grey with white tips. I take it all in. Feel it fill me up. I wonder if I'll ever swim again, then push it away. For the moment, I am home.

A short while later, my phone rings. It's my dad.

'Where are you?'

'On the beach.'

'For God's sake, what are you doing down there?' A pause. 'Are you OK?'

'I've never been better, Dad.'

I can hear his relief down the line. 'I'll have the kettle on.'

'See you in a bit.'

I sit on the damp sand and wonder why it took me so long to get back here.

RUBY

Small-town life. When I ran away to Dublin, I was lost in the crowd. Invisible. I wanted someone to see me, but no one did. I came to High Hills to find some semblance of the life I used to have. At least that's what I think now. Only in High Hills I was still invisible. Here, back at home, I have become the person everyone looks at but no one sees. I am a curiosity. I am the girl who ran away one day in June and came back eight years later. I am the girl who broke her mother's heart and made her old before her time. Though she says she was always old. I am the girl the whole place spent days searching for, I am the girl they mourned while she was still alive. I am the girl that while she was away galvanised a population. Now that I'm back, no one knows what to do anymore. I have to get used to being a curiosity. Get used to people trying not to look, trying not to whisper. I tense up every time someone looks in my direction. Mam says that it will pass, that being looked at is hard, that she never liked it, but that it's part of her life now and it gets easier.

Going into a shop with my mother the day after the news was broadcast was terrifying. Even though people made me welcome and said how great it was that I was back, it didn't feel real. Their unspoken questions were the loudest part of the conversation. I was aware of the irony of the role reversal. My mother leading me out of the house.

So far, no one from my old life has spoken out. Maybe the

other cleaners didn't see me either. And the people on Max's road might not want to get embroiled in my life. I feel bad that I've brought it on them.

And Max. I can't even think about Max. I miss him like a limb. I miss his caustic humour and his badass attitude. Already he seems part of a dream of another life. He hasn't rung me since I rang him, even though my number must have been on his caller display. I thought he might. Maybe I seem like a dream to him too. I can't blame him if he wants to forget the whole time around his breakdown. If he has to forget me to do it, well then, fine. I just want him to get well.

I make all these resolutions but then, ten days after I get back, I open the paper and see the perfect excuse to ring him. And what's more, it's not putting pressure on him or making him think he has to do anything for me. My heart sings as I dial his mobile.

It rings and, finally, quite an upbeat, 'Yo!'

'Max? Is that you?'

'Sandy?'

I love the way he says my name. 'Yes. I just called to say that I think it's really decent what you did.'

'What did I do?' He sounds surprised.

'Laura Morley? The singer. She's in the paper today full of praise for you.'

'Laura? In the paper? That's two very dangerous things right there.'

'She says, and I quote, "Max Coyle took me on and then told me that I wasn't his type of act. Even though he had a massive breakdown and went mental, he still found the time to email me a list of every agent in town who he thought would be suitable. I found one and am now hoping to record my first single."'

'She's telling everyone that I had a massive breakdown and went mental?' He sounds horrified. 'Bloody hell.'

'She's telling everyone how decent you are. You dope.'

He chuckles. 'Yeah, well, I was pretty hard on her, I thought the least I could do would be to help her out.'

'You're so nice.'

'So are you.'

The way he says it send shivers up my spine. I tap dance around a response. 'You think?'

'Yep.' That's all he says. Firm and definite. I don't know how to respond. Should I thank him or would that be stupid? The silence stretches.

'I'm at home,' he says then, 'planning on doing some bridge-building.'

'You're in Wexford?'

'Not too far from you.'

More silence. Is he waiting for me to say something? 'That's great.'

'I know.'

'Going home. That's exactly what Ian said to do.'

'Can we forget for one second that I had a breakdown? Is that possible?'

His sharp tone, coming out of nowhere, makes me flinch. 'I wasn't—'

'You were. I am doing my best to get on with things and—'

'I know.'

'I don't need protecting or patronising or—'

I cut him off. 'Don't talk to me like that.'

'Then stop treating me like a moron. I'm not some kid that has to be constantly reminded to do what my shrink said.'

'Fine.'

'Fine.'

'I've got to go.'

'So go.'

The line goes dead.

I'm too stunned to cry.

MAX

It's been a week and I haven't yet returned to Dublin. Instead, I've been with my dad in his place in Wexford. I'm not sure if there is a lot to go back for now. I've missed the beach and sea more than I realised, and Sandy isn't in Dublin anymore.

Her phone call the other evening killed me. I was buoyed up when I saw she was ringing me, killed because I tried to gauge how she felt about me, and nothing. No 'That's great, you're in Wexford' or 'What do you mean by you think I'm nice?' I don't think I was being subtle. Instead, I got a lot of crap about what Ian wants me to do. It's like she's turned into my dad. I snapped at her the way I do at him and she snapped right back at me. I don't know how to make it right. Probably I should have rung her back, but I didn't. I was afraid of the hurt, I think.

Is she scared to be with me? Did our kiss give her pause for thought?

She and her mother are still making the papers. My heart lurches each time I see Sandy in a photo. I spend longer than I should staring at her picture and I realise that I don't know this new girl. It's like the person who stayed in my house and visited me in hospital has faded away.

Some reporter is trying to piece together where Sandy was all these years and so far they've traced a few cleaners who remember her. Though I think they're spoofing. Sandy was good at being invisible. The folks on my street are keeping schtum, though a few people that she dealt with in shops and things have talked of seeing a girl fitting Sandy's description around.

It's like it was all another life. Which it kind of was. I really miss her, though. Like, really miss her. Or miss what I thought she was.

I'm getting to know my dad all over again but I can't see us going off into the sunset. He drives me mad. He refuses to let me buy takeout, instead he makes me peel spuds and chop carrots. I haven't had a decent Indian meal in a week. He says if I want to eat Indian I have to learn to cook it. When did this man turn into Masterchef?

Sandy is not the only thing I miss, I miss work too. Even one decent showbiz client would fill the gap. Laura is with Peter Quirke now and when I looked in the paper, she was pictured with her horrendous boyfriend on the town. Both of them waving at the camera.

Please, I say to whatever is in charge of the universe, find me a client I can experiment on. In a good way. I'd do things differently now. Way differently. I'd do everything differently.

Finally, someone talks. Or some intrepid journalist digs deep enough and the truth about what Sandy has done since she left home is unearthed. A lot of it is unremarkable, sad, the story of life in a big city with no home, crap wages and a hand-to-mouth existence. It's the part where she stayed in my house that grabs the attention of the whole nation, though. I suppose it is a bit unusual, a hotshot agent letting a homeless girl bunk in his house. For the first time, I bless my breakdown because it could have been a whole lot worse.

Questions might have been asked about my motivation. I'd never have been able to shake off the suspicion of what might have been going on in my house. As it is, I can declare proudly to the journalists who gather outside my dad's house the day the news breaks, 'I had a breakdown. It was massive. Ask my counsellor. Ask all my neighbours, they'll be delighted to fill you in.'

'But why did you let her stay in your place?' some kid with acne asks, as he holds a tape machine under my mouth.

'What can I say? Underneath the obnoxious exterior, there beats a human heart.'

They laugh and jot it down and fling some more questions at me. Finally I close the door and turn around to see my dad staring at me. 'You're not obnoxious,' he says as he sips on a cup of tea he's made for himself.

'Not now,' I concede.

'You never were.' He says it as if he means it. 'I was always really proud of you, Max. You were always such a kind boy and a great kid.'

I want to tell him that, sadly, I grew up.

'And even when you grew up, you did your best.' He nods. 'Didn't you?'

I guess he's right. I had always done my best.

'Well, then,' he says.

And we leave it at that.

RUBY

'Hello!' Bill, the man from Casey's, says as he deposits my mother's messages just inside the front door. 'Welcome home.'

I glance up at him and I have a sudden flashback to a day fifteen years ago. I'd forgotten about it until right now, but seeing Bill, standing in the sunlight, framed by the door, brings it rushing back. He'd come into the house behind the ambulance men and scooped me up in his arms so I wouldn't run after them up the stairs. He'd hired a taxi to drive us to the hospital and spent the trip singing silly little songs to make me smile. He'd stayed with me all day until the puppet lady arrived.

He'd bought my mother daffodils when she'd come home.

'It's good to see you again,' I say.

'I thought you might like these.' He grins and pulls seven lollipops from one of the bags. 'All for you.'

I laugh, ridiculously touched that he remembered. 'Like old times.'

'No,' he says. 'Better.'

And it is. Here, anyway.

I'm in the paper. Max is in the paper. A black and white picture of a very handsome man. I feel loss like a live thing in my belly, scrabbling about. I don't know what I did wrong and he hasn't rung me.

'Is that him?' my mother asks.

'Yes.' The headline reads: *Max Coyle Admits He's Human.*

My mother frowns. 'What does it mean, "admits he's human"?'

'He has a bit of a reputation for being an asshole,' I say. Then add, 'It's not true.'

She's leaning over my shoulder, reading the piece. 'He had a breakdown? You never said that.'

'I guess I never thought of it as a breakdown. He had some problems. He's fine now.' Then I think, he was always fine. It was just life that was shit.

I read the rest of the paper but my eye keeps returning to his picture. He looks good. Solid. Steady. Though pictures are deceptive. His eyes are laughing, as if he finds it all very amusing. I touch his face.

'You like him, don't you?' It's a statement.

'Yeah, I do.'

'I meant more than like.'

A beat. 'Yes.'

'And him?'

'He wasn't well when he met me. He has a lot to sort out.'

'I'm sorry.' She caresses my shoulder.

'Don't be. I'm glad I know him.'

And I am.

The next day the paper is full of people I recognise. The whole front page is devoted to pictures of the residents of Church Terrace. They are standing in Max's back garden. Molly, a blanket around her legs, is in the middle of the group, smiling as if she hasn't a care in the world. Charles is on his hunkers, beside her. Patricia on the other side. Behind her stand Julian and Tar, both looking as if they're trying to be cool about their moment of fame. Clara, standing a little apart, dressed like a punk rocker, bleeds attitude. She's described as the 'friend and confidante of Ruby Fairbrother'.

Patricia seems to have adopted the role of spokesperson for the street.

Patricia McCabe, pictured left front, read a statement on behalf of the residents and neighbours: 'Max Coyle is a lovely man and a very good neighbour. None of us were at all surprised when he took in a homeless girl off the street. It's the kind of thing Max Coyle would do. His breakdown was very unfortunate but no one noticed anything different about him at all while he was having it. He has always been willing to pitch in and do his bit for the community. As for Ruby Fairbrother, we all loved her. She was shy when she came first but she slotted right in. We hope she is happy now she's back home.'

Ruby's long-time friend, Clara Ryan, said that Max met Sandy when he bought her coffee every day. 'I thought it sounded a bit weird at first but he's pretty sound.' And Molly Reynolds, who has motor neurone disease, told this journalist that Ruby Fairbrother was an exquisite reader of prose. 'She read to me each day about the world that I felt was being denied me. Little by little I wanted to find it again. She brightened my life.'

I hope she knows that she brightened my life too.

Dear Sandy,

Unfortunately I have to dictate this to Charles, so excuse the scrawl, he was always a terrible writer. (If she doesn't die soon, I'll kill her for that. This is Charles, btw ☺)

You'll always be Sandy to me. Charles has employed a new reader for me, a woman called Eileen, who lost her husband ten years ago. Apparently he died of some tropical disease that I've never heard of. But that's Eileen: if I had ten bikes, she'd have eleven. I've got motor neurone disease, but her husband had something far worse. Patricia's daughter hasn't written to her in two years, Eileen's daughter is in prison and won't write to her. (I made that bit up – but you get the idea.) Still, she reads well so I'll put up with her for now.

The other piece of news is that I met your friend Clara. It was during the shoot for the paper and Charles and I got talking to her. She made us all coffee afterwards and I asked her if she read. I was thinking of her as a reader (this was pre-Eileen). She got very cross and used a lot of bad language. Then she wanted to know if I was making fun of her. Me? I said. A woman who can barely move in a wheelchair? Make fun of her? That made her smile a bit. Anyway, it transpires that she can't read too well and so I've offered to teach her. She's quite eager, which is charming. In return, she is going to relieve Charles for two hours each day.

In other news, the view from my window has changed to autumn and the leaves are falling, which means I've survived another season. I keep expecting to die and don't.

Patricia told me it's about time I expected to live. She could have a point, for once …

(She does have a point! – Charles ☺)
All the best
Molly (and Charles)

Sandy,
How are you? I can't blive my luc to have Maxs house to myself. He left to go down to his da and hasn't come bac yet. He is one fucked up weirdo but nice. Hes been in weird form though so I was glad when he went off. I think he wishes it was u here and not me.

His da is gr8 though. A real da. One you can hav a laff wit. And talk to.

Molly is teaching me to read. And rite. She's OK but she looks out her window at me in Max's garden. All the time. Then she gets Charlie to call in with food to spy on me.

This is a nice street but I think I mite go home just for a visit soon. Maxs dad said that my ma thrung me out only because she loves me and thinks it's tough love. My ma agreed wit that when I talked to her. Anyway, I have to prove to her that I am not robin and I can go back to visit wit her anytime.

U can tell yer ma she'll have to watch out, I could start riting pomes.

This is the most I ever rote in my life.
See you soon.
Clara.

MAX

I'm standing at the bar in the place that was my local when I was a kid. It's a small shabby building that faces the beach. I like the way it has refused to move with the times. The carpet is worn, the lights are yellowed with old smoke stains and the seats still retain the odour of cigarettes. It's as if it gave two fingers to the Celtic Tiger and I admire that in a crappy pub. This is step two in the 'Get Max Back into Life' recovery plan.

I'm nervous, having arranged to meet Tom and John, my one-time buddies. I'm here deliberately early so that they're not hanging about waiting for me, not talking about me before I arrive. I order an orange juice and find a seat opposite the door so I can wave at them when they come. That's if I recognise them.

The first to turn up is Tom. He hasn't changed – he's small, almost delicate, like a girl. His hair is as black as ever, his skin dark from a warm summer. I wonder how he has survived being gay in this small town. I raise a hand and he raises one back, orders a pint and joins me at the table. He grins at me.

'Hey,' we both say together.

'John is on his way,' he says, 'he's running late. The little feckers he teaches are giving him grief.'

'Great.' Then I add, 'About him being on his way, not about the feckers giving him grief. Obviously.'

'Obviously.' Tom smirks at me good-naturedly.

I'm nervous, I realise. I have to get a grip. John arrives then, rushing. We are silent, waiting for him to join us. He crosses over with a pint and sits in beside Tom. 'The prodigal has returned,' he chortles. It breaks the ice and we laugh.

The night flies. They don't ask me why I vanished off the radar. They don't ask why I'm back. Well, in fairness they probably know most of it, it was all over the papers. Instead they tell me what I've missed. Tom talks about coming out to his parents. He'd only done it last year. He reckons they were the only people in Wexford who didn't know.

'They were,' John agrees.

'I thought the mother would take to the bed,' Tom grins at me over his pint glass, 'but she insisted on meeting Alan and now she says he's the daughter she never had.' The three of us laugh loudly at that.

'I'm only messing,' Tom says then. 'But they get on great. It's worked out good.'

John tells me that he's a PE teacher in a local school and loves it. He's married and has two kids.

It strikes me that we're all grown up now. Long gone are the days on the beach. I found it hard to leave them behind, taking them with me when I left. After a bit, talk turns to Shane. We drink a toast to him and hope he's doing well. I don't say that Shane killed himself. There is no need. The secret isn't a burden anymore.

When we part, it is as old friends. I might never see them again, but I'm OK with that.

RUBY

I have the picture my grandmother gave me pinned to my wall. The more I look at it, the more complex my emotions. I was so happy then and yet … I think of that eager little girl, desperate to connect without actually knowing what it was she wanted, watching the world from behind a pane of glass or the pages of a book. Later, she observed how people interacted with each other and tried to replicate it, never once being quite herself. No one had noticed. They'd all come out to search for her when she was gone, but it was too late then.

I don't want it ever to be too late again.

'Ruby?' My mother knocks on my bedroom door and something in my face must catch her attention. A flare of hastily dampened-down sadness.

'What's wrong?' she asks.

I don't answer immediately, just continue to look at the picture.

She comes closer. 'Tell me.' She is firm. 'I can handle it now.'

'It's just,' I shrug, at a loss to explain, 'everything is different now.'

'Is that not a good thing?'

'Sometimes I feel it's come too late.'

'Too late for what?'

'I've missed so much.' I look at her. 'My whole life, practically. What could have been.'

'I know. It's my fault.'

'Not completely. I should have come home.'

She takes my hand. 'We've all missed so much,' she says. 'The only thing left is to live with it and make the best of it.'

'I thought … I don't know …'

'It's simple, Ruby. I had to change when you ran away. I had to find you, and while your leaving was the most awful thing to happen to me, it brought great things back into my life. I found Susan again. I met my nieces. I got out into the world and reconnected in order to find you. I saw Ivy and, though it didn't work out, I'm glad I did it. I'm not glad you ran away, but having you back now, and having my life the way it is, I think it's worked out fine.'

'Really?'

She nods. Then says, 'So you have to figure out what will make you glad your life is like this. Figure out what you want. And I know we haven't broached the subject, but if you'd like to meet Ivy, do it. She's your sister.'

And there it was. The glistening, shining fish I'd been hoping to catch. She'd just handed it to me. When I'd seen my mother embrace Susan, I think I'd known that one day I wanted to embrace my own sister. My mother understands much more than I'd given her credit for. 'You won't mind?'

'It wasn't that I ever minded,' she says, taking my hands and giving them a squeeze. 'It was just …' she pauses, 'in order to tell you about her, I had to face what I did and I wasn't able to.' She smiles shakily. 'If you want to meet Ivy, you go and meet Ivy.'

We smile at each other. And that is that.

I want to tell Max about it. Ask him how he felt facing his own sister after so long, but I pull back. Twice I've rung him now. Twice he's been off with me. It's like we shared some private bubble of togetherness for a few glorious months, but now real life is pulling us along in its current and neither of us can swim.

MAX

My dad asks me where I'm going. 'Out!' I tell him.

'There's no need for that tone,' he grumps. 'What the hell is wrong with you?'

I am in the middle of pulling on my jacket. 'Nothing.'

'Well, if there is nothing wrong, you can tell me where you are going.' He bangs some plates into the sink.

'I happen to be grumpy because I'm finding it hard to get work.' It's easier to admit that than tell him where I'm going. Or why I'm so grumpy.

'I'd say it's hard to find work when you spend days walking on the beach.' Dad bangs some more plates into the sink. I watch as he puts the tap on and water splashes everywhere. He is grey, just like the weather outside. I watch as he swirls the water around, making the sink fill with suds.

'Dad?' I venture.

He turns.

'Sorry. I'll be in better humour when I come back, right?'

'I worry.'

'Well, don't.'

'I wouldn't if you'd cop on and be in good form. You're talking to Maya again, you've met your old friends in the pub, what else is the matter?'

The matter is that I can't just take up the past and put it on like a coat. I've changed since then. I'm not that Max anymore, no matter how much easier it would be. I've met Sandy, for one thing, and I don't know what to do about her. I'd ring her if I thought we had a chance, I'd ring her if

I thought she could see beyond my breakdown. But I don't think she can.

My dad is still looking at me.

'See you, Dad,' I say as I close the door.

He raises a hand up. I leave. Today is the day, I think. Time to face the last of my past and move on.

It's the fourth time I've walked this beach in the last four days. It takes time to pluck up courage. Today will be the day because it's not a nice one. There are not many people about and those that are are bundled up in coats and scarves, concerned more with staying warm and making their way to wherever they are going than looking at me. I'm the same, wrapped up too. On my way to the place where Shane jumped.

I reach the spot after twenty minutes. A place three quarters of the way up the pier. There is nothing now to say anything ever happened here. No marker to the past. No scar. All about me is life – parents and grandparents, kids and dogs. The jangle of berthed boats and the screech of birds.

I sit on the pier wall and look out to sea. Something in me stills. I feel my phone vibrate with a text message. Foolishly I wonder if it's her.

Got new role in big-budget film. Want a client? Vic

Not Sandy, but good enough to make me smile. I wonder if the God of the universe is real, then decide not to think about it. I'd only go mad.

I text back: *You jammy bastard. Yes, I would.*

So I have a job. And this time it will be different.

RUBY

I arrive before Ivy. I've insisted on coming here on my own. Though my mother did say she'd wait for me in a coffee shop around the corner, the truth is, I want to do this alone. I don't know how I feel about having a sister. I think of Nan, Nelly and Nora and I know that it's probably too late for me and Ivy to have that kind of a relationship, but if we meet and can be friends, that'd be good enough.

We've arranged to meet in a hotel in Dublin and it's strange being back in the city whose streets I slept on not so long ago. No one gives me a second glance, which is good. I have a book of my mother's poems in front of me. The one she dedicated to her daughter by way of apology. I realise that she was making that apology to both me and Ivy.

The hotel foyer is large and I've taken a seat just opposite the front door; that way I can see everyone who goes in or out. Each time the door opens, I glance up, but so far no one fitting Ivy's description has arrived.

I've seen a picture of her. A close-up shot that she sent over email. Her eyes are the same as mine and my mother's, her face is rounder, her cheeks chubbier. Her hair is short, choppy, dyed a mixture of reds and pinks. She looks way too cool to be related to me. My mother says she always looked more like Joe than her.

At five minutes past eleven, in she walks. I recognise the hair. She's wearing a pair of overlarge sunglasses that conceal a lot of her face. She's stick thin and wears black skinny jeans and flat boots, a black biker jacket over a siren-red top. She spots me, hesitates and after I raise a hand in a wave, she crosses over.

She walks at high speed. I tuck the poems away in my carrier bag before standing up to greet her. My legs shake. I really hope we like each other.

She stops two feet away and looks me up and down. Or at least I think she does, it's hard to tell with the sunglasses. 'Hey,' I say. My heart is hammering wildly. I desperately want to feel a connection with her.

'Hello,' she says back in an English accent, which I hadn't actually been prepared for, which makes me sound really dumb.

We stand there. A beat of silence. People pass us.

'Should we hug?' I ask, flashing an awkward grin.

'We could try,' she says back.

And so we embrace a little awkwardly. Her biker jacket squeaks as she moves. She smells of roses. I never thought to wear perfume. All that girly stuff seems to have bypassed me. We pull apart and she sits down opposite me. We smile again.

'Can I get you a coffee?' I feel I have to ask, to be polite, but I don't want to leave her, not for a second. The feelings sweeping through me are overwhelming.

'No, thanks.' I watch as she removes her jacket. She has a tattoo on the back of her wrist. 'So, you returned home,' she says matter-of-factly as she folds up her coat.

'Yes.'

'Makes a change for her to have someone run off on her, I bet.'

The words are bitter. I flinch. 'She did love you,' I say. 'She wasn't well.'

'She never came back.' She tosses it out.

'She did. Eventually.'

'I hated her for leaving us.'

'I bet you did.'

'Don't go getting any idea of trying to reunite us or you'll never see me again.'

I'm a bit stumped at that. 'Tell me about my dad,' I say instead.

It's the right thing to do because the hard line of her mouth softens into a smile. 'I was only nine when he died but it was as if he was around for much longer.' She tells me that he made things grow, all sorts of things. Their garden was filled with the most exotic plants that largely died when he did. He'd run a successful gardening business in England before being killed in a car crash. 'My mother told me that he'd just found out about you at the time, that he was determined to meet you.'

'I know.'

'And when he died, my mother made it her mission to meet you instead. Your mother never replied to any of her letters except to tell her to leave her alone.' Again the bitter tone.

'Is he buried in England?'

'Cremated. He wanted his ashes divided between Ireland and England.'

'Where in Ireland?'

Ivy hesitates. 'You'll think this is really odd ...' Her voice trails off.

'What?'

In response, she pulls an envelope from her expensive-looking leather bag and holds it out to me. It's yellow with age. 'He wanted you to scatter some of his ashes too.'

It's a second before I take the envelope from her. I see my name on the front in flowing letters, the black ink a little faded. 'Is this …?'

'I was meant to wait but you did ask, so …'

'His ashes?'

She nods.

I rub my fingers over the envelope, hold it tight in my hands. It's more than I'd ever hoped.

'You're freaked?'

'No.' I look up hastily to see her studying me. 'I'm …' I scrabble to find the right word for how I feel, 'humbled, actually.'

Ivy makes a strange sound, like a gulp. Then I see a tear trickle down underneath the glasses. And another.

'Ivy?' She turns away. 'Please don't cry. This, us meeting, it's great.'

'Sod it.' She whips off the glasses and I see that her eyes are swollen and red from crying. 'Sod it,' she says again.

I want to hug her but I'm not sure she'd want me to. 'Come on,' I say instead, standing up.

She looks up, still sniffing. 'What?'

'Come on.'

She gathers up her things, replaces her glasses and together we walk out of the hotel and into the Dublin day.

A little while later we are outside the Botanic Gardens.

'This is where he worked when he married my mother,'

I say. 'She says he loved it here.' I lead her to the rose garden and we stand in silence for a bit, just the two of us, side by side. There is no one else around and the scent of roses is heavy in the air.

'It's lovely.' Ivy speaks for the first time since we left the hotel. 'Will you scatter his ashes here?'

'Not just me,' I say to her. I pull the envelope from my bag. 'Catch hold too.'

She looks at me and I nod. Taking her sunglasses off, she stuffs them into her bag. Then she takes an edge of the envelope and together we shake it.

And a part of me that I didn't even know was missing suddenly clicks into place.

MAX

Maya's boyfriend, lover, soon-to-be-husband is alright, I think. He's younger than her by three years, which I don't think Maya likes to admit, because when he calls himself her toy boy, she elbows him so hard that he spills his beer over his T-shirt.

'Gee,' he says, 'I'll never get the stain out.'

'No, you won't,' she says, 'because you never do the washing, do you?'

He laughs. 'Good one, Maya.' Then he leans over and nuzzles her ear.

I like him for that. He loves her, grumpiness and all.

'Piss off and make the dinner,' she tells him and he laughs some more, drains his beer and gets up. When he's left, she turns to me. 'So, Dad says you've been a grumpy fecker.'

I almost laugh as Dad chokes on his pint and splutters out, 'They were not the words I used.'

'The hell they weren't.' Maya makes a face. Then to me, 'What's the story?'

'No story, I'm grand. Got a new client.'

'So why the face?'

'Only face I've got, sadly.'

She studies me, head to one side. She lies back on the sofa and slides her legs up to curl them under her. She decides to leave it, which is good. Instead, she asks, 'How long are you planning on staying home?'

'Are you hoping to get rid of me?'

A long, slow Maya gaze. 'No. I hope you'll stay like this. But I also hope that when I go up to Dublin that you'll be in the house for me.'

'I will,' I promise. If I ever go back …

'Then that is all I need to know.'

We smile at each other, our relationship better than it's been in years, though I admit it has a way to go. I don't think she'll trust me for a while, but I promise myself that she will eventually.

Oliver arrives in with plates of pasta and a mountain of garlic bread. 'I wasn't sure how much you'd eat,' he says to me, 'so I made loads.'

'That's great, because I eat loads,' I tell him.

The four of us sit around the coffee table, plates on our knees, and I wonder why the hell it has taken me so long to do something as simple as have dinner with my sister and Dad. I was always rushing too fast before.

'So, you're not in bad form over that girl who was in your house who turned out to be Ruby Fairbrother?'

I should have known Maya wouldn't leave it. I don't want to talk about Sandy. I can't even think about her. I totally messed up and I'm not even sure how. OK, I was grumpy with her but she hurt me. I feel abandoned by her, if I'm honest.

'Well,' Maya asks. 'Are you?'

'Nope.' I stuff some garlic bread into my mouth to save me from anything else she might ask.

'I liked her,' Maya says.

'You did not!' I half-laugh, half-choke. 'You thought she was trying to steal my house.'

'I never said that.'

'You didn't have to,' my dad chimes in.

'You told me she was a gold-digger,' Oliver says, and earns another dig.

'So, what's the story with her?' Maya deftly gets back on track. 'You seeing her again?'

'Dunno.' *Shut up, Maya*, I want to say.

'She lived in your house and then dumped you?' She's outraged.

'She didn't dump me.'

'She hasn't rung you,' Maya mutters darkly. 'User.'

'She did ring,' I say, the garlic bread jamming a little on the way down. It hurts like hell. I take a glug of water.

'But she hasn't even called over to you and she lives, what, two miles away? Is she going to meet you?' Maya presses. She's like a dog with a bone.

'I'm not a mind-reader.'

'I think she's a right cow if she stayed in your house and can't be arsed ringing you or meeting you just because her life is all squeaky clean now.' Maya twists her pasta savagely onto her fork. 'A cow.'

'Maya, please.' I throw a hopeless glance at Oliver.

'You were so good to her and she just used you.' She jabs her fork in my direction.

'Maybe she thinks I'm too much of a nutter for her.' I try to make it sound like a joke but it doesn't sound at all funny.

'I doubt Sandy would think like that,' my dad chimes in. 'She cared a lot about you, Max. When I said to her that you had a lot on your mind, she backed right off.'

The words swoosh in and out. 'Sorry?' I say. 'What?' I look at my dad.

'I'm saying that Sandy is a very nice girl. She cares about you. Maya should know by now to stop judging.'

Oliver makes some crack that earns him a wallop from Maya and they all laugh. But all I can hear is the echo of my dad's words in my head. 'Did you say that Sandy backed off? Backed off what, exactly?'

The air stills. I think my dad senses the annoyance in my voice. I catch Maya throwing a look at Oliver.

'She wanted you to go to Wexford with her.'

'She was going to ask me to go with her to Wexford and you told her to back off?'

'You had a lot on your mind.'

'You told her I had a lot on my mind and she backed off?' My voice rises.

'Yes. She didn't want you stressed.'

'Where do you get off interfering in my life?' My voice is sharp. Cross. And yet, there is a dazzle inside my head. Sandy did back off but it was because she cared. About me. She really did. And the knowledge is like being baptised in warm water.

'I wasn't interfering. I just reminded her that you had a lot on. She seemed to think you were ...' his voice drains off, 'normal.'

I have to swallow a lump of hurt. 'I *am* normal. I *was* normal. I liked that she thought that. Now you've gone and made her think—'

'Whether you want to admit it or not, you were sick, Max.' It's my dad's turn to sound annoyed. 'You almost died.

You drank, popped pills. Your mind collapsed on itself. I do not want it happening again. I liked Sandy, she was a lovely girl, but you …' his voice breaks, 'you are my son.'

'And I am fine.'

'You were really sick,' Maya says, and she sounds as if she could cry.

'I have to go.' I look around for my jacket.

'Where?' Dad thinks I've lost it. I can see it in his eyes. Serve him right.

'To see Sandy. To tell her that you should never have interfered.'

'He had to!' Maya snaps. 'You were sick, Max. Really sick. Look at yourself, you're so different now.'

'I've never seen someone look as bad as you and survive,' Oliver says.

'You saw me?' Oh sweet Jesus, this gets worse.

'You probably don't remember,' Oliver goes on. 'It was—'

'I'm fine now,' I cut him off. I yank my sleeves into my jacket.

'For now,' my dad says.

'Isn't now all we've bloody got?' I pull up the zip, stare hard at the three of them. 'I can't steer clear of trouble or helping people because I was once sick.'

'No one is asking you to,' Dad says.

'You are. You need to get out of my life, Dad.'

He sighs like a building collapsing. He stands up. 'I'm your father. I can't. Whether you want to know or not, each minute you are away from me, I am consumed with worry over you.' He swallows hard. 'I can't help it and I can't lose you, Max.'

'You made me think Sandy didn't want me. That I was too much of a loser for her.'

'You really like this girl?' Maya says, the penny dropping. I ignore her.

'That's not want I wanted to do.' My dad looks at me desperately. 'And she doesn't think you're a loser. She cares that you get better.' He suddenly looks like an old man, a worried, terrified old man. I have caused it.

Guilt sideswipes me. 'I will be fine.'

'I want to believe it.'

'So do. You can't monitor every second of my life. If I fuck up and have another meltdown, then I do, but at least I'll be living, Dad.'

He looks at me hopelessly.

'That sounds all very positive,' Maya deadpans, and it raises a smile.

'I don't want that breakdown to define the rest of my life,' I say then, voicing my deepest fear. I don't want people to remember Max the nutter and never let me be normal. Shield me from the world. From heartbreak. If Sandy is going to break my heart, then maybe I should let her.

'I just worry,' Dad mutters.

'I feel the best I have since I was eighteen.'

His eyes tear up. Oh God. I love my dad, I do, but I don't want a hug or anything like that.

'Can you give me your car keys so I can get to Sandy?'

'You really, really like her,' Maya says.

'Yeah.' I eyeball Maya. 'I really, really like her and I'm going to find out if she really, really likes me.'

'Give him the keys, Dad,' Maya says. 'This is like a frigging movie.'

Dad tosses me the keys. 'Take care.'

Take care? No chance. I'm out that door and into his car in seconds.

RUBY

I head upstairs and log on to the computer. I've become a little obsessed with emails – not that I get that many, but a few people from around have contacted me on my mother's email to welcome me home. Their good wishes give me confidence. Tonight, there is one message.

From: Louis@freemail.com
To:mfairbrother@wexfordlive.ie
Ruby
You came home! I knew you would one day. And I knew that when you did, I'd be able to say sorry. Sorry for the appalling way I treated you.

I was young, stupid, scared.

You were not needy, you were never needy; I flung that out at you because I was scared. I was a kid and when you told me all your stuff, I thought somehow you wanted me to sort it out for you. I should have known that wasn't your style, you were always a girl who looked after yourself. It was what I liked most about you.

I was guilt-ridden when you left, told the cops everything I'd done like it was confession. I'm glad you're back, I'm glad you're safe. Have you heard our song about you? We can change it now to Ruby, Ruby, Ruby came home.

You, Rubes/Ella, are a one-off. A free spirit. The Unconventional. I hope you still are and that my crass behaviour of a decade ago hasn't made a difference.

Maybe one day I'll see you in Rossclare and we can have
a pint together.
Cheers.
Louis

Louis. It gives me a little pang to think he took the time out to apologise. And yet, I realise that even if he hadn't, it wouldn't make a difference. I don't need his apology. His hold over me has diminished like a piece of frayed rope being constantly pulled. I am free of him. I have been for ages. I just know it for sure right now. Compared to what I feel for Max, it's nothing. My feelings for Max are so much bigger, so much deeper. If Louis is a stream, Max is an ocean.

I know Max needs to get better, but surely if I'm sorted now, and I think I am as much as I can be, I can help Max.

But does he want it? He told me not to treat him the way his dad does. And then, I think that maybe, like Louis, his reaction had nothing to do with what I said to him and more to do with what was going on inside him.

Despite all his bravado, there is a crack in Max. Imelda messed big time with his head. I love him, I can help him and if he decides he doesn't love me at the end of it all, if he doesn't love me when he gets better, then at least I've done my best. At least it's not too late. I can't let him go, not just yet.

Downstairs, someone hammers at the door.

SANDY AND MAX

Oh, shit. I've just hammered on Sandy's door. And it's late. And her mother is the nervous type. I flatten down my hair, which is a waste as it's shaved tight, before glancing down at myself. Red pasta sauce on my T-shirt. A big line of it. My jeans are clean, though.

The door opens and a tiny woman, with Sandy's face, only older, peers out. I watch her eyes widen before she pulls the door open a little more. 'Max, is it?' she says.

'Yes. Hello. You must be …' and it's gone. Her name has gone. Me, PR supremo, cannot remember the name of possibly the most famous Irish poet since Heaney.

'Ruby's mother, yes.' She smiles a little. 'Melanie.'

'Is she in? Sandy? Ruby?'

'Won't you come in?'

'Sure.' I step into the house. I'm edgy, every nerve jumping. I try to rein it in. I shove my hands into my pockets and concentrate hard on the front room, steadying myself. My eyes flick towards the twisty stairs as Sandy comes and stands halfway down. My eyes drink her in.

'Hiya.' It's Max, looking a bit dishevelled, a bit anxious, standing in my mother's front room. I can't stop my grin. 'What are you doing here?'

'Thought you might like a drive.'

'A drive?'

'Yeah.'

He makes it sound perfectly normal. 'OK.'

He looks relieved.

'See you later, Mam.'

'See you.' She's smiling at us, as if she knows something I don't.

'Bye, Melanie,' Max says.

And then we are outside and the night is darkening and the stars are bright in the sky. The moon hangs heavy and the air is fresh and it's like the world just shook me awake. The backs of our palms touch as Max leads me to his dad's car. Zing! We make no attempt to move away from each other.

'How've you been?' he asks.

I take a chance. 'I missed you.'

He flicks me a smile. 'I missed you too. It's good to see you.'

'Great to see you.' I nudge him with my elbow.

'Excellent to see you.'

'Very excellent to see you.'

He smiles. Silence.

I hop into the car and she hops into the passenger seat. I fire the engine and off we go down the long lane. It just feels right, her being here, beside me. It feels like she was always there, as if the last few weeks have vanished, swallowed up by the now.

We don't have to speak. I don't even have to refer to the phone call, I realise. Now that I'm with her, it doesn't matter. Occasionally I glance at her from the corner of my eye and each time I do, she's looking at me with 'Happy' spelled right across her face.

I pull the car in and we get out and walk through the streets that she walked through when she was a kid breaking out of her mother's house. We reach the beach and walk towards the edge of the tide. It washes in and out. Taking things with it, throwing things up onto the sand.

We stand for a bit just looking at the sea. Then he reaches for my hand. I clasp his.

'I can't be treated like a sick person,' he says.

'I can't be snapped at for caring about you,' I say back.

'I can't have you listening to crap out of my dad,' he says.

'Shut up,' I say.

He turns and looks at me, his brown eyes so black they pull me in.

'I'm mad about you,' I say.

A faint smile curves his mouth upwards. 'I'm just mad,' he says.

I won't let him make a joke of it. I turn to face him, my back to the water. 'You are brilliant, Max. I love you.'

He bites his lip. 'I mightn't be a good bet.'

'You're a good man.'

He swallows hard. 'And you don't think I'm too much of a nutter?'

'You're my kind of nutter.'

'Really? Because I love you, Sandy, but this,' he shrugs, 'sadly, is what you get.'

'This,' I grab a fistful of his T-shirt, 'is exactly what I want.'

His smile dazzles me; it's bright and affectionate and so brilliantly happy. He curls my hair around a finger. 'I adore you. I really do. I only hope that—'

'I only hope as well.'

Something good flares in his eyes and then, with exquisite slowness, he bends down and kisses me and it is the sweetest, loveliest kiss in the whole world. His thumb brushes my cheekbone.

'If it's any consolation,' Max says, softly, 'I'm glad you ran away.'

And there it is. I ran away and found Max. And he found me.

Sandy and me, we wade into the sea. At first my heart starts hammering and then I realise that I can swim. I've always been able to swim. I'd just forgotten how for a while.

So we swim.

Acknowledgements

Thanks to Colm, Conor and Caoimhe – love you lots.

Thanks to everyone involved in making this book as good as it is: my publisher Hachette Ireland, my editor for this one – Alison Walsh. Also to Ciara and Joanna, Breda, Ruth, Bernard and Jim. Thanks to Aonghus Meaney and Emma Dunne for their excellent skills and suggestions.

Thanks to the booksellers who do a fantastic job and who sold lots of *Things I Want You to Know* for me.

Thanks to Clare Dowling and Melissa Hill – two wonderful writer friends – for their lovely words about *Things I Want You to Know*. The biggest perk of this job is that you get to meet so many generous people.

Thanks to everyone who came to my last book launch – it was a great night and I'm so indebted to you all. Martin Higgins for arranging June Rogers, and June Rogers for being June Rogers! Terry and Bill for the music. The magnificent Clara Rose for her stunning singing. (Go see her everyone.) Tina O'Connor for the flowers. Stewart Dowling for the wine. McMahons pub, Maynooth, for the brilliant venue. Maynooth Bookshop for selling my books, and for their support over the years.

Thanks to Aideen and Vincent from *The Liffey Champion* who have been there from the off.

Thanks to the people I talked to for research purposes for this book. All wished to be anonymous! Any mistakes are mine.

And to you, the reader, I wrote this for you. I hope you enjoy it.

MARTINA REILLY

Things I Want You to Know

'Life-affirming and evocative'
Irish Independent

Sometimes love lasts
longer than one lifetime…

How do you pick up the pieces
after the worst has happened?

When Nick Deegan's wife, Kate, dies, leaving him with two small children to raise alone, he has no idea how he'll manage. But on the day of her funeral, he discovers a book Kate left for him, *Things I Want You to Know*.

Her instructions for raising Emma and Liam without her give him comfort, but her other plans for him seem much more daunting …

Five dates with five different women. Nick isn't sure his heart is in it … but as he tries to follow Kate's careful instructions, he slowly realises that it's not romance Kate wanted him to find, but something far more important.

Will Nick find the courage to take a second chance?

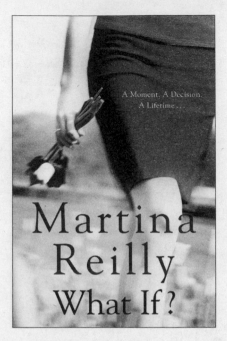

A Moment. A Decision.
A Lifetime...

Martina
Reilly
What If?

A single moment can change a life forever...

When seventeen-year-old Lily discovers she's pregnant, she has to make a choice that will determine the rest of her life. Now, nearly sixty years later, in the late stages of Alzheimer's, Lily has been admitted to Lakelands Nursing Home. Among her possessions, Zoe, a young helper, finds a diary with a note that it be read aloud to Lily's daughter Deirdre.

The diary holds the truth to Lily's past and, as secrets are uncovered, a tale of fate and responsibility unfolds that binds the three women together.